DAVID GEORGE CLARKE

THE DUST OF CENTURIES III

fatal consequences

clarkeFiction

For my wife Gail, for my family and for many dear friends,
with grateful thanks for all your support in so many ways

The Dust of Centuries

Quincentenarian

The Delusion Gambit

Fatal Consequences

The Cotton and Silk Thrillers

Irrefutable Evidence

Remorseless

The Cambroni Revenge

An Imperfect Revenge

Non-Fiction

Hong Kong Under The Microscope

A History of the Hong Kong Government Laboratory 1879–2004

FATAL CONSEQUENCES

Prologue

500 BCE

The high priest intoned a hypnotic chant in a language known only to him, his rich, resonant voice amplified by the natural amphitheatre of the hillside surrounding the sacred ground. The two dozen acolytes kneeling before him in front of the altar struggled to follow, their heads bowed, their eyes closed in concentration as they coaxed their tongues to shape the unearthly sounds, their throats to utter the rasping tones.

For the watchers, the ordinary folk of the island, the content of the incomprehensible ceremony mattered little. It was the result that was important: the perfectly timed sacrifice of a newborn child, a sacrifice that would save them.

Glaring menacingly from under his heavy eyebrows, the high priest, Cyrus, let his eyes roam slowly around the throng of frightened humanity staring obediently back at him. The entire population of the island: four hundred and thirty-five men, women and children. Even the very old and infirm were not exempt, brought carefully on cloth litters, while tiny babies were suckled to keep them from crying, their terrified parents not wanting to attract attention to themselves.

At the front of the gathering, ten metres from the altar, a man and a woman stood nervously facing Cyrus, knowing they were the focus of his attention. The woman, Iola, was holding her newborn child to her breast, a boy named after his paternal grandfather just that morning according to custom, the seventh morning after his birth. Pelagios. The sea. The boy's father, Karpos, a huge man nearly two metres tall, stood next to his diminutive wife, his right arm curled protectively around her shoulders.

The high priest's gold-embossed staff tapped firmly on the altar stone and immediately the tone of the chant changed, the beat increasing and the volume slowly rising. Karpos felt his wife lean into him as she gathered her precious baby even more tightly to her. He was terrified that she would faint, casting a bad omen on an already cursed family. The law dictated that the child had to be ready at his mother's breast at the time of transference. If the light could not pass directly into his eyes, half his spirit would be lost forever and he too would have to be sacrificed. Karpos tightened his grip, clamping Iola's upper arm and shoulders. Now, even if she were unconscious, he could hold her with one powerful arm, while the other crossed in front of him to help her cradle the baby.

As the chant slowly reached a crescendo, seven pairs of acolytes standing on seven evenly spaced stone plinths arranged in a wide semicircle behind the altar each lifted a highly polished, bronze disc above their heads. The heavy, one-metre-wide discs had each been beaten into a concave form to capture and focus the power of the sun as it reached its zenith. The pairs of acolytes on either end of the semicircle pulled the sun's rays onto the altar itself, while four more pairs sent their beams directly onto the crowd behind Karpos and Iola, causing a tangle of arms to rise in a wave to shield dazzled eyes. The final pair of acolytes, positioned directly behind the altar, bided their time as they waited for the climax of the ceremony.

Despite being half-blinded by the beams of light, the crowd muttered in agitation as they became aware of the high priest bending to gather something from behind the altar. The chanting changed again into an insistent staccato as Cyrus lifted his burden into the air: a writhing child wrapped loosely in a white cloth. As the high priest's hands stretched upwards, he let the cloth fall to reveal a baby boy, shocked awake and now bellowing in distress. Karpos felt Iola tense as his own breath almost left him. The boy was their son, Pelagios' twin brother. Younger by three minutes, he was identical in all respects and by the laws and beliefs of the islanders, an evil drain on the spirit of his elder brother, a curse on them all. Redemption could only be achieved through sacrifice, the spirit of the younger child carried on a beam of light to its rightful owner at the moment of the child's death.

The bearers focussing the sun's rays onto the altar rotated their discs to move the beams directly onto the child, who responded with an even louder wail. The high priest then slowly lowered his arms, placing the child back into a wooden crib concealed behind the altar. When he raised his arms again, his hands were grasping the jewelled, golden hilt of a long, double-edged dagger. Spittle flew from his mouth as he cried out a prayer in his mysterious tongue and plunged the dagger downwards into the crib. A spurt of blood sprayed onto his face and robes. The chanting stopped as the crowd gasped and then fell silent. Cyrus withdrew the dagger and lifted it above his head with both hands, then he plunged it downwards a second time, and then a third before finally laying it solemnly on top of the altar.

The high priest then bent over and gathered the lifeless body of the child into his arms and once again lifted him into the air. At the same moment, the two bearers on the plinth directly behind the altar turned their disc, raising their beam so it intersected with the beams from the side playing onto the motionless mass of bloodied flesh. The beam passed across the dead boy and directly onto the child in Iola's shaking arms. Karpos knew his task, hating himself as he did it. He gently turned Iola, exposing Pelagios' head and eyes to the beam. As the rays penetrated the child's eyes, it screamed in terror. As one, the crowd surged forward, surrounding the desperate couple and their child, eager to witness and touch the twin who had been saved.

Suddenly the chanting was louder and even more insistent. All eyes fell again on the altar as the high priest stepped back, lifted the crib and held it out in front of him. The disc bearers had now become torchbearers. They moved alongside the priest as he turned to carry the crib towards a pyre of wood some metres behind the altar. As he placed it on top of the pyre, fourteen flaming torches were thrust into the kindling.

Iola angrily pushed several arms to one side, arms still insistent on touching her now blessed child. As the flames burst skywards, she screamed and fainted into the firm grip of her husband's arms.

The high priest edged back from the flames and stood motionless, watching until the crib and its contents were completely consumed. He turned to the spellbound crowd, walked in front of the altar and raised his arms.

"Karpos and Iola, hold up your child!" he ordered, pointing his staff directly at them.

Karpos carefully removed his son from Iola's grip and held him up above the crowd.

"The gods are appeased!" cried the high priest. "The spirit of your child, Pelagios, is now whole and the devil who would have consumed it destroyed. Your son is no longer in danger and our people are saved. Praise be to the gods of this island! Without their might, we would be cursed for all time!"

The crowd cheered in delight and swarmed again around Karpos who kept his child high in the air, his great height ensuring that the boy was well out of reach. He looked down into their eyes, seeing joy and relief, but he felt no such emotions himself. He had had no choice but to comply with the religion of the island, his birthplace and home, but in his heart he did not agree with it. He had looked into the eyes of his now-dead younger son many times over the last seven days and he had perceived no evil, just an innocent child.

Cyrus walked slowly away towards the dwelling beyond the sacred ground, trying to maintain an outward appearance of calm that he certainly didn't feel. At any moment in the last few minutes, the baby boy hidden in his robes might have awoken from the herbal sleeping draft he had given him and started to cry. But he hadn't and as Cyrus entered the seclusion of the dark vestibule, he allowed himself a sigh of relief. The substitution had worked. The baby he had stolen from the shepherd girl he had murdered on the far side of the island, a simpleton of a girl most people had forgotten existed, had been a perfect substitute. Ideally, he would have performed the swap earlier, but Karpos and Iola's younger son was permitted, according to the ritual, to remain with his parents until the ceremony, making Cyrus' scheme highly dangerous. However, everything had gone perfectly and now he was leaving with his followers.

The islanders knew nothing of Cyrus' plans, and they would be too busy celebrating for the rest of the day and into the night to notice his absence. By tomorrow he would be far away, heading for a temple on the mainland, well away from this island in the Dodecanese. And with him he would have a new slave. A baby now, but when he was grown, Cyrus knew this boy, whom he was calling Makar, the blessed, would be an acolyte like no other. The boy would be like his father, huge and strong among a population of short men and women. What better protection than his own hand-reared bodyguard, trained from birth to serve him in every way.

From the shadows of the vestibule, he took a final glance at the crowd and at Karpos, who now seemed to have relaxed and to be warming to the celebrations as he continued to hold his son high above their heads. Cyrus wished he could have taken both boys and their father as well. But that would have been asking too much.

He placed the still-sleeping Makar into a sling and slipped quietly out of the rear of his house where his trusted followers were waiting to go with him to the boats.

Chapter One

2012

Naomi Tripley pulled off the road onto the gravel track that led to her rented cottage. Like many of the homes described as cottages on Cape Cod, the three-bedroom, two-storey structure was a substantial house, far bigger than Naomi needed, but the price was reasonable and the owners, an elderly couple called Jake and Myra Higgins who lived across the drive in an even larger cottage, were friendly without being intrusive. Apart from the security lights that had come on as she approached, both properties were in darkness, Jake and Myra having left that morning to drive to Provincetown at the northern tip of the Cape to spend a few days with Myra's sister.

Naomi switched off the engine but remained sitting in the car, staring into the blackness of the woods behind the two cottages. What was nagging at her thoughts? Why did she feel so hesitant, so uncertain? She should be pleased. She had all but finished the two portraits promised to the pair of wealthy clients who had paid her so generously for her skills and now she was almost ready to leave for England to be with her daughter, her half-sister and her father, the family that a few short weeks ago she had no idea even existed.

After nearly five hundred years of living on her wits, she was used to change, used to moving on, used to reinventing herself. Just three months earlier she had been Cassie Gomes living in the tropical north of Brazil, but circumstances had forced her hand and now she was back in the US as thirty-year-old Naomi Tripley, a portraitist with her own art gallery in Falmouth. When her former psychiatrist from the 1970s, Nancy Wright, had materialised out of nowhere on the sand cliffs above Marconi Beach on the Cape's east coast, Naomi's reaction had been one of amusement: the now elderly Nancy was clearly staggered to find the patient she had known as Annie Carr had been telling the truth about herself all those years ago. But then the psychiatrist had dropped a bombshell: Naomi's daughter, Serena Peace, whom Naomi had last seen in 1970 when the girl was four and whom she'd been told had been killed some years later falling from a tree, was in fact alive and living in Boston. Sara Farsley, as Serena was now called, was a successful lawyer and married with a grown-up family. At an emotional reunion of the two women the following day, there had been another bombshell: Naomi had a half-sister, Lily Saunders, living in New York City, but who happened to be visiting the Farsleys. Born in Hong Kong in the 1880s, Lily had the same rare traits as Naomi and Sara: all three women looked no more than about thirty, their DNA programmed to maintain their youth and their perfect health.

While Naomi was still absorbing the fact that she was now a mother, sister and grandmother, Lily quietly dropped the biggest bombshell of all: her and Naomi's father, who was Stefano Crispi when he fled Naples in 1517 some months before Naomi was born, was still alive. Now John Andrews, he was an English artist living and working in the Lake District of northern England with a wife, Lola, and two young daughters, Sophie and Phoebe.

Sara's own discovery of her extended family was also very recent. At the time Naomi arrived on the scene, Sara and her husband Pete, together with their children Julie and Matt, were about to go to England with Lily to spend time with John Andrews and his family. As busy lawyers, Sara and Pete had rescheduled their workloads and were ready to go, but their timeframe was limited. Not wishing to delay them, Naomi promised to follow them as soon as the two portraits she was contracted to finish were completed.

Nevertheless, John had flown immediately over from England

to meet Naomi, the daughter he had dreamed of finding for nearly five hundred years. When they met, they spoke to each other in a sixteenth century Neapolitan dialect. Naomi called her father Tata — Daddy — while John called his daughter by her original name, the only name he knew for her: Paola.

Shooing her father away to return to England with the rest of her new family had not been easy, but Naomi insisted. The plans had been made and she would soon join them. What she didn't reveal was that even for her, she found so much change overwhelming. She needed time to adjust, to think herself into her new persona. That must be what was nagging at her, she thought. Usually when she created a new identity in a new place, she would make up a history to match it. However, she had revealed much about her past to Nancy Wright back in the '70s when she was trying to convince her she was delusional and not competent to stand trial following her brutal stabbing of the commune leader Ty Donnington. Wright had written up her story in a textbook and shown the Farsleys all her notes. Later, John and Lily had seen them too, so they were all aware of Naomi's often-violent past, of the times when she had killed to survive. Or at least they were aware of some of it. There was much she hadn't told Nancy Wright: too much information might have unsettled the psychiatrist.

Having registered no movement for a predefined number of seconds, the security lights obeyed their programing and switched off, allowing the darkness to regain its hold and envelop the car. Naomi jolted out of her reverie with a start. She sighed and thought again of John. He was a gentle, kind man who was overjoyed to have found the daughter he had been convinced for centuries was still alive. They were all good people: her father, the Farsleys and Lily, her half-sister. She had adjusted to many extreme circumstances in the past. She could adjust to these.

She climbed out of the car, the movement triggering the security lights once again. She paused for a moment, breathing in the crisp air, a taster for the winter temperatures that would soon cool the Cape. As she walked towards the house, the only sound in the stillness of the night was the soft crunch of gravel under her shoes and the distant hooting of a solitary owl from deep in the woods. She smiled; she had heard it before. It seemed to be welcoming her home. She pulled open the screen door, unlocked the main door and switched on the hall light. Then, as she dropped the keys on the hall table and her bag on the floor, she suddenly froze. Something wasn't right. There was no noise in the house, no unusual smell, nothing out of place, but her senses were screaming at her. She carefully opened a cupboard set in the wall to one side of the hall table and put her hand into the darkness to find the four foot long rattan punishment cane left there by a previous tenant. When she'd first found it, she'd wondered at her predecessor's predilections. She wrapped her hand around the leather grip and turned towards the living room, peering into the darkness as she did, but she could see nothing beyond the beam of light from the hall. As she reached the open door, she felt for the light switch.

The light flooded the room to reveal a middle-aged woman standing on the far side. The woman looked up and smiled.

"Ah, there you are, Naomi. You're late this evening."

"Who the hell are you? And what are you doing in my house?"

"I'm Edith, dear, Edith Cooper. I've come to help you pack a few things. You won't need much; we'll provide almost everything."

"What the hell are you talking about?" Naomi's voice had risen in pitch. She ran her eyes rapidly over the woman. She was holding something in her left hand, trying to conceal it.

Naomi increased her grip on the cane and took a step towards the woman, but a voice from behind stopped her in her tracks.

"I'm afraid I couldn't wait two months, Ms Tripley, or should I say, Annie Carr. You see, I need some of your time right now."

Naomi whisked around to see a man standing in the doorway to the hall. She recognised his face; he had visited her gallery a week ago and completely spooked Mary Murphy, her assistant. She felt her pulse rise as she glared at him, trying to remember his name. Charles Creed, that was it. He had bought a painting and claimed he wanted to commission more, but she hadn't believed him. She remembered there being something very cold and threatening about him, his jet black eyes boring into her just as they were now.

Naomi had learnt long ago that the best form of attack is surprise. An apparently stronger opponent who assumed an upper hand would be expecting caution, discussion even, some sort of exchange. She knew she probably had one chance since she could feel the middle-aged woman treading cautiously towards her from behind. In a blur of motion, Naomi whipped the cane across the man's face. He was quick; he saw it coming, but reacted too slowly to ward off the blow. Her aim was good and the cane bit deeply into the thin skin covering his left cheekbone and the flesh of his cheek, blood welling up immediately from the wound. He yelled in pain but Naomi didn't wait. She ran towards the open kitchen door and shot across the kitchen to the rear door of the cottage. Sometimes she left the key in the lock, but today she hadn't. She turned; it would be in a drawer in the unit next to the door. But as she reached for the drawer, she saw the woman had followed her and was standing about three metres away. She still had a benign smile on her face as if she were collecting for charity.

"My, you have got a temper on you, dear. We'll have to watch that. There's nowhere to go, you know, and if you resist, I'll have to shoot you."

The woman reached her right hand towards her jacket pocket, but just as she did, the house phone on the wall about a foot from her ear started to ring. In the fleeting moment that the woman's eyes wandered involuntarily towards the sound, Naomi leapt forward, raised the cane and whipped it down on the woman's left arm. But it was less effective through a thick tweed jacket. The woman grabbed the cane, wrenched it from Naomi's grasp and flung it to the floor behind her. Naomi glanced to her side, remembering the cooking knives in a nearby drawer. She jerked the drawer open and grabbed the handle of an eight-inch filleting knife. Continuing the movement, she shifted her arm's direction and the tip of the blade flashed millimetres from the woman's throat.

Edith Cooper was no longer smiling. Her eyes pierced into Naomi's as her right hand shot upwards in a blur and clamped around Naomi's wrist, twisting it hard. Naomi yelled and dropped the knife, but managed to snatch her arm away and take a step back. The shrill ring of the telephone suddenly stopped and in the calm that followed, the woman seemed to relax again. She opened her left hand and placed the syringe she had been concealing on the countertop next to her. Then she spread her feet to balance her body, crouching slightly, ready to spring. But Naomi's attention was firmly fixed on the remaining knives in the drawer. Spinning round, she seized a vegetable knife and as she completed the spin, threw it hard at the woman's chest. Edith's reactions were good. She chopped her arm across the path of the knife, preventing it from finding its mark, but the razor edge caught her hand, cutting it deeply. Without pausing to consider what damage she might have inflicted, Naomi took a third knife from the drawer, a ten-inch carver. This one she didn't throw. She calmly stepped forward so she was within easy reach and slashed the blade across the woman's throat, severing a carotid artery. Blood immediately pumped from the gash as the woman yelled in horror rather than pain, her hands flying to her throat. As Naomi regained her balance, the woman suddenly lurched towards her, pushed hard from behind by the man, who had now followed her into the room. Naomi dropped the knife and put up her hands to fend her off. She never even saw the fist fly out of the gloom from behind Edith. It connected squarely with her jaw, knocking her out.

Her strength leaving her, Edith slid down Naomi's unconscious body as it slumped to the floor. But the man was now moving with purpose. He grabbed roughly at Edith's clothing and pulled her out of his way, ignoring the blood still spurting from her throat. Reaching for the lapel of Naomi's jacket, he hauled her up and slung her over his shoulder. Then he turned to Edith whose terri-fied eyes were now fixed on his, pleading for the help she knew he wouldn't give.

"I'm sorry, Edith, there's nothing I can do. You were supposed to be the best. No one can touch you in unarmed combat you always said. Well, it seems you met your match."

The blood was still dripping from the wound to the man's face, but the adrenalin was also pumping and he no longer felt any pain.

He glanced around, saw the syringe on the countertop and with his free hand, pocketed it. He then turned on his heel and marched into the hall. Retrieving his cell phone from his pocket, he punched a speed dial key.

"Heston. You'd better get in here immediately. There's a hell of a mess to clean up."

Within seconds there was a grinding of gravel as a black van braked to a halt outside the house. Rodney Heston, two hundred and fifty pounds of muscle the man employed for what he liked to call 'housekeeping operations' on the East Coast, burst through the main door to the cottage. He was visibly shocked when he saw the wound on the man's face and the blood on Naomi's unconscious body.

"What happened, Mr Dayton? I thought you didn't want her hurt."

"That's not her blood," grunted Marcus Dayton, "it's Edith's. This feisty bitch killed her."

Heston pushed past his boss and ran into the kitchen. "Christ!" Dayton heard him yell.

"Heston! You can come back for her later. Right now, I need to get to the airfield in case anybody heard anything or the neighbours come home."

"I told you, Mr Dayton, the neighbours have gone up to Provincetown for a few days."

"Given our luck lately, they'll decide to come back. Let's go. Now!"

Dayton marched out of the house to the van, pulled open the sliding door and placed Naomi's body on the floor inside. But Rodney Heston didn't follow him. He had known Edith Cooper for a number of years; they had worked on many jobs together; trained other teams overseas. He knew that in their line of work there was always the risk of injury or being caught. However, they were both professionals and Edith could handle herself in most situations. The Tripley woman must be good. He stooped down by Edith's now motionless body, avoiding the blood surrounding her, and felt for a pulse in her neck. Nothing. He pushed his fingers a little harder, in case the surgical gloves he always wore on jobs were masking any faint pulse. But there was still nothing. Edith was dead. Just as he stood up, the phone on the wall started to ring again. He turned to it, angered by the intrusion into his thoughts. He reached out and ripped the cord from the phone, silencing it.

"Rodney, I'm sorry, but as soon as I saw the injury to her neck, I knew there was nothing to be done."

Marcus Dayton had returned to the kitchen, sensitive enough not to keep yelling for Heston to obey his orders.

"I feel bad about leaving her, Mr Dayton," said Heston, still hovering near the body.

"Rodney, you're a pro, act like one. We have to prioritise. And the number-one priority is to get that wildcat out there onto the airplane and out of the country. You can be back here within two hours and you'll have all night to remove the body and sort out the mess."

He nodded at the cane lying on the floor. "Make sure you lose that as well. The less there is to connect me with this place, the better."

An hour later at Packet's Field, a small airfield for executive jets on the mainland a few miles north of the bridge from Cape Cod, Naomi was sleeping soundly in her seat in the luxurious cabin of a Gulfstream G550. Dayton had given her an injection to ensure that she would stay asleep for the flight to Algeria. He would be injecting her again for the sea journey across the Mediterranean to a quiet port in Spain and then for the next flight into Italy.

Rodney Heston watched from where the van was standing near the small terminal building as the jet taxied to its take-off position. He remained motionless, although the anger at the way his colleague had been treated was boiling inside him. Once the jet lifted from the runway and the lights faded into the night sky, he got back into the van where he sat staring at the dashboard, his breathing rapid, his jaw set and his lips curled in a snarl. He suddenly threw back his head and let out an anguished scream of frustration as his clenched fists slammed repeatedly into the steering wheel.

. . .

It was almost eleven in the evening before Heston approached the lane leading to the cottage. Across the fields he could see the telltale flashing of blue and red lights playing on the two houses, while in the distance more lights were heading towards him. He cut his headlights and pulled into the shadows of some cedars. Dayton had been right to leave when he did: Myra Higgins had forgotten some important medication and sent her husband home to fetch it. He had noticed that the front door of Naomi's cottage was wide open and then discovered the body.

Something in the vehicle's footwell caught Heston's eye. The flashing lights were somehow reflecting off the large bloodstained knife he'd picked up from the kitchen floor and tossed into the van. He hadn't seen the others or he would have taken them as well. Next to the knife was the punishment cane he'd noticed at the same time. He grunted in frustration, wishing he could beat the Tripley woman black and blue with it before slitting her throat.

Unable to do anything further for Edith, Heston reluctantly slipped the van into drive and moved off, leaving his dead colleague to the police and the probing hands and hi-tech tools of the crime scene personnel.

Chapter Two

Mary Murphy drove into the small parking lot behind the gallery and raised her eyebrows in surprise. It was early, a few minutes before eight, but she had expected Naomi to be there. For the past week, Naomi had arrived before her every morning, keen to finish the large portraits for the two well-heeled local residents who had commissioned them. Walt Walton, billionaire, would soon be seventy and a huge celebration was planned with his portrait centre-stage. No less a party would follow on the heels of Walton's. Felix Crompton, cosmetic surgeon to the rich and gravity-challenged, was about to turn sixty and was intending for his own perfect, scalpel-assisted features, recorded flatteringly in Naomi's oils, to wow his several hundred guests and drum up even more business.

Mary unlocked the rear door to the gallery and switched off the alarm. She was heading for the studio to make coffee when she heard someone rapping firmly on the main door. The tourist season was waning so she was surprised: it was breakfast time, a little early for art.

She hesitated as she approached the door. The man looked crumpled, unkempt, like he'd slept in his clothes; he certainly didn't fit the normal customer profile. She caught his eye and he held up a badge. Police. Mary shivered. Naomi was late. Had something happened?

"Can I help you, officer?" she said, almost before she'd opened the door.

"I hope so ma'am. I'm Detective Mullins. I have a few questions for you." He walked in without being asked.

"Has something happened to Naomi, Detective? Has she had an accident?"

"When did you last see Ms Tripley?" asked the detective, his eyes roaming the studio as if expecting Naomi to appear.

"I ... I left her here last night when I finished work. At six. She's been working late all week. She's anxious to finish two portraits—"

"Anxious?"

"I mean she wants to finish them because she's heading off to Europe to see some friends."

"Europe?" echoed the detective, as if the notion were absurdly alien.

"When you say she's anxious, has she been agitated in some way? Has she said anything about being threatened?"

"I didn't mean she was anxious that way, Detective. It was just a turn of phrase. Threatened? Why should she be threatened?"

"I was hoping you could tell me, ma'am."

"It's Mary, Detective. Mary Murphy."

"That was my next question, Ms Murphy." The detective's slight smile was devoid of any humour. "Did Ms Tripley call you at all last night?"

"No, she never does. She's really very private, you know. Detective, would you mind telling me what has happened?"

"There was an incident at Ms Tripley's house last night. A—"

"An incident?"

Detective Mullins raised his eyes to Mary with a look that said controlled impatience.

"Sorry," offered Mary.

"A woman was killed." He put his hand up as Mary was about to interrupt again. "It wasn't Ms Tripley. We don't know who she is. She has no ID on her. We were hoping that you might know her."

Mary shook her head absently. "I think I want to sit down, Detective."

She walked to the rear of the gallery and sat behind a desk, indicating a chair on the other side for the detective. He sat down, saying nothing as he waited for her to calm herself.

"How do you know it wasn't Naomi?" said Mary, raising her eyes to Mullins.

"Her landlord took a look at the body. He's never seen her before. Reckons she's older too. Ms Tripley's, what, about thirty?"

Mary nodded.

"Well the victim is late forties, at least, but was in good shape, physically. Lean. But definitely not thirty. Does that description mean anything?"

Mary shook her head. "I'm afraid I know little about Naomi's private life, Detective. I've never been to her cottage."

"Do you know if she saw clients there?"

"I doubt it very much; she certainly never said so. I mean, I never heard her even give out her cell number. Her card just has the gallery's landline."

"Have you any idea where Ms Tripley might have gone?"

"You mean she's not at the house?"

"No, Ms Murphy, she's not. She's disappeared. Her car's there, the house was unlocked, the lights on, but no Ms Tripley. Just the body of an unknown woman."

"How did you find out about it?"

"A neighbour. The owner, in fact. He and his wife had gone away to Provincetown, but he had to come back to fetch his wife's meds. He saw the lights on and the main door open."

"Jake Higgins," nodded Mary.

"You know him?"

"Vaguely. He and his wife are quite old and forgetful, apparently. Naomi said they were good landlords, though. Let her be."

"Apart from her Europe trip, has Ms Tripley talked about going anywhere else?"

"No, she's been far too busy with the portraits."

Mullins looked around the gallery. "A lot of these paintings are of the sea. Does she make them up or does she go somewhere to paint them?"

"No, Detective, she doesn't make them up. They are from life. Until her friend contacted her and asked her to visit England, she was up there a lot."

"Up where?"

"Marconi beach."

"I thought it looked familiar. I'll send someone to check."

"You think she's gone there?"

"Ms Murphy. We have a dead woman in Ms Tripley's house. Although there's not much sign of a struggle, there's a lot of blood. There's no sign that anyone else has been there and Ms Tripley has disappeared. So she's our main suspect. Right now, I'm thinking that if she killed this woman, she might have hightailed it to somewhere quiet she knows about. If it's a beach in the middle of nowhere, once she realises the seriousness of her situation, I'm concerned she might harm herself. I want to stop her before that happens."

He took out his cell phone.

"But her car is still at the cottage, you said," objected Mary.

"Her car, yes, but how did the woman get to the cottage? Tripley has probably taken hers."

He made to punch a button when his phone trilled out its ring tone. He glanced at the screen and put the phone to his ear.

"Lieutenant." He waited, his eyes looking up to Mary's in a way that made her think the caller was talking about her.

"Yes, Ms Murphy's here. She's had no contact with Tripley since she left the gallery last night." He paused as he listened to the response, and then continued. "Around six, she says." He listened again, snorted dismissively and started nodding. "Good of him to share that with us." His tone was sarcastic. "Yes, Ms Murphy said he was forgetful." Another longer pause as he listened to his boss. "Ok," he said finally, "that's good. I'll show her, Lieutenant, as soon as it arrives."

He ended the call and turned to Mary.

"It seems the neighbour suddenly remembered he has a CCTV

system installed in the driveway. It slipped his mind last night." He shook his head.

"Does it show anything useful?"

Mullins nodded. "Maybe. It shows a man and a woman arriving at Ms Tripley's house. The angle's not good so you can't see the main door; it's in too much shadow. Then it shows Ms Tripley coming home and a short while later a van pulling up outside the door. A big, well-built man goes in and then he comes out with the first man, who is also tall, but not as well built. He's carrying a body."

"You mean the dead woman?"

"No, someone else. I'd like you to come downtown and see the tape, confirm that it's Ms Tripley."

"Was she alive?"

"Difficult to say, she was over the man's shoulder. But he placed her rather than threw her into the van."

His phone made the sound of a cock crowing. He winced. "My granddaughter's been playing with this thing."

He pressed a few buttons and then held up the screen to Mary.

"The lieutenant said she was sending through a picture. This is it. It's of the dead woman, taken in the morgue. Would you mind looking at it, see if you recognise her?"

Mary recoiled slightly when she realised she was looking at a dead person. But since the image showed only the head, the deep wound to the neck being screened with a white sheet, the woman just looked asleep. Mary took hold of the half-frame spectacles that were dangling from a cord around her neck and peered more closely at the face in the image. She shook her head.

"I'm sorry, Detective, I don't recognise her at all."

"That's OK, Ms Murphy. I somehow thought you wouldn't. Could we go along to the police station now? You don't seem very busy."

Mary smiled. "I'll just lock up the rear door."

"You leave that door open in the daytime, Ms Murphy?" He seemed shocked.

Mary nodded guiltily, as if she'd committed some kind of misdemeanour.

. . .

By ten o'clock, Mary had carefully watched the video recording from the CCTV cameras outside Naomi's cottage three times, asking Detective Mullins to rewind and replay some sections frame by frame. Only then was she able to confirm that the person being carried to the van could be Naomi. The image was very grainy, but the clothes looked like those Naomi had been wearing the previous day.

"How tall is Ms Tripley?" asked Mullins.

Mary thought about it. "I guess about five-five, five-six. She's a couple of inches taller than I am."

Mullins puckered his lips as he made a calculation. "That would mean the man carrying her is pretty tall. I'd guess around six-five, six-six. Quite well built but not gym-enhanced like the other one, I'd say. Has anybody like that been into the gallery?"

Mary's eyes widened as she remembered. "Yes, there was, about a week ago. He was really quite creepy. Naomi was in the studio but I asked her to come through since he was insistent he wanted to speak with her. He had the darkest eyes. Could have been good looking if his face relaxed a bit."

"Did he give a name, leave a card?"

"Gave his name, yes. Creed. Charles Creed. Oh, and he bought a painting. One of the seascapes."

"How did he pay?"

Mary realised she'd given him false hope. "Um, cash, I'm afraid."

The detective grunted.

"If I got a police artist down from Boston, do you think you could give a more detailed description so we can construct a picture? I could get him here tomorrow."

"Of course, but I think we could do better than that."

The detective tilted his head in question.

"I have an artist friend, Detective, here in Falmouth, who can sketch the most amazing portraits in no time at all. He's quite brilliant. Specialises in charcoal and makes his money sketching tourists. Cut his teeth in Florence many years ago."

"Does he have a studio?"

"He shares a premises with some other artists. But I'm sure he'd be happy to pop along here." She smiled at the detective, pleased she was helping.

Detective Mullins was waiting for his boss, Lieutenant Sharon Roper, as she walked into the detectives unit.

"This could be the perp, boss," he said, handing her the printout from the scan of the artist's sketch.

Roper gave him a withering look. "Eh, sorry, bo … I mean Lieutenant, Lieutenant."

"Can he tidy it up a bit?"

"He's doing that now, but after that I thought we could send it up to Maynard," he said, referring to the State Crime Laboratory. "They've got some fancy enhancement program that will render it more like a photo."

"Good idea, Kevin. Give them a call."

At three o'clock that afternoon, Mary Murphy was about to sit down in a rocking chair on the porch of her house in Woods Hole when her cell phone rang. She put her mug of tea on a side table and went inside to find the phone.

"Ms Murphy, it's Detective Mullins. I'm at the gallery but it's all locked up. There's something I need to show you."

"Sorry, Detective, I'm at home. I went back to the gallery briefly but I couldn't settle. I'm afraid I found all the events of this morning rather upsetting so I gave myself the rest of the day off. I'll be back there tomorrow morning. And Naomi has my cell number so I won't miss any calls from her."

"I'm afraid it can't wait, ma'am. OK if I call by your place? It won't take long."

"That's incredible," said Mary when Detective Mullins handed her the computer-enhanced image of the sketch. "It could be a photograph of the man who was in the gallery. Charles Creed. It's a perfect likeness. Exactly as I remember him."

"OK," replied the detective. "We'll put it out on the wires. Maybe we'll get lucky." He paused. "Ms Murphy. Thanks very much for your help with the artist. Having the image out there today, less than twenty-four hours after the killing, that could be very useful."

"You're very welcome, Detective. If there's anything else I can do, please let me know."

"Actually, Ms Murphy, there is one other thing. We searched Ms Tripley's house to see if there was a photograph of her, but there's nothing. We found her passport, which of course has a photograph, but there are no photographs anywhere of her or anybody else. You don't happen to have one, do you? Perhaps on your phone?"

Mary shook her head. "Sorry, Detective, I don't." Then she remembered. "But there is a photograph that should be useful to you. A little while ago a reporter from the local newspaper interviewed Naomi about the gallery. It was well written, I thought, when it was published. And the article included a picture of Naomi. I'm sure you can get a copy at the newspaper's office."

Chapter Three

John Andrews stood at the kitchen window watching the dawn rise over Thirlmere, but his thoughts were far from home. For the past two weeks, he'd spoken to Paola every evening on the phone but the night before last, she hadn't answered, and then soon after her phone was dead. Thirty-six hours later it was still dead and the only response he could get from her mobile was her voice message. He was beginning to worry: she hadn't said she was going anywhere and why wasn't she answering her mobile?

"Any luck, darling?" asked John's wife Lola as she wandered into the kitchen and headed for the coffee pot.

"Nothing," he answered, the worry sounding in his voice. "I've given up for now. It's after two in the morning in Cape Cod, so if I did get through, she'd hardly appreciate me waking her."

"You know, John, Paola does have a life; she's been a grown woman for a long time. Just because you've suddenly come into each other's lives doesn't mean she doesn't go out on the razzle occasionally." She walked over to him and ruffled his hair. "Without telling Daddy."

His mouth twitched, but it wasn't a smile. "I know. I'm being ridiculous. I just wish she'd been able to fly over when Pete and Sara did. It would have been so much easier."

Lola nodded. "Yes, but work's work, as you well know."

"The strange thing is that when I called at around 7.30 her

time Saturday evening, that's 12.30 yesterday morning here, the phone kept ringing. When I called a few minutes later, it rang twice and then suddenly went dead. Since then it's been giving an unobtainable tone."

"Perhaps they're having storms and the lines are down."

"I wondered about that, but there's nothing on the weather report for Cape Cod."

"It's probably some technical glitch. It's bound to be working later on; Americans can't live for long without the phone. They're lucky they don't live under the lottery of British Telecom's so-called service. How long was it we were without a line last winter before they deigned to drive the seven miles from Keswick? Three weeks?"

Telephones were something of a hobbyhorse for Lola.

"But what about her mobile?" persisted John. "And why is there no answer from the gallery. She has an assistant who's supposed to be there."

"Maybe she's lost the mobile and it was her assistant's day off." Lola opened a cupboard and passed her husband a frying pan. "Come on, Mr Andrews, the Farsleys will be down any minute eating us out of house and home. Time to get breakfast on the go."

John hadn't told the others about not being able to contact Paola; he didn't want to worry them unnecessarily over something that might turn out to be trivial and potentially cast a damper over their continued delight in exploring the Lakes. However, if he made no progress today, he would have to say something.

Over breakfast the exchange of chatter from the collection of adults and children remained as lively as ever. Eleven-year-old Sophie had taken up her regular spot next to Matt and as usual she was hanging on his every word. Technically speaking, Sophie and her eight-year-old sister Phoebe were Matt and Julie's great aunts, but familial relationships aside, an eleven-year-old's infatuation with a seventeen-year-old as congenial as Matt was inevitable.

Phoebe, meanwhile, loved her one-hundred-and-twenty-seven-year-old half-sister, their bond the rare traits they shared with their father. Unlike Sophie, Phoebe had pale grey eyes, was never ill, and was destined to live an extraordinarily long life.

Lily looked down at her young admirer. "Well, Miss Andrews, are you ready for school?"

"School?" said Phoebe indignantly. "Isn't it Saturday?"

"Not in this universe," said Lola. "Come, girls, let's hit the road."

"O-oh!" they cried in unison.

"I'll take them, Lola," offered Lily.

"Will you, Lily?" The girls were suddenly bouncing, their faces wreathed in smiles. Their objections forgotten in an instant, they rushed off to fetch their backpacks.

Lily grinned at Lola. "Fall for it every time, don't they?"

As Pete helped himself to more coffee, he decided to draw on what he considered to be John's inexhaustible font of historical experience. "What did you drink with your breakfast in the days before caffeine? I can't imagine a world without it."

John stared into his own coffee as his thoughts drifted back over three hundred years. "Coffee arrived in Europe in the mid-17th century. I remember first tasting it in Marseille in the 1650s. By the 1700s, there were some very smart coffee houses in many European cities. There was a particularly good one in Lyons that I went to with my son Michel, although he was called Charles by then."

Matt was, as ever, enthralled by the conversation. "Was he—"

"Like me?" said John, anticipating him. "Yes, both he and his brother were."

"What happened to them?"

"Henri was murdered by an alcoholic French painter in Paris and Michel was executed in the French Revolution."

"Wow!" said Matt, his eyes wide.

"And before coffee?" continued Pete.

"Some people drank beer, although it wasn't like the pint you get down at the pub, it was more like a slightly alcoholic soup."

"Yuk," said Julie.

"Yes, it wasn't great," laughed John. "Others drank red wine, again, fairly weak. You must remember that ordinary water was very dodgy, often contaminated, so people were loath to drink it. If they were thirsty, a fermented drink was far safer."

John spent the next few hours watching the clock, willing away the time until it was morning on the East Coast of the US. At one o'clock, he called Paola's house. It was now eight o'clock in Cape Cod; she should be up and around. But the line still gave the unobtainable tone. He tried several more times but by eight thirty he decided he might have missed her so he called the gallery's number. It answered almost immediately.

"Naomi?" The voice was urgent, full of trepidation.

"Er, no, it's John Andrews. I'm, er … I'm a friend of, er, Naomi. I was hoping to speak to her. I'm calling from England. Do you know when she'll be back? I've been trying her house, but the line doesn't seem to be working. And she's not answering her mobile."

"Mr Andrews, this is Mary Murphy. I'm Naomi's assistant. She's mentioned you to me; said she was going over to England soon to meet you." A pause. "Mr Andrews, I'm afraid something terrible has happened. Naomi's disappeared."

"Disappeared?"

"Yes. There was an incident at her house the night before last. A woman was killed, stabbed. Not Naomi, someone else. At first the police thought that Naomi had something to do with it. But now they think that she's been kidnapped."

"Kidnapped? Has there been a ransom demand?"

"No, nothing like that."

"What are the police doing? Do they have any idea what's going on?"

"No, none. They only have shadowy, poor-quality images from a CCTV camera on the driveway. They've shown them to me; I was at the police station yesterday. There are pictures of Naomi going into the house, and then of someone carrying her, or someone dressed like her, out of the house and putting her in a van. She's not struggling, so the police are assuming that she must be, well, unconscious or something. They don't know who the man carrying her is, but the image reminded me of someone who came to the gallery a week or so ago. He was big, like the man in the video. He gave me the creeps. I gave the police a description of him and I got an artist friend to sketch him. The police then rendered that image with their computers into a sort of photographic lookalike."

"What did he look like, this man?" asked John. "Could you describe him to me?"

"Yes, I can, but is it likely to be of much use? I mean, you're in England."

"It will probably be of no use at all, Ms Murphy, but it can't do any harm either. And just in case …"

"Yes, of course." There was a pause, then she added, "Rather than describe him to you, I could send a copy of the computer drawing. The police gave me one. I'll take a photo of it with my phone and email it, if you want." She sounded pleased with herself.

"That would be very helpful, thank you. He didn't give a name by any chance?"

"Yes, he did. It was Charles Creed. I think the police are following that up."

"I'm sure they are. Do you know what else they are doing?"

"Well, one of them spent yesterday morning with me, but as far as I know, the rest are still up at the house. The crime scene people are swarming all over it, to quote the detective I was talking to."

"Who's the dead woman? Did they say?"

"They don't know. They showed me a photo of her taken in the morgue, but I didn't recognise her. Oh yes, I forgot, the CCTV tape also showed her arriving with Creed, but at that time, there was no sign of the van."

"So there must have been at least three of them: two went into the house and one stayed in the van."

"Yes, that's what the police officer said too. Let me send you that photo, Mr Andrews. What's your email address?"

John quoted the address, thanked her again and rang off.

.   .   .

When Lola walked in fifteen minutes later, John was sitting impatiently by his computer.

"Any more news, darling?"

"No, I'm still waiting for the email. What's the woman doing?"

John had called Lola immediately after finishing his call with Mary Murphy and she had come straight home, leaving Lily to look after John's gallery in Grasmere.

"I'll make some tea," said Lola. "Shout when it arrives."

As she was pouring boiling water over the teabags she had put into two large mugs, Lola heard a ping from John's computer in his study. A few moments after that she heard his printer running through its warm-up routine followed by the sound of plastic spindles banging as the paper was mobilised. After that, there was silence.

"John," she called. "Have you got it?"

When there was no reply, Lola picked up the mugs and turned to head for the study. But John was now standing by the kitchen door clutching the printout, his forehead furrowed in a deep frown.

"John?"

"This makes no sense," he said. "No sense at all. It can't be."

Lola put down the mugs and ran over to his side. He held up the paper for her to see.

"What? That can't be right. It's ridiculous. There must be some mistake."

"I know, but how? The likeness is amazing. It couldn't be anyone else."

"Are you trying to tell me that Jacques Bognard is the person who took Paola?"

Chapter Four

John sat down on a kitchen stool and stared at the face in the print-out. While the image was no more than a computer-enhanced drawing, the likeness to his seafaring friend from seventeenth-century Marseille was uncanny.

Jacques Bognard had been a successful merchant with a fleet of ships plying the waters of the Mediterranean. A highly respected businessman, his skill as a sailor had been legendary among the trading community of the time. Serving as crew on one of his vessels was regarded as a rare privilege. John first met him in the 1640s when he came to Marseille from Paris as Philippe Laurent, and the two had quickly become firm friends. Philippe had painted a number of portraits of Jacques' wife, Mathilde, and was working on a new one in 1677 when a fatal fight in the bar where he lived with Arlette, his lover of many years, changed everything. Arlette and Georges, her son by her late husband, had been killed along with a number of drunken sailors in the bar. Jacques had spirited Philippe from the bar along with Henri and Michel, Philippe's sons with Arlette, and Henri's young lover, Gisèle. From their hiding place, they sought out Arlette's and Georges' killer and avenged their deaths, but they had then been forced to flee Marseille to avoid arrest and execution. Jacques had taken them to Italy where they started new lives.

Despite their closeness as friends, Philippe had not revealed anything about his extraordinary longevity to Jacques, and neither had he any idea that Jacques was the same as he was. Both men had good reason to be more than cautious about themselves, and while Jacques had his suspicions, he had let the matter ride. They had lost contact after Philippe fled to Italy and by the time Philippe returned to Marseille to visit Arlette's grave, he had assumed that his old friend was long dead. On that visit, he had learned that Arlette's, Georges' and Mathilde's graves — Mathilde died in the 1680s — were kept in immaculate condition thanks to a fund set up in perpetuity by Jacques. On another trip to Marseille over one hundred years later, by which time he was Pierre Labreche, Philippe was delighted to find that the graves were still perfectly maintained.

When Jacques, who was now Adam Fowler to his many business associates, contacted John unexpectedly in the Lake District in 2009, having been tipped off about his old friend by his shadowy protector from an arcane branch of the British Government, John was as utterly amazed as he was delighted. Not only was Jacques alive and well, but also John now knew with certainty that there were others who shared his rare traits who were not related to him. The surprise of Jacques' return into his life was only topped by the staggering information from Jacques that he was some two and a half thousand years old.

With their history, and from what he had learned of Jacques since their friendship had been renewed, John's trust in his friend was total. He was a man who had risked his life to save him and who had returned to his life in the present day full of bonhomie and kindness. To see a sinister version of Jacques' face staring back at him from the printout was beyond comprehension.

John became aware that Lola was talking to him, but he had registered nothing. The pain in his eyes as he lifted his gaze to Lola's was tangible, and Lola resisted questioning why he wasn't listening to her.

"Sweetheart," she said softly, putting her hand on his, "I was asking you if Jacques knows about Paola. You have mentioned her, haven't you?"

"Of course," said John, still distracted. "I spoke to him about her as soon as I knew. He was very excited about the news; said he couldn't wait to meet her."

"John, there must be some logical reason for this." Lola pointed to the printout. "Why don't you call him and see if he can come up with an explanation?"

"Yes, I will. I was thinking exactly the same," replied John, his eyes roaming the room for his mobile phone.

He walked over to it, swiped the screen and hit the favourites button and Jacques' name.

After a few rings, there was a click and Jacques' voice, genial as ever, burst into his ear.

"Philippe, my dear friend, how good to hear from you. How are you? And, of course, the lovely Lola."

John paused, puzzled by the conflict between the voice on his phone and the image in his hands.

"Jacques, something very disturbing has happened. Where are you?"

"Where am I? Of course, I forgot to mention it. It's about this time every year that I visit the US to keep up with my business contacts here. Of course, I talk to them regularly on conference calls, but there's nothing like a face-to-face meeting. I'm in Boston, Philippe. Well, south of Boston, to be exact. I've been over here for two weeks now. I've just had a cup of coffee at a roadside place on the freeway heading north. I—"

"You're in the States?" interrupted John.

"Yes, Philippe, the States. You sound surprised. It's not the journey it was once upon a time, you know. While I haven't lost my dislike for aeroplanes, they really are very convenient. However, this trip seems fraught with irritating problems. As you know, I avoid driving as much as possible. I use a driver whenever I can. But my regular driver here is sick, and I couldn't get a trusted replacement at short notice. I'm driving myself around, Philippe, and I hate it. Philippe? Are you still there?"

John realised he was nodding but saying nothing. "Yes, Jacques, I am. Jacques, have you been anywhere near—"

"Just a minute, Philippe," interrupted Jacques, "I need to sort out a little problem. There's a policeman here who seems very agitated."

John listened and heard Jacques say, "Yes, all right, officer," before the line went dead.

John raised his eyes to see Lola standing with her hands on her hips, her face a picture of confusion. "He's in the States?" she said.

"Yes," muttered John, returning his gaze to his phone and staring at it as if it were an alien object. "He said he's in Boston."

"Boston!"

"This is weird, Lola," said John. "I knew something was wrong when Paola didn't call back. She's not always there when I call in the early evening, as you know. She's been packing in the hours to finish her commissions. But she'd always call back later."

"Try Jacques again," suggested Lola.

John tapped the screen and held the phone to his ear. "It's going to his voicemail message, just like Paola's," he said. "What's going on, Lola, and what has Jacques got to do with it?"

"And who's this dead woman at Paola's house?" added Lola.

John raised his arms in a gesture of helplessness. "I don't know what to do."

The two police officers had just pulled their patrol car into the gas station and diner for a coffee break. The elder one, Stan Pasherly, parked the car near the exit and looked around. He was old school and liked to cast a relaxed, world-weary eye over the parking lot. You could learn much from checking out the vehicles and watching the behaviour of their drivers. His young partner, Carl Frazer, was, by contrast, totally unaware of his surroundings. His entire attention was focussed on his iPad as he scrolled through pages from a secure link to the police information centre with live updates on APBs, wanted persons, missing persons and so on.

"You know, son, we got enough hi-tech gizmos in this vehicle without that thing. If you get your nose outta the electronics for a few seconds and use those young eyes to look at the world around you, you might see some real stuff going on."

"I know that, Stan," said Frazer, without removing his gaze from the screen, "but with this App I can really keep ahead of the game. I don't even need to be in the car. Finding suspects and solving crime is all about information and this little beauty gives me that, wherever I am."

"You sound like some smart-assed instructor from the training school," growled Pasherly as his eyes roamed the parking lot.

Ignoring his cynicism, Frazer continued. "Take a look at these APBs, for instance. These perps all committed crimes in the last twenty-four hours on our patch. Well, sort of on our patch. That means there's a good chance they're still in the area, possibly drinking coffee at a place like this."

Pasherly stopped his scan of the parking lot and turned to Frazer.

"Wake up and smell the coffee, Patrolman Frazer. You think the kind of scum we deal with come here to drink coffee? Most of them crawl straight back to their rat holes to inject the shit they just bought with the cash they stole. They ain't inta sipping coffee." He threw his head back and guffawed.

"They're not all creeps," said Frazer, still scrolling through his screen. "Take a look at this guy. Wanted for homicide and possible kidnapping/abduction near Falmouth. He ain't no creep from the streets."

"Let me look at that thing, seeing as you think it's so good," said Pasherly, holding out his hand.

He took the iPad and studied the image on the screen.

"Yeah, he ain't no bum. How do I look at the others?"

When there was no reply, he turned to his partner to see him staring intently through the windshield.

"Jeeze," whispered Frazer. "I don't believe it. Read that description to me, Stan."

Pasherly followed Frazer's gaze and raised his eyebrows.

"You looking at that guy with the cell phone?"

"Yeah. Just read me the description."

"Says here the perp's big, about six-five and well built. That's him, Carl, that guy with the bandage on his hand, gotta be, he's a dead ringer for that mugshot. OK, let's take this nice and slow. Looks like he's headed for that black Lexus. He certainly ain't no punk, but he could be dangerous. Cover me."

They both quietly opened their doors and Pasherly walked towards the man crossing their path about ten metres away, drawing his gun as he did. Frazer remained by the patrol car's front passenger door, his gun also drawn.

Pasherly let the man walk past him and then called out. "Hold it right there, sir!"

Jacques Bognard half turned towards the voice to see if it was addressing him. He frowned. The police officer was holding a gun.

"Keep both hands where I can see them, sir."

"Yes, all right, officer," said Jacques as he pressed a button on the phone and then held up both hands. "What's the problem?"

"Turn and face the car, sir, arms and legs spread."

"What?"

"Now, sir! I don't want to tell you again."

Jacques did as he was told.

Pasherly stood motionless, watching Jacques carefully for any sudden move as Frazer slipped past and quickly but thoroughly searched him.

"No weapons, Stan."

"Cuff him."

In a smooth and practised action, Frazer grabbed both of Jacques' wrists and cuffed his hands behind his back.

"Right, turn around," ordered Pasherly.

"Look, officer, you are making a mistake, I—"

"Name?" demanded Pasherly.

"My name is Adam Fowler," said Jacques, his jet eyes piercing angrily into the older officer's. "Would you mind telling me what's going on?"

Holstering his gun, Pasherly took Jacques' arm and moved him towards the patrol car. "Just come and sit in the car, sir, while I call this in."

"Call what in?"

Pasherly ignored the question as he ushered Jacques into the plexiglass-screened rear of the patrol car. Leaving Frazer to stand by the rear door, he sat in the front and reached for one of the bank of radio handsets.

His conversation with his HQ was short. "Officer Frazer," he called, as he climbed back out of the car. "Instructions from the Chief that we need to check the trunk of this man's vehicle. He thinks the victim could be in there."

He leaned past Frazer into the rear of the patrol car.

"Key?" he said to Jacques, nodding his head in the direction of the Lexus.

Jacques returned the stare and waited a few seconds before he replied.

"Left jacket pocket."

Pasherly reached into Jacques' jacket, retrieved the key and tossed it to Frazer.

"Wait!" called Pasherly as Frazer headed for the Lexus.

"Out of the car, Mr Fowler, let's do this together."

Grabbing Jacques by the arm, he guided him over to the Lexus, his reasoning being that if the car was wired, the man would hardly be calm about standing next to it, unless he was suicidal, which didn't seem to be the case. However, Jacques showed no concern.

"Pop the trunk," said Pasherly to Frazer.

Frazer followed the instruction and the trunk lid clicked. Gingerly raising it, he peered inside.

"Just a travelling bag," he announced.

"OK, Carl. Don't touch anything else," said Pasherly. "What have you done with her, Mr Fowler?"

"Done with whom?"

Pasherly raised his eyebrows at what he regarded as fancy talk.

"Whom?" he mimicked. "The woman you took two nights ago. There's a video of you taking her from her house."

"Officer, I have absolutely no idea what you are talking about. I don't know who you think I am, but I can assure you that you've made a mistake."

Pasherly shook his head. "I don't think so. Come back to the patrol car."

He ushered him back and sat him in the rear.

"Pass me that electronic gizmo of yours, Officer Frazer."

He gazed in puzzlement at the blank screen and passed it back to Frazer.

"I don't know how to work this thing. Show me the mugshot, Officer Frazer."

Frazer turned on the screen and ran his fingers over it to bring up the drawing of the suspect. He then held it up to his partner.

Pasherly grinned at him. "Yep, that's him all right."

He took the iPad and showed it to Jacques, a smile of satisfaction on his face.

"I wouldn't say there's much arguing with that now, Mr Fowler, would you?"

Jacques stared in disbelief at the image on the screen. It was his face, even though he knew it couldn't be. He was still staring at it when the noise of sirens sounded in the distance, bearing down on the diner.

While Jacques was being transferred to the rear of an unmarked police vehicle, Lieutenant Sharon Roper was standing alongside the patrol car talking to Pasherly and Frazer.

"Good work, both of you," she said. "Your answer to the call for coffee was perfectly timed, and then your excellent powers of observation did the rest. You've saved the county a lot of resources by finding this creep so quickly."

Pasherly's face remained impassive. "I just need to take a quick glance at the sheets in the briefing room every morning, Lieutenant, and those faces are burned into my memory," he said casually. "Don't need none of the fancy toys the tech boys are handing out. Good old-fashioned police work always comes up trumps."

"Is that so?" replied Roper, trying to keep the amusement out of her voice as she winked at Officer Frazer.

Chapter Five

Paola Santini drifted slowly from a deeply sedated sleep into a troubled semiconsciousness. Disconnected sounds and images tumbled through her brain as a harsh white light drilled into her eyes. The throbbing drone of aircraft engines fought for dominance with a harsher pounding in her head. But it lost the battle, subsided and disappeared, only for the pounding to become more insistent. Then there was a duller, sicklier vibration, and a rolling and pitching. She was briefly aware of being on a boat in a storm, but then she was swamped again by wave after wave of a more rhythmic, insistent pounding from the hammers immediately behind her eyes, the vibrations so intense she could see the hammers hitting her skull. The hammers were at least familiar territory. She always reacted badly to any form of medication, particularly sedatives. Some idiot must have injected her.

As this image bounced and stretched across her mind, the white light intensified, swamping her thoughts and spinning faster and faster out of control, the screaming that accompanied it rising higher and higher until the sound was so high her ears could no longer respond. Her hands clasped at her head and she realised the screaming was coming from her.

Suddenly her eyes popped open and the hammers stopped. She stopped screaming and the silence rolled over her.

The room was cool but she was sweating. She looked out

through her fingers. The harsh white light that had come from within her head was replaced by shafts of sunlight playing onto the otherwise shaded walls of what appeared to be a large, sparsely furnished bedroom. She looked up to see a high ceiling of terracotta tiles held in place with rows of narrow wooden crosspieces that in turn were supported on huge, rough-cut chestnut beams that looked centuries old. Her eyes roamed the room. There were two large windows either side of a wide, plain wardrobe that also appeared to be old. Outside the windows, louvred shutters filtered the sunlight to give the room its soft ambience. Hinged, solid wooden panels on the inside of the windows hung open; closed they would have plunged the room into darkness. She frowned. The room had a distinctly Italian feel. How could she be in Italy?

She absently rubbed her jaw, only to wince as a jolt like an electric shock seared through the bone. A memory of explosive pain flashed through her mind. She knew she had been hit, and hit hard. Then scattered fragments of other memories: blood spurting, the lash of a cane whipping to find its target. Then the hammers started again behind her eyes. Her hands clasped at her head as she tried to shield herself from the insistent pounding. She lay back down and curled up into a tight ball, concentrating on regulating her breathing and ignoring the pain until she finally drifted into sleep.

Sometime later she jolted awake. The light was the same, but whether it was the same day, she couldn't tell. She suddenly felt very thirsty and she reached out to a side table next to the bed. The movement sent a wave of nausea through her and the room reeled. As it settled, she became aware of two figures standing on either side of a large, dark wooden door, their arms folded as they stared at her. They were dressed in nurses' uniform, but they looked more like wrestlers. Paola quietly surveyed them, instinctively calculating how she might get the better of them should she need to.

Without any warning, the door opened and a stick insect of a man in a white coat cautiously entered the room. He was gaunt to the point of being skeletal, with wisps of silver hair struggling to cover the parchment-like skin of his head. His bony hands were clasped behind his back. No more than five foot three, he almost disappeared beside the two mountainous nurses who were now looking down at him, waiting for any instructions.

The man's eyes fell on Paola's and the skin around his mouth stretched. She realised he was smiling at her.

"Signora Santini," he said, speaking in Italian, "I need to examine you. May I?"

"Who are you?" replied Paola. "And where am I? I need to know before I agree to any examination."

The man paused, as if considering his next move, then he took a step towards the bed. "I am a doctor, signora. My name is Ronaldi. Dottor Ronaldi." He bowed his head. "I just need to check your pulse and blood pressure. You have had a long journey."

"Can't one of these buffalo do that, or are they wearing nurse's uniform because they like dressing up?"

Paola saw the two women bristle.

The doctor held up his hands in submission. "Let's not rile them, signora," he said nervously.

Paola's laugh was caustic. "I assumed they were here to protect you, since you probably know that I'm not afraid to defend myself. But you seem to be more afraid of them."

Ronaldi walked up to the bed. "Please, signora, may I take your pulse?"

Paola sighed and held up her wrist.

"Mmm," muttered the doctor. "Good."

He turned and beckoned to one of the nurses who wheeled a metal trolley over to the bed. Ronaldi picked up a stethoscope and cocked his head in question at Paola.

"Go ahead, dottore, before I change my mind."

As he was listening to her heart and then checking her blood pressure, Ronaldi's eyes were focussed on Paola's face, a look of wonderment in his eyes.

Paola scowled. "What's so fascinating, dottore? I hope I'm not the first patient you've examined."

Ronaldi leaned towards her. "Perhaps we should speak in

English, Signora Santini," he said quietly. "These two only speak Italian and although your Italian is rather, well, quaint, they probably understand you. But they know little about you and it's better we keep it that way."

Paola's eyes darted to Ronaldi's. "What's that supposed to mean?" she said, switching to English as well.

"Simply that I've been told quite a lot about you. I admit I find it hard to believe, but it would be better, I'm sure, if these two women didn't know so much. In fact, it might be better if you didn't speak to them."

"Why? My Italian might be a little rusty, but I can still communicate."

The doctor smiled. "It's not so much rusty, signora, as … well … antiquated. You sound like you are reading the script from a seventeenth-century play. Very formal and polite, but not really the way we speak to each other these days."

Paola's eyes narrowed as she thought about the doctor's words. How much did he know?

"Now, signora," continued Ronaldi. "I shall need to examine you further once the effects of the drugs you've been given have worn off. I need to determine your monthly cycle."

"My *what*?" exclaimed Paola, raising her voice. Both nurses took a step towards the bed, but Ronaldi held up a bony hand to them.

"Your monthly cycle, signora. Could you perhaps tell me the expected date of your next menstruation?"

"Considering I don't know what day it is nor how long I've been here, it's a hard question to answer." Her eyes flared. "Not that I can see why it is any business of yours."

"All will be explained in due course, signora."

"Well until it is explained, you can keep your greasy little hands off me. I should be careful, dottore, unlike most people, my bite is far *worse* than my bark." She darted her head towards him and he immediately recoiled, flinching.

"Now," continued Paola, "it seems reasonably clear that I'm in Italy although I have no idea why. So where am I, exactly, and what is it you want from me?"

Ronaldi lowered his head in regret. "I'm afraid I'm not at liberty to tell you, signora. However, I'm sure that everything will be explained to you very soon."

"Then we don't have much to say to each other," said Paola. She let her eyes bore into him, knowing that he would back away and leave.

Once Ronaldi had left the room, the nurses remained, hovering by the door.

"What do you two want?" yelled Paola, switching back to her archaic Italian. "You'd better stay close to your little *medico*. Believe me, he needs your protection!"

The nurses' response surprised her. Initially they gave her a quizzical look, as if they didn't understand her. Then they smiled at each other as if exchanging a secret.

Paola shrugged, lay back on the bed and closed her eyes. She was soon asleep as the remains of the drugs in her system took over.

Chapter Six

Lieutenant Sharon Roper walked into the interview room at the Falmouth Police Department and sat opposite her suspect. She was feeling good. An arrest within forty-eight hours with strong identification evidence that would soon be backed up with DNA would help her ambitious career prospects no end. The Chief had already expressed his satisfaction, a definite feather in the lieutenant's cap.

The man whose ID said he was Adam Fowler was sitting at the table looking surprisingly relaxed. He had already been photographed and fingerprinted and a buccal swab had been taken for profiling his DNA. A detective was on the way to the Tripley Gallery to show the new photograph to Mary Murphy prior to her being brought in for a formal identification.

"So, you're a Brit, Mr Fowler. What are you doing in the US?"

"I've already told your colleague, Lieutenant, I'm here on business. I come over quite regularly; at least once a year, often more. My visa is fully in order, as you'll find out if you check it with your system."

This was all perfectly true and a check would back it up. What Jacques was not going to reveal was that he had several other completely valid identities that he also used in the US and elsewhere when he didn't want whatever business he was conducting associated in any way with the respectable businessman Adam Fowler.

"I see you've hurt yourself," continued Roper, nodding towards the bandage covering Jacques' left hand. "How did you do that?"

"I was preparing some food for myself a couple of nights ago. The knife I was using to cut a pineapple slipped. It was very sharp. Hurt like hell when the pineapple juice got into it."

"A couple of nights ago?"

"Yes, why?"

"Can anyone verify that?"

"No, I was on my own."

"Did it bleed much?"

"Yes, quite a bit. It probably could have done with a couple of stitches, but I butterflied it. I think it will be OK. Do you want to see it?" He held up his hand.

"Er, no thank you. But I'd like a medical examiner to take a look, if you don't mind."

"Not at all. Why are you so interested in my hand?"

"There's a lot of blood in the house you were filmed leaving. I was thinking that some of it could be yours."

"Whoever you filmed, Lieutenant, it wasn't me. And neither is any blood at your scene of crime mine. So test it all. When your laboratory confirms that it isn't mine, perhaps you will accept that I have nothing to do with the crime you're investigating."

"Where were you two nights ago, Mr Fowler?"

"I was in a motel. It's not something I would normally do but my driver is sick and I've been driving myself around, so I've stayed in the area to keep distances shorter. I dislike driving, especially at night. Normally my driver would have taken me back to my hotel in Boston."

Roper grunted and opened a file in front of her. She pulled out an envelope of photographs and removed one of the body of Edith Cooper lying on the kitchen floor at Naomi Tripley's house.

"Ever seen this person before, Mr Fowler?"

Jacques took the photograph and studied it closely. Roper watched his eyes as he did and was surprised by the care he was taking. Normally a perp would take a casual glance and sling it back.

"No, I don't think so. But she's covered in blood so I can't really see her face properly."

"Doesn't bother you, Mr Fowler, seeing a mutilated dead body?"

"I've seen dead people before, Lieutenant," said Jacques, handing back the photograph.

"Really, Mr Fowler? Where was that?"

Images from across the centuries flashed through his mind. The aftermath of massacres he'd witnessed, some of them over two thousand years before, wholesale slaughter in the name of religion he'd narrowly escaped being part of on more than one occasion. Far more recently, the dead Arlette lying on a table in a room at the back of her beloved bar, her son Georges nearby her. He looked up into Roper's eyes. "It's of no relevance to your investigation, Lieutenant."

Something in Jacques' eyes told Roper that he was right. Usually she would pursue that line of questioning, not let the suspect get the upper hand. But there was a depth of feeling to the way Jacques had spoken the words that stopped her in her tracks. Instead, she fanned the photographs, picked out one of Edith Cooper from the mortuary and handed it over.

Jacques studied it. "No, I've never seen her before."

"Are you sure, Mr Fowler? Take your time."

"I'm certain, Lieutenant. I don't know her. Who is she?"

"I was hoping you'd be able to tell me, since the CCTV footage shows you going into Naomi Tripley's house with her. Tell me, Mr Fowler, what sort of business is it that brings you to Cape Cod?"

Jacques shook his head. "I have no business in Cape Cod; I've never been here in my life until today when you brought me."

"And Ms Tripley? What sort of business did you have with her?"

"I don't know any Ms Tripley, Lieutenant. I've never heard the name before."

"I'm talking about the woman we have CCTV footage of you carrying out of her house, the tenant of that house, Naomi Tripley. Tell me about her, Mr Fowler."

"I told you, I've never heard the name before."

He was telling the truth. When John Andrews had called him about Paola, he'd only referred to her as either Paola or Annie Carr. The name she was currently using wasn't mentioned.

"You know, Mr Fowler, you're really not helping yourself."

"I can't tell you things I don't know, Lieutenant."

At that moment, the door to the interview room opened and Detective Mullins came in. He glanced disdainfully at Jacques and then leaned over to talk into the lieutenant's ear. She listened carefully and nodded.

As Detective Mullins left the room, Roper gathered her thoughts and sat back on her chair.

"Mr Fowler, I don't know how it works with the police over there in Britain, but here in the States, if someone is facing serious charges — and it looks as if you are — things go much better if the person admits what they've done and helps us out. The DA and the courts will take a more understanding view if you just come clean.

"Now, I've just been told that the lady who gave us your description from when you visited the Tripley Gallery a couple of weeks ago has been shown the mugshots we took of you earlier. She is in no doubt that you are the man she described, but she says that you used the name Charles Creed."

Jacques let his gaze penetrate the lieutenant's eyes. "That's totally ridiculous. I've never heard the name Charles Creed before. I don't know anyone of that name."

Roper shook her head. "Like I said, Mr Fowler, Creed, whatever your name is, you're not helping yourself with these denials. However, I'll give you one more chance to help me. Tell me what you've done with Ms Tripley; tell me her whereabouts. I'll see that the information gets taken into consideration. You see, if you haven't killed her, even though she looked pretty lifeless in the CCTV footage, then you've put her somewhere. Now, here's the thing. If she's hurt or bound and your partner's hightailed it somewhere, then when you don't come back — and you're not going anywhere, I can assure you — when you don't come back, Mr Fowler, she could die. That will make this case a double homicide."

She paused to watch her suspect's reaction, but the expression on his face didn't change, so she continued.

"You tell me where she is, Mr Fowler, and I'll send a patrol car right away. It may save her life. Do you want her death on your hands as well?"

Jacques put his hands together in front of his mouth for a few moments as he gathered his thoughts. Then he sat back.

"Lieutenant, I repeat what I said earlier. I have nothing to do with this woman's disappearance. Before this morning, I'd never been to Cape Cod, and I certainly have nobody's death on my hands. The suggestion is utterly ridiculous."

Sharon Roper shrugged and tidied the contents of the file.

"Do you have a lawyer here in the States, Mr Fowler? Because it looks to me as if you're sure going to need one."

Chapter Seven

Paola Santini was dreaming about her mother in Naples. It was a dream that recurred whenever she was troubled, uncertain of her situation. It was 1534; she was sixteen years old and she had plucked up the courage to ask her mother about her father, knowing it would probably end with her mother screaming abuse at her.

"I've told you, Paola, that you are not to speak of him. His name is never mentioned in this house, indeed in this city. He was evil, a weak man who gave in to the temptations of the Devil and became his slave."

As ever, Francesca Santini started to cross herself vigorously. Her voice rose.

"I fear for you, child, especially now that you are hardly a child but a young woman. Who will want to marry the daughter of a man who was the Devil's servant? Who? You are too much like him, Paola, what with your ridiculous good health. I shall be watching you carefully as you get older to make sure the years take their rightful toll on those good looks."

"But Mamma, I only want to know a little about him. Aunt Anna thinks that underneath he had a good heart, that—"

"Your aunt Anna has no right to say such things. She didn't know him as I did. I've paid the Church a fortune to ensure that you have inherited none of his evil ways, that all trace of his spirit is banished from your body. How many exorcisms does it take to scour him from your mind? I thought that was over. Do I need to arrange another?"

Paola scowled at her mother. The exorcisms and other rites dreamed up by the priests and bishops were raw scars etched into her memory. They had all seemed to necessitate a detailed examination of her body. When she was a child, she just found it embarrassing, but at the last ceremony two years ago, when her body was advancing into womanhood, it had been more than embarrassing; she had been revolted by their undisguised ogling and leering, their touching and probing. She hated them.

Her mother was shouting now. She had taken hold of her shoulders and was shaking them.

"Is that what you want?" she screamed.

Paola tried to push her hands away. "No, never again! I'll kill any priest who tries to lay a hand on me!"

"Signora?" The hands were shaking her roughly, taking pleasure in giving her discomfort. "Signora. It's time to get up. The boss wants to see you."

Paola opened her eyes, and the image of her mother's face twisted in anger faded from her mind, replaced by the face of one of the nurses about six inches from hers. She glared at the nurse, still disturbed by the echoes from the distant past.

"What makes you think I want to see him?" she spat and turned her back.

"You have to get up. Now!" The nurse shook Paola's shoulder roughly. Paola grabbed her wrist and spun it around. The nurse yelped in surprise.

"Back off," growled Paola. "I can get myself up. Shake me like that again and I'll break your arm."

The nurse took a step back and put her hands on her hips.

"I look forward to seeing you try, *signora*. We've been told to be gentle with you, which is difficult, believe me. But when there's no one else around, gentle might be forgotten. Now get up and get yourself ready, unless you want me and Maria to scrub you down in the tub and force you into your clothes. You, with your fancy way of talking, you're nothing but a murdering bitch."

Paola had drawn her legs under her on the bed and was ready to launch herself at this woman, to scratch and tear at her, but then the door opened and the second nurse, Maria, came in. Maria took one look at the scene in front of her and slammed the door.

"Patrizia!" she barked. "What's going on? You'd better back off. We've been told to deliver her to the boss; he won't be pleased if she's injured. There'll be plenty of time for that later."

She turned to Paola.

"Perhaps Your Majesty would deign to raise her aristocratic backside off the bed and head for the bathroom. After you have prettied yourself up, your two maids-in-waiting can help you to dress. Which powdered wig would you prefer today, Madam?"

Paola frowned at the nurse's performance, not understanding the reason. "What the hell are you talking about, you fat oaf?"

"Your fancy ways, of course, Contessa. Tell me, where did you learn all this flowery talk? Some ancient count who still thinks the aristocracy is special? Have you spent your life screwing him and picking up his posh ways?"

Paola suddenly remembered her conversation with Doctor Ronaldi. Her Italian. She hadn't spoken the language much since the early seventeen hundreds, the only times being in Rio when she'd posed as an Italian in one of her policeman friend and protector Rodrigo Barros' little set-ups to break down a suspect. She'd thought the occasional incomprehension had been a dialect problem; it hadn't really occurred to her that her language was archaic.

The nurse Maria walked over to the wardrobe and pulled open the doors.

"Your clothes are in here, bitch, and the bathroom through that door. We'll be back in twenty minutes. You'd better be ready. We don't want to keep the boss waiting, do we?"

Anxious to be on time, the nurses were back within fifteen minutes and hurrying Paola from her room. They escorted her along a corridor that led onto a grand, wooden staircase and then descended two floors to a large entrance hall whose walls were adorned with numerous bucolic scenes of rural Italy. From there they walked along another corridor to a large sitting room. Here, picture windows looked out over a wooded valley in the distance and a more formal garden nearer the house. Several of the windows were open, allowing the crisp autumnal air to permeate the room. From the shadows she could see in the garden, Paola decided it was probably early afternoon.

"Ah, Annie, you're awake. How are you feeling after your long journey?"

Paola turned in the direction of the voice to see Marcus Dayton, the man she knew as Charles Creed, sitting at a large walnut desk at the far end of the room. Behind him and on his left were floor-to-ceiling shelves filled mainly with leather-bound books.

Dayton stood and walked round the desk.

"I hope you are feeling better now that you have freshened up. Are you hungry? You must be after our long trip."

He pointed to a long table to the left of the door through which she'd entered. It was laden with fruit, bread and cheese. "Please, help yourself to a snack. Or if you prefer, I can order something more substantial for you."

He smiled, but Paola could see no warmth in his eyes. She turned in the direction of the table of food and noticed a well-built man who could only be a guard standing at the far end, positioned close to an array of cutlery. She let her eyes linger on him, assessing his weight and fitness. He looked like he could handle himself. She'd need a weapon if she took him on. Turning back to Dayton, she noticed a large scar on his left cheek that was still raw, only partially healed. A memory of her whipping the cane across his face flashed across her mind. Her eyes creased in satisfaction.

"How's the face, Mr Creed? You turned your head just in time back in my cottage. If I'd found my mark, you'd be blind in one eye now."

Dayton's left hand instinctively rose to the wound. "Then perhaps I should consider myself lucky, Annie."

"I can see you are taking precautions," said Paola, nodding towards the guard. "This brute is there to deter me from taking the silver, is he? Or is he part of your protection detail along with these two mountains of brainless muscle?" She waved an arm towards the two nurses who were standing by the door.

"You're very gung-ho, Annie. I should be careful if I were you. You killed their colleague; they would dearly love to get even with you."

"Ah, that explains their gentle caresses in my room when they woke me up," said Paola.

She thought back to the scene in the kitchen of her house in Cape Cod. So the woman was part of a team. She remembered her deceptively calm and friendly tones, with their underlying threat. *I'm Edith, dear, and I've come to help you pack a few things. You won't need much; we'll provide almost everything.*

Paola looked down at her clothes. They had indeed provided everything. The wardrobe in her room was full of new tops, jumpers, trousers, jeans, shoes and underclothes, along with some warm jackets and scarves. All her size. There was even a woolly hat.

"Why did you find it necessary to kill her, Annie?"

She snorted. "You break into my home and threaten me and you honestly expect me not to resist. I'd have killed you as well, given the chance."

"There was no need to kill anyone, Annie," reprimanded Dayton. "Edith had a family, you know."

"Then she should have chosen a safer profession. Now, I want to know where I am and why I am here."

"Well, Annie, you know already that you are in Italy, but where exactly is of no consequence."

"Like hell it isn't!" she barked, causing the guard to turn his head slowly in her direction.

Dayton ignored her outburst and continued.

"It's of no consequence since I have a number of houses like this in a number of countries that I could have chosen for the task. It's just that here is the most convenient."

"Convenient? Convenient for what?"

Dayton took a step towards her and dropped his voice, even though they were speaking in English and he knew that none of the three others in the room understood a word.

"Annie, you must understand that I know about you. All about you. I have not only read Dr Wright's book but I took the opportunity to examine all her notes. They make fascinating reading and I can assure you that, unlike the doubting psychiatrist, I had no trouble in believing them, for the most part, anyway."

"Really? Why is that, Mr Creed? Why should you so readily accept them?"

"Well, firstly, Annie, I also saw all the photographs that Dr Wright took of you both. I know they are genuine and that they were taken in the early 1970s. I have also seen Dr Wright recently, an elegant lady of over seventy years of age. But you, Annie, you haven't changed one bit since those photographs were taken. But even without that excellent evidence, there is another reason why I am ready to accept your tale as the truth."

Paola waited, wary. Wondering what was coming.

"You see, Annie," continued Dayton, "the simple fact of the matter is that I am the same as you are."

Paola threw back her head and laughed. "Is that right, Mr Creed? Well now, perhaps you should go consult Dr Wright. She'll readily diagnose you as delusional and have you locked up. Whatever makes you think you are hundreds of years old like me? You're not really Napoleon, are you?"

Dayton laughed. "No, Annie, not hundreds of years—"

"Oh, I see, you've just realised that you're like me, have you? A sudden change in the way your body works?"

"You're not listening to me, Annie. I said not hundreds of years because it's more than that. I am well over two thousand years old."

Paola raised her eyes to Dayton's. She knew hers could be devastatingly penetrating, their distinctive pale grey having cowed many an adversary. Creed's eyes, by contrast to hers, were jet black. She remembered them from his visit to the gallery. And she remembered the comment she had made to Mary Murphy about him having the dust of centuries about him. She gasped quietly to herself. She was inclined to believe him, but she wasn't giving in yet.

"That's easy to say, Mr Creed, especially after you've had the benefit of reading my life story, or some of it. You don't really think that I told Dr Wright everything, do you? Or that everything I told her was the truth. It was quite sanitised in places, you know."

A thin smile formed on Dayton's lips. "That's very interesting, Annie, perhaps we can talk more about that later. But for now, let me ask you this. You have, I imagine, tried to explain yourself to people you thought you could trust a number of times throughout your life, and I should think that on many of those occasions you have met disbelief, to say the least. Now that the boot is on the other foot, Annie, and you're hearing a similar tale from someone else, are you not open-minded enough to believe it?"

"Why should I?" said Paola. "You're just offering your word at the moment, no evidence. After the way you've treated me, why should I believe or trust anything you say or do?"

Dayton nodded. "You are right. Why should you just take my word?" He glanced at the two nurses and the guard. They were poised, ready to spring in case of trouble, but clearly not understanding any of the conversation.

Bringing his attention back to Paola, Dayton said, "I will show you some things that I think will convince you, things that I keep very secret. But first, Annie, I want to strike a truce. I want you to promise me that you won't try to grab the nearest object and start beating me over the head with it. If you do, I can assure you that my guard dogs here will jump to my defence and they *will* subdue you, and they won't do that without hurting you badly, firstly to teach you a lesson, and secondly because of Edith. And if by some chance you did manage to kill me, they would in turn kill you. It's as simple as that, Annie." He held out the palms of his hands. "So, no violence. Can we agree on that?"

Paola sneered a victorious half smile at him. "I seem to have got you and your staff very worried, Mr Creed. And look at me, a slip of a thing."

She paused and raised an eyebrow in question.

"OK, I'll agree, but tell me one thing. Why do you keep calling me Annie? I was only Annie Carr for a few years. It's hardly my name."

"What would you prefer that I call you? Naomi? Mali? Dolores?"

"I'd rather you didn't call me anything. I'd rather be sufficiently far away from you that it didn't matter. But since you seem to have the upper hand for the moment, I'd prefer Paola. It is, after all, my real name and the one I've used whenever I can."

"Paola it is, then," he replied, tilting his head graciously.

She studied his eyes once again, remembering all the recent events that had changed her life so much. Meeting her father for the first time, and before that, meeting Lily, her half-sister, and Sara, her daughter. She rapidly ran through them in her head and wondered just how much Creed knew. It seemed very likely that he didn't know about John or Lily. He certainly hadn't made any mention of them. So far he seemed to be relying on Nancy Wright's notes as his main source of information. She realised that she would have to be very careful about what she said to this man, that he would pick up on every nuance and would have the resources to follow up on everything. She still didn't know why she'd been taken. Regardless of why, escape would be her number one priority, but she didn't want to endanger any of the others in her family.

She smiled at him, appearing to relax. "Thank you," she said. "But while we're into show and tell, I certainly don't believe that your name is Charles Creed. I'm sure, like me, you've had many names if you are as old as you say you are. What should I call you?"

He absently rubbed the still-tender wound on his left cheek.

"Charles Creed is just for the games of smoke and mirrors," he said. "Here my name is Marcus Dayton."

Chapter Eight

John Andrews stared at the phone in his hand, willing it to ring, but it remained stubbornly silent.

"Anything?" asked Lola as she came back into the kitchen.

"Nothing. Both Jacques' and Paola's phones are still going to voicemail and now there's no answer from the gallery."

"This assistant who works in the gallery—"

"Mary Murphy."

"Yes. She didn't give her mobile number?"

"No. I forgot to ask. What time is everyone getting back here from wherever they've gone?"

"In an hour or so. Pete wanted to see the Cumbrian coast. I told him it's pretty underwhelming, but you know what he's like; he wants to experience everything. I think they were intending to browse the shops in Keswick as well. It's a pleasant enough day, so I expect they won't be hurrying."

"I think I should call them. Sara really should be told about what's happened to Paola."

Lola pursed her lips. "Yes, of course you must, although we don't actually know what's happened to her yet. But since they are both lawyers, Pete and Sara might have contacts in Massachusetts who can tell us more."

"That's a very good point," said John. "I'll call Sara now."

· · ·

Lola was right. Taking advantage of the mild weather, their visiting family had driven south down the coast from St Bees as far as Seascale and found it as unexciting as Lola had described. The presence of the Sellafield nuclear power station looming behind Seascale had hardly enhanced their experience. Giving up on the coast, with Matt engrossed in the maps and with the help of a satnav guiding them, they had worked their way inland to Lake Windermere and the dramatic views of the hills beyond. They were exploring an antiques shop when Sara's phone rang.

"John. Hi. Guess what? The boys managed to get us all the way from the coast to Windermere without going via London."

John heard a howl of protest from Matt in the background.

"Is that where you are now?" asked John.

"Yes. I'm resisting the temptation to buy a whole load of wonderful antiques."

John snorted. "Don't buy anything until Lola's with you. She knows all the dealers and will get you the best prices. Listen, I'm sorry to interrupt your afternoon, but something's happened that you all need to know about. Could you cut it short and head back here, to the cottage? It'll take you about half an hour."

"Sure, we'll jump straight in the car. What is it, John? Is it serious?"

"I don't know yet; I hope not. As you know, I haven't been able to contact Paola for a couple of days, but just now I spoke to her assistant in the gallery who told me there's been some kind of incident. Paola's disappeared. It could be nothing; a mistake ..."

"We'll be right there, John," said Sara.

They were back at the cottage within half an hour. John heard their car roaring down the lane just five minutes after Lily returned from Grasmere, Lola having called her to tell her to close the gallery and head home.

"Whatever's happened, John?" panted Pete as he rushed into the kitchen. "Sara says that Paola's disappeared."

John sat them down and told them everything he knew.

"I thought you'd been distracted, Papa," said Lily once he'd finished.

"I was," agreed John. "But I didn't want to say anything in case I was worrying about nothing. After all, telephone lines go down all the time."

"We should go back to the US immediately," said Sara. "I can't sit here wondering where my mother is. I've spent too much of my life without her; she's not disappearing out of it again."

"You're right," said Pete. "But first, I can make some calls. I know the DA in Boston pretty well; we've worked together on many occasions. Although it's not his patch, he's bound to know the DA down in Falmouth."

"It'll be the DA for Barnstable County," said Sara. "His area covers Falmouth. The detectives unit from his office will be investigating the homicide of this woman who's been killed."

"I'd forgotten. You had a case down there, didn't you?" said Pete.

Sara nodded. "Yes, several years ago. It's a different DA now. I don't know him. It'll probably be better if you ask your contact to approach him. You know how touchy people can be if they don't know you, especially in the early stages of an investigation."

"That's true," agreed Pete. "We're hardly in a position to explain why we're so interested in the woman they'll know as Naomi Tripley. All we can really say is that she's an artist friend."

Lily was quietly drumming a finger on her chair, running ideas through her head.

"You could say that she told you she was about to visit England, to see friends, say, not that she was visiting her father. If you'd told her that you were coming here as well, you could have all agreed to meet up. That would be a reason for you trying to get in touch, to check on her travel dates and so on."

"That's good, Lei-li," said John, calling Lily, as he always did, by the original Chinese name he and his former wife, Mei-ling, had given her when she was born in Hong Kong in the 1880s. "I think Paola told Mary, her assistant, something along those lines. That she was visiting friends, I mean. Mary will have told the police so if Pete comes up with a similar story, it won't seem strange."

"OK," said Pete. "I'll make those calls."

"Use this phone, Pete," said John, tossing him the cordless handset for the house phone. "I have a deal. Calls to the US are free."

"Thanks," replied Pete as he caught the phone and headed for the sitting room.

From the expression on Pete's face when he returned about twenty minutes later, they knew he hadn't been very successful.

"The DA was in court but I spoke to one of his assistants, Daryl Wiseman, whom I know pretty well. He didn't push too hard on why I was interested and he seemed OK with the story I gave him — I'm glad we discussed that; it helped it to slip off my tongue very easily. He called a contact in the DA's office in Barnstable who would only initially tell him that the investigation was ongoing, which of course means that he didn't want to say anything."

"Why so cagey?" asked Lola.

"Hard to say," said Pete. "I guess they don't get too many big cases down there; it's a pretty peaceful place. So when there is one, they must be concerned that it'll be taken out of their hands. However, Daryl is a fairly persistent sort and his contact did tell him that someone had been brought into custody and that they were extremely confident — their words — they had got the right man. However, they had no clue of any motive."

"Christ!" said John, the worry clear in his voice. "That must be Jacques he's referring to. They've arrested Jacques. That's what was happening when he broke off our call. He said that there was an agitated police officer approaching him. They must have identified him from that drawing that Mary Murphy sent through."

"Did Jacques say what he was doing in the area?" asked Sara.

"No, the conversation didn't go that far. He said that he was on a business trip. I didn't get a chance to tell him about the drawing or to ask why he thought it would look so much like him."

Pete sighed, trying to weigh up all the information.

"John, setting aside for a moment why anyone would want to abduct Paola, and it does seem to be an abduction since there's been no ransom demand. That was the other snippet of information that Daryl wheedled out of the Barnstable office."

"Pop," interrupted Matt, "there could be many reasons why someone might want to take her, especially if they'd found out any of what we know."

"I know, Matt," said Pete, "but we'll come back to that." He turned back to John.

"I know Jacques is a very old friend of yours, but, if you'll forgive me for being blunt and playing the devil's advocate, just how much do you know about him? Enough to have total trust in him?"

"Absolute and total trust," said John, rather affronted by the insinuation.

Pete held up his hands in submission. "Sure, but how much do you really know about him? From what you've said, I think he's a pretty rich businessman. What's his line of business?"

"He's quite an entrepreneur, always has been," said John. "Most of it revolves around shipping and the sea, although I know he has fingers in a number of other pies. He's accumulated wealth over the centuries and secreted it around the world in a number of safe havens so that if he needs to disappear, change identities, he can access whatever he needs. We're talking about someone who's been around a long time, Pete, and who expects to be around for, well, I don't know how long. When Jacques formulates a game plan, he's looking at decades at the very least, sometimes centuries."

"Sounds like he's even older than you are," said Matt.

"Matt!" cried Sara, shaking her head.

John forced a slight smile at Matt's guilelessness. "Yes, he is. I'd forgotten that you weren't in the room when I told your mom and pop about him. I got to know Jacques in Marseille in the 1640s. He was a merchant sailor with several ships. He ended up saving my life in 1677, but I didn't see him again until just three years ago. You see, we didn't know about each other's rather strange condition in the 1600s. It wasn't something you talked about. Still isn't, except to a trusted few.

"Anyway, Jacques has spent much of his very long life on the sea. He's the most amazing sailor; totally at one with the ocean."

"Wow!" said Matt again. "Exactly how old is he?"

"Exactly, I can't say, but he was born in the times when Greece was still a major world force, in the West, at least. He's around two and a half thousand years old."

"Two and a half thou … that's so … cool," said Matt, his voice drifting away as he realised his enthusiasm wasn't appropriate.

John turned to Pete. "Look, Pete, I understand what you're saying, but really, you have to trust me on this. I knew Jacques for over thirty years back in the sixteen hundreds and I've got to know him well in the last three years. He's a powerful man but he's not a criminal. No, whatever's happened, there must be a rational explanation — a case of mistaken identity or something like that. Jacques simply wouldn't abduct Paola; he has no reason to."

"I agree," said Lola. "I've only known Jacques for three years. He is charm personified, and I'm not saying that because he's cast a spell on me. I know a smooth talker when I meet one; I've come across a few customers in the gallery over the years who've tried to sweet-talk me and I know how to deal with them. It's true that Jacques has a charisma about him, a presence. There's a quiet confidence that makes you believe in him. Christ, it's not surprising when you think about all the things he must have seen in his life. But it's all based on an underlying goodness. You should hear him talking about Mathilde, for example. He was devoted to her. And there have been others like her, not loads, a select few, in fact. But in each case, he was a wonderful and devoted husband and father."

"OK," said Pete, "I'm convinced. I'd really like to meet this man, especially given our joint love of the sea. Look, I'll get back to Daryl Wiseman, see if I can persuade him to wheedle the name of the man they've taken into custody from the DA in Barnstable."

"What about Digby, John?" said Lola. "Surely with all his contacts he should be able to help."

"Yes, of course," added Pete. "I'd forgotten about Digby Smith, our very own spook. He has contacts everywhere."

"I'll call him," said John. "But given that it's all only just happened, I doubt he'll get much further than you, Pete. And knowing Digby, he'll see it as a diplomatic nightmare. He told me once that he finds the American government very difficult to deal with."

Lola raised her eyebrows in surprise. "That's quite a revelation, given our Digby's penchant for secrecy. If I didn't know that he avoids even sparkling water in case the bubbles make him light-headed, I'd say that he'd been drinking when he told you that."

"That's another point, Lola," said John.

"What? Drinking?"

"No, of course not. You referred to 'our Digby.' Our Digby isn't Jacques' Digby. He has his own and he probably doesn't even know what's happened. I'll call now. Our Digby can pass on the information."

Pete was lost. "How many Digbys are there?"

"Good question," replied John. "We know of two, although of course we won't ever meet one of them."

"Right," said Pete, not understanding at all.

Chapter Nine

At nine the following morning in the holding cells at Falmouth Police Department, Jacques Bognard, known to the police and most of his current business associates as Adam Fowler, was sitting on his bed while his lawyer, Bryan Meecham, was standing with his substantial back to the bars of the door that faced into the corridor. Meecham was a corporate lawyer, unused to dealing with the police and criminal proceedings, but he was savvy enough to be keeping a watchful eye on the whereabouts of the custody sergeant, in case he was trying to listen in on any conversations.

It was with this concern in mind that the man perched on an upright chair between Meecham and the bed where Jacques was sitting had insisted that their discussion with their client be in the cells, not in the interview room. Kyle Drover, one of the best criminal defence lawyers on the East Coast and one of the most expensive, was concerned that, while it was against protocol, the lieutenant might not have been averse to listening in on their conversation from the other side of the one-way glass, the mics accidentally switched on.

Drover undid the button of the jacket of his five-thousand-dollar business suit and eyeballed his client.

"Mr Fowler, I've spoken with the lieutenant to see if they're holding anything back. As far as I can see, their case is entirely circumstantial without a shred of hard evidence to implicate you. We'll post bail, no problem."

Jacques was watching him quietly, unfazed by the display of wealth, wondering if his confidence was merely an act for his benefit or whether he could make a good case.

Drover continued. "It's well known that eye-witness testimony is inherently unreliable and the Murphy woman is not even a witness to this case. All she's done is describe an unrelated incident that occurred two weeks ago in a place completely unconnected with the crime they want to accuse you of. Her testimony isn't worth squat."

Jacques shook his head very slightly. "The problem, Mr Drover, is that she gave an extremely detailed description of the man in the gallery, a man who bears an amazing likeness to me. And now she has confirmed that by identifying me directly."

"Doesn't mean a thing, Mr Fowler. Proves nothing about the homicide whatsoever. She gave a generic description from which a portrait was drawn. It's not even a photograph and it could have been any one of thousands of men. A couple of patrolmen looking for glory think it might be you, and suddenly everyone agrees it is you. This gives Murphy such confidence that when she sees you, she's convinced, even though your face might not have been close. If it gets to the witness box, I'll destroy her. ID-ing you is of no relevance, rest assured. The CCTV footage they have is poor quality; I've seen it. It's very grainy and the people shown in it could be anyone. You can't see any of the faces, so just because one person has a vague physical similarity to you, it means nothing. There are tens of thousands of people of your height and build in this country. If they come up with nothing else, then you're outta here, my friend. I take it there is nothing else you can think of that might explain the confusion, is there?"

"Nothing, Mr Drover. It's as baffling to me as it is to you."

"OK, we'll head up to the interview room, but let me do the talking with the lieutenant. She's a hard-nosed bitch, but a flimsy case is still a flimsy case, and she knows that's all she's got."

. . .

Lieutenant Sharon Roper deliberately kept them waiting, much to Drover's annoyance, and when she did appear she was clutching a file that seemed to Jacques to be substantially bigger than it had been the previous day. She took her time settling into her chair before she looked up at her suspect.

"Lieutenant," started Drover, "I—"

Without moving her head, Roper let her eyes turn to the lawyer's. She put up a hand to stop him. "Mr Drover, as much as we all appreciate the sound of your voice, I have an important question to put to your client. Once we have an answer to that question, we'll see what you have to say."

Drover bristled as the lieutenant stared him down. "Get on with it then, Lieutenant. My client is a busy man and doesn't want to waste any more time here. What is it you need to put to him?"

Roper gave him a mirthless, slightly mocking smile. She turned her attention once again to Jacques.

"Mr Fowler. You told me yesterday that you have never been to Cape Cod, let alone to the cottage rented by Ms Tripley. You told me, effectively, that this is a case of mistaken identity."

"Lieutenant," interrupted Drover, "We've been through all of this. If you've nothing—"

"Patience, Mr Drover, please," said Roper, holding up her hand once again to stop him without taking her eyes off Jacques. "Well, Mr Fowler?"

Jacques turned his head to Drover who considered the options and then nodded his agreement for Jacques to respond.

"Nothing's changed overnight, Lieutenant," said Jacques. "I haven't suddenly realised that I was suffering from a memory loss when I spoke to you yesterday. What I told you was completely true."

The lieutenant shook her head slowly.

"Well what has changed since yesterday, Mr Fowler, is that we have the results of the lab tests on the blood at the scene. There are two distinctly different DNA profiles found in the blood. One, as you would expect, agrees with the victim. But the other blood found at the scene in several locations including outside the main door to the cottage, blood that must have been spilt as Ms Tripley's unconscious or dead body was carried from the house, has a DNA profile that matches your blood exactly. I'm not talking about a possibility here, Mr Fowler. It's your blood. Just how do you explain that?"

Her voice had risen as she was talking, her tone as she finished very accusing.

Drover countered immediately. "I need to see those results, Lieutenant. I need a copy of all the profiles to show to my experts. There's clearly been a mistake. The blood cannot possibly be my client's; your lab must have got the samples mixed up. It's contamination of some sort. Happens all the time with DNA."

"No, Mr Drover, it doesn't. Contamination is very unusual now that the proper procedures are followed to the letter. If it happens at all, it's when we're dealing with microscopic traces of blood from a scene. And I can assure you that isn't the case here. There is no mix-up, no contamination. These are substantial bloodstains we're talking about here, not traces. They are from one person and one person only, Mr Drover, and that person is your client, who I'm about to charge with homicide and abduction."

"There's nothing to support abduction," stormed Drover. "There's just a grainy video of a person — you can't even be sure it's a man — carrying another person you can't identify."

The lieutenant leaned forward. "There's blood, Mr Drover, a lot of it, right at the spot shown in the CCTV footage. And your client has a recent and deep cut to his hand that by his own admission bled profusely."

"Where's that cut hand in the video, Lieutenant? I couldn't see any cut hand."

"It's hidden by the body he's carrying."

"How convenient for you. Well, I'm not so sure. I'll have that video enhanced so it's as clear as a Hollywood 3D movie, and you'll find that not only is the person not my client, but also that you'll see his hand and there'll be no cut on it."

The lieutenant shook her head. "Nice try, Mr Drover, but you're just spinning fairy tales now. You have no idea what an enhancement might show. In the meantime, I'll be charging your client and the DA will be opposing bail. That's certainly not going to be a problem for him in the light of the violent circumstances of the case and a rich, foreign businessman who might just be tempted to flee the country."

She held up her hand again as Drover blustered his objection. "*I'm* not saying your client would do that, Mr Drover, but that will be the DA's pitch, trust me."

Jacques was silent. He was staring at the lieutenant in disbelief while his head was spinning with the information he'd just been told. There was no way any blood from Naomi Tripley's house could possibly be his, and yet the results, according to the lieutenant, were unequivocal. He played various scenarios in his mind and rejected them all except one. And that one, which made no sense at all, was that the whole thing was a set-up. But why should Roper and her colleagues manipulate or plant evidence to implicate him? He had no history with them, no connection whatsoever. It didn't add up.

He continued to stare at the lieutenant, but her face didn't register in his consciousness as he wrestled with the information. As his awareness of the room and the people in it returned, he realised that the lieutenant was looking extremely angry. Kyle Drover was waving his finger in her face and yelling.

"This is all bullshit. What about DNA from Tripley? Where's that? Are you trying to tell me that there was a violent fight in which the dead woman was hacked viciously and another person, who you're suggesting was my client, was also badly cut, while the woman abducted was unharmed? This whole thing stinks, Lieutenant, and I shall prove it."

"Firstly," yelled the lieutenant in retaliation, even though she was trying hard to be calm, "I'm not suggesting your client was at the scene; I'm telling you. The DNA is totally unambiguous on that. As for other injuries sustained by other parties, that's pure speculation. For all I know, Tripley was in on the homicide, got knocked unconscious somehow and Fowler was carrying her from the scene. He certainly appears to be treating her quite gently. It's her cottage, Mr Drover, so any DNA of hers found there is of no great significance."

As she sat back, fuming, Jacques held up a hand.

He spoke quietly, forcing her to pay attention. "Lieutenant, before you charge me, would it be acceptable if I had a word with my lawyer in private? It won't take a moment."

Roper sighed heavily. "Go ahead, Mr Fowler, you might try instilling some manners in him." She got up, turned on her heel and left the room.

Jacques turned to Drover. "You tried your best, Mr Drover, but that was an unexpected broadside. I know your expert will be reviewing the results, but I doubt they have made an error. There must be some other explanation. Now, if you don't mind, there's something I need to discuss with Bryan."

Drover made to object, but then remembered he was being paid substantially whatever the outcome. He adjusted his suit jacket and stood. "I'll wait outside and entertain myself watching that dragon breathing fire."

Once he'd left, Bryan Meecham sat down next to Jacques.

"How can I help, Adam? This is all rather out of my comfort zone. I'm used to fighting your corporate battles, not your personal ones."

"We'll leave that to Kyle, Bryan, my old friend." Jacques smiled. "I'm sure he'll regroup and come up with something. I am innocent after all. I hope you believe that."

"I have known you for too many years to doubt it, Adam. Now, what can I do for you?"

Jacques leaned forward to speak softly into Meecham's ear. He too was uncertain who might be listening and there was no way he wanted what he was going to say to be overheard.

"It's a simple phone call, Bryan," he whispered. "There's a man in London I need you to call and explain everything to. I can't tell you who he is, apart from his name, nor can I tell you what he does or for whom he works. Suffice it to say that if he cannot help me, then no one can. Would you like to write down his number?"

Meecham retrieved a notebook and an engraved fountain pen from his jacket. He unscrewed the cap of the pen and raised an eyebrow to Jacques, who dictated the number.

"And his name?"

"Smith," said Jacques very quietly, "Digby Smith."

Chapter Ten

"Marcus Dayton?" said Paola, the disbelief apparent in her tone. "Surely that's a modern name. I can't believe it was your original one."

Dayton smiled. "You are right, Paola. I have only used the name Marcus Dayton and variations of it in relatively recent times. I have no idea what my original name was, that is, the name given to me by my parents. I never knew them, you see."

Paola peered into Dayton's jet black eyes. Was there a waver of emotion there, something she could capitalise on?

Dayton sighed. "It's a long story, Paola and not one I want to tell you today. Another time, perhaps. But there is something I'd like you to explain to me, if you will."

She waited, wondering what was coming, knowing he was still probing. What he said next made her think he'd been reading her mind.

"Tell me, as a relatively young artist trying to establish herself in the rather seasonal climate of Cape Cod, how come you were suddenly so keen to head off to Europe? What was the great attraction?"

"Well, you know very well that I'm not a relatively young artist, as you put it—"

"Don't pretend you didn't understand my meaning, Paola. You are cleverer than that. You know very well that I'm talking about your Naomi character. Why should she want to rush off to Europe?"

Paola shrugged, trying to appear nonchalant. "It's actually none of your business, but I met an old friend. She came into my gallery in Falmouth. I hadn't seen her for a few years and she invited me to her home in England."

Dayton laughed. "A few years or a few hundred years? Come on, Paola, you can do better than that. Your story makes no sense. If you hadn't seen this person for a few years, then you must have known her when you were Cassie Gomes. You see, I know about Cassie Gomes. And if she knew you as Cassie Gomes and turned up in your Falmouth gallery, she must have been very shocked, unless she knew your secret. Perhaps she was like you, Paola. Are there others like you?"

"Not that I'm aware of," she lied.

Marcus laughed out loud. "There you go again, Paola. Your default position can't always be denial. Surely you realise that I know about your daughter."

A dark cloud descended onto Paola's face and her entire demeanour changed.

"If you so much as lay a finger on my daughter, I'll kill you, Dayton, have no doubts about that."

"Whoa!" said Dayton, holding up his hands. "I wouldn't dream of hurting your daughter. But you still haven't answered my question. Not with a truthful answer, anyway. Why the urge to see Europe?"

Paola felt uncomfortable with the way the conversation was going. He was pushing and she needed to take him somewhere else.

"Like the story of your original name, Marcus, it's a long one and it's something I don't really want to talk about today," she said, her smile angelic.

"Touché," said Dayton. Then he stood.

"Come," he said, beckoning her. "I said I'd show you some proof of my being the same as you. Let's move into the more comfortable sitting room next door."

Paola stood, her eyes taking in the present room again. It seemed perfectly comfortable to her. However, when they walked through a large oak door into the adjacent room, she understood Dayton's remark.

This sitting room was considerably larger than the first, with several well-stuffed leather sofas positioned to take in the view through the large picture windows. Her eye was taken naturally over the limits of the garden to the forest below it and the hills beyond, a spectacular panorama of one hill rolling into the next. It was like looking at a huge mythical monster, its many limbs cascading into the distance, its feet resting in the valley below them.

Paola rapidly searched the landscape for any clue as to where they might be. However, apart from the forest stretching away into the distance, there were no obvious landmarks, no signs of habitation. There was nothing nestling among the branches, no roofs or breaks in the density of the trees.

"Beautiful, don't you think," said Dayton, interrupting her thoughts. "We are completely isolated. Not another soul lives in those woods for as far as the eye can see."

"Knowing the Italian male's love of hunting, don't you find rather a lot of people wandering through the paths that must be there?"

Dayton laughed. "They would certainly like to, believe me. The place is teeming with wildlife; some of the boar are really quite large. But no, no one visits those woods. They are surrounded by a very effective fence that is well patrolled. Everything you can see and several kilometres beyond. The estate is vast. It costs me a lot to keep the authorities away, but they have learned to appreciate the things I can do for them in return for their cooperation."

"Italy doesn't change then," retorted Paola.

"How very cynical of you." Dayton smiled. "Come, sit on one of these sofas; the leather is wonderfully soft." He walked over to an antique desk and pulled a bunch of keys from his pocket.

Paola looked back towards the room they'd just left and saw the three guards standing by the door. She understood why Dayton wanted to use this room. It wasn't simply to impress her with its comfort; it was so large that the guards would be unable to see any detail of anything he showed her, and neither would they be able to hear any of the conversation.

She sank into the upholstery of one of the sofas and watched Dayton retrieve a folder from the desk. He sat down opposite her and placed the folder on the low table that separated them. Inside was a sheaf of photographs, the top one of which he handed to her. It was a professionally taken, present-day studio portrait of him.

"Very nice," she said, glancing at it briefly before tossing it onto the table. "Why should this interest me?"

Without answering, Dayton handed her another, a black-and-white shot of himself with a 1950s Hollywood film star.

"Do you recognise her?" he said.

"Of course," said Paola, "who wouldn't?"

"We were lovers for a while," he continued. Paola said nothing but couldn't fail to note that the Dayton in the photograph looked no different from the man sitting opposite her, apart from the change in fashions over sixty years.

He passed her another, this time a sepia shot from the 1920s or '30s. Again, the main subject was clearly Dayton. He was wearing a double-breasted blazer over an open-necked shirt and a cravat. His trousers appeared to be cream or white and his shoes were two-tone brogues.

"Quite the dapper sailor boy," remarked Paola.

"That was in Portofino on a yacht belonging to one of Mussolini's bully boys. He liked to relax in style."

He retrieved another. "And this one was in Monte Carlo around 1900," he said, looking up at Paola and waiting for a reaction.

However, she merely shrugged and tossed away the picture. "So you're good with Photoshop, or one of your minions is. Virtually anyone can do this sort of thing these days. It's all too easy."

Dayton smiled at her cynicism.

"Look at them carefully, Paola. They are not fakes. Every one of them is completely genuine. Why should I go to so much trouble? As you can see, I keep them locked away. You are the first person to see them since …" He paused, his voice catching slightly.

She waited, but he didn't explain further.

"For a long time," was all he said as he gathered up the

photographs and put them back in the folder. "There are others in here that go back to the early days of photography in the 1840s, but you clearly need other proof. I'll show you something else that can't fail to convince you, but I really must emphasise your agreement to behave yourself, Paola."

She held his eyes for a moment, her lips pressed together in amusement. Then she raised her arms in submission. "I said I'd be a good girl and I will."

Taking the folder with him, Dayton stood and walked towards a door in the far corner of the room. He retrieved his keys once again, unlocked the door and opened it. He then punched a series of numbers onto an electronic device on the key ring. There was a soft swish from beyond the door as a large steel panel slid back.

"No one else is allowed in here," he said, turning to Paola.

Paola looked back at the guards, but they hadn't moved.

"They have no knowledge of what's in here," said Dayton, following her eyes, "and that's as far as they are allowed to come."

He held the door for her. "Come," he said.

Paola walked past him into a huge, windowless room some twenty metres in length and about twelve wide. Unlike the room she had just left, this one had no beams or terracotta tiles, nothing to attract insects or dust. The walls and ceiling were white while the ceramic floor tiles were a soft grey. A gentle hum from a number of vents high in the walls told of a sophisticated climate and air quality control system. This visual information flashed in Paola's consciousness for a mere fraction of a second, since her attention had immediately been drawn to the large number of paintings hanging on the walls. She turned to her right and as she approached the closest, she heard a faint click behind her as Dayton closed the outer door, but the significance of their being alone in a closed room escaped her notice as she gasped at the painting in front of her.

"This has to be a Picasso," she said, touching the frame. "It's brilliant, but I don't recognise it."

Dayton nodded his approval of her knowledge. "You're right, it is. And you don't recognise it because it's never been on public display. It exists in no catalogues or books of his work. It's one of several in here he produced for me personally."

Paola couldn't hide her amazement. "You have an impressive list of friends."

"I don't think I'd call Picasso a friend, not a close one, anyway. He and his crowd were rather too Bohemian for my tastes. But I love his work and he appreciated my knowledge of painting. Although of course I never told him I'd acquired it directly from many famous artists through the centuries."

Paola moved along to the next painting, a dark portrait of a noblewoman. "Rembrandt?" she said, turning to Dayton.

"Exactly, Paola. You have a good eye," he replied, tilting his head slightly to emphasise his approval.

"And this one's a Vermeer, I'm sure of it," she said, unable to take the wonder out of her voice. "And like the Rembrandt and the Picasso, totally unknown to me. Are all the paintings in this room like that? How many are there?"

"There are two hundred and thirty-one, and, yes, they are all unknown to the outside world. I have accumulated them slowly over the centuries and kept them in a number of locations, ensuring they are protected by the latest technology."

Still unable to take it all in, Paola walked to the left side of the room, stopping in front of a portrait of a young woman. "Now this one I can't identify. It looks old, about sixteenth century, but although I don't recognise the style, there's something very familiar about the face."

"Interesting painting, that one," said Dayton. "You're right, it is sixteenth century. It's by a Tuscan artist called Tommaso Perini. He's almost completely unknown these days, but for me that portrait rates as one of the finest works I have in this collection, despite all the famous names. I picked it up from a dealer in Florence centuries ago and it's always stayed with me."

Unknown to Paola, she was looking at a portrait of her half-sister, Gianna, painted as a young woman in her twenties. As she took in the detail, she realised that it was familiar because the face was very like hers. Tommaso Perini, she thought. Was that one of

John Andrews' former personas? The style was certainly like his, even today. Could this woman be a relative?

She suppressed the feeling and walked on. She felt in danger of letting her guard down and revealing more than she wanted to Dayton.

She lifted her eyes to scan the rest of the paintings, taking in for the first time that most of them were portraits. She walked farther down the room, away from the door through which they'd entered. As she moved from one painting to the next, the main reason for the gallery hit her. Of the more than two hundred paintings, around fifty were portraits of Dayton, the range of style covering most of the major developments and schools from the present day back to the very early Renaissance.

Dayton had walked over to where she was now standing in the centre of the room, her eyes darting from one painting to the next.

"I see from your reaction that you've recognised the subject in many of these," he said. "You're not going to accuse me of Photo-shopping them, are you?"

She ignored him and marched over to one particularly large portrait. "Is this by Titian?" she said, awestruck once again.

"Yes," replied Dayton, "You really do have a remarkable eye. Unfortunately I only commissioned it after he had become famous. It cost me a lot of money. The man had a good head for business and as he became better known, his prices soared. But it's worth it, don't you think? It's a wonderful piece, even if the subject is me."

Paola smiled. "He's made you look rather handsome," she said. "Did you really know all these artists? Wasn't it a problem, you know, hiding the facts about yourself? I have found it a constant headache, and I can always resort to make-up. For a man, it must be even more of a problem."

"It is, most definitely, although I'm pretty adept in the use of make-up as well. But of course, I didn't meet any of these artists with any of the others. And for the most part, I appeared in their lives, commissioned a painting, and moved on. They were paid generously, and so they were happy. I don't suppose they gave me another thought. Only occasionally did my dealings with them continue over a longer period of time, as with Picasso."

"Quite the narcissist, aren't you? Do you enjoy sitting in here and admiring yourself?"

"I didn't commission them because of the subject matter," retorted Dayton. "They are an interesting ongoing experiment through the centuries. Give the same subject to a succession of master artists and see what sort of job they make of it. The results so far have been really rather interesting. Some of those artists considered to be the last word in portraitists have, in my opinion, not always made the grade. I think the best portraits of me are by a couple of lesser-known artists. However, art is very subjective and that is merely my opinion." A smile only a whisker short of supercilious drifted across his face.

"Not much point in an experiment spanning centuries if you don't publish the results," said Paola.

"I'm hardly in a position to do that, Paola. You know as well as I that it doesn't pay to advertise our unusual condition."

A thought occurred to Paola and she ambled back to the portrait of Gianna, hoping not to be too obvious in her behaviour. "Did the artist for this piece—"

"Perini."

"Yes, Perini. Did he paint your portrait?"

"Sadly no, he didn't. I only came across his work after he was dead."

"Dead?" She sounded almost shocked.

"Yes, he died in the late fifteen hundreds, as I recall."

"Oh." Paola's quiet reply wasn't lost on Dayton. He frowned slightly as he looked from Paola's face to the Perini portrait, the threads of a connection starting to intertwine.

Again, Paola realised she was on dangerous ground, but she had to know. She marched up the gallery, scanning the portraits of Dayton, trying to find one in what she was now thinking of as the distinctive style of John Andrews. But there was nothing.

"Looking for anything in particular?" asked Dayton.

"Ever been to the Caribbean?" she improvised.

He laughed. "Of course I have, many times. I own an island there. But I never met your friend Cazabon, if that's what you're thinking, the artist you described to Nancy Wright."

"Just a thought," she replied.

Dayton stood and watched while Paola moved from masterpiece to masterpiece.

"Huh!" she exclaimed. "A Joshua Reynolds. I'm not sure the powdered wig suits you."

Dayton smiled. "I thought it rather fetching at the time."

Paola continued to scan the paintings, hoping her behaviour would distract Dayton from her reaction to the Perini painting.

"Ah, there," she said, pointing to yet another portrait of Dayton. "A Renoir. I was hoping there would be a Renoir. I love his work. I should like to have met him, but I'd moved to the Caribbean by the time he was born and I never returned to Europe."

She turned to face Dayton, who was across the room from her.

"An impressive collection, Mr Marcus Dayton. No, more than impressive, it's outstanding. Unique. But it only goes back to the early Renaissance, just a couple of hundred years before I was born. Yet you are claiming to be much older. Have you nothing that's pre-Renaissance?"

"As you well know, the skill of painting realistic portraits of people only really developed with the Renaissance. Giotto is generally credited as the first to move away from the stylised paintings of the medieval and Byzantine eras and focus on emotions and natural representations of the human form. I have a number of portraits of myself from the tenth to twelfth centuries, but I'm afraid they don't look much like me," he laughed. "For that reason, I keep them elsewhere."

He paused. "However, I agree that magnificent though it is, this collection is incomplete as a record of my life. Perhaps I need to show you something else."

Chapter Eleven

Bryan Meecham punched the red button on his cell phone to end the call. As the screen reverted to the wallpaper photo of his two Maine Coon cats, he continued staring at it, as if hoping the animals that ruled his house and his private life might clarify the conversation he'd just finished.

"Damn Brits," he muttered. "It's like they're still playing the Great Game."

He had left the Falmouth Police Department, watched Kyle Drover's fawning driver usher his boss into his sleek Bentley, and then opened the door to his own preferred barrier between himself and the world around him: a top-of-the-range Toyota Land Cruiser. Once he had settled in the firm leather driver's seat, he called the number in the UK that Jacques had given him a few minutes before.

The call was answered after two rings.

"Four seven one three," announced a voice that Meecham immediately classified as upper class Brit: it was dripping with superiority, confidence and the British public school system.

Whoever answers their phone by reciting the last four digits? thought Meecham. Don't these people use their names?

"Hello, yes, I'd like to speak with Mr Digby Smith."

"Speaking."

Quite the conversationalist, thought Meecham.

"Mr Smith. My name is Bryan Meecham. I'm a corporate lawyer representing the interests of Mr Adam Fowler in the United States. He gave me your number and asked me to call you."

"I see. Is he unable to call me himself?"

"Precisely, Mr Smith. He cannot call you."

"Why is that?"

"Well, the fact is he has been arrested and is now in police custody. He's being charged with homicide and abduction. He is allowed calls, but not international ones, and he was adamant that calling you was his best hope. In fact, his only hope, according to him."

"Would you mind telling me what's happened?"

Meecham clenched his teeth. There was that tone again: the landed gentry talking to one of their peasant farmers. It might have sounded like a polite request, but it was an order.

Meecham gathered his thoughts and spent the next five minutes giving Smith a clear and concise summary of the events of the past three days. During that time there was total silence from Smith, not even the sound of him breathing. As Meecham finished talking, the silence continued.

"Mr Smith? Are you still there?"

"What? Yes, of course I am. Mr Meecham, I am indebted to you for passing on this information as soon as you were asked. If you get the opportunity to speak again to Mr Fowler, I should be most grateful if you would convey to him that I shall be pursuing the matter with the utmost expediency."

"I'm sure he'll be very reassured to hear that, Mr Smith. Um, I wonder, might I ask in what capacity you will be pursuing the matter?"

"The capacity is subordinate to the purpose, Mr Meecham. And the purpose is to gain Mr Fowler's release from these charges. I shall start the task immediately. Thank you so much for contacting me. If there is anything else you discover that you think might be relevant to Mr Fowler's case, please do not hesitate to call me. May I wish you good day."

With that, the line was cut and Meecham found himself staring at his cell phone.

Digby Smith was the name by which Jacques knew his protector, the man who worked for a particularly secretive arm of the British Secret Service. At least that was what Jacques assumed; he didn't know for sure. Smith had been assigned to Jacques five years before when Jacques' complex system of passport substitution had failed him in Cairo and the Egyptian authorities had arrested him. The British Embassy in Cairo had been contacted and Jacques' file, in the name of Adam Fowler, had ended up on the desk of the Senior Liaison Officer, who was also the main MI6 man operating out of the embassy. The SLO turned out to be a very thorough man who started delving into the records of names Jacques had given him. For once in his long life, Jacques had made a mistake and given the SLO too much detail, enabling him to make comparisons of passport holder photographs, dates of birth and subsequent dates of death. The SLO had become convinced he was dealing with a very secret operative who might well not be working for his own government.

Jacques was flown back to London under guard and interviewed at a secure country house secluded in dense woods in the Surrey countryside, south of London. Like John Andrews two years later, Jacques' life was becoming increasingly difficult in the light of the ever-improving security surrounding passports and other identity documents. While there were still several ways of circumventing the system, the situation was only going to become more and more difficult. Once his interviewers were convinced that he wasn't working for a foreign government, Jacques decided he would try to convince them about his true situation in the hope it would give him a long-term solution to his unusual problem. A very sceptical Digby Smith had been assigned to him and it was only when Jacques took him to a number of his own secret locations around the globe, where he had archives of material that supported his claim to be immensely old, that Smith broke into a smile and opened the resources of Her Majesty's Government to him in return for his unique fund of historical and other information.

Digby Smith was not Jacques' protector's real name. Part of the smoke and mirrors game that he and his colleagues played was to use aliases and code names, and one particularly arcane habit among the small band of Smith's colleagues engaged in handling what they referred to as 'special charges' was that they all used the codename Digby Smith. It had started as an in-house joke, harmless enough since none of the special charges was ever likely to meet another and even then would never reveal his protector's name. It was only when John Andrews was assigned his own Digby Smith, following John's rescue from the hands of Wallingford Peterson and his introduction to Professor Frank Young's secret world, that the joke backfired. Courtesy of both Jacques' Digby Smith and John's, Jacques was put in touch with John and they were reunited after over three hundred years. They were highly amused to discover that their protectors had the same name, even though they were different people.

Jacques' Digby Smith, Martin Pettigrew-Wyatt, stared through his office window at the view of the Thames and wondered about his special charge. Having known him for five years, and being in the unique position of knowing a huge amount about Jacques' two-and-a-half-thousand-year history, he was convinced that his man was not a killer. That was not to say Jacques hadn't killed during his life to extricate himself from a life-threatening situation — kill or be killed — but that didn't make him a cold-blooded murderer.

The call from Bryan Meecham had not been a surprise: John Andrews' Digby Smith, whose real name was Samson Blythe, had told Pettigrew-Wyatt that his own charge had called him asking for his help. And when Meecham's call came, it was to a number that Pettigrew-Wyatt had given Jacques to use only when he was in serious trouble — thus ensuring that even if Jacques was unable to talk, the simple fact of the number ringing would alert Pettigrew-Wyatt to the existence of a problem.

Both Pettigrew-Wyatt and Blythe had the same background of

Eton and Oxford, although they differed in age by ten years. And they had both ended up in the same highly secretive cloisters of the security services, following their recruitment while still undergraduates. Pettigrew-Wyatt had been largely responsible for training Blythe. However, regardless of their background and relationship as colleagues, neither would ever reveal to the other anything more than was absolutely necessary about their special charges, including their charges' names.

Ever distrustful of telephones and office walls, Pettigrew-Wyatt turned from the window and walked out of his office, locking the door after him. He strode along a short corridor to Blythe's office and tapped on the door.

"Come!"

"Roof, old boy," was all that Pettigrew-Wyatt said as he popped his head round the door.

They had both discovered that there was a particular corner of the roof that was almost guaranteed free of the possibility of eavesdropping. It wasn't overlooked, there were no bugs — they checked regularly — and London's nearby traffic roar meant the sound of their subdued voices would be inaudible to even the most sensitive of long-range microphones.

"There's something of a problem, Samson, old boy," said Pettigrew-Wyatt quietly, speaking inches from Blythe's ear. "I've had a call from my man's lawyer, as you predicted might happen following your man's call to you. Seems that my man has either severely blotted his copybook or the cousins have made an enormous blunder. Thing is, they have my man present at the scene of what appears to be the cold-blooded murder of a woman who was slashed deeply and expertly across her throat, and the abduction of another woman, the one who rented the house where it all happened. It's all very strange. There's been no ransom demand, so the authorities are not treating it as a kidnapping, not that the abducted woman has any money, apparently."

Samson Blythe nodded, pursing his lips. The protocol was a nightmare. He knew from John Andrews that the abducted woman was Paola, but because of the strict rules of secrecy, he couldn't reveal what he knew about her to Pettigrew-Wyatt. Jacques may be his colleague's charge, but all the others in the equation had become Blythe's responsibility. Under normal circumstances, a guardian like him would have just one charge, but no sooner had he taken on John Andrews than he automatically had Lily Saunders and Phoebe Andrews, and then later Sara Farsley, plus assorted extras. He hadn't yet met Paola Santini, but he knew she was destined to be one more on his burgeoning list.

"What I understood from my man," said Blythe, "is that the evidence against your man comprises an identification by an assistant from the missing woman's art gallery."

"I'm afraid it's far more serious than that, old chap," replied Pettigrew-Wyatt. "The police have confirmed that my man was at the scene of the murder from his DNA. Apparently he was injured at the scene and not only does he have a deep cut on his hand that supports that suggestion, but also some of the blood found at various locations around the scene is his. According to the police there is no doubt about the match. However, according to his lawyer, he's absolutely adamant that he wasn't there, knows nothing about it."

Samson Blythe rubbed his chin. "You said your man might have blotted his copybook. How sure are you of him? Is he capable of something like this?"

"I suppose given the right provocation and circumstances, we're all capable of it," replied Pettigrew-Wyatt.

"Of course," said Blythe, shuddering slightly. "But you said the dead woman was slashed expertly across her throat. Could your man have been responsible?"

"Obviously I can't reveal any details of his life, old boy, but I can say that he's been in some scrapes. So he might well have picked up the skill set, yes. However, knowing him as I do, I'd be extremely surprised if he'd kill in cold blood in this way, even if provoked or cornered. He's far too streetwise for that. I'm sure there must be some other explanation that makes sense."

Blythe straightened and paced the area of the roof they regarded as their safe haven, considering what to do. In his mind, he replayed his earlier conversation with John Andrews. John had sounded extremely worried about the disappearance of his daughter as well as the possible predicament with Jacques. Blythe had numerous contacts in the academic world to whom he could turn, but this was a sensitive issue; he would rather keep it in-house. He nodded to himself; he had one excellent source on whose expertise he could draw.

He stopped pacing and turned to Pettigrew-Wyatt. "Like you, Martin," he said, "I'm no scientist, so I can offer no explanation. However, I do have a close contact who might be able to shed some light on the matter. If there's any alternative explanation, she should be able to provide it."

Chapter Twelve

Marcus Dayton watched as Paola continued to examine the price-less paintings lining the walls of his personal gallery. Her abduction temporarily forgotten, she appeared to be soaking up the experience, delighting in each new piece as she moved from one to the next.

"You know, it's outrageous that these are totally unknown to the world," she said, turning to him.

The corners of Dayton's mouth twitched downwards. "I don't see why," he said. "I either bought or was given every single one of these paintings. Just because most of them are by artists who are now very famous doesn't mean I have any obligation to share them. You must see that by keeping them here, out of harm's way in this controlled environment, their condition will be preserved for centuries. They will probably be around in pristine condition long after many of the works in the major galleries of the world have succumbed either to lunatic vandals or over-zealous restorers. And anyway, if they were all by obscure artists, like the Perini over there, you wouldn't care anything for them. You are assuming a value simply because their creators are famous."

"Actually," said Paola, "I'm in awe of that Perini. I simply cannot understand why he is not better known. Even from a cursory look at the brushwork and the form, it's clear that he was a master as brilliant as any of these others."

Dayton smiled to himself. This was a Paola he had not expected. Her enthusiasm for her art had not been reflected in Nancy Wright's notes, and in his three brief encounters with her, she had been cold and distant at the first meeting in her gallery, dangerously violent in her house in Cape Cod, and today, until they entered the gallery, she had been calculating and guarded. He wondered how long this genial mood would last. He decided to capitalise on it, reinforce it while he had the chance.

"Come, Paola," he said, "We can return here later. I said I wanted to show you evidence from further back in history of my being the same as you, considerably older, in fact."

He took the bunch of keys from his pocket and walked over to a solid wooden door at the far end of the gallery. As he unlocked it, he turned to see if Paola was following. But she had stopped by yet another portrait.

"This is by François Boucher!" she exclaimed. "I'd know that style anywhere. He painted my portrait too, in the early 1760s in Paris. I had an English husband, an aristocrat, at the time. Boucher wanted me to pose nude; he had quite a reputation. Richard nearly threw him out, but I implored him to let Boucher continue his work. He relented, naturally, but insisted on sitting with us for every session. I was fully clothed, of course."

Dayton laughed. "That portrait of me was painted around 1759, as I recall, but I was in and out of Paris for a few years after that. It's a wonder we didn't bump into each other at a soirée."

He pointed towards the room beyond the gallery. "Please, Paola, tear yourself away for now. I think you'll find what's in here is really rather special."

Like the gallery they had just left, the windowless room was large with a high ceiling, but the air was cooler.

"This room," explained Dayton, "has an even more sophisticated climate control, and even with that, there are one or two pieces that have extra protection."

He pointed to a small group of paintings hung near the doorway. "These are all on wood, of course. Canvas and oil were a

Renaissance invention. So much has been lost from the times when these were painted. There are not many around the world in this good a condition."

Paola studied the first two, peering at the detail. "When were these painted?" she asked, the surprise at what she was looking at sounding in her voice.

"Those two are both by the same artist, one is of me, of course, the other, the noblewoman, was my wife. Her name was Eloise. I think you will be amazed to learn they date from the eighth century."

"The eighth century! Where were they painted?"

"In France, by a young man I knew near Lyons. Of course, Lyons wasn't part of France at that time. He was a remarkably talented artist, as you can see, painting at a time when there was very little interest in art, even from the aristocracy. He was the son of a merchant I had dealings with, forever scratching designs on parchment he prepared himself from the skins of various animals. It was a medium that was very prone to damage and decay, so he also painted on wood to produce portraits like these. The Church didn't like it, needless to say, and it was down to luck that I managed to save him from certain death at the stake. I smuggled him out of his village and took him to Marseille."

"What happened to him?"

"He decided to try his luck at sea. The unfortunate ship he set sail on sank in a storm off the coast of Spain, all hands lost."

"How sad. He clearly had an innate gift. These paintings are not in any way the iconic style you'd expect from that time. They are, well, very realistic."

Dayton laughed. "As I told you, Giotto might have been a major force in the commencement of the Renaissance, but he didn't invent realism. There have always been people like my young friend who simply painted what they saw instead of complying with the dictates of the Church or local customs. The further back you go, the more examples there are, relatively."

He turned and pointed farther into the room. "However, the main features of this room are not paintings but sculptures. Most of them are marble, that wondrous material, and most date from

Roman times. The oldest Roman one was produced around 150 BCE, as it is now called in these ridiculous times of political correctness, and they cover a period of about four hundred years, until around the fall of Rome.

"And there's one, sadly just one, that dates back even further to when I was still a relatively young man in Athens. As a sculptress yourself, I'm sure they will fascinate you."

A smile flickered briefly across Paola's face. "You're quoting from Nancy Wright's notes again. It's true that I've dabbled with sculpture on and off for many years, but it was only really as Mali Whittaker in the nineteen forties that I took it seriously."

As she was speaking, she turned her attention to the twenty statues standing before her. "These are incredible," she said, "and so much colour."

"Yes," replied Dayton. "They're not like most of the statues you see these days in museums: grey and lifeless. In Roman times, statues were mostly painted. Michelangelo got it wrong, you know, with his statue of David. He should have painted over the marble."

"That's a very contentious statement," said Paola, raising her eyebrows.

"Not really, Paola. The Renaissance was in many ways a resurrection of the classical world. Much of the sculpture echoes the work of Roman times when even expensive marble was often painted with carefully formulated pigments. Not so much to obscure the stone, but to use it to show skin textures and tones with wonderful subtlety."

He let Paola wander among the sculptures, examining each one closely.

"The pigment is in remarkably good condition," she commented.

"Yes, I have protected them carefully over the centuries. When I saw the effects of just a few years on so many excellent works, I was determined not to let my statues go the same way. They have probably not seen more than a few days of natural light in two thousand years."

"Given the turbulent history of Europe, wherever did you keep them?"

"It wasn't easy. Through the centuries I have had a number of very obscure, very well-hidden, well, addresses, I suppose you'd call them. As I accumulated more and more statues and then later paintings, it became increasingly difficult. In fact I lost many pieces; my collection should be four times this size."

Paola stopped by one statue, tilted her head to study it, and then turned to Dayton. "Marcus Dayton in a toga, with a very Roman hairstyle. You'll be telling me next you were an adviser to Julius Caesar."

He laughed. "No, I certainly wasn't; I've always avoided politics and politicians. They couldn't be trusted then any more than they can be trusted now. But I did meet him. He was a very charismatic man; there was an aura about him that drew people to him. It helped that he was quite tall, for a Roman, that is. At a guess I'd say he was about five foot nine, which is not so much by today's standards, but with the average Roman around five inches shorter than that, he certainly stood out. His eyes were like mine, very dark. It was the first thing he noticed about me, he even commented on it. However, I didn't hang around in his company. People my size were unusual to say the least, and they often ended up fighting for their lives as gladiators in bloodbaths like the Colosseum."

"I must say the likenesses are excellent," said Paola. "It's the eyes, I think. Because they're painted, they are animated. Not like the pupil-less versions you generally see on statues or busts."

"I agree," replied Dayton. "It makes all the difference." He tilted his head in question. "Well, Paola, do you believe my story now?"

As Paola ran a hand through her hair, a scene from Marconi Beach in Cape Cod flashed across her mind. The moment was the unexpected arrival of Nancy Wright on the clifftop, the first time she had seen the psychiatrist for thirty-seven years. Wright had been stunned by Paola's appearance and, in a matter of seconds, all her years of refusal to believe what she regarded as Annie's delusional tale evaporated. *Do you believe my story now, Dr Wright?* Paola had asked.

Paola sighed as she thought of the irony of now being asked

the same question herself. "To tell you the truth, I'm speechless," she said. "Either you are totally delusional and you have used what is clearly your considerable wealth to fabricate an entire history, or you are telling me the truth."

"I can assure you that it's the truth," said Dayton. "A detailed scrutiny and analysis of this work would reveal that, not that I'm about to have them subjected to a battery of tests. No, for obvious reasons, they must remain our secret. You see, you are only the second person to whom I have ever shown this collection."

"Who was the first?"

"The first was my daughter Emma. Once I realised that she was like me and once she had grown up, I wanted to show her the wonderful benefits a staggeringly long life could bring. She was fascinated." He paused and shrugged his shoulders. "How could she be otherwise? She wanted to start adding portraits of herself."

"Where is she now, your daughter? Is she here?"

Paola had been idly peering at one of the statues as they were speaking, but when there was no reply to her question, she turned to Dayton. His eyes burned into her for several seconds, then he diverted them to one side and she saw the sadness that had enveloped his whole stance. She immediately understood. To her surprise, instead of seeing his grief as an opportunity, she actually felt sorry for the man.

"What happened?" she said in little more than a whisper.

Dayton sighed deeply. "She died," he said.

"But …"

"What I mean is, she was killed. There was an accident, about two years ago, in the Caribbean."

"I'm sorry, that's tragic."

"Yes. I had planned so much for us. I am very wealthy, you see, and I had intended … her life was only just beginning."

He paused, gathering his thoughts. This wasn't a conversation he'd had with anyone before. He looked up and sighed. "It happened only a few months after I'd explained about myself to her and how she was the same. Obviously she didn't believe me at first, but after seeing all this and realising that like my health, her own incredible health was something very unusual, she had accepted it."

"But you must have had other children. Did you reveal nothing about yourself to any of them?"

"I have had many, but none was like me, like Emma. I tried to tell some, but mostly I didn't. It's a very difficult concept to understand, and, as I'm sure you have found, it can cause many problems. You must remember that for most of my life, society has been steeped in superstition and profoundly strong and inflexible religious dogma. Our so-called enlightened times are a very recent phenomenon. They are taken for granted now in the West, but things could easily regress and revert." He paused and then swept an arm around the room. "I certainly never got as far as showing them any of this."

"You're a secretive man, Mr Dayton."

Paola stood watching her captor, focussing her full attention on him, the priceless art surrounding her temporarily forgotten. She was aware she had let her guard slip in these two amazing rooms and she knew she had to be careful. But she was also aware that Dayton had let his own down. And now she had discovered the vulnerability in his steely exterior, she wanted to learn more about him, what was driving him. She would keep him talking.

"You said you were a young man in the time of the Greek Empire. Do you know exactly how old you are?"

"Not exactly, no. Dates were recorded very differently when I was young and since then there have been many systems. Historians have pieced a lot together and we blithely tend to quote or refer to dates as if they are absolutely accurate. They are not, believe me.

"In those days, people had a very different perspective on time passing and of course there were none of these ridiculous BC or BCE dates, as if the apparent date for the birth of Christ was the most significant event in the history of man. The system we use now in the West was in fact invented by some monk over five hundred years after the assumed date for the birth of Christ, a date for which, I should point out, there is very little agreement. So you can imagine how prone to error it is."

"For some it is," interrupted Paola, "the most significant event, I mean, although I admit that after my dealings with numerous representatives of the Church over the centuries, I am not one of them."

"For some, yes," agreed Dayton, "but they are in the minority, a large one I admit, but still a minority if you consider all the other major and minor religions in the world, let alone atheists, who use our present system of recording dates purely as a matter of convenience. You don't think people in the time of Julius Caesar thought in our dates, do you? People then didn't say to each other as, for example, 54 BCE drew to a close, 'gosh, the year has flown, in a matter of days it will be 53 BCE'."

Paola laughed. "That's really quite amusing."

"So in answer to your question," continued Dayton, "it was difficult to keep track. The ordinary people didn't really care that much. Most of them couldn't read or write, so their lives related mainly to seasons and harvests, not the birth of some prophet or other. But taking all that into consideration, I estimate that I am around two and a half thousand years old."

Paola raised her eyebrows. "And I thought I was old. But are you telling me that in all that time you have only had one child like yourself? Have you met anyone else, not related to you, who is the same?"

Once again, deep in the blackness of Dayton's eyes, there was a sadness, a weariness.

"Apart from Emma, you are the first, Paola. Until Emma was born, I had become convinced that I was simply a freak occurrence, a one-off, as the British say. Then after she died, I became obsessed with finding others. I knew they must exist."

Paola pursed her lips as she absorbed the information. "I wonder why you've never fathered others. OK, I've only had one child like me, as you know from Dr Wright's notes. In that respect, I was telling her the truth. But my father—"

"Your father?" interjected Dayton rather too forcefully. "What do you know about your father?"

Paola clenched her jaw. She'd said too much. It was bad

enough that Dayton knew about Sara; she didn't want him to know any more.

"I ... I know nothing about him," she stammered. "I never met him. It was rumoured, according to my mother, that he was like me, but I don't know. I suppose if he was like me, he could have fathered others like me, who knows? Before he died."

"Died?"

"My mother said that the Church caught up with him, executed him ..." She faltered. She felt sure he knew she was making it up. She raised her chin and returned Dayton's stare. "Have you any idea why we are like we are?" she said, hoping to deflect his attention. "Do you know if two ordinary people can have a child like us? Or if ..."

She stopped as she remembered the conversation with the skeletal Dr Ronaldi, his interest in what he had called her monthly cycle. Her thought processes raced ahead of what she had been asking Dayton and she suddenly realised why she was there.

"What is it you want from me, Dayton?" Her voice had hardened, her guard back up. "You drag me from my home and drug me, some of your heavies appear to be nurses and there's that creep of a doctor. Is this some sort of clinic? What's really going on here? This place obviously isn't just a private retreat where you can reflect on your lonely past."

Chapter Thirteen

Claudia Reid tapped her pen against her lips as she studied the data on her monitor. It was good, but not good enough. And there were some anomalies. The run would have to be repeated, which would mean several hours of meticulous extraction of the very sensitive DNA required for her tests.

Her elbows on the desk, she rested her head in her hands and scowled at the numbers, searching for inspiration. Then she sat back and ran her hands through her strawberry-blonde hair. She had let it grow again after experimenting with a boyish cut the previous year. She'd disliked it before she'd even walked out of the salon, not consoled by the words of her best friend, Sally Fisher, who had talked her into it in the first place. "It's only hair, Claw, it'll grow."

Well, it had grown and now it was getting in her way. She fished in her desk drawer for a hairband and tied it back, trying to refocus her attention on the screed of figures that seemed to scroll on forever.

"Jeff!" she yelled to her assistant.

"Claudia," came the far softer reply. "I'm on the other side of your desk, not on the other side of Lambeth."

"What? Oh, sorry. Yes. Listen, do these figures make any sense to you?"

"Most of them, yes, but I'm not the prof, Claudia. I can't look at a partial set of results, which is what these are, and predict with unerring accuracy what the rest are going to be and then what they mean."

"No, of course you can't. But the prof's not here, so I thought you might have some idea, 'cos they're bugging me."

"I known what you mean, Claudia, but at least they're consistent with the data we've got so far. They don't conflict."

Claudia's reply was a noncommittal grunt.

"I'm going to fetch a coffee, Claudia, do you want one?"

"Love one, thanks. Here, I've got some change."

"No, no, it's, er, it's my treat," stuttered Jeff. Now he'd moved from laboratory business to a personal level, his confidence had floundered. He'd meant to sound cool, relaxed, hoping Claudia would look up from her screen and see the warmth in his eyes, but it never quite worked. He was crazy about her, but his natural reserve coupled with no indication that Claudia really noticed him at all made him absurdly cautious. His adoration seemed destined to bounce around the laboratory and out the door. Certainly none of it appeared to stick to its target.

Claudia looked up, smiling to herself as she watched him go. She was perfectly aware of Jeff's feelings for her; he was as subtle as an air horn. The problem was that he simply wasn't her type, although with her succession of disastrous relationships with men over the years, she had no real idea what her type was. She just knew it wasn't Jeff. She shrugged and pulled a face. She'd better find her type soon; she was nearly thirty-five and her clock was ticking.

She turned her attention back to the monitor, sighing as she absently removed the band from her hair and tied her unruly locks into a loose knot. Her boss, Professor Frank Young, was away in Australia giving a plenary presentation at a cutting-edge genetics conference. Claudia was in charge during his absence. Their team was small but elite: six of the best geneticists in their field working on the highly classified research that had resulted from the discovery and interpretation of John Andrews' DNA profile back in

2009. Claudia had been at the root of the discovery, having profiled John's DNA while she was working for the now-disbanded Forensic Science Service. Her refusal to accept that John's profile was just a strange quirk of what was then regarded as junk DNA had led her to John and to the unravelling of his secret. Sally's then-boyfriend, Ced Fisher, now Sally's husband, had shed a different light on John when, through his ground-breaking art forgery software, he found a series of artists dating back to the fifteenth century, all of whom proved to be John. The prof had tied all the strings together when he applied his brilliant mind to the problem and proved how John and anyone else with his very rare DNA would defy ageing and live for hundreds, if not thousands of years. The prof and Ced Fisher had then found themselves very much outside their comfort zones when they located and helped rescue John after he was kidnapped by the pharmaceutical industrialist Wallingford Peterson.

In the aftermath, Frank Young had used his connections in the rarefied world of Whitehall's more secret corridors to broker a deal between John and Samson Blythe, whom both John and Frank knew only by his code name of Digby Smith. John's problems over changes of identity were now solved in return for his unique accounts of life, language and history over the past almost six hundred years. In John's wake and under Digby Smith's purview were Frank, Ced and the others who had come to learn John's secret. Claudia was part of this very special group.

None of this information was at the forefront of Claudia's mind as she continued to scrutinise the data on her screen. Why did the most difficult problems always arise when the prof was away? It was only when her mobile phone pinged for the third time that the sound penetrated the barriers of her consciousness and registered. She turned her attention away from the strings of numbers on her monitor to check the screen on her phone, only to find the message was yet another string of numbers. She recognised the sequence, it was a prearranged code, but since it was the first time it had been used she was momentarily taken by surprise. Then her lips pressed together in a knowing half-smile and she replied with another sequence of numbers that indicated she was alone, safe and could talk. Seconds later, another text arrived with yet another sequence of numbers. She studied them and then dug into her handbag to retrieve a different phone, one that was reserved for a very special purpose. She turned it on and waited. After ten seconds, a text arrived containing just a double-digit number: 53. She waited for a ping on her computer as an email arrived, one with nothing sensible in the sender's box. The email was a list of a hundred pairs of book titles and authors. She ran her eye down to number 53, hit the reply button on the phone and typed the letters CR, her initials, and waited. Her phone rang almost immediately.

"Pollyanna," she said, quoting the book title against number 53.

"Anthony Trollope," replied the caller, quoting the name of the author of the work one down the list at number 54.

"Digby!" exclaimed Claudia, relaxing now the protocols had been satisfied. "I wasn't expecting a call from you until next week, and certainly not one using this rigmarole. I take it that it's not a test, from the code numbers."

"Quite, Claudia, my dear," replied Digby Smith. "I hope you don't mind; I have a little matter that I'd appreciate your help with. I'm not interrupting you, am I? I wish to draw on your profound knowledge of DNA."

"Tell me more," replied Claudia, wondering why Smith couldn't have just called her direct. She could never get her head around all the cloak-and-dagger arrangements that he insisted on. Her laboratory and all its phone and Internet lines had been fire-walled and encrypted to a staggering level of security by Smith's people. Surely that was enough.

"I wonder if I could put a hypothetical situation to you regarding DNA profiling," continued Smith. "Imagine, if you will, that there is a substantial amount of blood recovered from various locations at the scene of a crime. The blood is profiled according to the normal procedures and is found to have the same profile as a suspect in the case, a person for whom there appears to be CCTV footage placing him at the scene. This is a good profile, one in fact that the DNA laboratory involved is quite excited about since it appears to contain some very rare … groups, do you call them?"

"Alleles," corrected Claudia, remembering only too clearly when she herself was in that situation when she first saw John Andrews' DNA profile three years before.

"Alleles," repeated Smith carefully, as if practising the word. "Exactly. Well, the problem is that the man in question, who has now been arrested for the crime, which was a murder, denies most emphatically that he was in any way involved. He says, in fact, that he was not even near the location of the crime at the material time."

"Does he have an alibi?" asked Claudia.

"No, he doesn't. He was alone throughout the entire timeframe of the incident and indeed was relatively close to the whole thing. He claims to have been about fifty miles from the scene."

"Well," said Claudia, nagging at her hair until it collapsed in her hand, "if the profiles match and they contain a number of rare alleles, I should say that he's not telling the truth."

"That is exactly the police perspective, Claudia, and I agree that they appear to have a strong case. The reason I'm calling you is to ask if there are any conditions or circumstances under which, despite the result, the blood profile could not have come from this man."

Claudia smiled to herself; the answer was obvious. "Well, I'm assuming that contamination and a general cockup on the part of the police or the lab can be ruled out—"

"Completely," interrupted Smith.

"And that the blood could not have been planted in some way or for some reason—"

"Definitely not. There is no suggestion of that and nor does there appear to be any reason for it to have been done."

"In that case, if your man is telling the truth, the only explanation is that he is an identical twin, a homozygous twin. For such twins, the DNA profiles used for crime investigation would be identical."

"A twin," repeated Smith. "That's an interesting thought. That will have to be explored. But am I right in assuming that if identical twins' DNA is identical, then everything else about them is identical?"

"No, you are not. You can't assume that at all," said Claudia. "In fact, there's recent research, which we have confirmed here in this lab, that even their DNA is not going to be identical in all respects. However, as far as DNA profiling for criminal purposes is concerned, it *will* be the same since that profiling doesn't target the areas where there will be differences. It requires some pretty expensive and sophisticated technology to show the differences."

"Mmm," mused Smith. "And you can do it, you say?"

"Yes, of course," said Claudia. "But there's a far simpler and easier solution than DNA profiling."

"There is? What is it?"

"Fingerprints."

"Fingerprints?"

"Yes. You see, fingerprints are formed in the foetus between the thirteenth and nineteenth week and the process leads to some differences occurring that make the fingerprints of identical twins very similar but not the same. There should be observable differences that will distinguish one twin from the other. I suggest that the investigating police check all the prints from the scene and compare them with your man. Any competent fingerprint examiner should be able to separate them immediately if he is in fact telling the truth."

She paused, thinking through the scenario.

"Tell me, Digby, if you can," she continued. "Do I know this man? I assume that because we're having this conversation, it must be connected to John in some way."

There was brief silence from the other end of the phone as Digby, ever cautious, considered his words.

"As it happens, Claudia, you are right, although I might just have been making an enquiry with respect to something quite unconnected, taking advantage, shall we say, of our special relationship and your undoubted expertise."

Claudia pulled a face and stuck her tongue out at the phone. Pompous ass, she thought.

"However," continued Digby, "yes, it is connected to John, although you needn't worry, we're not talking about John himself. To answer your question, you know of this man but I am fairly sure that you have yet to meet him."

"That's a relief," said Claudia. "Although I'd have been very surprised if you'd told me it was John since there has never been an inkling of a twin. But if we are talking rare alleles here and I know of the man but haven't met him, am I right in thinking that we are talking about John's friend from the seventeenth century, the one who these days is called Adam Fowler, but who in his past I think was called Jacques Bognard?"

She heard a deep sigh breathing down the phone. She was once again putting Digby Smith on the spot.

"I wouldn't usually be privy to that information, Claudia, but those names have come out during my extensive conversations with John."

"And he has a twin," said Claudia. "What a fascinating idea."

"We don't know that," cautioned Smith. "I'm afraid that I know little about the man and his history."

"Think of it though, Digby. I remember that he was considerably older than John. Imagine if he had a twin brother and that he is still alive. What are the chances of that? Does John know about any of this? Am I permitted to discuss it with him?"

"I don't see why not, given the confidentiality of our group," said Smith. "If you could give me an hour or so. I need to relay your information about fingerprints to the appropriate authorities first and then speak to John. After that, I think he would very much appreciate a call from you."

Claudia sat back in her chair and thought through the conversation, the jumble of data on her monitor quite forgotten. She was somewhat surprised that the issue of fingerprints hadn't occurred to the authorities involved. They must have been carried away with the quality of the DNA profiles and put fingerprints on the back burner. If that were the case, there would soon be a considerable spatter of egg on a number of faces. She frowned; something was nagging her. Yes, she thought, Digby's final remark. What had he meant by saying that John would appreciate a call? From the way he said it, John might have a problem.

Chapter Fourteen

Marcus Dayton was taken aback at Paola's change of mood. From being calm, almost friendly, and expressing great interest in his unique collection of paintings and sculptures, she was now, in a matter of moments, dark and angry.

He quietly cursed himself for not controlling the conversation more carefully. He had wanted to move slowly towards his reasons for abducting her, to make it as acceptable as possible. He thought it had been going well, but suddenly her whole demeanour had shifted. He thought back through the last ten minutes and remembered her mentioning her father. She had started a sentence about him, changed her mind and then tried to cover her tracks. Why was that? He would have to explore it, but whatever the reason, it had led her to ask questions about people like herself and Dayton, as well as the inevitable questions of why they were like they were and under what circumstances they might be created. He needed to pacify her.

He held up his hands. "Paola, let's go back to the sitting room and talk this through. It's more comfortable in there."

"And your Rottweilers can keep their eyes on me in case I start trying to break the place up?" Paola snorted. "No thanks, I'd rather stay in here where you don't allow them."

She glowered at him and then her eyes shifted to the statues. "Don't worry," she sneered, "I wouldn't dream of breaking your precious collection, although I'd be more than happy to break your neck."

Dayton held out his arms as if he were welcoming her. "Feel free to try, Paola. But be warned, I've learned a few survival skills myself through the centuries. Like you, I've been in many sticky situations I had to fight my way out of. Remember the punch to your jaw that floored you? My reactions are fast; I don't think you even saw it coming."

Paola tossed her head. "You're not so fast. You should remember the cane." Her smile was pure malice. "In fact, you'll remember it every time you look in the mirror, no matter how long you live."

She took a step towards him, pointing a finger. "Why have you brought me here? What exactly is this place?"

Dayton replied with another submissive gesture. "You needn't worry, Paola, the room you woke up in isn't the tip of some secret research establishment iceberg. I'm not planning to take over the world. The truth is that I'm more than happy to keep a comfortable distance between most of the world and myself, except when necessary. Especially given that the world in general is never likely to understand me.

"What I want, Paola, is simple. For most of my life I have been wealthy and I've been able to take on various personas in various parts of the world, usually for decades at a time, in order to deal with what I thought was my unique situation. These days, with the benefit of my own air and sea transport, I can move around effortlessly and in luxury and, unlike in the distant past when my choice of location was more limited, the entire world is now available to me. I have enough connections through my various aliases to keep ahead of whatever sophisticated security is incorporated into identity documents and the data associated with them. It's still, as it always has been, just a matter of paying the right price to the right people. But ultimately, as you have said, it's a lonely existence. I—"

"So you want me to be your friend?" mocked Paola. "A soul mate? Someone like you?"

Dayton shook his head. "No, Paola, I cannot expect that. Friendship is something that develops slowly; it is born out of mutual respect. It's not … it's not something I am used to achieving. And given the circumstances under which we met, and perhaps now because of how I have treated you, I could not expect friendship from you."

"Then what do you expect from me?" She was becoming exasperated by his prevarication. She was sure she knew what was coming but she wanted him to say it. "I insist you tell me."

Dayton paused and took a breath.

"What I want from you, Paola, is a child."

"A what? You mean you expect me to …"

"No, no, please. I expressed that badly. I am not intending to force myself upon you. If I'd wanted to do that, I could have done it while you were unconscious. I don't even want you to bear my child. What I want from you is that you allow Dr Ronaldi, who is an expert in the most advanced IVF techniques, to harvest a supply of your eggs that will be fertilised by my sperm in the laboratory I have installed here for him. After that, the resulting embryo will be implanted in a young woman who has consented to the procedure. She will be paid handsomely and once the child is born, she will have nothing more to do with it. It is a form of surrogacy, you understand."

"Understand? What I understand, Dayton, is that you're mad! Why ever you should think that I would comply with your wishes, I don't know. Do you honestly think that I would allow you or some so-called doctor to invade my body? You're out of line, Dayton. I absolutely refuse."

Paola folded her arms across her chest and spun on her heels to pace the floor of the gallery, the anger radiating from her.

Dayton let her pace, watched her vent her steam. After a few minutes, she stopped and returned to stand in front of him.

"How long have you been planning this? You can't have just set it all up."

"Of course not. It's taken a lot of effort. It started soon after I learned of your existence; it was an obvious plan."

"Obvious! It's not obvious to me. All that's obvious is that you want that creep of a doctor to get his grubby little hands on me, to take unacceptable liberties. If he so much as touches me, I'll break all the bones in his pathetic body."

Dayton's eyes bored into hers and for the first time, Paola felt unsure of her ground. It was now Dayton's demeanour that had changed.

"It is regrettable that you feel the way you do, Paola," he said, his voice becoming cold and emotionless. "I don't think the conversation went according to plan. I won't beat about the bush. There are two options open to you. One is for you to comply; the other is that I bring your daughter here and harvest her eggs instead. In fact, I'm beginning to regret not doing that in the first place."

"What do you mean? I've told you I'll kill you if you touch Sara."

"I heard you the first time, Paola, but I'm afraid you are not calling the shots. What I mean is that I was within a heartbeat of bringing Sara here when the news arrived that you had been located. You wouldn't believe how close it was."

"Did that woman have anything to do with it?"

"Edith? The one you killed? Yes, she did. I wish now I'd gone ahead with the plan. Edith would be still alive and I might have a more compliant donor for my plans. Sara doesn't appear to be quite the ruthless killer that you are."

As they faced each other, Dayton was concerned that Paola was losing control. The last thing he wanted was for her to attack him. It wasn't that he thought she would overpower him; that was extremely unlikely given his superior strength. But he didn't want to hurt her or antagonise her further.

Watching her carefully for any sign she was about to pounce, he held up his hands again.

"Paola, please, let me explain. I'm not intending or wanting any harm to come to you or to Sara. How much do you know about IVF? The process involves no risk to you and it is entirely painless. It's simply a question of getting timing right. You see, once Dr Ronaldi has charted your monthly cycle, preferably over two or three months—"

"Three months! You intend to keep me here for three months! That's totally unacceptable. I have commitments. And anyway, how do you know that my eggs are even usable? I *am* four hundred and ninety-four years old, you know. Maybe I'm past my prime." She spat out the words, trying to sound as dismissive as possible.

"I doubt it. After all, you had Sara only forty-six years ago and she was the first of your children to be the same as you. Maybe you are just coming into your prime. Maybe I am too, given that Emma was born so recently."

Paola said nothing, but her rapid breathing showed she was far from being appeased.

Dayton continued. "You see, Paola, I am a reasonable man with two and a half thousand years of patience. But I am also a man who ultimately gets what he wants, if it is achievable. And, thanks to the most amazing advances in modern science, it is. So I can assure you that I will have my way."

"I don't see what's reasonable about snatching me from my house and bringing me here for your sinister purposes and then blackmailing me by threatening to do the same to my daughter if I don't comply with your wishes."

Dayton steepled his hands and tapped his lips with the ends of his fingers. "Paola, think about it. I could have confined you to your room, held you prisoner there, sedated you, if necessary, for as long as it takes for Dr Ronaldi to obtain the data he requires. But I haven't done that and neither do I wish to. Rather, I should prefer that you are comfortable here, relaxed, so that you can enjoy the beauty of this house and its grounds. They are very extensive, as I have explained, and you are free to wander. The boundaries are very well secured so you can neither get lost nor disappear to the nearest village."

"That counts as imprisonment as far as I'm concerned." Paola was still growling as she glowered from under her eyebrows, but Dayton felt he could sense a softening of her tone: less anger and more resignation. Maybe mention of Sara had worked despite the threats Paola had hurled at him.

"In my experience, prisoners are not usually given such freedom. I can provide you with anything you want; there is no need to feel idle or bored. Maybe you'd like to work. Just let me know what artist's materials you would like."

"You're all generosity, Dayton. I suppose you want another portrait for your collection. You wouldn't be impressed with my version of you; it would have horns and an arrowed tail."

Dayton allowed himself the ghost of a smile; the atmosphere had thawed fractionally. "Come, Paola," he beckoned, "will you come back to the sitting room now? If you wish, I can call Dr Ronaldi and have him explain the details of what the process entails."

Paola grunted in compliance and took a step towards the door. She knew if she riveted her gaze on Dayton, if would be unlikely to affect him; there had been no indication of that so far. But the doctor, he was altogether different. She would do all she could to intimidate him with her eyes in the hope that he might be too nervous around her to carry out his work. However, what had given her hope from her caustic exchange with Dayton was the news that she was free to roam the grounds. She had plenty of experience in forests; she felt sure she would find a way of escaping, even in the presence of guards. They weren't going to shoot her; she was no use to Dayton either dead or incapacitated.

She glanced at the gallery of portraits as they made their way back to the large sitting room. Dayton was a complicated man, a potentially dangerous adversary, but she was beginning to understand his weaknesses, to learn how she might play him.

Chapter Fifteen

Two hours after his call to Jacques' Digby Smith in London, Bryan Meecham was parking his car in the basement of his office tower in downtown Boston when his cell phone rang. It was now late afternoon in London and Meecham assumed that the Digby Smith types, whoever they were, would be heading for their clubs, certainly not still working in their offices. He was, therefore, very surprised to hear Smith's patrician tones in his ear when he answered the call.

"Mr Meecham, Smith here, we spoke earlier," announced Pettigrew-Wyatt. "Before we go any further, would you mind awfully reciting the number you called me on earlier? Can't be too careful; want to be sure I'm talking to the right person and all that. Last four digits will do."

Meecham shook his head as he pulled his notebook from his pocket. The Great Game continues, he thought.

"Four seven one three," he read.

"Excellent," announced Pettigrew-Wyatt. Meecham thought he might follow with a score out of ten.

"Can you talk?"

"Talk?" replied Meecham, puzzled.

"What I mean is, can anyone else hear your side of this conversation?"

"No, I'm just parking my car. I'm alone."

"Jolly good. Now, I've made some enquiries and I've been advised to ask you about the fingerprint results."

"Fingerprint results? I haven't been told of any. So far, the police have been emphasising the DNA. Surely that is far more important."

"Not so, apparently, if our mutual friend is as innocent as he claims."

"I don't understand."

"Well, to be perfectly honest, neither do I. All this scientific mumbo-jumbo leaves me rather cold. Can't get my head round it. But I am assured that the fingerprints could shift the focus of the whole investigation."

"I'm afraid I still don't understand."

"I'm not in a position to discuss anything I know about Adam Fowler, Mr Meecham, but there are of course many things I don't know. Maybe you have the advantage of me here, perhaps you might know something germane to this enquiry that is of crucial importance."

Meecham kept quiet. Presumably the man would eventually get to the point of his verbiage.

"You don't happen to know if Fowler has an identical twin, do you?" continued Pettigrew-Wyatt.

"Identical twin?"

"Yes, you know, identical in every way and all that."

"No, I'm afraid I don't. But I can certainly ask him."

"Good idea. Listen, I have a feeling that he'll be out of wherever your police are holding him pretty soon. Would you be so kind as to remind him to give me a tinkle?"

"A tinkle?"

"Yes, a tinkle. A call. On the telephone. Doesn't matter what time it is. Always available and all that."

Meecham immediately called Kyle Drover, smiling to himself as the criminal defence attorney whooped in pleasure. He could smell victory. Drover insisted that he call the lieutenant himself. He was going to enjoy listening to her wriggle, even though he was only going to tell her the minimum over the phone.

Lieutenant Sharon Roper was eating a late lunch in her office when the call came. She groaned inwardly when she heard Kyle Drover's voice sounding cockier than ever.

"Lieutenant. Kyle Drover. There's something we didn't discuss this morning. I hope you weren't keeping it from me."

"You certainly have a knack for ruffling feathers, Mr Drover. However, I'm not clairvoyant, so unless you tell me what it is you think I'm not telling you, I won't know, now, will I?" She pulled a face at the receiver as she waited for the attorney to answer.

"Fingerprints, Lieutenant. I'm talking about fingerprints. I don't recall you making any mention of the results from the scene of the homicide and abduction. I need to know, and I need to know now, whether or not the fingerprints corroborate the DNA results you say put my client at the scene."

As Drover's voice boomed in her ear, Roper pressed a button on the phone's base to put it on speaker. She grabbed the file and jerked it open. She couldn't remember seeing anything about fingerprints and there was something about Drover's tone that worried her.

"Damn," she muttered under her breath as the papers spilled across her desk.

"I can assume they have all been examined, can't I, Lieutenant?" Drover continued, knowing full well they could not have been.

"I'm sure I've seen something about fingerprints," stalled Roper as she frantically searched the papers. "And I'm sure they will corroborate the DNA results."

"Are you now, Lieutenant? Well, I want to see those results in black and white, so I'd appreciate it if you would fax them to my office. Any time in the next two minutes will do."

Roper ran her hands through her hair. The damn results weren't there. "Mr Drover, I've only got part of the file here on my desk," she lied, "my detective's taken some of it to write a preliminary report. I'll locate the fingerprint sheet and send it to you. But I really don't see why it's so important; the DNA says it all."

"Lieutenant Roper. I'll conveniently forget that I heard you say you are spreading the contents of a confidential case file around the building *if* you get those results over to me now."

"It was just for photocopying," she replied lamely as she beat her head with her fist.

"I'll be waiting, Lieutenant," said Drover and rang off.

"Detective Mullins!" yelled Roper as she slammed the handset back on its base.

"What's up, boss?" said the detective as he looked warily round her office door.

"How many more times, Detective? Stop calling me 'boss'! You've been watching too many of those British TV series. And don't even think about 'ma'am'. I'm Lieutenant, got it?"

"Sure thing, Lieutenant," said Mullins carefully as he noted Roper's panic-stricken eyes. "Is there a problem?"

"Have you taken anything from the file, detective?"

"Of course not, Lieutenant, I wouldn't do that without your consent."

"Well, where are the fingerprint results?"

Mullins scratched his head as he trawled his memory of the file.

"Fingerprints? You know, I don't think the lab's given them to us. I can only remember seeing the DNA results, and of course all the stuff from the CCTV and the sketch of the perp and—"

"But no fingerprints," snapped Roper. She lifted the phone and punched the numbers so hard that Mullins winced.

Roper drummed her fingers on her desk as she waited for Barney Crummins, the forensics officer heading the lab work, to pick up.

"Crumm—"

"Barney. It's Sharon Roper—"

"Hi, Lieutenant, how ca—"

"The Naomi Tripley case, where—"

"Great results, huh, Lieutenant, I mean, conclusive or what? Especially given your perp's got a profile that redefines rare."

"It's the 'or what' I'm concerned about, Barney, not the rare."

"Whadya mean, Lieutenant? These profiles are the sweetest."

"Well, stop writing your ode to them, Barney, and give me the rest of the results."

"Rest?"

"The fingerprint results, Barney. They're not in the file. Where are the fingerprint results? I assume the prints were all lifted."

"What do you take us for, Lieutenant?" said Crummins through his teeth, the elation in his voice replaced with hurt professional pride.

There was a pause, then, "We're still working them up, Lieutenant; the report's not ready yet."

"Well, what have you got so far? Toss me a crumb."

Silence.

"Barney?"

"Thing is, Lieutenant, I got two men off sick and Charlene starts maternity any day now. I'm short-handed. I had to prioritise and the DNA was the way to go. I don't get it; the results couldn't be better. I was going to start the fingerprint comparisons in the morning. I—"

"Start! You mean you haven't started them yet?"

"There's no need to shout, Lieutenant. I'm under a lot of pressure here."

Roper shut her eyes and took several long, deep breaths.

"Lieutenant?" Crummins' voice was hesitant.

"Barney. OK, I understand, but here's the thing. I just had Fowler's attorney bawling me out on the phone for the fingerprint results, wanting them, like, yesterday. He knows how good the DNA is so perhaps he's clutching at straws, going for something procedural, which won't wash, believe me. But there was something about his voice. It was as if he knew something we don't. Got any ideas what that might be?"

Crummins stared through the glass partition that separated his office from the lab. There was only one of his team in view, the heavily pregnant Charlene working with an intensity that bordered on hurried, her three colleagues being out at other crime scenes and the rest off sick. Crummins scratched at the stubble on his chin. DNA and fingerprints? He had an idea what might be behind it, but he wasn't going to tell the lieutenant right now. He might be wrong; he hoped he was. He'd had enough of her yelling at him. Damn; he'd been on a high that morning. Fowler's profile was the weirdest he or any of the others had ever seen. He'd been dreaming publications, his name on a significant scientific paper. But all he'd got so far was a bucket of cold water from Roper bringing him back to reality.

"No, Lieutenant, I don't know what it could mean. Listen, I'll get on to the prints now. There's a lot of them, mostly partials, so it'll take a while, but I promise I'll have something for you by first thing in the morning."

He put down the phone and sighed deeply. It was going to be a late night.

At nine the following morning, Detective Mullins walked into Sharon Roper's office to find her sitting with her head in her hands, her fingers massaging her forehead.

"You ok, bo— Lieutenant? You look like you got a migraine. My wife gets them." He stopped, deciding it would be better to say nothing more.

Roper stirred and swept her hands through her hair. She looked up at him, her mouth puckered tightly.

"A migraine would be better than what I'm feeling right now, Detective."

Mullins waited, knowing that what he had to tell her would probably bring on more than a migraine.

"Sit down, Detective. This case is beginning to piss me off. I need some good news."

"Anything on the prints?" stalled Mullins.

"Still waiting. Now, bring me up to speed. Have you traced the name of the victim yet, the homicide victim, I mean?"

Mullins shook his head. "No, Lieutenant, we've drawn a complete blank. It's like she doesn't exist. Her prints aren't on any database, so she doesn't have a criminal record. Her DNA doesn't show up anywhere. I've got someone trying to trace her through dental records, but nothing so far. It's weird. But without a name, there's a limit on what we can find. The Doc says she's had at least a couple of kids, some years ago. For her age, she was in top condition, must have worked out a lot. I've got her photo circulating through gyms and fitness centres, but do you know just how many there are?"

"No, but I can imagine. Anything else?" she added as she teased the corner of the case file in front of her.

When Mullins didn't answer, she looked up at him. "Detective?"

"Yeah, there is. I just got off the phone. I've been talking to a contact in Chicago."

"Chicago? Why?"

"Lieutenant, we have a problem with the Tripley woman."

"Of course we do. We don't know where she is."

"I mean, with her identity. She's not who she says she is."

Roper exhaled slowly, shaking her head. She opened her hands, indicating for him to explain.

"According to the Falmouth Business Registration Office," continued Mullins, "she took out a licence for the gallery three months ago. She told them she couldn't give any references because she'd just come back from an extended trip abroad. Many years, is what she told them. She paid all her bills upfront so they weren't too fussed. Anyway, I checked with immigration and the only Naomi Tripley who's entered the US in the last few months arrived from Rio de Janeiro, in Brazil."

"I know where it is."

"Right. Well, the thing is, I got to thinking about the name Naomi Tripley and it struck me as being pretty unusual. So I started checking with Social Security and I found only one Naomi Tripley in the whole of the US who's the right age. She hails from Chicago. I called a contact in Chicago who traced Ms Tripley's parents and they said she's disappeared."

"When?"

"About three months ago, in Rio. She'd been travelling in South America. She'd kept in regular contact with her parents, but suddenly her emails and calls stopped. I faxed the passport details to my contact who showed them to the parents. They confirmed that it's their daughter's passport. So I sent the photo we got from the Falmouth News. When he showed them that, they didn't think it was their daughter. And I think they're right."

"Why so sure?"

"Because Naomi Tripley from Chicago is short, about five-two. Now Ms Murphy said our Naomi Tripley was about five-five or five-six."

"So Tripley is using a missing woman's papers," said Roper. "Which means we don't have any idea who the abducted woman is?"

"That's about the size of it, Lieutenant."

"It must be connected. I mean, she must be on the run from someone who's caught up with her. Fowler would be my guess. We need to interview him again."

"I'll call his lawyer," said Mullins.

As he got up to leave, Roper's phone rang. She lifted the receiver and eyeballed Mullins. "Barney," she mouthed, motioning for the detective to sit down again.

Mullins watched Roper's face, hoping for an indication of something positive, but the signals weren't good.

Roper took a pen from a container on the desktop and scribbled some notes as she listened. She grimaced as she underlined a few of the words. Finally she spoke.

"You're absolutely sure of this, Barney? I mean, you're not going to come back to me later with something different?"

From the way Roper briefly lifted the handset from her ear, Mullins assumed that Crummins had not appreciated the remark.

"OK, Barney. Yes, I know you've been up all night. I do value what you're doing. It's just not the kind of news I wanted to hear." A pause. "Yes, thanks, if you could get the preliminary report to me in an hour, that would be great. Thanks, Barney."

She waited for Crummins to ring off and then she slammed the handset into the phone cradle.

"Shit!" she yelled. "Shit! Shit! Shit!"

Mullins waited until her eyes were less wild, then he waited some more.

Eventually Roper sat back. "You'd better make that call, to Fowler's lawyer, I mean."

"What is it, Lieutenant?"

Roper sucked her top lip into her teeth. "I mean that it looks as if Fowler could be telling the truth, weird though that may seem. Barney says that while the DNA from the scene matches Fowler's, the fingerprints from the same locations, the ones associated with the blood from which they got the DNA results, do not match."

"That's crazy."

"Apparently not. You see, the fingerprints almost match. They are very similar, but they are not the same. The differences are subtle, but enough to say that the prints and, therefore, according to Crummins, the DNA, are not his."

"You've lost me, Lieutenant."

"Identical twins, Detective. We're dealing with identical twins, and the one who is the perp in this case is not Fowler. His big-mouth lawyer is going to be over here like a shot and I'm going to have no other choice but to release him."

Mullins nodded slowly. "It might not be all bad, bo—, Lieutenant. After all, if Fowler has an identical twin, he must know where he is and how we can find him."

"I wouldn't be so sure, Detective, nothing in this case is that easy. Remember, Fowler is a Brit, which means his brother is too, presumably. The brother will be long gone, probably out of the country."

"Yes, but with a name, the British authorities should be able to trace him."

"*If* we get a name. There's no guarantee of that. Look at the rest of the case. We've got an abducted woman who's disappeared who isn't who she claims to be, a suspect who's no longer a suspect because his twin brother is now a suspect instead and a dead woman who's a Jane Doe."

She looked down at the notes she'd scribbled when she'd been talking to Barney Crummins. She tapped at the page. "The lab also said that the DNA from Fowler and from the brother are both very weird. Full of something odd. Eels or something. Whatever."

She closed the notebook and slammed it on the desk. "Right,

Barney might have been up all night but we need to get a team back to the house. I want it searched again from top to bottom. I want all papers found and checked for anything that might help us identify who Tripley really is. And I want a sample of something from Tripley: hair, a toothbrush, something that will give a good DNA profile. Whoever she is, she must be on record somewhere."

Soon after midday, Jacques was leaving the Falmouth Police Department accompanied by Bryan Meecham and Kyle Drover, the events of the morning still playing in his mind.

Once Meecham had received the call from Mullins — Roper had been too angry to call herself — he had contacted Drover and they made quick time back to Falmouth. Drover went for the jugular, intending to give Roper no quarter.

"Lieutenant, I shall be making a full and comprehensive complaint to the police commissioner over your incompetent handling of this case. The fact that you failed to obtain crucial fingerprint evidence at the earliest possible stage and relied on flawed DNA evidence is totally unprofessional. You have attempted to intimidate and threaten my client, you have put him under unacceptable psychological pressure and then when you did have irrefutable proof of his innocence, you delayed releasing him until Mr Meecham and I arrived."

"I needed, still need, to interview him further, Mr Drover, and I couldn't do that without you being present."

"Firstly, my client will answer no further questions about something that has nothing to do with him and of which he has absolutely no knowledge, and secondly, even if you did want to interview him further, there was no reason to keep him locked up in a cell."

"We returned all his possessions, let him make calls. We don't have a lot of space here."

"That's baloney. You could have put him in here."

"He's not the only person we interview in a day. This room gets used a lot."

"I can't exactly see a line outside the door. Where are all these criminals? No, Lieutenant, you—"

"Kyle," said Jacques.

"What?" said Drover more forcefully than he intended. He had been working up to his finale and the interruption was unexpected. "Sorry, Adam, what is it?"

"Kyle, I know where you're coming from but really, the lieutenant and her team were only doing their job. Put yourself in their position. They are facing a puzzle tied up in a conundrum. I think they were right to focus on the DNA evidence. I would have. There's no harm done, I haven't been locked up for years and my sojourn here has not resulted in any financial hardship for me, except that I have to pay you." He caught the lieutenant's eye as she suppressed a smirk.

"Now, Lieutenant," he continued, "I am delighted to be free to walk away from this and I really doubt that I can help you. But you indicated that there was something you wanted to ask me. Please, feel free while you have the opportunity."

"Adam—" started Drover, but he stopped when Jacques held up a hand.

Roper was startled at the offer. She coughed in embarrassment.

"Er, well, thank you, Mr Fowler, for your understanding. What I wanted to know is this: can you give me a name and an address for your brother?"

As they stopped by Drover's car, the lawyer turned to Jacques, a puzzled expression on his face.

"You know, Adam, the lieutenant really didn't seem to like the fact that until today you didn't even know you had a twin. I must admit, it's a strange sort of thing not to know."

Jacques smiled. "As I told Ms Roper, my mother never even knew who my father was and she gave me away at birth. She must have done the same to my brother, but to a different family or organisation."

"Adam, I don't mean to be disrespectful, but that tale doesn't really have a ring of truth about it. I can see why the lieutenant pushed you a little on it."

Jacques said nothing.

Drover persisted. "Sharon Roper is something of a terrier, you know, so I've heard. She'll probably follow up your story, want it verified."

"I wish her luck. It all happened … rather a long time ago and I doubt the records still exist. Now gentlemen, I see my car has arrived and that my usual driver has recovered his health. I am indebted to you both."

Meecham extended his hand. "It's your contact in Britain that you are indebted to, Adam. He did the ferreting and came up with the information about the fingerprints."

"Yes," agreed Jacques. "I thought I could rely on him."

"Before we go our separate ways," said Meecham, "I'd like to ask you one question, Adam, if I may. Your contact, Digby Smith. I mean, who the hell is he? He didn't sound like he belonged to the real world. After speaking to him, it was as if I'd spoken to a ghost."

The corners of Jacques' mouth twitched in the slightest of smiles. "You're closer than you could imagine, Bryan."

Chapter Sixteen

Jacques gave a parting wave to his lawyers and walked over to his car. Kenton, his regular driver, was standing by the nearside rear door holding it open for him.

"Kenton, it's very good to see you. Are you fully recovered?"

"I am, sir, thank you. I apologise for my absence at a difficult moment for you, sir. My illness could not have come at a worse time."

"Not to worry, Kenton, it has been an interesting experience, although not one I wish to repeat in a hurry."

"Thank you for your understanding, sir. Are we heading back to the hotel in Boston?"

"No, I think I need a day to relax in the comfort of my own surroundings. We'll go to the apartment in Manhattan. I still have some unfinished business here in Massachusetts, but it can wait for a few days."

"Very good, sir."

As they drove away from Falmouth, Jacques settled back in the leather-upholstered luxury of his limousine and thought over the events of the past two days. It had come as a shock to learn that he had a twin brother; it was something his parents had never told him. As with John Andrews, Jacques' rare traits included a most exceptional memory, enabling him to recall events from his distant past perfectly clearly. And two and a half thousand years was distant. Even so, his earliest memories, like everyone's memories of very early childhood, were fragmented. He let his mind drift back in time. He had left the Greek Island in the Dodecanese with his parents at the age of three, following rumours of an invading sea force from the mainland. Their departure had not been too soon: only two days after they set sail to the south west in the direction of Crete, their island had been overrun and all the remaining islanders slaughtered.

His father, Karpos, a huge muscular man who stood over a foot taller than most of his contemporaries, was an expert sailor and it was through him that Jacques, or Pelagios as he had been first called, learned to love the ocean. It was a love affair that had remained with him throughout his life and one that had sustained him and made him a rich man.

His mother, Iola, a quiet, withdrawn woman, with sadness almost permanently in her eyes, had died when Pelagios was twelve. The boy would never know she had been broken by the sacrifice of her other son, the hidden but fatal wound to her mind eating her like a cancer.

By then, Karpos had a small fleet of trading ships providing a steady and reliable supply of goods in demand to many Mediterranean ports and islands. Serving everyone, he managed to avoid the necessity of allegiance to any one particular country or group. His size helped: rumours of his strength preceded him and he was treated with enormous respect.

With no siblings, Pelagios worked with his father, learning everything he could about trading and the ways of the sea. When his father died of a fever in his fifties, the young man, who had grown to the same stature and who had the most remarkable health, took over the fleet and gradually expanded it, amassing a considerable fortune as he did. The first of many. But never in all his long talks with his father at the helm or when the sun had gone down, was there any mention of a brother.

.   .   .

Jacques watched the scenery flash by his window as they took the Interstate to Providence, Rhode Island and then along the Connecticut coast. A brother, an identical twin who was still alive. It seemed too absurd to be possible. Yet if he had lived an incredibly long life, overcoming many potential disasters, why not his brother? Was this brother a killer? The police seemed to think so: he had been involved with the apparent murder of one woman and the abduction of another. Jacques himself had been forced to kill on occasions in order to save his own life or those near to him at the time. It was inevitable, although it had happened far less frequently in the last two hundred years than in more ancient, lawless times. He wondered what had really happened and he wondered if his contact, his version of Digby Smith in London, would be able to help him find out.

However, although speaking to Smith was important, he had a more pressing call to make. At the time of his arrest, he had been talking to his old friend, John Andrews, whom he still called by his seventeenth-century name of Philippe. He had sounded worried, preoccupied.

His call to John was answered almost immediately.

"Jacques, I'm so relieved to hear your voice. Have you been released?"

"Yes, mon ami, I have. And if you knew that I'd been locked up, I assume that your Digby Smith has been in touch with you."

"Yes, he has. I was very concerned."

"There was no need to worry. I felt sure that sooner or later my Digby Smith would work his way under the skin of the American authorities and secure my release. Did your Digby tell you the remarkable news that I have a twin brother?"

"No, he didn't. It's not in his nature to pass on more than is absolutely necessary. But Claudia Reid did, with Digby's blessing, she assured me."

"Ah, the enigmatic Dr Reid. Do you know that I've never met her? Somehow our paths haven't crossed even though we have both visited you quite frequently in the Lakes. How come she is involved?"

"Digby called her for advice, told her the circumstances and she raised the possibility of a twin and the fact that the fingerprints would be different."

"Then she is the one I must thank. I'll send her some flowers and ask her out to dinner. Do you think her boyfriend will mind?"

"I don't think she has one," replied John, dropping his voice, "I can never fathom Claudia's love life. All I know is that both Lola and Sally are always offering her advice, but it doesn't seem to have resulted in anything."

"The mind of a woman is a mystery, mon ami, even to someone as old as I am. If you could give me her number I'll call her."

"You can thank her now, if you like, Jacques."

"Really?"

"Yes, she's here, in the Lakes. I think she still feels guilty about what happened three years ago when she first uncovered my strange DNA and the events that followed which ended with my being taken by Peterson and his cronies. When she heard about Paola's disappearance, she immediately offered to help where she could and drove straight up here. She arrived this morning. Would you like me to put her on?"

"Yes, of course, that would be delightful. But what do you mean by Paola's disappearance, mon ami? What has happened since I was locked up?"

"You don't know? That was the reason I was calling you when you were arrested. Paola has been abducted. I'm surprised that the police didn't tell you."

"Why should they tell me? They were too busy fussing over a murder and another abduction in Cape Cod. The one where they found the blood they thought was mine. The woman abducted was called Naomi Tripley, as I recall. She was an artist with a gallery in Falmouth, Cape Cod—"

"Jacques, Naomi Tripley is the name Paola has been using since she returned to the US. Naomi is Paola."

"Philippe, I had no idea. This is bizarre. You must have thought it very strange when you called me to tell me and you discovered I was near Cape Cod."

"Yes, at that stage, I did. Paola's assistant from the gallery had given a very detailed description of a man who visited the gallery a couple of weeks ago and whose general description fitted a figure they could see in a CCTV recording from Paola's house. The assistant emailed me a copy of the artist's drawing enhanced in some way to look like a photograph. I was stunned. The similarity to you was uncanny."

"So you thought I had taken Paola?"

"Of course not, Jacques. I knew there had to be a plausible explanation; I just couldn't imagine what it was."

"So what does this man, my twin, what does he want with Paola?"

"I don't know. All I can say is that I think he has been planning it for some time."

"Well, whatever the reason, we must do everything we can to get her back. I take it the police have no idea where she's gone."

"None at all. There has been no communication."

"Philippe, mon ami, we shall solve this problem. But my head must be clear; I need a good night's rest. I really didn't sleep well in that police cell; I've known more comfortable tombstones. We'll talk in the morning. But before that, would you be so kind as to ask Miss Reid if I may talk to her?"

The voice in Jacques' ear was hesitant.

"Hello? This is Claudia."

"Ah, Dr Reid, this is Adam Fowler, or as our friend John would have it, Jacques Bognard. Actually I think I prefer Jacques Bognard. Dr Reid, I wanted to thank you at the first opportunity for working out the cause of my dilemma. I am not a scientist and I should never have known about DNA and twins and so forth. I am indebted to you. Your perspicacity and profound knowledge enabled me to be whisked away by my Rottweiler of a lawyer from the grasping clutches of the Massachusetts police. I can assure you they were very reluctant for me to leave their company."

He heard a soft giggle down the line.

"Mr Fowler—"

"Adam, please."

"Adam. I did no more than any biochemist would have done. I'm surprised that it's not more common knowledge that homozygous twins have DNA that is identical as far as profiling is concerned."

"Oh, Dr Reid—"

"Please, Adam, it's Claudia."

Jacques smiled at the sound of the soft break in her voice, and then continued. "Claudia, if you could have seen the look on the dragon of a lieutenant's face when she told me I was free to go. She was breathing fire, believe me. It made the whole incident worthwhile.

"Now, I intend to return to England as soon as possible and I should like to ask if you would do me the honour of coming to dinner with me. There is a wonderful French restaurant I know in Knightsbridge. I am sure you would enjoy it. You do eat French food, don't you?"

"I love French food, Adam, yes, thank you." Then she panicked and wondered if she was being too gushing. "But there's really no need, you know. And Knightsbridge, gosh, that sounds very, um, exclusive."

Jacques' deep resonant laugh sounded in her ear. "Yes, I suppose it is. Good, that's settled then. Now, John tells me that you are applying your considerable intellect to the problem of the disappearance of his daughter, whom I only knew as Paola, which is why when I heard the name Naomi Tripley from the police it meant nothing to me. What are your thoughts, Claudia? Would you share them with me?"

"Well, there's nothing very profound in my thoughts that make them any different from anyone else's. I've been trying to work out the wheres and the whys, applying a little lateral thinking. Where would Paola have been taken and why was she taken. Now, we know that Charles Creed—"

"Charles Creed?" repeated Jacques. "Yes, I recall the lieutenant mentioning that name."

"It was the name given by the man who visited the gallery in Falmouth two weeks ago," said Claudia. "I shouldn't think for a moment that it's his real name or the name he regularly uses. Anyway, we know now that he is, well, like John and like you."

Jacques laughed. "You can say 'incredibly old', Claudia. I won't be offended."

"Actually, I was going to say 'very special'. What we don't know is whether he knows about Paola, that she's the same. But really, what other reason could there be for his interest in her? It can't be just her paintings. He'd hardly take her because of those. And then there's the woman who was killed."

"Yes, I didn't recognise her."

"You've seen her?"

"Her photograph, yes. The police took a shot in the mortuary. Her face meant nothing to me."

For a few moments there was a silence from the other end of the line. Then Jacques spoke.

"Claudia, I can almost hear your brain ticking away."

"I was just wondering if we could get a copy. We know what Creed looks like, since, of course, he looks like you. Having her photograph could be useful if indeed she was working with him."

"Leave it with me, Claudia, I think I know someone who can organise it. Now, about the dinner. I'm thinking of getting on a plane tonight once I've freshened up. When would suit you?"

"That's so kind, Adam, but let's wait until we've got Paola back. It wouldn't seem right going out to a special dinner while John is so upset and distracted, let alone Sara."

"Of course, you are right, my dear. How insensitive of me. Perhaps I shall come straight to the Lakes to be with you all."

"Actually, Adam, it might be better if you remained there. The Farsleys are returning to Boston tomorrow and John is thinking of going with them. He hasn't decided yet. I'm sure you could be of great help to him there."

"Ah, I didn't realise the Farsleys were in England. If that's the case, Claudia, you should come as well. I think you could offer much."

"Me?"

"Yes, I insist. I'll talk to John first thing tomorrow."

"Do you want to talk to him again now? He's only in the sitting room. I can take the phone through."

"Thank you, but no. I've had a trying forty-eight hours. I want nothing more than to soak in a steaming bath and, if I'm going to do that, I'd rather have the echo of your voice in my head than John's, dear friend though he is. I'll talk to him in the morning. Bonsoir, Claudia, and I thank you from the bottom of my heart."

Claudia walked back into the living room where the others were gathered around an open fire.

"You look very pleased with yourself, Dr Reid," said Lola, a knowing look on her face.

Claudia blushed and averted her eyes. "I've just been invited to dinner at an exclusive French restaurant in Knightsbridge," she said coyly.

"Ah," nodded John. "That will be Mathilde."

"Mathilde?"

"The restaurant. Jacques named it after his wife."

"His wife?" whispered Claudia, her face crumbling.

"Yes," laughed John. "His wife in Marseille in the seventeenth century."

"Oh, I see. What do you mean he named it after her?"

"Didn't he tell you? He owns it."

Chapter Seventeen

At eight the following morning, Claudia gave a huge yawn as she wandered into the Andrews' kitchen. John was there with his daughters Sophie and Phoebe, who jumped up to give Claudia a hug.

"Hi, Auntie Claw!" they squealed, enjoying using the familiar name that they'd heard Ced and Sally Fisher call Claudia. They thought it was really cool.

"Hi girls. What are you eating for breakfast?"

"Eggs from our chickens," said Phoebe, "and bacon from, er …"

"The freezer," laughed John from in front of the cooker. "I forgot to get the packets out last night. Want some, Claudia?"

"Yes, please, if that's OK." She loved breakfasts at the Andrews' cottage.

"Well, the hens have been working overtime with four ever-hungry Farsleys here, but there are still enough eggs to go round. Did you sleep well?"

"Brilliantly, as always. The air here is so much better than London and, of course, it's so wonderfully quiet. No traffic noise. I could sleep for a week. I wonder if I could persuade the prof to move the lab up here."

"And pollute our waters with his mysterious experiments?"

Claudia laughed and waved her forefinger back and forth at

him. "Now, now, I'll have you know that we have excellent waste treatment in the lab; you could drink the water flowing into the drains."

"I think I'll stick to the water from our borehole," said John, wrinkling his nose. "It doesn't taste of chlorine like London water or, for that matter, the normal water from the taps from round here."

"Are you sure your borehole isn't affected by the run-off from the nuclear power station? Doesn't glow in the dark, does it?"

"Digby Smith had it tested for me; it's as pure as any mountain spring water." He watched in amusement as Sophie scrutinised the glass of water in front of her and then took it to the darkness of the pantry to make up her own mind.

"I hear you are coming with us to Boston, Claudia," called John over the sound of the sizzling bacon.

"Gosh, has Adam called already?"

"Yes," replied John, "a couple of hours ago. It's just as well I get up early. Of course, it was very late for him, but he wanted to persuade me that I should go and that I added you into the arrangements. Oh, heavens, have you got your passport with you?"

Claudia's mind was elsewhere as she stared at the hills beyond the cottage.

"Claudia?"

"What, oh yes, sorry. Miles away," she said with a self-conscious smile. "I have, luckily. I don't usually carry it but when I was throwing things into my bag I saw it in the drawer and it kind of said 'take me with you, just in case'. The ESTA visa thingy is up to date as well."

"That's a relief," said John. "I think it's a great idea, Claudia. You might be able to suggest a few things if you see Paola's house. Jacques — Adam — said he'd make sure that a ticket will be waiting for you at the airport. And he said that if you haven't brought enough clothes up here with you, you are not to worry. He'll take you shopping. I think you've impressed him."

Claudia blushed. "I haven't done anything except put him straight about the DNA and fingerprints of identical twins," she said, fussing with her hair. "And I don't think the police would appreciate me sniffing around their murder scene."

Just then, Lola walked into the kitchen carrying a huge bunch of roses.

"What's going on, Dr Reid? These have just arrived along with other flowers for all the ladies. But this bunch is really rather special. I think you have an admirer."

"Don't be silly, we've never even met," said Claudia, colouring further as she took the bunch of exquisite buttermilk roses. "These are so beautiful, Lola," she added, touching the petals to her nose.

Lola caught John's eye and they grinned at each other.

As John was serving up Claudia's breakfast, his mobile phone pinged with a message. He walked over to the shelf where he'd left his phone in a wicker basket with other phones, bunches of keys, wallets and purses.

"It's a message from Digby Smith," he announced, running his eye over the screen. "At least, I think it is. His enigmatic codes change so frequently that I can't keep up. I'll just reply. Heavens, all this cloak-and-dagger stuff, it takes ages."

He waited for another message. "Ah, this one's in plain English. He says there's an email coming with something we should find interesting. I'll go through to the study to check it on the computer."

"Digby says you spoke to Jacques about this, Claudia," said John as he returned clutching a single sheet of A4 paper. It's a photo of the dead woman found at Paola's house."

"Is she dead, Daddy?" said Phoebe, rushing over to take a look. "That's so gross." Then she pulled a face, disappointed. "She just looks like she's asleep. How do you know she's dead?"

"Phoebe, come and finish your breakfast," said Lola, widening her eyes in reprimand at John.

"It's OK," said John defensively, "there's nothing gruesome about it."

"Adam said that when he saw it, the face meant nothing to him," said Claudia. "Sorry, Lola, I said it might be useful for us to see it too."

"Well, I'm afraid I don't recognise her," said John. "What about you, sweetheart?" He passed the sheet to Lola.

"Mmm. Middle-aged, ordinary looking woman. No, I've never seen her before."

"Nor me," added Claudia, who had walked over to where Lola was standing.

"We'll ask Sara and Lily when they come down," said John as Lola handed him back the printout. "After all, the murder was in their neck of the woods, loosely speaking."

"Murder!" echoed both Sophie and Phoebe.

"Off you go, you two," said Lola, still not happy about them overhearing so much of the conversation. "Time to get your stuff together for school. Kitty's doing the run in her wagon this morning; we mustn't keep her waiting. She's picking up some others too."

"You mean it's still not Saturday?" complained Phoebe as she reluctantly followed her sister out of the room.

John put the printout on the end of the table and returned to the cooker. "More eggs, anyone? Bacon?"

"On the button, Mr Andrews, sir," said Pete Farsley, striding into the room. "I'd far rather have some of your wonderful British farmhouse cooking before getting on an airplane than any airline food, even if we are travelling business."

"If I know you, Pete Farsley, you'll take advantage of both." Sara had followed her husband into the kitchen. "Good morning, everyone. There seem to be flowers everywhere."

"Read the cards with them, there's a bunch for you as well, Sara," said Lola, her eyes twinkling in amusement as she saw Claudia dissolve into blushes again. "You can thank Dr Reid. Have you seen her roses? How Jacques manages to locate so many beautiful blooms *and* have them delivered here in the middle of nowhere at such short notice while he is on the other side of the world beats me completely."

John smiled. "He probably owns the florist and the delivery company."

As Sara walked to the table carrying a bowl of yoghurt and fruit, she glanced at the printout. She stopped and picked it up, frowning. "I know this face. I've seen her somewhere. Who is she?"

She nodded as John explained. "I'll remember by and by," she said.

She sat down by Claudia who was unsuccessfully trying to grind pepper onto her eggs and bacon.

"Am I missing something with this thing?" she asked.

"Probably peppercorns," said Lola, "there's a packet in the cupboard on the wall behind you."

Claudia stood and opened the cupboard door. At five foot one in her shoes, most wall cupboards defeated her and this one was no exception. She could see the packet on the top shelf but her arms wouldn't reach.

"Can I help you?" asked Lily, as she walked into the room and noticed Claudia's dilemma.

"That's it!" exclaimed Sara.

"What?" said Pete.

"'Can I help you'," repeated Sara. "That's what I said to the woman when I opened the door to her. 'Can I help you?' And she replied 'I do hope so'."

"Who did, sweetheart?" asked Pete. "You're not making any sense."

"The dead woman, Pete," She reached over for the printout and pointed at the face. "She came to our house, knocked on the door and I asked what she wanted. She seemed a little flustered, hesitated for a moment, and then asked if I knew her friend, Lorna Whitely."

"Who?"

"You wouldn't know her, Pete, but I've met her at some residents' thing. She lives on Brookton, the same street number as ours."

"When was this?" asked John.

"The day Lily came over to Boston to go over arrangements for this trip. It was before we met Paola. Don't you remember, Lily? You'd caught the early train and were arriving late morning. I imagined that you would walk through town since it was a lovely day, so when the doorbell rang, I thought either you'd caught a cab or the train had arrived early. Anyway, I thought it was you so I was rather surprised to find this woman standing on the doorstep."

"She's the one who was found dead at Paola's house in Cape Cod?" asked Claudia. "It can't be a coincidence. Did anything else strange happen that day?"

"There was the gate to the yard," said Matt, who up until then had been fuelling up with breakfast. "You know, these eggs are amazing."

"It's because they're freshly laid in the henhouse out there," said John. "The one we share with our neighbour."

"Wow, what do you feed them on?"

"Can we stick to the point, Matt?" admonished Pete. "What was it about the gate?"

"Oh, yeah, the gate. I thought I told you. When I got back from the wild goose chase at the phone company sorting out roaming plans for Mom's cell here in England, a phone that I think has only rung once, by the way," he added, raising his eyebrows. "When I eventually got back after pumping up both my tyres outside the phone shop — I mean, whoever gets *two* flats? And they weren't flats; someone let them down. Well, anyway, the gate to the yard was wide open, which it never is. I know for certain that I closed it and locked it, so I assumed that Julie had gone that way and forgotten to close it."

"Never!" Julie was indignant. "I *never* leave the gate open. Anyhow, that morning I left with you and when I came back, I used the front door."

"Was there any sign that someone had been in the house, Sara?" asked Claudia.

"Not that I noticed," said Sara, shaking her head.

Claudia tapped her chin lightly with the side of her balled hand.

"I can't work out why she would come to the house and then ask for someone else," she said. "Maybe there was a change of plan."

"What do you mean?" asked John.

"Well, supposing she came to the house as part of a plan to abduct Sara."

"Sara?" said Pete, taking his wife's hand.

"It's not beyond the bounds of possibility, you know," said Claudia, her eyes roaming the table top as she processed various scenarios. "If the gate was open, it could indicate that someone had come in through it and perhaps a bit later left in a hurry, forgetting to close it."

She nodded to herself as the ideas clarified.

"Yes. Somehow, for some reason, there was a change of plan and the woman backed off with a story about your friend."

"Lorna Whiteley," prompted Sara.

"Yes," said Claudia. "Gosh, she would have to have been very well prepared. But I'll bet if you showed Lorna Whiteley this photo, she wouldn't know this woman."

"Wow!" exclaimed Matt. "Is this what you do all day? Work out weird scenarios to solve crimes?"

Claudia laughed. "Certainly not! It's the last thing I normally do. I was just applying a bit of logic combined with lateral thought."

"Maybe I won't be a historian after all," said Matt.

"You know, you've raised a very worrying matter," said John.

All eyes turned to him.

"If there was a plan to take Sara that changed suddenly and unexpectedly for some reason, then whoever's behind it might still want to go ahead with it in the future. After all, we know nothing of their motives, and they *have* taken Paola, who is Sara's mother. I think it might be better if you don't return to the States for a while, Sara, until this is all sorted out. The chances are that no one knows you're here which means you should be safe. I can contact Digby

Smith and if he agrees, which I'm sure he will, he could arrange some sort of protection to the cottage."

"You mean armed guards at the door?" said Lola indignantly, "I don't think so."

"No, sweetheart, I think Digby would be more subtle than that. You'd probably never even see them."

"I can't just stay here while all of you go home," objected Sara.

"I'll stay with you, Mom," said Julie as she absently picked up the print of Edith Cooper's face and studied it. "If that's OK with Great Grandma Lola," she grinned.

"Not if you call me that," said Lola, narrowing her eyes at her.

"I think it's really cool," said Julie.

"In that case," added Matt, "I think I should stay too. There's not much I can do in Boston and staying here, I can look after you both."

"Thank you, Matt," said Sara, taking his hand.

"It makes sense, sweetheart, your staying here I mean," said Pete to Sara. "It would mean that I could focus on chasing up the police and other contacts without constantly worrying about whether you are all right."

"I wonder why she was killed?" said Julie, still staring at the printout. "I mean, if she went to Paola's house with Charles Creed, or whatever his name really is, with the intention of abducting her, how come she ended up dead?"

John sat back in his chair and rubbed the muscles on the back of his neck. "Well," he said, "we know there was a fight since Creed was also injured. Hence the blood that led to the confusion over the DNA. We also know that Paola isn't averse to using a knife to fight her way out of trouble."

"How do we know that?" asked Claudia, looking shocked.

"From the information she gave to Dr Wright, her psychiatrist, which Wright published in her memoirs about delusional patients," explained John.

"That's how we found out about my mother in the first place," added Sara, "when Matt got hold of a copy of the book. By her own admission, rather than having a delusional past, my mother has something of a murderous one. All in self-defence, of course."

Claudia rested her face on her hands as she thought the conversation through.

"If you got hold of a copy of the book — I assume it's on public sale?" she said, turning to Matt.

"I located it on Amazon, although it came from an academic books supplier," replied Matt.

"OK, if you got it so easily, then perhaps this Charles Creed did too. You've spoken to Dr Wright, haven't you, Sara?"

"Yes, of course. I visited her at her practice in New York City. Once she realised who I was, she gave me everything she had, or at least photocopies. All her notes, the complete set, as well as a number of photographs she took of my mother in the early 1970s. Of course, my mother looked exactly the same then as she does now. But it was only when Dr Wright caught up with her again three weeks ago that she finally accepted my mother's story. It was Dr Wright who turned up at our house on that wonderful day. Heavens, was it only three weeks ago? So much seems to have happened."

"Do you have the notes here with you?" asked Claudia, "I could read them on the plane."

"No, they're all at our house in Boston. Pete could pick them up tonight when you arrive."

"That would be great," said Claudia. "It would be good to know more about Paola." She paused as something else occurred to her. "Do you think that Charles Creed has ever visited her? Dr Wright, I mean."

"I don't think so," said Sara. "She certainly didn't mention it."

"She might not know," said Claudia quietly, more to herself than to the others.

"What do you mean?" asked Sara.

Claudia turned to John. "Dr Wright seems to be a key to this whole puzzle. I think one of the first things we should do is to make an appointment to see her."

Chapter Eighteen

The meeting with Doctor Ronaldi in the spacious sitting room did not go well for the timid specialist. Paola had already decided that she wanted to delay whatever processes Dayton was planning to set in motion for as long as she could. Talk of the grounds and her freedom to explore them had excited her: she was sure she would be able to find a way out. For that, she wanted to be free of interference from the doctor and the nurses.

As soon as Ronaldi entered the room, Paola fixed her eyes on him, her expression dark and menacing. Despite his timid exterior, the doctor was a kindly soul with impeccable manners, and he found it impossible to talk to someone without looking them in the eye, especially if that someone were a patient. It was simple courtesy. But even before he sat down on the sofa opposite Paola, he had become aware of her eyes. Dayton was aware of the tension building and he tried to defuse it by inviting the doctor to outline the processes involved in IVF and how they impacted on the donor of the eggs.

However, no sooner had Ronaldi started to explain than he began to falter, stuttering over his words, wringing his hands and generally becoming increasingly uncomfortable. Dayton felt he had no choice but to intervene.

"Are you feeling unwell, dottore?" he asked. "You appear distracted."

Ronaldi shuffled in his seat. "I regret that I had a restless night, signore," he lied. "I hardly slept a wink."

"Is the bed too hard? Too soft? I will have it changed immediately," said Dayton, knowing full well that the doctor's bed had nothing to do with the problem.

"The bed is perfect, thank you," replied Ronaldi, horrified at the thought of losing his wonderfully comfortable bed. "It was my own fault, I turned the heating up too much, but then I was concerned about opening the windows to cool the room down. The insects, you know."

"There are insect screens on all the windows, dottore, you simply have to pull them down."

"Of course, how stupid of me."

"Perhaps we should reconvene tomorrow, dottore. After you've had a chance to catch up on your sleep."

After Ronaldi had hurriedly left the room, Dayton turned to Paola, his face thunderous.

"What the hell do you think you're up to? You're like some witch out of the Dark Ages putting your hex on someone. The man was quivering under your gaze."

Paola laughed, the sound metallic, harsh. "I suppose I am a witch from the Dark Ages, well, the sixteenth century. Does that count?"

Dayton was dismissive. "Far too recent; it seems like only yesterday. You might think you're good, Paola, but I've seen far better, in the real Dark Ages. The witches then would have eaten you for breakfast."

"You must tell me about them sometime, the Dark Ages, I mean," replied Paola, pleased to have riled her captor.

Dayton let out a sigh, forcing his irritation to subside. Getting angry only worked to Paola's benefit. "I'd be pleased to," he said through clenched teeth, "but not if you're going to carry on like you did just now. You might think it gives you some sort of advantage, but I'll counter by simply restricting your freedom. Do you want to be confined to your room, strapped to the bed?"

"Is he the best you could find?" asked Paola in her most patronising tone as she deliberately ignored his threats. "Surely someone a little more confident, more assertive, would have been better."

She was rewarded with a flash from Dayton's eyes.

"He's the best there is, the top in his field," he snapped. "Assertiveness doesn't equate to competence, you know. It's often the opposite. I can assure you that once he dons a mask and gown, he is brilliant. So treat him with a little more respect."

"I'll think about it. Now, talking about freedom, you said I could explore the grounds. I should like to do that; I need some air."

Dayton pinched at his top lip, considering his reply. "Here's the deal, Paola. I'll agree to you exploring the grounds as long as you stop trying to intimidate Dr Ronaldi. Let him do his job, which I should like to see him start as soon as possible, and the grounds are yours. Is that fair?"

"I don't think fair has anything to do with it. Fair would be letting me walk out of here, back to my life."

"Which will happen, Paola, once Dr Ronaldi has successfully completed his task. Everything you do to slow him down, every tantrum you throw or hurdle you sling in the way will only serve to ensure that you stay here even longer. Do you understand?"

"What I understand is that it could take years for him to complete his task. From the little I know about IVF, there is no guarantee of success. Just how long do you intend to keep trying if Ronaldi fails?"

"He won't fail," growled Dayton.

Despite her aggressive stance, Paola understood she was on shaky ground. If she became too difficult, Dayton would resort to capturing Sara, something she wanted to avoid at all costs. She would have to give a little.

She sighed in apparent resignation. "All right," she said, "I'll allow him to start his tests tomorrow. Now, I really need some air."

"OK," said Dayton, relaxing. "Take a warm jacket; these autumn days are deceptive. In the sun it's fine, but much of the estate is well shaded, and it can be cold, even on a pleasant day like today."

"I'm pleased to hear you have my welfare so much in mind," sneered Paola.

Dayton paused and forced a smile. He needed to get beyond Paola's constant hostility.

"Will you join me for dinner this evening?" he asked.

Paola narrowed her eyes at him, momentarily surprised at the change of direction of the conversation. She still needed to learn about this man, find his weak spots. Understand your enemy, she thought.

"If the alternative is sitting in my room to eat, yes I will."

"It's not; I can have your meal served in here or anywhere you wish. But I'd be very pleased to share the time with you. Shall we say seven o'clock?"

Shortly after seven that evening, Paola made her way to Dayton's dining room. It was smaller than she had imagined, given the size of the sitting rooms. The centre of the room was dominated by a dark walnut dining table that looked centuries old. About four metres in length, it could comfortably seat twelve people. Tonight it was set for two. On one side of the table was a long credenza, while on the other a fire blazed in a large, open fireplace.

Dayton jumped up from one of the two armchairs by the fireplace where he had been sitting reading.

"Paola! Are you refreshed from your walk?" he said, forcing his tone to be amiable and hoping that his words wouldn't be slung back in his face. "Please, sit here by the fire. May I offer you something to drink? A glass of wine, perhaps? I have just opened a most delicious red from a tiny vineyard not far from here. It's an excellent blend, perfectly balanced: Merlot and Cabernet, with just a little Sangiovese to give it an edge. I discovered it some years ago and since then I think I have taken the lion's share of their production."

Paola's shrug signalled her indifference. "I'm not much of a wine drinker, but I'll give it a try," she said as she sat in the armchair opposite Dayton's.

Dayton poured the wine into a tulip-shaped crystal goblet and placed it on a side table next to Paola, together with a plate of nibbles. "These are taralli, very special ones I have sent up from Puglia. They are delicious. Try one. The Puglians like to dip them in their wine."

She took one, tried it and nodded in appreciation. "Delicious. Melt in the mouth. Quite different from the bagel-like versions I've had in the States and in Rio."

"Excellent. Now, tell me, how was your walk?"

"To be honest, Dayton it—"

"Paola, please, I haven't lost sight of the inevitable gulf between us for all the reasons we've discussed, but now that you are here and will be for … well … could we be, perhaps, more relaxed? Could you bring yourself to call me Marcus?"

"Marcus," repeated Paola slowly, testing the word. She picked up another tarallo and rolled it in her fingers. "I suppose I can live with that, but don't think you are going to achieve a kind Stockholm effect here, a captor-captive bonding. I've been in situations like this before and they always ended badly for my captors. I see no reason why this one should be different."

"I most certainly do not underestimate you, Paola, but we can at least pretend to be civilised. Now, you were telling me about your walk."

"Yes, *Marcus*, I was. Frankly, I was disappointed. I expected to be roaming the grounds on my own, not to be trailed and watched at every turn. Just how many guards do you employ? Even in the woods there seemed to be one behind every tree. It's very inhibiting."

Dayton smiled and took a sip of wine. "It's a very large estate and the guards are here mainly to keep people out. Watching you is a new role and they have possibly taken their instructions rather too literally. I forget exactly how many there are, but the number is considerable. Of course, there is a physical barrier at the borders of the property as well: a substantial electric fence. There are also many security cameras, but all that only goes so far. Having guards patrolling is far more effective than having them sitting on their backsides watching CCTV monitors. They get fat and lazy doing that. So, while the guards are out in all weathers keeping fit — they also have a forestry work schedule they are obliged to follow — I have a cutting-edge computer program scanning the CCTV for any unexpected variations to the images. It's relentless, obedient and it doesn't doze off."

"Whatever they're up to, I'd prefer it if they kept their distance."

"I'll have a word," said Dayton. "Now, Paola, something you mentioned earlier intrigued me. I wonder if I could ask you to elaborate."

Paola moved her gaze from the fire to Dayton. "It rather depends."

Dayton smiled, still trying his hardest to play the congenial host. "When you were talking about your conversations with Dr Wright, you said that some of them were sanitised. What did you mean? What was it you didn't want her to hear? Were you perhaps referring to your times as a nun? You told her that you spent a total of over a hundred years in various nunneries. I thought that even given you were trying to hide, it seemed rather excessive."

"Very perceptive of you, Marcus." Her reply still had a grudging edge. She wondered how much she should tell him. Then she decided it didn't really matter; he was hardly going to report her to the authorities. She took a sip of wine and caught his eye over the rim of the glass.

"You're right, I didn't spend over a hundred years in nunneries without a break, although I did spend several decades in them, when you add up all the time. No, I should have gone crazy in that suffocating world if I hadn't escaped occasionally. But given the turmoil in those times, and given I was still finding it hard to come to terms with the fact that I wasn't getting any older, nunneries were a very convenient hiding place."

"So why did you tell Dr Wright that you spent so much time there?"

"I didn't know how much checking of my story she would do and I didn't want her looking into incidents in Italian nunneries in the seventeenth century. So I covered the time period by simply saying that it was all spent hiding in the nun's habit. A bland existence that wouldn't be very interesting or easy to research."

"What were you trying to hide?" said Dayton, a glint of amusement in his eyes.

"Why do I have a feeling that you already know?" she replied.

Dayton took a sip from his glass. "I was in southern Italy on and off throughout the sixteen hundreds. I heard of a couple of, what shall we call them, shocking incidents? When I read of nunneries in Dr Wright's report, I was reminded of them. Anything to do with you?"

Paola smiled, although her eyes were still cold. She held out her wine glass. "You are right, Marcus, this wine is delicious. May I have another glass to help me remember?"

"Of course," he said, jumping up.

Paola stared into the flames of the roaring fire. "The first one I regret, in part," she said. "I didn't mean for so many of them to die. I was less experienced with herbal concoctions at that stage and I didn't know that the mother superior would change the dining arrangements on the very day I'd added the brew to her evening meal. I'd put far too much of the mixture in the pan from which she and her cohorts would be served. You see, she always insisted that her food and the food for the other seniors was prepared separately from the gruel most of us had to endure. I knew there would have to be some who would die who perhaps didn't deserve it, but it certainly wasn't intended for the younger, more innocent women. Some of them were little more than girls. But then a delegation from the bishopric turned up unannounced. The mother superior became very flustered and burst into the kitchen insisting that the quantities of food in her pan were increased to accommodate the visitors. I didn't care about the delegation: they had come visiting with a view to sampling more than the food and I could see the younger nuns were nervous. But then the bishop leading them insisted on a couple of the novitiates sharing his food. There was nothing I could do. Within minutes, the mother superior, the priests, the bishop and the unfortunate novitiates were all writhing in agony on the dining hall floor with no chance of survival. I knew I had to escape since once the shock of what had happened abated, they would know I was to blame.

"I ran to the stables to alert the delegation's horsemen that they needed to ride for help. The best rider and the fastest horse were chosen and I said I would run to the gate to open it. I had a bag with ordinary clothes hidden under my habit and when the rider got to the gate I pretended I couldn't open it. He climbed off his horse to help me and as he concentrated on the lock, I cut his throat. I was off and away into the night immediately, stopping only to discard my habit and put on my ordinary clothes, and to shed the disguise that made the nuns think I was approaching my fifties. They searched far and wide for the murdering middle-aged nun, but the young woman I had become slipped past them all."

"It must have been an effective poison. What was it?"

"Nux vomica. Strychnine. The seeds had been available in Europe for over a hundred years, having been imported originally from Asia. It causes a horrible death with violent distortions of the body."

"Where did you go? To another nunnery?"

"No, not immediately. My son Luigi was still alive and living about a hundred kilometres to the south. I managed to get word to him and he found me, took me in. He introduced me as his cousin in mourning for her late husband. It worked as a subterfuge for a while."

She stopped and looked up at Dayton. "It was an accident, Marcus, I had no intention of killing so many people."

"Why did you want to kill any of them?"

"I had been there for twenty-five years. I'd told them I was twenty-one when I arrived, which was after I fled Naples with Luigi, so I was really in my late eighties by the time of the poisonings. The mother superior had always been a witch. She was a domineering, vicious woman who would think nothing of beating the novitiates or insisting they satisfy the local priest's sick fantasies.

"She had started to notice my perfect health, the fact that whenever there was sickness around, I never fell ill. She began to watch me more closely. I knew what she was like; she had a way of blaming everything on the Devil. If she had realised that I also wasn't ageing, she would have decided that I was working for the Devil. I should have been summarily burnt. It was a desperate situation; I had to resolve it."

"Of course, it wasn't the first time you'd killed, was it, Paola?"

"No, it wasn't. But I told Dr Wright all about that. I'd killed Cardinal Alvaro in 1582; that was the reason I left Naples and went into the nunnery in the first place."

"There was another such incident that I remembered earlier, around 1685, in a nunnery near Ancona. That one anything to do with you?"

Paola shrugged and took another sip of wine.

Dayton raised his eyebrows, inviting her to tell him.

"It was a very similar tale, Marcus, and a very long time ago." Her tone was dismissive. She wasn't sure about the wisdom of revealing so much, but she had whetted Dayton's appetite; he was clearly not going to let it go.

She sighed and continued. "I had honed my craft by then; my skills had gone beyond inadvertently killing off a load of innocents. I'd expanded my armoury of poisons over the years and I could now dispatch an unwanted priest or overbearing mother superior in far subtler ways, ensuring that the finger of suspicion would never point at me."

Dayton half closed his eyes in question. "I seem to remember that the Ancona killings totalled nearly fifty people. Another accident or intentional?"

"Intentional. Very. The entire sisterhood had ganged up against me. Hypocritical, self-righteous sycophants, they would do anything to please the mother superior. They locked me in a cell in the cellars of the nunnery. They were planning to report me to the Church and have me executed. I had one chance: a very young novitiate whose life I'd saved twice when she fell ill. She was a weak, sickly waif of a thing and she idolised me. I persuaded her to add a concoction to the food so that I could escape. I told her how to prepare it and said it was just a sleeping draught, enough to buy me some time. She was traumatised once she realised she'd killed them all, babbling incoherently with horror, but she insisted she come with me. Sadly, she wasn't much on a horse. She fell when we were riding fast through some woods. Broke her neck."

She finished the glass of wine as she watched the flames.

"Some more wine?" asked Dayton.

"No, I'll be drunk. I don't know if you are the same as me, but any drug seems to have an exaggerated effect on my body. Alcohol is no exception. That's one reason why I seldom drink very much."

"How unfortunate for you," was all the information that Dayton would offer.

He reached for a bell. "Let's eat," he said. "My housekeeper and my cook make a wonderful team, and," he added with a smile, "I can trust them implicitly with what they put in my food."

Chapter Nineteen

Thirteen hours after being picked up in Thirlmere by a car provided by Digby Smith, a travel-weary threesome of John, Claudia and Pete found themselves heading for the immigration lines at Logan Airport, Boston. As a US citizen, Pete joined a different line, but the processing for him was almost as long.

"I've asked Digby on a number of occasions whether any of his contacts can speed this process up for us," said John, turning to Claudia, "but it seems that even his reach only goes so far; we just have to wait our turn."

"It's quite a disincentive for coming all the way to the US," said Claudia. "I don't make too many intercontinental trips, to here or elsewhere, but when I do, I've learned just to switch off, stay in limbo in a sort of suspended animation until after I arrive. However, these endless queues don't help."

"It's the jet lag that I find difficult to cope with," continued John. "Changing time zones so abruptly is an assault on the senses. But I suppose you have to balance the convenience of air travel against that. The first time I crossed the Atlantic in this direction was on a smelly steamer in the 1870s, from Genoa to what was then called The Brazils. It seemed to take forever."

Claudia giggled as an elderly man standing in front of them turned to look quizzically at John.

"Whoops!" mouthed John, raising his eyebrows in amusement

as the man moved forward to create more space between himself and the clearly deranged person behind him.

Finally the three of them emerged into the greeting area to be met by a beaming Jacques Bognard.

"Philippe, mon ami!" he exclaimed as he enveloped John in a huge hug. "It is so good to see you, despite the circumstances. But where is Lily?"

"She decided to stay in the Lakes. She loves it there and like Sara, she felt that there was little she could do here. She's right, of course, and it's an extra pair of eyes to watch out for Sara."

"Yes," agreed Jacques, "a wise decision."

He stood back and turned towards Claudia. "Now, Philippe, I demand that you introduce me to your travelling companions."

"Of course," said John. "This is Claudia, to whom you spoke yesterday on the phone. Claudia, this is my old and dear friend, Jacques, or, as you know him, Adam Fowler. And this is P—"

Jacques wasn't listening. He immediately took Claudia's hands in both of his and bent towards her, his six-foot-five frame towering over her.

"Claudia, I am so delighted to meet you at last, having heard so much about you from this rogue and his charming wife, and, of course, having spoken to you on the telephone. Once again, I should like to thank you for your brilliance in resolving an extremely difficult and really quite embarrassing situation for me."

Without giving Claudia time to reply, Jacques turned to John. "Philippe, I am at a loss for words."

"That," said John, "I very much doubt."

"Philippe, you must explain why in all the times you have spoken of Claudia to me, you have never once mentioned her beauty." He turned back to Claudia, still holding her hand. "I think his artistic skills must finally be deserting him, Claudia. After all, no true artist would ever fail to mention a young woman's beauty in the first breath he draws in describing her."

He waved an admonitory finger at John while Claudia laughed quietly at the display of Gallic charm. As she did, she found herself staring intently at his face. Knowing his approximate age, and having spoken to him on the phone, her mental image of him was of a far older man, even though she understood that he had the same rare traits as John. Contrary to that image, here, standing before her, was a very tall and well-built handsome man who was apparently in his thirties. He was, perhaps, a somewhat old-fashioned in his choice of clothes, being casually dressed in an expensive jacket and trousers, but he was, nevertheless, a man in his prime. His hair was very dark and his skin naturally tanned, and although his eyes were jet-black, very different from John's, there was warmth radiating from them.

"You look confused, Claudia," said Jacques, a concerned note in his voice. "Has the flight worn you out? Do you need to rest? I am sure you must. We'll head straight for the hotel."

He turned and waved. In the distance, a car engine started.

"I am fine, thank you, Adam," said Claudia, trying not to show how flustered she was feeling. She was inwardly fighting to control the blush she could feel flooding her face. "Actually, the flight was amazing, so comfortable. I've never flown business before; it's another world from cattle class, where even I feel cramped. You would find it impossible."

Jacques threw back his head and laughed. "I have no doubt, but I can assure you that I have no intention of experimenting with it. I think I should rather go in the hold, sedated in a suitcase."

"I'm sorry if I was staring," continued Claudia. "I'm still somewhat overwhelmed by the whole idea of you and John, even though I've known about it for over three years now and, of course, I fully understand it."

"I am sure there is no one on earth who understands it better than you, Claudia," said Jacques, his eyes beaming at her.

"Well, I think the prof ..." she started. "Anyway, to meet you in the flesh, so to speak, while at the same time knowing your secret, is, well, pretty amazing." She paused and looked up at him from under her eyelashes. "And you look much younger than I imagined."

Jacques laughed loudly again and, as he did, he noticed Pete standing back from them by the suitcases, amused by their performance.

"My dear man," said Jacques, taking a step towards him and holding out his hand. "I do apologise. You must be Peter, Sara's husband. I am honoured to meet you."

He turned to John. "Philippe, how could you?"

"What?" said John, but Jacques had already turned back to Pete. "You will agree, I think, Peter, that it is every man's lot to have to take a step into the background when in the presence of a beautiful woman."

"I couldn't agree more," said Pete, noticing out of the corner of his eye that Claudia was still blushing. "But it's Pete, not Peter. I think the only time I've ever been called Peter was when I was christened. And while we're talking names, I'm perplexed. Should I call you Adam or Jacques? It's all very confusing."

"An excellent point, Pete, and I can understand just how confusing it must be. I know that whatever you call me, I shall always be Jacques to Philippe, but why don't we let Claudia decide. I think she too has found it confusing. What do you say, Claudia, my dear?"

Claudia looked up at him. "You know, I'm not sure. Where did you get 'Adam' from? I don't know that it suits you. I suppose you've had dozens of names, hundreds perhaps, but let's not confuse the issue by going there."

She dropped the corners of her mouth as she thought it through. Then she smiled, her eyes lighting up as she noticed Jacques quietly gulping as he watched her. "If we are not intruding on your special friendship, I think I'd prefer Jacques. May we call you that, amongst ourselves at least?"

She turned to John. "But just to confuse the issue, Mr Andrews, I'm afraid that there's no way I can ever call you Philippe, any more than I can call you Luca or Stefano, Tommaso or Giovanni. You'll always be John. Oh dear, it's really very confusing, isn't it?"

They all laughed and turned toward the car that had just drawn up.

"Ah," said Jacques, "here is Kenton. Leave the bags, Pete, Kenton will stow them." He put his arm around their shoulders.

"Come, Philippe, come Pete, we have serious business to attend to, once you have all had a good night's sleep. We are the Three Musketeers accompanied by our beautiful forensic detective. We are invincible and with our combined efforts, we shall soon have Paola back in the fold."

As he guided them into the car, he added, "I knew him, you know, Dumas, a very close friend. Wonderful fellow; great sense of humour. He could spend hours talking about himself — very French — and of course he was a brilliant writer."

John smiled quietly to himself as he saw Claudia and Pete stare at Jacques in awe.

Chapter Twenty

On the fifteen-minute drive from Logan International to the Mandarin Oriental in Boston's Back Bay area, Jacques apologised to Pete for his presumptuousness in booking him a room as well.

"I realise you might prefer the comfort of your own bed in your own house, but I thought it better to hedge my bets and include you. I keep a suite there and I thought that we should probably all want to discuss our plans at breakfast."

Pete looked at him sideways at the mention of a permanent suite in one of Boston's top hotels. He'd often toyed with the idea of taking Sara there for a special weekend luxuriating in the spa treatments on offer. He certainly wasn't going to turn down the chance of staying, even if Sara was still in England.

"It sounds perfect, Jacques. I wasn't looking forward to going back to an empty house, and we'll certainly need to put our heads together first thing."

He paused, then remembering their conversation that morning at the Andrews' cottage, he turned to Claudia and added. "There is one thing. I was going to get you the file with Dr Wright's notes, Claudia. Are you up to reading them tonight?"

She smiled and shook her head. "Thanks Pete, but it's really not essential I see them before our meeting with Dr Wright. I'll need my wits about me to concentrate on them and at the moment

I've got that kind of out-of-body feeling that comes after a long flight with a big change of time zones."

"Good," beamed Jacques, "then everything is settled."

John wasn't so sure. "Jacques, I don't think Digby is picking up the tab for our hotels, just the flights."

"Mon ami, there is nothing to worry about. The manager is a personal friend; he gives me very good rates. It is my pleasure that you will all join me in my home away from home. Now, I know you are all tired but in my experience, after a long flight there is nothing better than the luxury of a gentle massage. I have again taken the liberty of arranging personal treatments for you all, after which I guarantee you will sleep most soundly and awake completely refreshed. I should hate for any of you, particularly our forensic super-sleuth, to remain out of your bodies for longer than is necessary."

The following morning at ten saw Jacques, John and Claudia once again in Jacques' car as Kenton drove them to New York City for an appointment with Nancy Wright. Sara had called ahead from England to confirm that the psychiatrist could see them and had arranged an appointment for early afternoon. She had explained briefly who John was and added that Claudia was a forensic expert friend who was helping them out. Pete had stayed in Boston to lean on his police and legal contacts for whatever information they had. What he discovered after several hours of frustrating calls was that very little progress had been made. Although they doubted that Naomi Tripley had been spirited out of the country, the police had checked ports and airports, and in particular, small airports servicing private jets. But Marcus Dayton had covered his tracks well. Nothing of significance to connect Charles Creed or anyone of his description with a flight could be found on the day of the abduction or on any date since.

They had also failed to make any progress regarding the dead woman found at Naomi Tripley's house.

"Like the lieutenant said, she's a Jane Doe," Pete's contact in the DA's office had told him. "We simply don't know who she is.

There's nothing on file and no one of her description was reported missing anywhere in the US, either on the date of the murder or since. And for the third man who showed up in the CCTV footage, the image is far too grainy for an ID. The only one we were sure of was Creed and now we've been assured that he is not involved."

"Why's that?" asked Pete, hoping his tone was sufficiently innocent.

"Something to do with DNA and identical twins. They're saying that the fingerprints are different between Creed and the scene. Me, I think they've screwed the whole thing up. I wanted the prints checked for quality and integrity of match, but it's too late. They've let Creed go, although of course he was still claiming that he'd never heard of the name Creed. Anyway, since he's a Brit, we'll probably never see him again."

"So where are you going from here?" asked Pete.

"Good question, Pete. In fact, I was going to ask you, how well do you know Naomi Tripley?"

Pete was immediately cautious.

"To be honest, I've never met her. It was Sara who visited her gallery and struck up a conversation with her, made some loose arrangements for seeing her when we are in England."

"When was that?"

"I'm not sure exactly. A few weeks ago, I think. Why?"

"Well, the thing is, Pete, that the Tripley woman is not who she was claiming to be either. She's stolen her ID, so we have no idea who she really is. It's very weird. It's like these were people who didn't exist, that appeared from nowhere, and then went straight back there."

They arrived in Manhattan in time for Jacques to insist on a light lunch at La Danseuse in Greenwich Village. As they sipped their coffee after what Claudia declared to be the most delicious Caesar salad she had ever tasted, Jacques told them that he was passing on the visit to Nancy Wright.

"I've been considering it as we drove over and I'm concerned that it might be rather intimidating for three of us to turn up in her office and ask her questions. She doesn't know about me or how I fit into the story, so perhaps it would be better left that way, rather than make up some nonsense. And, as it happens, following my little holiday with the Cape Cod police, there are several pressing matters I need to catch up with here in New York."

Shortly after three o'clock, as Kenton drove John and Claudia to Nancy Wright's ageing office on the Upper West Side, John noticed that Claudia seemed to have gone into her shell.

"You're very quiet, Claudia. Is there something wrong? Are you still feeling the effects of the time change, even after that wonderful massage and a good night's sleep?"

Claudia ran a hand through her hair as she turned briefly to him. "I slept very well, thanks. I think it must be the time change."

She attempted a smile but her mind was elsewhere. She had surprised herself by realising she was very disappointed Jacques wasn't with them, but she was hardly ready to admit it to John. She was having a hard enough time admitting to herself that she was very attracted to a man who was around two and a half thousand years old.

The traffic was mercifully light and they arrived within twenty minutes. As Claudia got out onto the tree-lined street and looked up at the row of brownstones, she sighed, telling herself she had to focus on the coming meeting with the psychiatrist. John said nothing as she continued to avoid his eyes. He was fairly sure he knew what was distracting her.

Nancy Wright welcomed them warmly and sat them on the large sofas in her consulting room. At seventy-four, she looked very different from the pictures John had seen of her from when she was photographed with Paola in the early 1970s. Even his artist's eye found it difficult to associate the elegant but ageing woman sitting in front of him with the young woman pictured with Paola.

"It's very good of you to meet with us at such short notice, Dr Wright," he said, watching her in quiet amusement as her eyes took in every feature of his face. "I hope that we haven't put you to any inconvenience."

"Not at all, Mr Andrews. When I heard from Sara about Annie's, sorry, Naomi's disappearance, I wanted to meet you and help in any way I could. I can assure you that I'm thrilled to meet the father of the woman I knew as Annie Carr, the man she said was called Stefano Crispi at the time she was born."

John smiled. "That's correct, Dr Wright, I was. It's good to be able to discuss it openly with someone who accepts the truth about me and about my daughter."

"Oh, it took me a long time to accept the truth, Mr Andrews. Far too long. It was such a hard story to believe. Annie was very convincing, you see, as a delusional patient, and convincing myself of the truth of that was far easier than accepting what the truth eventually turned out to be."

Claudia leaned forward, focussed now and eager to get to the point of their visit.

"Dr Wright," she said, "the police have made very little progress with the abduction, except unwittingly to have arrested an innocent man. That has now been resolved, but neither they nor we are any closer to discovering who is involved and where they might be. We were wondering if we showed you a couple of photos whether the faces might mean anything to you."

She took the photograph of Edith Cooper from her bag. "This is the woman found dead at Naomi Tripley's house, the one who appears to have been killed during the abduction."

The psychiatrist studied the face carefully. "This is clearly a post mortem photograph," she said, "which means the features will have changed subtly from a living person, but no, I'm sure I have never seen her before."

Claudia took back the photo and replaced it with the image rendered from Mary Murphy's description of the man calling himself Charles Creed. She could see that Nancy Wright didn't recognise the face even before she'd finished explaining it.

Nancy Wright studied it, but continued to shake her head. "No," she said, "I think I'd remember that face, he has strong features. He's a handsome man although those eyes look cold."

Claudia wondered whether to show the psychiatrist a shot of

Jacques she'd taken with her phone that morning, but she realised that explaining it could complicate matters.

While Nancy Wright had been examining the faces, John had been letting his eyes drift around the consulting room. They stopped on the painting of a far younger Nancy.

"That's Paola's portrait of you, painted in the 1970s. I've seen a photograph of it. May I take a closer look?"

"Please do, Mr Andrews. It's not every day that I get a genuine Renaissance artist assessing a portrait in my office."

"Thank you." John stood and walked over to the painting.

"Yes," he said after a few moments of peering closely at it. "It's every bit as good as I thought it would be. Paola has a natural talent."

Nancy Wright handed the printout with the image of Marcus Dayton back to Claudia.

"I'm so sorry that I can't help you further, especially since you've come so far to see me. Did you think perhaps that one or both of these people had come here to see me?"

"I doubt they would have done that," said Claudia, "but they might have taken an interest in you if their source of information on Naomi was your book."

Nancy thought about it. "Perhaps it would be worth showing these to my secretary. Unlike me, she's here every day and she knows far more about the comings and goings in this building than I do. Not that I think there are many. I'll ask her to come through."

She stood and walked over to her desk to press a button on the intercom box.

Maureen, Nancy Wright's secretary, shook her head as she looked at the photograph of Edith Cooper.

"No," she said, "I'm sure I've never seen her before."

She turned her attention to the rendered drawing of Marcus Dayton and her eyes lit up. "But this face, yes, this one I do recognise."

"You do?" said both John and Claudia together.

"Yes. I only saw him briefly on the stairs one evening. Frankly he seemed rather put out when I almost bumped into him. Perhaps he thought everyone had gone home, but on that particular evening, I was working late. I think he was the boss of the company that rented the space upstairs."

"The space upstairs?" said Claudia.

Nancy explained. "It was a lawyer's practice for many years, but the firm moved away when the principal partner died and the offices were empty for some considerable time. Then a short while before I finally met up with Annie, just after Sara came to see me, it was rented."

She paused. "I wonder if that's significant," she mused absently. Then she continued. "The leasing agent explained that it was only going to be used by a couple of people working on the Internet. She assured me there would be no noise. You see, I've gotten used to the peace and quiet around here and I didn't want my patients being disturbed. Well, she was right; I never heard a thing. I still don't. I assume they are still there, Maureen?"

"I think so," replied her secretary. "But come to think of it, I haven't seen anyone for a few days."

"Do you know anything about them?" asked John. "The name of the company, for example."

"No, nothing at all." Maureen shook her head.

"Perhaps we should go and take a look," said Claudia, starting to get out of her seat.

"I'll go," offered Maureen. "I'll talk to the security people as well."

After she'd left, Claudia put the heels of her hands together and drummed her fingers against each other.

"Don't you think it's rather a coincidence that the man we are looking for, the man who has been involved in Paola's abduction, should have rented the offices directly above you, Dr Wright?"

"I certainly do, Dr Reid. It's strange, very strange indeed. Do you think he was spying on me?"

Claudia nodded. "Possibly. Has there been any sign of a break-in over the last few weeks? Has anything gone missing?"

Nancy Wright looked worried. "Not as far as I know," she said, glancing nervously around the room. "Everything seems to be as it should be." Then she added quietly, "I'm sure I'd notice." But she didn't sound convinced.

Claudia stood, wanting to fill the time before Maureen returned. "Would you mind if I had a look at your portrait, Dr Wright? I don't know a lot about art, although a close friend of mine has tried very hard to educate me."

"Thank heavens he did," said John as he thought about Ced Fisher's role in seeking him out three years before.

When Maureen returned, she was looking puzzled.

"Anything?" asked Nancy Wright as she looked across the room expectantly.

"Maybe," said Maureen. "It's all very strange. The offices are locked up and there are no lights on, no sign of any activity at all. I went down to the desk and the guard told me he hadn't seen any of them for several days. The last time he remembers seeing anyone was when the two main occupants of the offices, a young man and a young woman, were carrying two computers out of the building to a waiting taxi."

"Could you call the leasing agent, Maureen?" said Nancy. "Check if the lease has been cancelled? Oh, and Maureen, have you noticed anything odd in my offices lately? Has anything disappeared or been moved unexpectedly?"

Maureen looked concerned. "Actually, Dr Wright, I wasn't going to say anything because I thought perhaps it was me being forgetful, but a few weeks ago when I came to work, I got the distinct impression that things weren't exactly as I left them. I remember it was a Monday morning, so I'm talking about how I left them on the Friday evening. You see, I always leave my chair straight and tucked in under the desk. I'm very particular about it. That morning it was slightly out of position. And the papers in my desk drawer, I don't know, they just weren't quite right."

"So you think someone could have been in here?" asked John.

"The alarm system is a sophisticated one," said Maureen. "They'd have to be pretty good."

"Where do you keep your patients' files?" asked Claudia, turning to Nancy.

"The main ones are kept outside with Maureen, in the filing cabinet there. But I also have some very confidential ones locked up in here." She pointed at a single four-drawer filing cabinet. "Only I have access to those."

"Would that include Naomi Tripley's notes?" asked Claudia.

"Yes, well the notes from when she was Annie Carr." She suddenly realised that her secretary was still in the room and looking puzzled. "It's a very old case, Maureen, involving a severely delusional patient. Would you mind checking on one further point with the guard downstairs? Could you ask him what happens to the recordings from the CCTV, where they are kept and so on?"

As Maureen left, Nancy smiled guiltily at John and Claudia. "Neither Maureen nor any of her predecessors know anything about the Annie Carr case, and they don't even know the files exist. In fact, the only times the files have been looked at recently were when I was writing my book and when I showed them to Sara."

"Could you check them?" asked Claudia. "See if they have been disturbed in any way?"

Nancy stood, walked over to the cabinet and unlocked it. Claudia followed behind her and suggested that she take her time. "Just look first and then carefully remove the folders," she said. "Actually," she added, "do you have any surgical gloves? I was thinking that if someone else has handled them there could be fingerprints on them apart from yours and presumably Sara's. It would be better not to touch the folders any more than necessary."

"Yes, of course," said Nancy. "I wouldn't have thought of that."

She fetched some disposable gloves from her examination room, put on one pair and handed another pair to Claudia. Then she opened the top drawer. "It all looks OK," she said. "Everything is neatly in its place."

She pulled out the first folder of Annie Carr's notes, laid it on her desk and opened it. "Mmm," she said. "This isn't right. They are not in the right order."

"Are you sure?" asked Claudia. "It's very important."

"Quite sure," said Nancy. "I have a meticulous system for storage and I know that after Sara and I had finished photocopying these notes, everything went back in the correct order. Let's have a look at the photographs."

"Photographs?" asked Claudia.

"It's a long story, Dr Reid, but there are photos of Annie and me back in the early 1970s when I was trying to set up a comparison of the effects of the years on both of us. It didn't get very far because I moved here and then there was the fire in which I thought Annie had died, but they are still in the file. I can remember that the top one should be … yes, that's right. It's this one. But the one underneath is upside down and shouldn't be the next one anyway."

She turned to Claudia and saw that John had joined her.

"This filing cabinet has definitely been broken into, although …" She paused to look at the lock. "No, nothing appears to have been forced."

"I'm afraid that a lock like that would be child's play for anyone with a little knowledge of lock picking," said Claudia.

She turned to John.

"This is very significant. If Charles Creed's fingerprints are on these files, it would show that he hasn't just read Dr Wright's book, but he has seen all the notes as well as the photographs that Dr Wright just mentioned of Naomi, er, Annie. Oh, so many names!"

John smiled. "But will that take us any further forward, Claudia?"

"I don't know," said Claudia, pursing her lips. "Perhaps Creed had an accomplice who also left his prints, and perhaps he has a criminal record. Who knows? We're searching a trail of crumbs in the hope that they lead us back to something more significant. I could get these files fingerprinted; I have a friend here in New York I could beg a favour from."

Nancy Wright looked up from the file she was still studying. "Since my office has been broken into, don't you think it would be better if I report it to the police and ask them to take the fingerprints?"

Claudia shook her head, "Actually," she said, "I don't think that's such a good idea. You see, all the police know is that someone called Naomi Tripley has been abducted. They know nothing about her, or about who she really is and her connection to John, and nothing about how Sara fits into everything. Nor, for that matter, do they know anything about your connection with Paola, Dr Wright, and we certainly don't want to have to tell them. Frankly, I think it unlikely they would come here at all. After all, you didn't even know there had been a break-in until just now. They'll probably think that you have mistaken the order of the notes and photos. But if they do come here and they find finger-prints, they will eventually match them through the database with Charles Creed, or whatever his name is, and they will start asking awkward questions."

She paused and smiled self-consciously, realising that her ideas had poured out in their usual rush. Then she continued. "I think that would be best avoided. Let me talk to my friend. I'm fairly confident he will be able to make use of his own contacts in the police and check anything we find with the fingerprints of Charles Creed they have from Paola's house."

As Claudia was talking, Nancy had turned her head back to the file she was holding. Seeing this, Claudia caught John's eye and shook her head very slightly. John nodded almost imperceptibly. Clearly there was something Claudia didn't want to discuss in front of the psychiatrist.

"Would it be OK if I contacted my friend and asked him to call round, Dr Wright? He's very good and won't disturb you for long."

Nancy looked up. "Whatever you think best, Dr Reid. In fact, I feel very privileged to be included among the people who know about Annie and her family and of course I understand completely the need for secrecy." She smiled. "Let's do it your way."

Chapter Twenty-One

Paola sat back in her dining chair and took a sip of water. The meal of locally produced prosciutto, home-made tortellini and a veal cutlet fried in a very light dusting of breadcrumbs had been delicious. Dayton had deliberately refrained from asking her more about her past, instead telling her something of the history of the house, which he had first bought in 1253 from a nobleman fallen on hard times.

"Of course," he explained, "officially the ownership has moved around. For a long time now it's been under the name of an obscure charitable trust that ultimately I control. However, the paper trail would quickly become a maze for anyone trying to unravel it. But as long as all the appropriate taxes are paid, there is no reason for anyone to even think of trying."

He suggested they return to sit by the fire. "I'll fetch a plate of cantucci biscuits. Can I tempt you to a glass of the most exquisite Vin Santo to go with them? It's from the same vineyard as the red wine we had earlier. Surely a small drop won't affect you adversely and it's the perfect way to end a meal."

"It's a long time since I drank Vin Santo," said Paola. "Several centuries, in fact. Make it a very small drop."

She sat down in the armchair by the fire, drawing her legs up under her. "You realise that you've just confirmed that we're in Tuscany," she said, turning to him to watch his reaction.

Dayton cocked an eyebrow.

"Vin Santo?" said Paola.

He smiled. "When were you last in Italy, Paola? Vin Santo might well have originated in Tuscany, but it's fairly widely available throughout the country these days."

Paola ignored the rebuff; she knew she was right. She picked up a biscuit and snapped it in two. "OK, Marcus Dayton, I've told you something of my somewhat murky past. What about yours? You told me in the gallery of statues that you were around two and a half thousand years old. That's a hell of a long time. Tell me about your early life. Where were you born?"

Dayton poured two glasses of Vin Santo, his own fairly large, and sat back in his chair.

"In Greece, when that country was still powerful. But where exactly, I don't know. From the rumours I heard, I think it was an island."

"Rumours? Didn't your parents tell you?"

"I never knew them. I was separated from them soon after my birth and placed in the hands of the high priest of an obscure sun-worshipping sect. I was brought up in a temple where there were no other children. From a very early age I was expected to serve Cyrus — that was the high priest's name. I was seldom allowed to leave the temple and when I did I wasn't allowed to play with the other children in the town. Initially I couldn't understand them since they were speaking Greek and all I spoke was Cyrus's mother tongue, which was a form of ancient Turkish.

"By the time I was about fourteen, I was head and shoulders taller than Cyrus and any other man in the town. I was strong too, and it slowly became clear to me that Cyrus had marked my role in life as his protector. He must have known I would grow to be tall so I assumed my father had been the same. I searched for other men with my stature, but there were none. He must have had my father killed.

"He refused to educate me, so I couldn't read or write, but he did have me trained in the use of a sword and a dagger, as well as unarmed combat. He understood that while most men would have weapons in a fight, if you lost them, it was essential that you could use your hands and limbs as weapons in order to survive. I was good and I think he was proud of me. Certainly no man would have challenged him while I was around."

Paola watched him closely as he stared into the fire, those ancient days almost reflecting in his pupils.

"But I was lonely, Paola. And although I was feared, because of my lack of the most rudimentary form of education, I was regarded as a simpleton. My contemporaries laughed at me behind my back and they could lose me easily with their words. I would hit out, hurt them physically, but it didn't stop them. They would get the girls to do their bidding, knowing I'd stop short of striking them. Then one girl befriended me, felt sorry for me. We started to meet in secret and she would teach me things. She quickly realised that I was no idiot, that I had simply been deprived, so she made it her mission to educate me. It was difficult; my duties with Cyrus occupied much of my time, while Thera, that was the girl's name, was very tied to her family duties.

"We continued for two years and, of course, we fell in love. We were both sixteen; how could it be otherwise? By then, the resentment I felt for Cyrus for depriving me of my true parents and bringing me up to be his slave was festering within me. I developed a hatred for him that took me over like some beast invading my body. Thera could see the change in me and it frightened her. But once I'd explained the evilness of the man, she agreed with my plan to kill him and run away. She wanted to come with me, to leave the family that she loved.

"We decided we would steal two horses and ride to the sea. We knew it was about two days' ride. There we would steal a boat and disappear into the Mediterranean. We were extremely naïve."

"Sounds like the plot of one of the second rate silent movies I was involved with when I was Dolores di Napoli in Hollywood about a hundred years ago," said Paola, injecting a heavy dose of sarcasm into her voice. "But unlike those worthless pieces of rubbish, I suspect that your story didn't end happily for all parties."

She saw Dayton glance briefly in her direction and then look away. She knew she was right.

Dayton sighed and then continued. "Cyrus saw a change in me, began to suspect something. He kept me on an even tighter chain, making me stay with him almost every hour of the day. At night I was to sleep outside his door in full sight of his two trusted guards. It was like being in prison without the walls and bars. He made enquiries, found out who I'd been seeing, who my friends were. He was very cunning. He knew instinctively a girl was involved and so he gathered six of the girls I knew, but deliberately didn't include Thera. He had them brought to the temple where, in my presence, he berated them about loyalty, religion, duty and the wrath of the gods. He threatened them with torture in the present life and for eternity in the afterlife if they didn't tell him who I had been seeing. It didn't take them long to cave in and give up Thera's name.

"Thera was dragged to the temple along with her hapless parents. She was accused of the foulest things, of being a whore, of treason and worst of all, of incurring the anger of the gods who would in turn put a blight on the entire community. Thera knew she had no chance, that she was going to die. So in the midst of Cyrus' rants, she rushed at him, pulling a dagger from her toga. But he saw her coming, drew a sword and cut her down."

"You mean you stood by and watched your lover sacrificed?" Paola was incredulous.

"I tortured myself with questions like that for many years. You must remember I was little more than a boy; I had no experience of fighting authority. I had been waiting for the right moment, but seeing her dying on the temple floor, seeing the sneer on Cyrus' face as he turned to me, I knew my time had come. I had no interest in living or dying; I just wanted to kill Cyrus before any of the guards stopped me. I charged at him, knocking the sword from his hand and, grabbing him by the head, I lifted him off his feet. Then as his arms flailed, I spun him round and crashed him to the floor, still grasping his head. His neck snapped and I felt him go limp. I could hear the guards rushing me — there were only three — so I hauled Cyrus's body into the air and hurled it at them, following on in a charge with my now-drawn sword. Almost before his body crashed into them, I had cut all three down. I didn't wait, didn't care how many others were coming. I ran back over to

Thera and knelt by her. I lifted her into my arms, but she was dead. I carried her to her parents, who were just standing there horror-struck. Somehow, her father found the strength to take his daughter's body from me. 'Go!' he insisted. 'Go! Run! You have to try, for Thera's sake.' I didn't need telling twice. I turned and ran and, in the confusion, I somehow managed to escape. To tell you the truth, I have no idea how, but when I regained my senses, I found myself on a horse riding at full pelt into the countryside."

He stopped, his face taut.

"Did you ever find out about your origins, your parents?" said Paola, surprising herself that she was taking a genuine interest in Dayton's story.

"Never. I tried, followed rumours, stories, but nothing came of it. But Thera's tuition led me to an understanding of business. You see, her father was a trader, a merchant of some standing. Unusually, he had taught his daughter the principles of trading and doing business, and she passed that onto me, whetting my appetite. I found I had a natural aptitude for it and once I'd stopped running and accepted that no one was running after me, I settled in Athens where I apprenticed with another trader, a ship owner who sent me to sea for a few years where I made him a lot of money. He rewarded me by giving me half his business. I've had many businesses over the centuries, Paola, made and lost fortunes, but I've always managed to accrue wealth."

He stopped and shifted his gaze from the still-blazing logs to Paola. Her eyes were fixed on his, her expression neutral. He could read nothing from it.

For her part, Paola was fighting her emotions. Her default position in any threatening situation was always to escape, and if that meant fighting or killing to achieve it, she would not hesitate. There was even now a demon within her telling her to attack Dayton where he sat, but she kept it at bay, knowing that even if she overpowered him, she could not escape his house. She would be killed. However, interwoven with her instinctive reaction was a sense of fascination for this man. He was absurdly old, had experienced more than anyone could imagine. Yet he had been denied the one thing he had wanted for almost all his long life, and when his dream had finally been fulfilled, it was cruelly snatched from him. With unlimited wealth and being used to getting whatever he wanted, he had followed his natural instincts. He had found her and then had taken her against her will. He was used to no other way.

She shuddered inwardly. What he wanted was unacceptable, outrageous. What right did he have to take away a product of her body and allow her no further contact, to use her like a machine? Fascinating or not, she would resist, find a way to compromise Dr Ronaldi's work. Or if it were successful, to claim the child. She would, after all, be its mother with as many if not more rights than Dayton. Better still, she would stick to her earlier thoughts: lead Dayton along, let the preliminary tests commence, and make her escape.

She stood. "An interesting tale. In spite of my continuing anger over the reasons why I am here, I should like to hear more sometime. But now, I'm tired and I'm going to bed."

She paused by the door and looked back at him.

"We shall make formidable adversaries, Marcus Dayton." She let her eyes linger on his for a few moments. "Don't let your guard down."

Dayton watched her leave, realising as he did that for the first time since he had known of her, he was suddenly thinking of her as an attractive woman rather than a commodity, the source of something he wanted. He was perfectly aware of the danger that lurked in such a feeling; he needed very much to follow her advice and keep on his guard.

Chapter Twenty-Two

As John and Claudia made to leave Nancy Wright's office, Claudia had a nagging feeling that they were missing something. They had established that Charles Creed had been spying on the psychiatrist, but they had little more. She thought over their conversation and realised they hadn't examined all the possibilities.

"John," she said, "I've been thinking. It might be an idea to check inside the offices upstairs, the ones that appear to have been abandoned, if only to establish that they are empty rather than the occupants all being on holiday."

"Perhaps if they are abandoned, your friends here in New York could look for fingerprints there as well," said John.

"Good idea," replied Claudia. "But there could also be something up there that is of use to us right now. I don't know, writing paper with the company logo on it, something like that."

"The guard should have the keys," said Nancy. "Maybe we can persuade him to let us in. I'll ask Maureen to come down with us; she seems to know the guard. Perhaps we should start by showing him the photos."

Fernando, the Mexican guard, was six foot two with a mop of luxuriant jet-black curls and a self-assured radiant white smile that homed straight in on Claudia. As she passed him the photos, he made sure his hand lingered on hers for long enough that she would look up into his dark brown eyes.

"I am very observant, señorita. If these people been here, Fernando, he see them," he said, flashing even more of his teeth.

Claudia offered him a broad smile in return. "That's very reassuring, thank you so much."

"Hey, where you from? You speak like the Queen of England. She a very special lady."

"She is," agreed Claudia, "but I'm not sure that I sound very much like her." She paused and then tilted her head at the set of prints. "The photos?"

As he tore his gaze from Claudia to look at the post mortem shot of Edith Cooper, Fernando's heavy eyebrows closed in one another in a frown, his face taking on a distinctly Neanderthal appearance.

"I never seen her. Man, she don' look too well."

He put the photograph down on the counter before he focussed on the next one. Claudia suppressed a wicked thought about one brain cell being able to process only one piece of information at a time and having to clear its limited capacity before attempting a second task. She jumped as he bellowed his reply.

"Yeah! This dude I seen. He come here coupla times with a greasy-haired geek type and a very attractive young lady. Much more classy than the geek," he added as he straightened with a swagger to indicate that whoever the young lady was, she was worthy of his consideration. "Say this for the geek though, he know his stuff with computers. When the CCTV break, he fix it in no time flat." He returned his attention to Claudia, but Maureen was ready to divert him.

"Fernando, dear," she said with her most winning smile. "I have a little favour to ask. It would really help us enormously if you could assist us, wouldn't it, Claudia?"

Claudia nodded enthusiastically as she flashed a coy smile for the guard.

"Just name it," said Fernando, suddenly wary of all the attention.

"Well," continued Maureen, letting a note of concern into her voice, "We're rather worried about the offices on the top floor, the ones immediately above Dr Wright's practice. As you know, there doesn't seem to have been anyone around for a few days, but Dr Wright did hear some noise up there, a sort of scraping sound. We did wonder if it would be a good idea to take a quick look around the door, just to make sure that everything's all right up there."

Fernando frowned deeply, his eyes almost disappearing under the overhang of his eyebrows.

"I'm not sure, I mean, I'm not supposed to open up offices to other people."

"Of course you're not, Fernando," interjected Nancy. "But we're hardly other people. I've been a tenant in this building since the 1970s, since before you were born, in fact. I have the best interests of the landlord at heart, and of course the tenants on the top floor. Given that I'm probably worrying about nothing, it seemed easier for us to check now rather than worry either the landlord or the tenant."

Fernando was still frowning as he slowly processed Nancy's reasoning. What they were asking for was against regulations, and for Fernando, regulations were everything. He wondered why it needed four of them to check if there was really nothing to worry about.

"I think maybe I should call the boss, Dr Wright," he said, "I don' know if he like it."

"Naturally, you must," said Nancy, surprising him. She took her phone from her jacket pocket. "I'll tell you what, why don't I speak to him? Reassure him that we're not up to any mischief. What's his number, Fernando?"

Claudia felt sorry for the man. This kind of decision-making process was clearly making him uncomfortable, although now Nancy had taken some of the responsibility, he seemed to be wavering. She thought she'd help him along.

"Of course, we won't touch anything," she said, smiling at him reassuringly. "They've probably left a window open and a bird's got in. They can make a terrible mess."

A plausible and innocent reason. It was good enough for Fernando; in fact it gave him cause for action. "OK, whatever you say. I'll fetch the key from the safe. They don' got an alarm they told me about."

As soon as she walked into the offices, Claudia knew she was wasting her time. There was nothing but empty desks and a couple of easy chairs. No papers, no computers. Nothing that could tell them anything about the company that had been there or what they had been doing. She turned to where the others were waiting by the entrance. "Panic over," she said for Fernando's benefit. "There's nothing to worry about here, and all the windows are secured."

"I must have been hearing things," added Nancy, smiling at the guard. "These old buildings, you know, they creak and groan a bit."

Out of the guard's view, Claudia caught John's eye and shrugged in disappointment. "It was worth a look," she said to him quietly.

They returned to the entrance lobby and were about to bid their goodbyes when Claudia thought of one more point.

"Fernando," she said, turning to the guard. "We forgot to ask you. You don't happen to know the name of the man in the photograph, do you?"

"No, señorita, he never introduce himself."

As his forehead furrowed, Claudia worried that she was over-taxing him again. But suddenly a light switched on in his eyes. "But I did hear the greasy-haired geek talking to him on his cell a couple times. Called him sir and boss a lot, and yeah, a name. Let me think."

This time when Claudia caught John's eye, her excitement had returned. She held her breath as she watched Fernando trying to recall the sequence of the geek's words, mouthing them to himself as he did.

"Yes, sir, boss, Mr ... Clayton? No, Layton, er, Payton. That was it!" he cried. "Mr Payton. The geek said, 'yes sir, boss, Mr Payton', all together, like that."

"Payton," repeated Claudia. "That could be extremely useful. Thank you so much, Fernando, you really have been such a help."

He flashed his toothy smile again and puffed out his chest.

"Does the name Payton mean anything to you?" asked John, turning to Maureen.

Maureen shook her head. "No, sorry, nothing at all. Except for the movie of course."

"Movie?" asked Claudia.

"Before your time, Claudia," said John. "Maureen's referring to Peyton Place."

"That's right, Mr Andrews, I am," agreed Maureen. "Lana Turner; she was wonderful, although I'd have thought it would have been before your time as well."

"Nothing like those old movies, Maureen," said John, remembering seeing it in early 1958 in London. "I can't get enough of them."

They thanked Nancy Wright once again for her time and walked out into the crisp autumn sunshine. As John lifted his hand to hail a taxi, there was a shout from the guard as he ran from the building.

"Señorita! Señor! I remembered! I remembered his name. It's not Payton. I got it wrong. It sounded a bit like Payton but it wasn't. It was Dayton. I remember now. He always said, 'Yes sir, boss, Mr Dayton', or something like that. But it was definitely Dayton!"

Chapter Twenty-Three

"The Carlyle, please, East 76th Street," said John to the taxi driver as they sped off down the tree-lined street of brownstone buildings from Nancy Wright's office. He turned to Claudia who was staring through the cab window, her mind clearly elsewhere once again.

"What was all that about your contacts here, the ones you want to do the fingerprinting?"

She surprised him by laughing. "I don't have any contacts here, but I really didn't think it a good idea to have the police talking to Dr Wright. Apart from anything else, it wouldn't be fair on her. She seemed rather flustered by us, so I don't think she needs any extra hassle."

"So what are you intending to do about the fingerprints?"

"I was rather hoping that Digby Smith might be able to arrange something. He seems to have fingers in pies everywhere. Do you think that's possible?"

"Yes, I should think so," agreed John, "but I'm not sure if he'll be able to breeze his way into the US fingerprint database."

"We can worry about that later," replied Claudia. "In fact we don't need to compare the prints against their database, we have Jacques."

"Jacques?"

"Yes. Because they are identical twins, Jacques' fingerprints are almost identical to Creed's, or Dayton, as I think we should now call him. So we can use Jacques as the control. There's no need to compare any prints from Dr Wright's office with the crime scene. If they are similar to Jacques' prints, then we'll know for sure that Dayton has been there."

"That's brilliant, Claudia. But what about this other person; the greasy-haired geek that the guard described?"

"Let's see what turns up. If necessary, maybe Digby can arrange something."

"OK," said John. "Anyway, it was good to find a name, don't you think?"

"Definitely," replied Claudia. "Dayton. It's pretty unusual, I should say. I wonder how easy it will be to track him down."

"Well, you must remember that it will not be his real name. If he is who we think he is, he'll have had many and will be very used to changing them. I've had to do it enough times and he's been around for far longer than I have."

"Yes," said Claudia, "but let's look positively at it. He's got to be using one name or other and if his computer person is calling him Dayton, then that must be the name he's using routinely. He might well have used it in the company he's running. If so, he could be traceable."

"It's possible," said John. "That's always assuming he is running a company."

"John, you're being very negative. We're going to sort all this out, you know." She paused, realising she'd been rather abrupt. She put a hand on John's arm. "We'll find Paola," she said more softly. "Now listen, Dayton's bound to be doing something here. Like Jacques, he has to make a living, unless he is mind-blowingly rich and doesn't have to work." She pulled a face, realising she was defeating her own argument.

"Let's see what Jacques has to say," said John.

"Is that where we're going now?" said Claudia, taking in the view for the first time. "Where *are* we going now, in fact? Is this Central Park? I don't know New York at all; I've only ever transited at the airport, seen it from the air on take-off and landing. It's really exciting to actually be here."

John smiled to himself at Claudia's usual gushing enthusiasm, her ideas all coming in a rush.

"Yes, this is Central Park. We must find time to take a stroll through it. You should see it on a Sunday; it's full of New Yorkers relaxing in weird and creative ways. Where we're going is just on the other side of the park, on the Upper East Side. It's a hotel that's one of Jacques' favourites for afternoon tea, so I've no doubt it will be smart."

He laughed as Claudia immediately began teasing her hair with her fingers. She dived into her handbag. "Gosh, I wish I'd known. I don't even have a hairbrush with me. Ah, here's a comb; it'll have to do. What's that building over there?"

"It's the Metropolitan Museum of Art."

"Wow! I hope we can go there. Some of your work's hanging there isn't—"

She faltered as John touched her arm and put a finger to his lips. His eyes flicked to the cab driver.

"Sorry," mouthed Claudia.

As they left the park, she turned to John. "Have you ever lived here, John? In New York, I mean."

"Not really, no," he said, talking quietly. "Other parts of the States, yes. Virginia mostly. Let me think, before my recent trips to see Lily, the last time I was in New York was in 1939. I stayed at the Waldorf Astoria with my wife Catherine, before we took the Queen Mary to England. I couldn't have timed it worse, really." His eyes clouded as his thoughts drifted back to the WWII bombings in London and Catherine's death.

"Ah, here we are," he said looking up.

As he leaned forward to pay the driver, the man turned to him. "Excuse me, sir, I wasn't snooping or nothing, but I couldn't help overhearing. It's sometimes useful to overhear things in case my fare's a tourist who's lost and I can help. But did you say 1939?"

John smiled and shook his head. "No, you must have misheard. I said 1999."

The driver gave him a strange look. "Coulda sworn you said …" Then he shrugged. "You have a good day, now."

• • •

Jacques was sitting in the hotel lobby waiting for them. As they came through the hotel door, he stood and walked forward to greet them.

"Claudia, Philippe, you have found something I think. Claudia, my dear, you have a twinkle in your eye. Come; let's walk through here for some afternoon tea. The restaurant is called The Gallery and the decor is exquisite. Its design is based on the Sultan's dining room from the Topkapi Palace in Istanbul, you know. I was there, the palace, I mean, many years ago now. The designer of this place did a remarkably good job."

A waiter who clearly knew Jacques picked them up and guided them to a table in a prime position.

"I have taken the liberty of ordering a selection of their delicious afternoon tea treats," Jacques informed them, "and we shall have three or four of the most divine teas. Michael here will ensure that each is brewed to perfection, won't you, Michael?"

"Certainly, Mr Fowler." The waiter bowed his head in deference.

Jacques was waiting for the waiter to complete his task and leave before he quizzed the pair over their visit, so he described the contents of the trays to them and then offered them round. Finally the first of their teas was judged ready and delicately poured into bone china cups.

"Right," said Jacques rubbing his hands together and leaning forward as the waiter departed, "tell me what you've found."

"Not a huge amount, but what we have is pretty exciting," said Claudia as she wiped her mouth with a heavily starched napkin. "We're pretty sure that Charles Creed broke into Dr Wright's offices and examined her files. If he did, he probably made copies of everything in an office he appears to have had set up on the floor above her practice."

"Then that confirms the connection," said Jacques. "I take it that he didn't meet with Dr Wright?"

"No, she didn't recognise him, but her secretary did, and the guard at the entrance."

"And the guard gave us another name that Creed was using," added John. "The name Dayton."

"Dayton," repeated Jacques, rubbing his chin. "Just Dayton?"

"Yes," said Claudia. "No first name. He also seems to have had a computer person working with him."

Jacques nodded and took a cell phone from his pocket. "Excuse me for a moment, please, I have to make a call. I don't like using these things in restaurants; it seems rather impolite, somehow. I'll go through to the lobby. Please help yourselves to some more of these bits and pieces."

"Thank you," said Claudia, "they're delicious and I'm starving. I think it must be the time change and the nervous tension."

"You don't seem nervous, Claudia, my dear," said Jacques. "In fact you seem very much on top of things."

There was a flash that looked like annoyance in Claudia's eyes, but it passed almost before Jacques could register it. "I think I just mean it's all so exciting," she said biting into another sandwich.

Jacques laughed the moment off. "The Three Musketeers are very lucky to have you working with them. I knew you wouldn't return empty-handed. Now, before I make the call, I'll tell you what I'm doing."

He shifted forward in his seat and leaned his head towards them, speaking in a low tone. "From time to time, I use the services of an excellent private investigator. He is totally discreet and very professional. He is not one of these types who sits around in a car all day smoking dozens of cigarettes and never washing. No, Max is a real gentleman. Anyhow, I took the precaution earlier of warning him that we might need his services, so he's expecting a call. Let's see if he can find anything about the name Dayton."

"We could always get one of the Digby Smiths onto it," said John.

"There's more than one?" said Claudia, turning to face John in surprise.

"Whoops," replied John. "You didn't hear that, Claudia."

Jacques sat back and chuckled, then he leaned over to Claudia while keeping his eyes on John. "Mon ami, you shouldn't worry. Claudia is one of us and her discretion is absolute."

Then he looked straight into Claudia's eyes and, keeping his voice almost at a whisper, said, "It's quite simple, Claudia, my dear.

All three of us have the amazing luxury and good fortune to know Digby Smith. Where indeed would we be without him? The bizarre twist is that my Digby Smith is not the same person as yours and John's. Amusing, no?"

"I'm speechless," she said, her eyes flashing angrily again for the briefest of moments.

The moment passed and she continued. "Actually, I'm not. I've just had a thought. Your private investigator, is he up to lifting fingerprints?"

"I'm sure he is," said Jacques. "Why?"

Claudia explained her thoughts about the possible prints in Nancy Wright's office and comparing them with Jacques'.

Jacques clapped his hands. "Excellent idea, and it will prevent dear Digby, whichever one we choose, from the headache of having to jump through what would no doubt be a host of diplomatic hoops. Is there anything else, my super-sleuth?"

"Actually, there is," said Claudia, her eyes roaming the table as she thought something through. "I've just remembered that Dr Wright asked her secretary to check out the CCTV records in her building. She didn't mention it again, so the chances are it won't happen. Could your man Max do that as well?"

"Right up his street," grinned Jacques. "I'll tell him to search the recordings to see if someone just like me is on them."

For the next forty-five minutes, while he waited for a reply from his private investigator, Jacques fussed over more varieties of tea, finishing with one he insisted would be the perfect to aid their digestion now that they had probably eaten their fill. He had also been regaling them with tales of afternoon teas in the smartest hotels all over the world through several centuries.

"Can I order either of you something else?" he asked. "They have the most delicious cheesecake."

"If I eat any more, I'll burst," said Claudia, patting her stomach.

"Me too," added John. "I must bring the girls here when we come to New York. They would love it."

At that moment, Jacques' phone vibrated in his pocket with a text. He took it out and read the screen. "Remarkable," he said. "Max does not disappoint, He says he might have found something. He wants me to call him immediately."

Jacques' face was quietly confident as he returned from the lobby.

"Progress indeed," he said, sitting down. "Max has made an appointment with Dr Wright for tomorrow morning to look at her filing cabinet. In the meantime, he said he'll look into the CCTV recordings and the premises above Dr Wright's tonight. Mmm, better we don't delve too deeply into that one. Right now, we're off to meet him outside a luxurious office tower about thirty blocks south of here. I'll just text Kenton and we'll head off."

"Wow!" said Claudia. "I'm impressed. Your Max doesn't hang around."

Jacques smiled as he completed the text to his driver and while still looking at the screen, he said, "I told you he was good. Now, are you sure you don't want any more, either of you? Claudia, my dear? That cheesecake really is wonderful."

When there was no reply, he looked up to see Claudia biting her bottom lip.

"Is everything all right, Claudia, my dear? You suddenly look very troubled." His voice was edged with concern.

Claudia looked down at her hands. "Yes, of course. I mean, gosh, things are really moving along at a pace."

She glanced up at Jacques, catching his eyes for a moment before looking down again.

"Then what is it?" said Jacques, leaning over to her.

She fidgeted with her napkin as she stared at a spot on the carpet. Without moving her eyes, she said very quietly, "Jacques. You and I are, well, sort of the same age. I mean, I'm thirty-four and I know you're not, of course, but it's like you are and that's all you look, which is great, but, well, you … you keep on calling me 'my dear', which is very sweet, but it's like I'm your favourite niece or something."

She paused, wringing her napkin in her hands. Then she slowly lifted her eyes to his. "You see, that's the problem; it's like you're sixty or something and, well, I don't want you to act like you're sixty or fifty or anymore than thirty-four, or to think of me as your favourite niece. I want …"

She trailed off, blushing deeply and not finishing the sentence.

For a moment Jacques was speechless. Then he shook his head. "Oh, my … Claudia, what can I say?"

"Look," said Claudia, her eyes searching the room. "I really must find the loo before we go."

As she rushed off, covered in confusion, John caught Jacques' eye.

"Well, well," he said with a knowing smile. "Who'd have thought it?"

Jacques sighed heavily, but his eyes were twinkling.

"Ah, mon ami, it might not be springtime, but … I haven't felt like this for a long while. I didn't dare think that Claudia might feel the same."

Chapter Twenty-Four

The morning after the dinner with Marcus Dayton was crisp and bright, the forest beyond the house a rich canvas of autumnal colours. Paola made her way out of the main gardens and into the damper cover of the trees that marked the start of the estate's extensive forest. She had got up at first light, demanded an early breakfast from one of the huge female guards who was stationed outside her room, and then dressed for the woods.

As she made her way along the moss-covered undergrowth of the first of the shaded paths, the rising sun caught myriad spiders' webs criss-crossing the branches and bushes around her, a labyrinth of sparkling filaments stretching in all directions. She marvelled at the thought of so many small creatures following their daily routine of life and death, of the literally millions of spiders waiting patiently in their webs throughout this huge expanse of woods and the tens of thousands of hectares beyond. They were always there, of course, but there were only certain times of year when they could be so easily seen.

Following her berating of Dayton about the over-zealousness of his guards, Paola wanted to test the outcome: had he really instructed them to keep their distance? Over the centuries, she had acquired excellent survival and tracking skills, having hidden in woods and forests throughout Western Europe on many occasions. But it had been a while since her skills had been put to the test, over forty years since she had been in the commune in the forested foothills of the Rocky Mountains in Colorado. However, she had little doubt she would be able to outwit her guards. Wherever they placed themselves, she intended to lead them on a dance through the woods to see how good they were.

She also wanted to confirm her observations of the previous day when she had been looking for any security cameras. She had seen none so far and she suspected they were probably only along the perimeter fence.

Firstly, she wanted to know how many guards were following her, since, if they were good, only some would have let themselves be seen. After half an hour of a cat and mouse game, she had the measure of them. There were six guards in total trailing her, reporting quietly to each other through walkie-talkies, although as she stepped up her elusiveness, the level of the guards' voices increased as they became more frustrated.

Running lightly along a hidden track, she increased her distance sufficiently to give herself time to lay a couple of false trails that would lead two of the guards off one way and two in another. However, they would then find that the trails they were following doubled back, so that they literally bumped into each other.

After two hours of successfully testing and increasingly outwitting the guards, Paola decided to circle back to the house, leaving them searching for her deep in the woods. One trail she had left led to where she thought the nearest perimeter point would be, hoping that the guard following it would think she might have escaped.

She made her way quietly to the control post on one side of the house and surprised their supervisor who was deep in urgent discussion with his team through the radios.

"Looking for someone?" she said quietly as she leaned on the door frame.

The supervisor whipped around, the shock of seeing her there quickly replaced with anger at the humiliation of his team.

"You should be careful, signora," he said, the threat heavy in his voice, "my boys are trained to apprehend any intruders by force. If you surprise them in the forest, they might hurt you by mistake."

"The only surprise would be if they managed to find me," sneered Paola. "You should be grateful to me: their morning's training should have sharpened their skills."

She turned and left the guard snarling down his radio at his team.

Making her way to the smaller of the two sitting rooms, she issued curt instructions to one of her indoor minders that she wanted an early lunch. She had no intention of attempting much courtesy with any of the staff; she wanted to remain aloof, disdainful of their very presence; she wanted to see resentment in their eyes, anger in their body language. Angry people were careless people.

As she finished eating from the selection of pecorino cheeses, salami and salad leaves, she saw the rather dejected squad of guards returning to their post, no doubt to be told their fortune by their supervisor. It was one o'clock and time for their lunch. They looked hungry. Paola smiled. Time to test them again, she thought, nothing like an empty stomach to bring on more mistakes. She picked up her jacket and left the room through a pair of large French doors that led onto a terrace. From there she walked casually down a few more steps that led onto the grass, making sure that she lingered long enough to be noticed.

Her goal that afternoon, apart from confusing the guards, was to check out the perimeter fence. She knew from what Dayton had said that it would be some distance, but she didn't expect to walk nearly six kilometres to find it. As she approached it, staying behind the cover of the trees, it wasn't the lack of height that surprised her — it was less than three metres to the top of the rolls of barbed wire that embellished the steel chain-link — it was the attention to detail on both sides of the fence. Designed as much to keep a person in as it was to keep intruders out, it had numerous trip wires and sensors on either side. In addition, the fence itself clearly continued for some way below the ground, sufficient to deter any animal or human from trying to dig underneath it. She pulled out a pair of binoculars she had found in a drawer in the sitting room and let her eyes take in detail that from ten metres away was hard to see with the naked eye. Although there were no warning signs, the fence was clearly electrified, the circuitry subtle, almost as if it were not meant to be noticed.

She stood motionless, taking in everything, wondering about vulnerability. Then it occurred to her that the fence's sophistication was its vulnerability. Everything about it, from the electrification and trip wires to the CCTV cameras every thirty metres, it all required power. If the power were cut, it would take seconds with a pair of bolt cutters to be through it. She would have to look into the power arrangements. Someone as savvy as Dayton would inevitably have several layers of back-up, generators covering all levels of failure, so it wouldn't be easy. However, she had plenty of time to reflect on the problem. Dayton had no intention of letting her go in the immediate future.

She wondered if there would be any other entrances to the property apart from the main gate, which she assumed was heavily guarded. There was a track on either side beyond the trip wires where a four-by-four could patrol and provide maintenance to the fence, but surely there had to be another gate somewhere: the circumference of the property must be at least fifty kilometres. She decided she would have to walk the perimeter, preferably without the knowledge of the guards, so it would need to be done indirectly. She shrugged: again, she had time. For today though, she thought that having left the guards running around the woods looking for her, it would be prudent to let them find her, to make them think they were better than they thought. Otherwise more might be drafted in, or worse, Dayton might start restricting her movements. However, she didn't want to be found too near the fence so she headed back towards the house.

Chapter Twenty-Five

John followed Jacques and Claudia through the Carlyle's revolving door and cast a rueful eye along East 76th Street towards the escalating traffic on Madison Avenue.

"I don't remember it being this busy when we arrived," he said. "Have we hit the rush hour?"

"It will get busier than this, mon ami," laughed Jacques. "This is just the mini-rush hour with mothers in large wagons on school runs. There are several exclusive private schools in this area and they all finish their day about now. Fortunately, this is a one-way street leading onto Park Avenue where we can turn right and head in the direction we want. Kenton knows every inch of Manhattan, so a little traffic won't bother him in the least."

He held open the door for Claudia and John, and then followed them into the car's spacious interior. As he sat down, he glanced across at Claudia, only to find her staring pointedly out of the window, her eyes blinking fast. He thought about her outburst in the tearoom. She was clearly still embarrassed by her display of feeling for him and so he sat back in his seat and remained uncharacteristically quiet as he watched her discreetly.

However, within a few seconds, John broke the spell.

"Where did you say we are heading?" he said as they accelerated away from a stop light.

"It's a very smart location on Forty-fifth Street," replied Jacques. "It's called the Trevelyan Building."

"Trevelyan?" John turned his face abruptly to Jacques.

"Yes, do you know it? Does it mean something to you?"

As he replied, John noticed Claudia had also turned towards him, her embarrassment temporarily forgotten as she tuned into their conversation.

"The name does," he said, nodding his head slowly, "not the building."

He paused as distant memories flooded into his consciousness.

"I had a dear friend once, in Hong Kong. Fiona Trevelyan. Her father was a very wealthy trader. But there can't possibly be a connection."

"Her father wasn't William Trevelyan, by any chance?" said Jacques, the corners of his eyes creasing in amusement as he saw the surprise on John's face.

"Yes … Yes it was," stuttered John. "You're not going to tell me you knew him, are you?"

Jacques threw back his head and laughed. "I am indeed. But I didn't just know him; he was a close friend for some years. I met his daughter too, but she was only a girl at the time."

"Jacques, are you telling me that you spent time in Hong Kong?"

"No, Philippe, not at the time I knew William Trevelyan, although in the past forty years I have often been there on business, as well as China. It was when I was trading in Calcutta in the 1850s and '60s that I first met William. His business was just starting to take off. He was an ambitious young man and I was tempted to join him."

"Join him?"

"Yes, he wanted me to become a partner in his business, but I had a number of other irons in the fire and I couldn't see myself based in the backwater Hong Kong was at the time."

"And you met Fiona?" John was still incredulous.

"Yes, she was a delightful child. She came on a couple of trips with her father in the 1860s. She must have been ten or twelve. Strong-willed girl, even at that age. She adored her father."

"Yes, she did. Her mother was far less of an influence since she spent most of her time as a missionary in China. How incredible, Jacques. Just think, if you had set up in Hong Kong with William, you would have been there when I arrived in 1877."

"Imagine," said Jacques. "That would have been something. Our lives now might be altogether different." He smiled to himself as his eyes caught Claudia's. She was looking horrified at the thought.

"Tell me," continued Jacques, "what happened to Fiona? I heard she had a Chinese lover."

John nodded. "She did. Kwok Fu-keung. He was murdered in 1905, soon after I was forced to flee Hong Kong. Fiona died a couple of years later of typhoid contracted in one of the hospitals she devoted herself to."

He glanced round at Claudia as he heard her shift in her seat, laughing when he saw her wide-eyed gaze.

"Something wrong, Claudia?"

"Nothing, except I have to keep pinching myself to know I am awake and not dreaming your bizarre conversations. Listening to you both talking about events of well over a hundred years ago as if they happened yesterday is, well, gobsmacking."

Both men laughed.

"It's good that we can share it all with you, Claudia," smiled Jacques.

Claudia briefly caught his eye and blushed again. Then she turned to John. "Have you been back since? To Hong Kong, I mean. Is it as fascinating as people say?"

"I haven't been back, no," said John with a sigh, "but I'm sure it is."

"I was there only last year," added Jacques, "and I can assure you that it's as amazing as ever. How could it be anything else?" He leaned towards them and took one of Claudia's hands and one of John's.

"We should take a trip, once all this is over."

"Gosh," stuttered Claudia. "That would be brilliant. I've always wanted to go there."

"That's settled then," smiled Jacques. *"Méi wèn tí, Kè láo dí yà. Wǒ jué de nǐ fēi cháng piào liang."*

"What?" said Claudia, her eyes half closing in suspicion.

"That's Chinese," laughed John. "Or rather, Mandarin, which is the language of mainland China. It means 'no problem'. At least the first part does. I'll let Jacques translate the rest of it."

Claudia turned to Jacques in expectation, but he simply grinned mischievously. "There's a Cantonese equivalent, of course, but my Cantonese is not so good." he said. Then, glancing out of the window as the car drew to a halt, he added, "We're here."

Kenton jumped out of the driver's seat and was quickly round the car to open the rear passenger door. As they got out, Jacques pointed upwards. "Fifty-five floors of luxurious high-tech offices. I'm impressed if our Mr Dayton is here. This is a very exclusive address. We could be getting somewhere, mes amis."

He turned and scanned the wide piazza in front of the building. "Now, I wonder if … ah, yes, there he is." He lifted an arm and waved at a man walking towards them. "Here's Max."

Max was middle-aged and sandy-haired with an eminently forgettable face. He was of medium height and quietly dressed in a medium-grey suit. He reminded John of Digby Smith: he was almost invisible. Jacques shook his hand. "Punctual, as ever, Max. What progress is there?"

Max didn't seem to expect any preamble or introductions. In fact, he hardly appeared to notice Claudia and John, although Jacques knew he would have assessed them thoroughly as he approached.

"I'm afraid that we might be a too late, Mr Fowler," said Max, looking up at Jacques. "The offices occupied by Dayton are being vacated as we speak. I've had a preliminary look around and it appears there's a secretary organising things. But I thought it better to wait for you before going in."

"Quite right, Max," said Jacques. He turned to the others. "Shall we go?"

He made to walk towards the entrance, but Claudia hesitated.

"Um, Ja— Adam, can I have a word?" she said quietly as she glanced at Max.

"Of course, Claudia," said Jacques, putting an arm around her shoulders and moving her a few steps to one side.

"Sorry," said Claudia quietly, "but I don't know how much your friend Max knows. You see, I was thinking. If Dayton is who we think he is and he has been using these offices, if you walk in, then the people there who know him, his secretary and so on, well, they'll think you're him. And then they will quickly realise that you're not. Now, we don't know yet if Dayton knows of your existence, but if he doesn't, we don't want to run the risk of someone like his secretary alerting him. After all, it would seem pretty weird for his double to turn up in his offices just as they were being vacated. He's bound to be suspicious. Don't you think it might be better if you stayed in the car while John and I go up there with Max? What does the company do? We can say that we're looking to do business with them."

All this came out in a rapid-fire Claudia rush. Jacques felt his heart pounding; he wanted to hug her. Instead, he turned to face her and put his hands on her shoulders.

"You are absolutely right, Claudia," he said, looking down into her eyes and grinning. "You really are a super-sleuth. That's impressive thinking. I would have gone blundering in and probably caused all sorts of problems. But I think you can do better than pretend that you have business with the company. The secretary will soon realise that you don't and might get suspicious anyway. Why don't you say that the leasing agent has told you that the premises are being vacated and that you have been instructed by a client to see if they are suitable for his needs?"

"Yes," agreed Claudia, "that's a much better idea. It's suitably vague and no one can take exception or be suspicious."

Jacques took the opportunity to put his arm around her shoulder again and guided her back to where John and Max were standing.

"Gentlemen," he announced, "I have decided to stay in the car while the three of you inspect Mr Dayton's offices, or what's left of them. Claudia can explain your cover story in the elevator."

A flicker of a question appeared briefly on Max's face, but he said nothing. He was far too discreet to ask about matters that were of no concern to him.

Emerging from the high-speed elevator that had whisked them silently to the fortieth floor, they were greeted by the stylish logo of MDCorp engraved on a glass entrance door. Beyond, the entire office suite was a hive of quiet activity as removal personnel and office staff went about the task of vacating it. Several teams were carrying furniture to a cargo elevator while others were sifting and stacking piles of documents. As Max pushed the door open, a security guard appeared, raising a hand.

"These are private offices, folks, I'm afraid I have to ask you to turn around and take the elevator back down. Unless you've gotten out at the wrong floor."

Claudia and John hesitated, but Max strode on confidently.

"It's OK," he said to the guard. "I'll square it with Ms Turner over there."

The guard looked puzzled. "She didn't say she was expecting anyone."

Max smiled as he glanced at the name on the guard's lapel. "Well, with respect, er, Rick, I doubt she shares all her appointments with you."

He continued walking towards the far end of the open-plan office where a harassed-looking woman was standing holding a clipboard. John and Claudia hung back, more or less forcing the guard to stay with them.

"How did he know the secretary's name?" whispered Claudia to John.

"He's a private detective; I imagine he's good at his job," said John with a shrug.

Max strode up to the woman, his right hand extended. "Ms Turner?" he said, making sure the guard couldn't hear him.

"Can I help you?" said the woman as she looked up briefly from the clipboard.

"I'm sorry to disturb you," said Max, "I tried to call ahead, but there was no answer. I thought perhaps the offices had already been vacated so my colleagues and I," — he waved a hand in the direction of the elevator — "we thought we'd pop along since time is short."

Still puzzled, Doris Turner began to focus her attention on Max. "I'm sorry, I don't quite—"

"The leasing agency," interrupted Max, smiling warmly at her. "They advised us about this suite, knowing our client would be very interested. I apologise, we've obviously come at an inconvenient time. Pity though," he added, rubbing his chin. "Our client's flying off to Europe tonight and really wanted a heads-up before he left."

The secretary thought about it for a moment and then decided. "Well, since you're here and we don't have a huge amount more to do, I don't see any objection. All the sensitive things have gone." She turned and waved to the guard. "Rick, it's no problem if these people have a look around."

While Max was talking to Ms Turner, Claudia had taken the opportunity to glance around the office suite, noting the positions of the main offices. As soon as Ms Turner called out, she marched off in the direction of the southwestern corner. "Come on, John," she called back over her shoulder. "You know the CEO's office position and view is a deal-breaker; we might as well start there."

John smiled at the guard. "She's the boss," he said, and followed after Claudia.

Marcus Dayton's large corner office had always been minimalist. Now it was even more so, with just his all-glass desk remaining.

"Quite a view," said John as he saw Claudia looking out at the view of Lower Manhattan.

"Breathtaking," she replied, turning to face him, but as she did, her eyes immediately focussed on the wall behind him. "Oh, I wonder who that is."

John turned to see the huge black and white photograph that dominated the wall and faced onto Dayton's desk. "I think I can guess," he said, his artist's eye noting a number of features. "She reminds me—" He stopped suddenly as Ms Turner came into the room.

John smiled at her. "We were just admiring this superb photograph. She's a beautiful young woman."

"Yes," replied the secretary. "We're down to the last few items of furniture now, but I'm really not sure what to do with that."

"Who is she?" asked Claudia.

Doris Turner looked wistfully at the photograph. "Her name was Emma. She was Mr Dayton's daughter."

"Mr Dayton?" said John.

"Yes, Marcus Dayton, the head of MDCorp. The owner, in fact."

"You said 'was'," said Claudia. "Has something happened to her?"

The secretary nodded, her eyes sad. "Yes," she said quietly. "She was killed in a terrible accident. I don't know the details, but I do know that Mr Dayton was heartbroken. She was only twenty. I don't think he had any other family. His wife, Emma's mother, died when Emma was born."

"That's terrible," replied Claudia as she peered more closely at the image to see if she could register the likenesses that John had clearly noticed.

"This is an excellent suite of offices," said John, his words breaking through the gloom that had descended on the room. "Why are you moving? Do you need more space? I can't imagine a location better than this one."

"Yes, the view is rather special," said Ms Turner wistfully. "But we aren't moving. This is my last day with MDCorp. The corporation seems to have closed its doors. I have been paid well to oversee the final removal, but after that, I'm out of a job. I can't pretend to understand it. One day it was business as usual and then the next, I'm instructed that it's all to stop. The important files were removed instantly; the others, like the ones the team was packing up down the way, are scheduled for destruction."

"But surely MDCorp must be setting up somewhere else," said John. "Big companies don't just stop."

"If it is, I don't know where. Mr Dayton has left me no other instructions."

The secretary turned her eyes away, and as she did, John looked over to Max, who had just come into the office. He indicated with a movement of his eyes that he wanted Max to distract the secretary. Max acknowledged with the slightest nod and walked over to Ms Turner, letting a puzzled frown form on his face. "I'm sorry," he said. "But we were told that the suite is thirty thousand square feet, but this space seems nothing like that. Is there some more?" As he was talking, he was quietly guiding the secretary out of the office.

"Yes," John heard her reply, "of course. This is only half of it. There's another floor upstairs. There's an internal staircase, let me show you."

After Ms Turner was well out of earshot, John turned to Claudia. "Would you mind taking a couple of shots of that photograph of Dayton's daughter, Claudia?" he said, holding out his mobile phone.

Claudia smiled at him. "Already done," she said, patting her bag.

"Really? I didn't notice."

"That's the whole point," she said with a nonchalant shrug. "It's all part of being a super-sleuth, you know."

Back at street level, John followed Claudia into the car, while Jacques remained outside in conversation with Max.

Once he had finished and taken his seat next to them, John turned to him. "That was rather disappointing. I really thought there was going to be a breakthrough, but the elusive Mr Dayton has slipped through the net."

"If he's anything like me," said Jacques, "he'll have had a contingency plan well in place. It won't be the first time over the centuries that he has had to disappear in a hurry. He'd know that the police would find his name sooner or later; it's just that we managed it first. I should imagine that the business of MDCorp will be quietly re-established somewhere else under a name or names that will have no connection. It's not as difficult as you might imagine, once you have the contacts and the resources to pay for whatever is necessary."

He paused and smiled at his two friends. "It isn't necessarily criminally-based, you know. It's not easy to survive for over two millennia without a little subterfuge. Dayton will certainly have covered his tracks well, but even so, I've instructed Max to find out everything he can about him. Now, don't look so downcast, both of you; you didn't come away entirely empty-handed. Max mentioned something about a photograph."

"Yes," said Claudia, "I took a couple of shots of it on my phone. It was a huge print of Dayton's daughter on his office wall. It must have been a couple of metres high. She's beautiful, or at least she was. His secretary said that she was killed in an accident."

She passed the phone to Jacques. As his eyes fell on the image, Claudia saw them widen briefly. He swiped the screen to enlarge the detail.

"What is it?" asked Claudia. "John obviously saw something in the face that he recognised, didn't you, John? And now you, Jacques, look as if you've seen a ghost."

"That sums it up perfectly, Claudia," said Jacques distantly, the wistfulness sounding in his voice. "What was her name?"

"Emma."

"Emma," he repeated softly. "Yes, it suits her. I had a daughter once who looked remarkably similar, startlingly so, in fact. I could be looking at a twenty-first century version of her."

He passed the phone back to Claudia who took it but let her hand remain on his.

"How long ago?" she asked softly.

"About five hundred years. I was living in what is now Hamburg."

Claudia gulped. "Gosh. Was she ... you know ..."

"Like me?" said Jacques. "No, she wasn't. I have had a number of children over the centuries, Claudia, not as many as perhaps you might imagine, but nevertheless, a fair number. But unlike my old friend Philippe here, I have never passed on my traits to any of my children. Not one has been like me."

"Dayton clearly adored his daughter," said Claudia. "I wonder if she was like him; had the same traits as the two of you."

"Could be," said John. "If she did, then he certainly would have been devastated to lose her." He paused. "I've been thinking. Do you think we should somehow let the police know about Dayton? If they can get hold of his fingerprints, it would help to underscore the fact that you had nothing to do with the homicide and abduction, Jacques."

Jacques shook his head. "No, I see no reason to assist them. If I indicate to them that I am following the case up, they will only want to know why and start suspecting me of some sort of involvement. I don't think there'll be anything to gain from telling them. I'm confident Max will dig deeper and more quickly than they will." He raised his eyebrows in question.

"Agree?"

"Absolutely," said Claudia. "They've given you enough hassle. I didn't like the sound of the lieutenant."

Jacques laughed. "Oh, we shouldn't be too hard on her. She was only doing her job. Her dragon character goes with the territory. Now, my friends, I think there is not much else we can do today. I think that rather than making the long drive back to Boston tonight, let's have a good dinner, stay overnight, and go back refreshed in the morning."

"That sounds wonderful," said Claudia, sitting back in her seat. "I could do with a soak in a hot bath to reflect on what we've got so far."

"Recharging your super-sleuth's batteries," nodded Jacques. "An excellent idea."

"Yes," replied Claudia, "but no amount of reflection is going to help with what you said to me in Chinese earlier. It sounded like an awful lot of words for 'no problem'. What did the rest mean?"

Jacques laughed as he caught the look of amusement in John's eye. "The first part meant 'no problem' — *Méi wèn tí*. After that, I used a transliteration of your name. The Chinese use combinations of the monosyllabic sounds of their words to approximate to Western names. The result doesn't necessarily mean anything, although they'll try to make it something good if they can. In your case, the Mandarin is *Kè láo dí yà*. If you say it fast, it sounds quite like Claudia."

"So, 'no problem, Claudia' is what you said to start with. What about the rest?"

Jacques gave her an enigmatic smile. "Just a compliment on your looks, Claudia," he said.

Unable to resist, John leaned over to her. "The important bit is *fēi cháng piào liang*, which means 'very beautiful'."

Chapter Twenty-Six

When Jacques' car drew up outside the Waldorf-Astoria on Park Avenue, John shook his head at his old friend. "I suppose I shouldn't be surprised that if you were going to book a hotel for me here in Manhattan, it would have to be this one."

He cast a nostalgic glance at the building. "It's been a long time," he said, "but the old lady is looking good for her years."

"Maybe she has our traits," said Jacques.

"Time will tell," said John. He followed Jacques and Claudia through the revolving door, half expecting Catherine to be standing in the lobby waiting for him, full of news of her day shopping in the smart Fifth Avenue stores.

Somehow, Jacques had already checked them in and they went straight to their rooms to freshen up. However, the soothing waters of their steaming baths proved too much. Jet lag and tiredness caught up with them and Jacques' plans for dinner were cancelled.

At eight the following morning, John and Claudia were enjoying a buffet breakfast in the impeccable art deco surroundings of Oscar's Brasserie, both of them feeling refreshed after a good night's sleep. John kept looking fondly around the room, its classic lines and decor reviving many memories for him from more than seventy years before.

"You don't think Jacques is offended, John, do you?" said Claudia as she buttered a warm sourdough roll. "I know he really wanted us to have dinner with him, but once I got into that bath, the tiredness came over me in waves. It was all I could do to get myself to my bed."

John laughed. "I felt the same. But don't worry; Jacques will have experienced his fair share of jet lag, even though he tends to travel in luxury. He'll understand perfectly."

"This breakfast is wonderful," said Claudia. "Having missed dinner, I could eat a horse."

"It could probably be arranged," said John.

"I'll stick to more traditional fare, I think," laughed Claudia. She glanced around the room. "I wonder where Jacques is?"

She had just poured them both a second cup of coffee when their host appeared looking fresh, his eyes sparkling.

"Good morning, both of you. I see the guilt of having forced me to dine alone hasn't affected your appetites."

"Jacques, I—" started Claudia.

He stopped her with a hand on her arm.

"Claudia, I am teasing you. I was surprised you even entertained the idea of dinner. You must have been shattered. I always think that the jet lag crossing the Atlantic is worse than going halfway around the world, to China or Australia, for instance."

He put up his hand to attract a waiter's attention and order a cup of black coffee.

"Not having any breakfast, Jacques?" said John.

"I already had a bite in my room a couple of hours ago. I've just spent some time on the phone with Pete and then I caught up with some of what Max found out overnight. I'm still waiting for the rest."

He paused to take a sip of coffee. "You know, that sourdough bread looks very tempting, Claudia."

"Help yourself," she said, holding out the breadbasket.

A hovering waiter saw the move. In an instant a side plate and cutlery appeared in front of Jacques and the breadbasket was refreshed.

"As far as Pete is concerned," continued Jacques as he spread some butter on his roll, "he hasn't got any further. In fact, his contact in the DA's office is becoming rather suspicious about why Pete is so interested in the case. Pete said he thinks it would be better if he didn't call him again for a while."

"And Max?" asked John.

Jacques chewed on a piece of the roll and then wiped his mouth with a starched napkin before answering.

"Max has unearthed various bits and pieces. Firstly, he looked further into MDCorp's business and found that our Marcus Dayton operated a complete smokescreen out of that office to the extent that even his personal secretary didn't know the truth. He must have had another set-up somewhere feeding this apparent front company enough information to make them think they were doing business."

"What sort of business?" asked John. "It all sounds very vague."

"Exactly, mon ami," agreed Jacques. "It was rather vague: stock forwarding, middlemen stuff; nothing concrete and, I suspect, nothing very real. It's the classic front for obscuring something that you want to keep very well hidden. I have operated such businesses myself, but long before these days of computers and the Internet when anyone can check up on almost anything anywhere in the world. In the past it was somewhat easier."

He smiled to himself as he noticed a sideways look from John.

"As for Dayton, he's more like the shadow of someone, which makes him difficult to investigate. Max has discovered that his entire business is structured around other names in other places. Anybody tracing the name Dayton will find that he is American, but further than that, he's invisible. He has no credit cards or driver's licence; he doesn't even have a passport. So according to the records he has never been overseas, which is patently absurd. He must therefore have multiple identities. His secretary did at least confirm that Marcus is the given name he has been using and Max has found the record of the birth of a Marcus Dayton in Seattle in 1975. But there's nothing else. Max has also run the same searches for Charles Creed, with the same negative result. This man is elusive and in order to achieve this he must be very wealthy, since constantly revising and faking identities in these times of electronic scrutiny is an expensive matter if you don't happen to be a government."

Jacques paused and called a waiter for some fresh coffee.

"Do you mean that he has effectively just disappeared off the face of the earth?" said John.

"Don't look so surprised, mon ami, you have done the same yourself more than once, as I have and as Paola has. It's what we do."

John looked a little sheepish. "I hadn't really equated it with my own situation. I was thinking of it on a grander but shadier business scale. But of course, yes, you're right. Marcus Dayton is just doing what he's always done; he's surviving in the face of a world that is never going to understand him. Unfortunately, he's chosen rather less salubrious methods of operation, or so it would appear."

"I'm not sure how you operate, Jacques," said Claudia, "but it sounds very much more complicated than the way John has dealt with the problem of changing identities and moving on, from what he has told me of course. I mean, I think it's one identity at a time, isn't it, John?"

John nodded his agreement and Claudia continued. "With Dayton, it seems that looking into his world is like peeling back the layers of an onion, with each layer completely different from the last. But this onion has many of the layers fully operational at any given moment. It must be very confusing."

"I agree," said Jacques. "It takes some planning to be able to just disappear the way he has and trust that the pieces will be picked up and sorted out by his well-trained minions. He disappeared on the night that Paola did and no one, according to his secretary, has seen him since. However, she did tell Max that she spoke to him on the phone on two occasions. They were short calls, very businesslike. In the first one he just gave her a number to call and a one-word message to deliver, and in the second, he told her that MDCorp was closing its office. He told her to comply with the instructions of the men who turned up to retrieve things and not to ask any questions. He then informed her that since the company was closing, all the staff would be losing their jobs, although he promised very generous golden handshakes. Ms Turner, in particular, would be extremely well compensated if she got the whole thing completed efficiently."

"What about phone records?" asked Claudia. "MDCorp must have used the phones extensively, no business can operate without them. I thought they were easily traceable."

Jacques shook his head. "He used an encrypted landline in his office but even then every call was bounced through a number of places so who he was really calling was lost. Incoming calls were also sanitised so that the sources are going to be virtually impossible to trace."

"And his mobile calls?" said Claudia. "Surely they should be easier?"

Jacques laughed. "On the contrary. His secretary had two numbers for him, which no longer work, and the records for those numbers were the records of two other people. One was the mayor of Orange County on Long Island and the other some actor in a second-rate soap opera, if that's not tautologous."

Claudia smiled. "Mr Dayton seems to have a sense of humour."

"Either Dayton or someone else," said John as he reached for the coffee pot. "To manipulate phone records like that must involve some pretty sophisticated computer skills. I've been wondering about the greasy-haired geek, as I mentioned yesterday. Do you think he could be pressing all the right buttons for Dayton?"

"You are right, mon ami," said Jacques. "That was something else Max mentioned. He also thought that Dayton must have a computer expert working for him and Dayton's secretary confirmed it. She told him that there was a scruffy young man who Dayton called his pet nerd. He spent a lot of time sequestered in a darkened room in the office suite, a room full of computers."

"Does he have a name?" asked Claudia.

"He does. It's Palo Melliff, and guess what: he doesn't exist. So either he was in cahoots with Dayton in the anonymity game or he arrived in Dayton's life with a totally fictitious name."

"Wow!" exclaimed Claudia, sitting back in her chair and running her hands through her hair. "That's pretty impressive. You know, we should run all this through Ced in England. He's a genius with computers. I mean, look at his style signature program. Without that, I don't think we'd be sitting here now."

"If we can find a way in for him," said John. "I suspect that any site relating to MDCorp either no longer exists or has been sanitised."

"If there's a way, Ced will find it," said Claudia, her voice full of confidence.

At that moment, Jacques' phone buzzed with an incoming message. "Ah," he said, "a message from Max. He's been following up on something else."

This time Jacques ignored his customary courteous behaviour and called from where he was sitting, although he kept his side of the conversation to the minimum. He listened for several minutes to what was clearly another detailed report from Max, nodding his head and looking pleased one moment and then frowning in concern the next. Finally he thanked Max and rang off, telling his private eye to keep on searching.

He sat silently for a few moments, reflecting on the call, as John and Claudia leaned forward expectantly.

"Well?" said John when he couldn't wait any longer.

Jacques drew a deep breath. "Nothing more on Dayton. But Max has just spoken again to Ms Turner — he has clearly impressed the woman and now it seems she can't help him enough. She said that recently she overheard Dayton having what sounded like heated conversations in Portuguese over the telephone — it seems her son-in-law is Portuguese and that she understands some of the language. She doesn't know who the conversation was with, but apparently Dayton was very angry."

"How long ago?" said Claudia.

"About three months."

"We know about this, of course," said John. "Paola told me that until recently she'd been in Brazil for many years. It could be that Dayton was on her trail. After all, she left because someone had discovered her secret."

Jacques pondered this as he sipped his coffee. "Brazil is a big place and I don't think we even have a name, do we, mon ami?"

"No," said John, shaking his head. "Paola didn't tell me much about her time there, nor did she tell me what name she was using."

Jacques nodded. "Pete's DA friend let slip that the police have been looking into Naomi Tripley's background and of course it doesn't go back very far. They have located the real Naomi Tripley's parents who have confirmed that their daughter is missing, last heard of in Rio, and that the passport Paola was using as Naomi Tripley was genuine, that is, it was the real Naomi Tripley's. So the police and the DA's office are now wondering who exactly the abducted woman really is."

"Unfortunately," added John, "events all happened too fast. Paola was supposed to have been meeting with Digby Smith who would have made sure that her history was watertight. However, I don't think that is the problem. The important thing is to get her back. Digby can then work on an identity for her."

Claudia put a protective hand on John's arm and smiled at him, but in her mind she was still sifting through all the information. She turned her eyes to Jacques. "You said yesterday that Max was going to look at the CCTV records last night. Did he come up with anything?"

"Yes, and no," said Jacques. "Somehow, he managed to gain access to the records stored, I haven't asked how, but the guard is probably a few dollars better off than he was yesterday morning. What he found was interesting. He searched the tape, or whatever it is, for comings and goings around the time that Dayton must have broken into Dr Wright's office. He found no footage of Dayton or anyone else connected to him. No one, for instance, that would fit the description of this Melliff person. The guard told you that Melliff had fixed the CCTV for him. Well, he must have fixed it so that all the recordings that included Dayton and himself were removed. There's nothing."

"No wonder Dayton called Melliff his pet nerd," said Claudia.

"It's a pity we can't give any fingerprints from MDCorp to the police, I mean any that might be in the room Melliff was using to do all his computing. Even if he was using a false identity, there's a chance that his prints might be on record from some crime or other he committed, perhaps when he was younger and more careless and using his real name."

"It's possible," said John, but his lack of enthusiasm was clear from his tone.

"You don't think it's a possibility?" said Claudia, bristling slightly.

"Oh, I agree with you entirely, Claudia, that the younger Melliff might have had a record," said John. "But with his computer skills, I should imagine that his fingerprints were wiped from any official database a long time ago."

Chapter Twenty-Seven

The day after Paola discovered the perimeter fence, Dayton was nowhere to be seen. Not wanting to be bothered with the nurses or the doctor, Paola took the opportunity to continue her exploration. To her surprise, the guards were less in evidence, so she took fewer precautions and covered a fair amount of ground. She was about to give up and return for a late lunch when she discovered what she had expected: a second gate to the estate. However, if she had thought it was going to provide a weak spot in the system, at first sight it seemed that she was wrong. The gate was strongly built, there were powerful-looking floodlights mounted on the posts on both sides, extra surveillance cameras and a guardhouse on the inside of the property. She studied the building for some time with her binoculars, noting the occasional movement inside as the bored guards stretched or got up to keep the circulation in their legs going. She suddenly realised there was a weak spot: there were only two guards. Now that really is worth some serious consideration, she thought.

The rain started just as she returned to the house and by the time she settled in the sitting room, where once again she had demanded rather than ordered her food, sheets of water were pounding against the windows. She felt like a caged animal, despite the size of the room, but there was little she could do except watch the weather vent its anger on the countryside.

. . .

At four a maid came to light a fire, despite the central heating keeping the room more than comfortably warm. Paola scowled at her and the maid kept a wary distance, scurrying from the room as soon as she had dealt with the fire. However, a few minutes later, she returned with a tray of tea and cakes. Paola noted there were two cups on the tray. She was about to investigate the cakes when Dayton marched in carrying a very large plastic portfolio.

"Ah, Paola, how good to see you. I missed you yesterday. I hear you were having fun and games with the guards."

Paola maintained her neutral expression and said nothing.

Dayton ignored the rebuff and put the portfolio down on the desk at the far end of the room. He walked over to the tray and indicated the teapot with his hand. "Tea? Or would you prefer some coffee?"

"Tea," said Paola.

"Tea it is. Tell me," he added, passing her a bone china cup and saucer, "what did you think of the perimeter fence?"

Paola's eyes explored his. She was startled but didn't want to show it. How did he know? Was he bluffing?

Dayton smiled and offered her the plate of cakes. "Did you think you'd shaken off the guards?"

"I did shake off the guards, so you're on a fishing expedition," she snapped, ignoring the cakes.

"How many guards did you confuse yesterday, Paola?"

"The entire squad. All six of them. I watched them for ages and I saw them come back. Twice."

"Six?"

"Yes."

"That would explain it."

"Explain what?"

"There were eight, Paola, eight. There were two you never even got a glimpse of. The same two who followed you round the fence this morning and watched you checking out the south guardhouse."

"I don't believe you; there was no one near me this morning."

"Maybe you're not as good as you think you are, Paola. It's been a long time after all."

Paola turned to the fire and sat in one of the two large armchairs. She was cross. She couldn't tell if Dayton was making it up or whether there really were two other guards. If there were, the next opportunity she had to search the woods, she'd find them.

Dayton put his cup and saucer on a side table and sat back in his chair. "We'll talk about the security system later, if you like. I'm perfectly willing to run you through it. Knowing how it works won't help you escape; it's too good for that. No, right now, I'd like to talk about your father."

Paola shot a glance at him. "I told you, my mother——"

"Yes, I remember. She told you the Church had put him to death, but I don't believe you. However, let me start at the beginning."

He paused, a condescending smile on his lips that Paola wanted to knock far into the forest.

"The other day when we were looking at my paintings," continued Dayton, "I couldn't help but notice your particular interest in that wonderful Perini portrait. We talked about it, if you remember. Well, yesterday, I went back into the gallery to have another look at it. Why would an admittedly remarkably good sixteenth century painting so attract your attention, I wondered. Then I realised. The exquisite young woman in the painting bears a remarkable resemblance to you. At first I thought perhaps it *was* you, but then I saw some differences that I think are significant, even considering it was painted a long time ago. And if it were you, I'm sure your reaction would have been a rather different. So I think that what you recognised, Paola, was that the subject was a relative." His eyes crinkled in mild amusement. "I nearly said 'an ancestor', but, of course, she will have been born after you."

Paola snorted her derision. "Given the style of painting at the time, I could probably find hundreds of portraits that look like me."

Dayton shook his head. "It's a possibility, but the likeness is really quite remarkable."

He stood and walked over to fetch the portfolio, then he

returned to the armchair and laid the portfolio on the large coffee table next to them. "Look at it, Paola," he said, taking out the Perini painting. It had been removed from its ornate frame, but was still secured on its stretcher.

She took it while he continued.

"I'd never given it much thought before, but it set me thinking about other paintings I have, ones that are not kept here. I have an apartment in … a nearby town, where I have some portraits hanging, so this morning I popped over to see them. One is a portrait by an almost completely unknown Venetian artist called Giovanni di Luca. Ever heard of him?"

Paola shook her head.

"Well," continued Dayton, "he would have been more or less a contemporary of Perini, perhaps a little older, and he was working in Venice when you were a young woman in Naples."

"So?"

"It's the subject. You see, it's another one of a young woman, very beautiful and about twenty years old. There are many similarities in the features with the Perini portrait, but not with you." He took a second painting from the portfolio. "Here, take a look."

"You've lost me," said Paola as she took the portrait.

"They were painted about thirty years apart. I think the woman in the di Luca painting is the mother of the one in the Perini. Compare them, side by side, you must see what I mean."

Paola was again dismissive. "Remember these are paintings you are dealing with; they aren't photographs. As I said just now, the style itself introduces similarities."

Dayton's smile was again condescending and Paola wanted to hit him. "Yes, I also thought that perhaps I was stretching the point. But then I remembered a painting I keep in a vault in another part of the city, another Perini, a portrait of a much older woman than the one in Perini you have there. I retrieved it and after studying it again, I now realise that the similarities with the di Luca painting are incredible." He removed a third painting from the portfolio. "It's the same woman in middle age."

"I still don't know where all this is leading," said Paola.

"I didn't just rely on my own eyes. I've a friend who's an expert in art forgery who lives in the same city. He's brilliant. With little more than a glance, he can tell the authenticity of virtually anything on canvas. I took all three paintings round to him and asked him for an opinion. I told him nothing about them; I just asked him to look at them. Well, within only ten minutes he looked up and told me that they were by the same artist. Not might be. Were. He was that sure."

He paused and held out his hands. "Are you following yet?"

Paola shook her head.

"I think you are, Paola. I got to thinking about your father, Stefano Crispi. He disappeared around the time of your birth. We know he was an artist, a brilliant one, in fact. Well, suppose he was like both of us and suppose he went to Venice and then later to Arezzo. Did I mention that Perini was based in Arezzo? If he became di Luca in Venice, then the second painting I handed to you, of the young woman, could be of his wife, while the third one, painted when he became Perini, is again his wife but in middle age. The young woman in the first Perini you saw in the gallery would be their daughter. She would have been your half-sister, which is why she looks so much like you. Crispi, di Luca and Perini are one and the same."

"But my mother said that my father died."

"No, she didn't. You made that up. If it were true then Perini couldn't be Crispi, since, by the time Perini was painting that portrait, your mother would have been long dead. Paola, you can't deny the similarity in those paintings, paintings a forgery expert has said are by the same hand. If Crispi, your father, was like you, then we have three of his personas. Was Crispi his first? Who knows, except why should it be? How many personas have you had, Paola? How many have I had? I realise, of course, that I'm not telling you anything you don't know. I think that you know that your father is still alive and I think you know where he is. But you don't want me to know."

He sat back, pleased with his argument.

Paola sat stock still, her eyes on the paintings now lying on the coffee table. She was trying not to betray any of her feelings.

"You've made a lot of assumptions from three paintings

produced over four hundred years ago. How would I know if he's still alive? Remember, he went out of my life before I was born."

"You'd know if you'd met him, and I think you have." His voice was more accusing now.

There was an awkward silence and then Dayton appeared to relax. "Paola, I can't really expect you to tell me but, fortunately, I have another avenue. I have a computer expert who works for me who's a genius at writing image comparison software. His program for comparing facial features from photographs is brilliant. That's partly how we found you in the first place and was how we caught up with you in Brazil and then in Cape Cod. There's nothing he likes better than a challenge so I have instructed him to write a routine and use it to compare as many portraits as he can from the past five hundred years to look for the similarities my expert found. To find out who the more modern personas of your father are. Who he is now."

Paola's laugh was pure scorn. "Oh, is that all you're asking of him? No doubt you'll have an answer by the morning. Ha! I hope your expert has the same traits as us; it's going to take him a couple of hundred years!"

"I think not, Paola. Once he's sorted out his program, it will be relatively quick."

"Do you know how many portraits there are in the world?"

"He can be intelligently selective, of course."

"Whatever that means. Tell me, Marcus, just supposing you find that my father is still alive, what do you intend to do? Start your own exclusive club?"

"That's a very good question, Paola. What shall we do with him?"

Chapter Twenty-Eight

With no trace of Marcus Dayton and with Max following tantalising but ultimately fruitless lines of enquiry into the impenetrable labyrinth of MDCorp, John, Jacques and Claudia decided to return to Boston to join Pete. They found him frustrated by his lack of progress and what he perceived as his inability to penetrate the wall of secrecy that had grown around the Tripley case. What he failed to understand was that he had almost all the information that the police and district attorney's office had unearthed; they were simply unwilling to admit how little progress they had made.

They compared notes over a light dinner in the Mandarin Oriental grill, where Pete was brought up to speed with the day's findings in New York.

"May I see the photo of Dayton's daughter that you took on your cell, Claudia?" asked Pete, once they had all finished. Claudia called up the image and handed him the phone. Pete scrutinised the photo carefully and then looked over to Jacques, studying his face.

"Interesting," he said. "I think I can see the likeness you mentioned. Is she really similar to your daughter from all those hundreds of years ago, Jacques?"

Jacques took the phone from him and studied the photo again.

"Remarkably so, Pete," he replied wistfully. "It's quite extraordinary."

"Strong genes," laughed John as he yawned and stretched. "I suppose they'd need to be to keep you going for more than a couple of thousand years. However, my relatively young ones are telling me that I need to get to my bed. This time change is still affecting me. It's never been this bad on the times I've come over to see Lily."

"Me too," added Claudia. "I can hardly keep my eyes open. I was going to read through Dr Wright's notes this evening, but I think her minute handwriting would be too much for me."

"You have the notes?" asked Jacques.

"Yes. Pete picked them up from his house earlier today, before we got back."

"Well, if you're not going to read them tonight, would you mind if I borrowed them? I'm not suffering the jet lag that you three have, so I don't think they would be too much of a challenge."

"Of course not. They're in my room. Why don't you come and get them?"

They all took the elevator to the floor of luxurious suites that Jacques had organised and Pete and John headed off.

Claudia walked along to her door with Jacques. "Nightcap?" she asked as she dropped the key card into the slot.

"Can you stay awake long enough?" he said, following her into the room.

"Oh, I think I can manage." She looked coyly up at him. "I'm suddenly not feeling quite as tired as I thought I was downstairs."

Jacques took a step towards her and reached out for her hands.

"Claudia, I ..." he paused.

"What is it?" she said very quietly.

"I ..." he stopped and laughed, shaking his head. "This is crazy. I'm two and a half thousand years old and I feel like a tongue-tied teenager on his first date."

"Wow! I don't think I've ever had that effect on anyone before. Where's all the Gallic charm, Monsieur Bognard?" she teased.

"It seems to have deserted me. Maybe that's because I'm not

really French." He stood very still, looking down into her eyes. "Claudia, I know we've only known each other for a few days, but, well, I think it must be obvious that I'm very attracted to you. I hope you don't think I'm being presumptuous, but—"

"I don't think anything of the sort," she interrupted, the huskiness in her voice surprising her.

"Then what *do* you think?"

She smiled. "I think we should get back to the tongue-tied teen. What would he want to do if he could pluck up the courage?"

Jacques pulled lightly on her hands as he stepped even closer.

"I think he would want to put his arms around you like this … and then gently tilt your head back, like this, so he could see into those beautiful eyes … then he would lean forward and very lightly brush his lips on yours … like this …"

"Mmm," she murmured, as she paused in returning his kiss. "I think this teenager is a little more worldly than he's making out."

"He's gaining confidence all the time," said Jacques as he lifted her off her feet. "You know, I think you might have to start wearing very high heels."

"We could always try the sofa," she replied, "or the bed."

Later, Jacques slowly disentangled himself from the remnants of their clothes and their intertwined limbs. Claudia was now sleeping soundly and rather than disturb her, Jacques took the duvet and laid it over her. He bent over, kissed her lightly on the top of her head and then tiptoed towards the bedroom door. As he quietly opened it, his eye fell on a side table and the file of notes that he'd come to collect. He pursed his lips in question and then smiled, shaking his head. Another time, he thought.

The following morning, all four of them were sitting in Jacques' suite discussing progress over endless coffee. Claudia was trying hard to focus, to give her thoughts to motive and method. But her eyes kept finding Jacques' eyes and she was struggling.

She decided the only way was to keep moving. "If you were in

Dayton's shoes," she said as she stood and paced the room, drumming her fingers on her folded arms, "where would you take Paola? Do you think you would keep her in the States or go elsewhere?"

Jacques sat back in his armchair to consider the question as he gazed in mild amusement at the flustered performance of the headstrong strawberry blonde who was suddenly occupying his thoughts in every waking moment.

"All things considered," he said after a few moments, "I think I'd leave the country. Dayton will accept it as inevitable that the police will identify him before long and of course they already know what he looks like." He held out his arms to indicate himself. "That would make moving around in the States more difficult for him since his face will be on police information notices everywhere. On the other hand, even if the police post his face — my face — to Interpol, the chances are that once he's moved into whatever country is his destination, the local police are not going to be as diligent as here. My guess is that he left the country on the night of the abduction and set into motion a carefully prearranged plan with respect to the decommissioning of his company."

"I agree," said Pete, looking up from the extensive notes he had been compiling on their findings, "but you know, it's a pretty big deal to shut down a company as large as MDCorp seems to have been. He must have really wanted Paola, and that want must have burned in him to the exclusion of everything else. What I can't get my head around is why."

Claudia had stopped pacing and was staring out of the window at the view over Boston. "I think I know," she said quietly. "But sadly for him, if I'm right, he's going to be disappointed."

She turned, walked over to where John was sitting and sat on the arm of the sofa opposite him. She knew her thoughts would not be welcome. The others immediately picked up on the seriousness of her expression.

After looking at each of them in turn, she focussed her eyes on Jacques, wanting reassurance from him as she spoke.

"We know," she started, "that Emma, Dayton's daughter, was very special to him. Of course, all his children might have been special, but just suppose for one moment that Emma was extra special, that she inherited his rare traits. If, like Jacques, he had never before had a child who was the same as him, wouldn't that explain his reverence for her and his devastation when she died? Especially if he felt in any way responsible. You see, Emma would have proved to him that he could have children like himself, that he wasn't alone. He would have changed his views from reluctant acceptance that he was a one-off to the exciting possibility of there being other people like himself. He'd waited two and a half thousand years for this and he would not relish the thought of having to wait another two and a half thousand. No, I think he took advantage of the vast body of information that the Internet has made available and used his resources to search for anything that would lead him to someone like him. And what he found was Paola, thanks probably to Dr Wright's book, although I suspect that if Melliff is as good as I think he is, he would have come up with something pretty soon irrespective of her memoirs. But Paola was elusive: he'd thought she was dead from Dr Wright's book, then perhaps he found she wasn't, but didn't know where she was. However, just as he was banging his head against the wall in the search for Paola, along comes Sara, whom he suspects is also like him."

"So are you saying," said John, his eyes fearful, "that Dayton has taken Paola somewhere to be his companion, to befriend her perhaps? If that's the case, he's made a poor choice, given the extremes of violence that we know Paola is capable of. She'd kill him at the first opportunity."

"Maybe he thinks that once she realises that he's the same as she is, she will be readier to accept him," added Pete.

There was a silence and the three men turned their heads to Claudia, who was staring at the floor.

"I think it's more than that," she said quietly.

"More?" said Jacques.

"Yes, I think he wants to have children with her."

"Children! My God, do you think he intends to lock her up and produce a brood of Emma substitutes?" John was aghast.

"I think it's a distinct possibility," said Claudia. "The problem for him is that it won't work."

"What do you mean?" said John.

Claudia sat back in her chair, still looking at Jacques as she started to speak. "One of the obvious lines of research the prof followed once we'd got John's and Lily's DNA was the likelihood of producing more people like them. Obviously, there has to be something pretty recessive about their genes otherwise the world would already be populated by others like them. Now Lily has only had a couple of children, neither of whom were like her, but once in a very small while, John has met and had children with a woman who has, by chance, exactly the right genetic make-up to bring his recessive genes to the fore. So what would happen if John were to have a child with a woman who was like him? In theory, the chances should be very high that they would have children who were the same. But we have looked at it at a cellular level and found that it simply doesn't happen. The cells become mutually destructive. There can be no offspring."

"Christ, how many years and attempts is it going to take before Dayton gives up the quest?" said John, standing to pace the room.

Pete turned to Claudia, a rising panic sounding in his voice. "If what you suspect is true, Claudia, Sara is also in danger. Not immediately, perhaps, but once Dayton finds that nothing is happening with Paola, he will look elsewhere. He has to be stopped. I think we need to head back to England as soon as possible and decide what we're going to do. Get the Digbys onto it; they must have many resources they can draw on."

"I agree," said John, "and it's not just Sara, although she would be the initial target. There's Lily to think of and, of course, Phoebe. So far as we are aware, Dayton still doesn't know about either of them, or about me. But that may change if this Melliff person is still helping him. However, as you say, Pete, it's unlikely to be an immediate threat, not unless he's making contingency plans already."

"We can leave immediately," said Jacques, "if you think it's really urgent. I can arrange a private jet."

"We shouldn't delay long," agreed John, "although I know that Digby already has people in place guarding the girls, at a discreet distance. But there is one thing I've been wanting to do, something that's been on my mind since we arrived. Perhaps we can do that first."

Jacques raised an eyebrow at him.

"I'd like to go to Cape Cod, to the gallery, and maybe to the house. I can't help feeling that there's something there that might help, something that would only be meaningful to us."

Claudia exhaled loudly, shaking her head in disagreement. "Well, Jacques can't go," she said firmly, "not to the gallery. It would raise too many questions. The Murphy woman would recognise him immediately. Is it really necessary, John?"

"I don't know, I just feel that if we, I, don't go there, something might be missed," said John, opening his hands in a gesture of helplessness.

"OK," she said reluctantly. "But I don't think the house is on the cards; the police are probably still there. It's a crime scene, after all. It would be most unwise to go near it."

Jacques nodded his agreement. "You are right, Claudia, we'll need to be very careful. I certainly shouldn't go to the gallery and in case anything goes wrong, I don't want you to go there either. The police don't know anything about you and I should prefer that it stay that way. Let's make a plan."

He looked at his watch. "If we leave now, we can be there before lunchtime; it only takes about ninety minutes. I'll make arrangements for a flight this evening. John can go to the gallery, perhaps with Pete?" — he glanced at Pete who nodded his agreement — "while you and I look at Falmouth."

"I think we should stay in the car," said Claudia. "You don't want to bump into your lieutenant."

Jacques laughed. "It's not against the law for me to be in Falmouth, especially with a beautiful super-sleuth on my arm. You said you were running out of clothes. We can stock up your wardrobe."

"Hardly necessary if we're going straight back to England afterwards," said Claudia, "and if anything, we should be shopping for clothes for you."

Jacques looked down at his impeccable handmade shirt and

trousers and frowned. But before he could follow up on Claudia's remark, she was organising them further.

"We don't need to come back here, do we? If we pack up our things, we can go straight to the airport."

"It'll be more of an airfield than an airport," said Jacques. "But yes, you're right. We'll go there directly from Cape Cod."

Chapter Twenty-Nine

As Kenton was parking the car in a side street a short distance from the Tripley Gallery, Claudia suddenly panicked. "Gosh," she said, "you don't think it's closed, do you?"

Pete laughed. "I called to check while you were in your room packing. It's open."

As John opened the car door, Claudia touched his arm. "Be careful, John. Wear some dark glasses. And if Ms Murphy seems suspicious, get out of there and we'll leave."

"Don't worry, Claudia," grinned John. "I've been in a few scrapes in my time. I think I can handle an art gallery and Ms Murphy."

As the opening door set the bell tinkling, Mary Murphy got up from the desk at the rear of the gallery and walked over to the two men who had just come in.

"Good morning," she said, wondering why the younger of the two was wearing dark glasses on what was a dull, overcast day. "May I help?"

"Hi," said Pete, "We saw the seascapes in the window and decided we'd like to see some more."

"Please." Mary smiled and waved towards the display boards. "Go ahead. I'll switch on some more lights."

She walked over to the bank of light switches, but her hand hesitated as she looked back at the younger man. There was something strangely familiar in the way he moved and tilted his head as he was studying the paintings. She decided she would like him to remove his dark glasses, so she only switched on a couple of the lights.

She walked closer to John. "These were all painted at Marconi Beach," she said. "Do you know it?"

"No," John replied, "I don't. This is the first time I've been here. These are really excellent seascapes. Are you the artist?"

"Heavens, no," laughed Mary in a well-practised reply. "The artist isn't here at present. Her name is Naomi Tripley."

John was peering at some detail in the colours of the sea and, realising he needed more light, absently removed his sunglasses, forgetting totally why he was wearing them.

"Will she be in today?" he said, turning his head to Mary. "I'd very much like to meet her."

"She's, um, gone away for a while," said Mary, trying not to gasp. She had immediately registered John's eyes and then the overall shape of his face. "I … I don't know when she's coming back." She took a step away from him. "Oh gosh, I've just remembered that I left the coffee pot on the stove in the studio. It will be boiling itself dry. Please excuse me for a minute."

As she rushed off, Pete turned to John. "She seems suspicious," he said quietly. "Perhaps we should leave."

"I think it's fine," replied John as he roamed among the paintings. "I haven't come all this way to see Paola's work only to leave immediately. Let's give it a few more minutes at least."

He looked up as Mary came back from the studio. "Coffee pot OK?"

"Yes, thank you." She smiled, trying to hide her nervousness.

"Tell me," said John, "apart from seascapes, does Naomi Tripley paint other subjects? Portraits for example?"

"She does," said Mary, "but only by commission. She has a couple in the studio she's been working on. If you are interested, I could show them to you."

"Thank you," said John, rather surprised by the offer. "I should very much like to see them."

He followed her towards the studio door.

Mary uncovered the two commissions Paola had been working on and John came closer to study them. "Remarkable," he said, soaking up the detail.

Mary watched him as she stood by the studio door. "Take your time," she said, looking back nervously into the gallery.

"I will, thank you," he replied without turning round.

John hardly noticed the doorbell sound as Sharon Roper hurried into the gallery. She glanced at Pete and then called out to Mary.

"Ms Murphy? Are you there?"

Pete looked up from the painting he'd been studying at the sound of the voice. He saw the woman looking at him and then in the corner of his eye noticed the man standing by the door. He had cop written all over him.

"Oh, hello, er, Sharon," said Mary as she walked from the studio. "I was just in here with another customer." Her eyes flicked to the studio door just as John walked out.

Sharon Roper took in his features in a glance and cocked her head, a slight smile on her face. Her interest was not lost on John. He sighed quietly to himself, wishing he had heeded Claudia's advice.

"Good morning, sir," said the lieutenant. "Is there something in the studio that interested you?"

"Yes," said John, "I was looking at a couple of portraits. Wonderful work. You're not the artist, Naomi Tripley, are you?" hoping his question sounded sufficiently innocent. He glanced briefly at Pete, who was looking wary.

"I think you know that I'm not," replied the lieutenant. "Let me introduce myself. I'm Lieutenant Sharon Roper of the Falmouth police, and this is Detective Mullins." She lifted her chin towards the gallery door.

"I don't understand," said John. "Can I help you in any way?"

"I think perhaps you can, Mr ...?"

"Andrews. John Andrews."

"Mr Andrews. And you, sir?" she said, turning to Pete.

"Er, Pete Farsley," said Pete.

"Really?" Roper smiled, but there was no amusement in her eyes. "Not the same Mr Pete Farsley who's been pestering the assistant DA for information about the disappearance of Naomi Tripley? Tell me, Mr Farsley, why are you so interested in Ms Tripley?"

"Er, my wife was here, in the gallery, a few weeks ago, and she struck up a friendship with Ms Tripley. She was very impressed by her work. Ms Tripley told Sara, my wife, that she was going to England hoping to meet some dealers. As it happens, we are going there soon and Sara knows a few dealers. She offered to make some introductions. Then we heard that Ms Tripley had disappeared, so I came down to see if there was any news."

"And you came here to the gallery for that rather than coming to the police, did you?"

"Well, it seemed like the obvious place to start."

"Mmm," grunted the lieutenant. "And you two are friends?" she said, turning to John.

"Yes, of course," coughed John.

"Tell me, Mr Andrews, have you ever met Ms Tripley?"

"No, I don't think I have. Why do you ask?"

In reply, the lieutenant turned to Mullins, who was holding a briefcase. "Detective?" she said.

Mullins opened the briefcase, retrieved a clear plastic folder containing some documents and handed it to her. Roper took a photograph from among the papers and held it up, comparing it with John's face.

"Interesting," she muttered. "Are you sure you've never met?"

"What's this about, Lieutenant?" said John, not wanting to lie again.

Roper turned to Mullins. "What do you think, detective?"

Mullins took the photograph and glanced from it to John.

"Yeah," was all he said.

"May I see, Lieutenant?" asked John, holding out his hand.

Roper passed it to him. The photo was full colour and high

definition. Paola's eyes stared back at him, a light smile on her face. Her resemblance to him was indisputable.

"Well?" said Roper.

"This woman's eyes are remarkably similar to mine, Lieutenant, if that's what you mean."

"Oh, it's more than just the eyes, Mr Andrews, you could be brother and sister. Are you?"

John opened his mouth to answer but the lieutenant immediately held up a hand. She'd had a hunch. She turned to Pete. "Mr Farsley, you don't by any chance carry a photo of your wife, do you? Sara, was it?"

"Yes, I do, of course," said Pete rather reluctantly. He took his wallet from his jacket and fumbled over pulling out a photo of Sara. He glanced nervously at the lieutenant, hoping she wouldn't see the other photo it contained, one of Sara and Paola together.

He handed the photo of Sara to Roper who smiled triumphantly.

"Well, now, gentlemen, please don't waste my time by telling me this is all a coincidence. Your wife, Mr Farsley, is the image of Ms Tripley who in turn bears a remarkable resemblance to Mr Andrews here. I'm guessing siblings, all three of you. Am I right? You're Sara Farsley's brother, Mr Andrews, aren't you, as well as Naomi Tripley's. That makes you Mr Farsley's brother-in-law."

John raised his eyebrows in apparent agreement.

"Now that's all very nice and cosy," continued the lieutenant, "but I'm investigating a homicide and abduction, and not only that, I've discovered, as I think you'll know, that Naomi Tripley is not the lady's real name. She's in the US on a stolen passport and living here illegally. How did your sister get hold of that passport, Mr Andrews?"

John heard Mary Murphy gasp at what the lieutenant had just said and took the opportunity to gather his thoughts before he answered. He glanced at Pete whose normal lawyer's courtroom cool had clearly deserted him. His face was ashen.

John looked directly into the lieutenant's eyes. The lie came easily; it wasn't the first time he had had to think on his feet. "We had no intention of trying to deceive you, Lieutenant, and we had every intention of coming to see you once we'd been to the gallery. You see, I'm an artist as well and I was very keen to see her work. It's been years."

"Years?"

"Yes. My sister Sara and I have been estranged from our sister, whose real name is Paola, for nearly ten years. During that time, we had no idea where she was. Then Sara called me — I live in England, you see — to say that she'd been here to Cape Cod and she was convinced she'd seen Paola walking in the street. She didn't dare approach her since the last time they'd met had been very difficult. There had been an argument and many regrettable things were said. I said I'd fly over immediately and come here with her. It was only once I arrived that we heard of the homicide and the disappearance of Paola, er, Naomi. Since both Pete and Sara are lawyers in Boston, they obviously have many connections with the police and the DA's office. Pete started to call around."

"You've been more than calling around, Mr Farsley, from what I've been told," growled the lieutenant. She turned back to John. "When did you arrive here in the US, Mr Andrews?"

"Five days ago."

"Five days! How come you're only now coming down here to Falmouth to check out where your sister worked? I'd have thought you would have been banging on my door to put pressure on me to find her, not just sit around and wait and get second-hand information from your brother-in-law."

John raised his shoulders submissively, his smile apologetic. "I, er, suffer dreadfully from jet lag, Lieutenant, every time I fly across time zones. I hate flying; it always takes me days to recover. I can hardly stand for the first two days." He tried to hold Roper's eyes, his excuse sounding very feeble to him. But, to his surprise, it struck a chord.

"Yeah, I'm the same," she grunted. "I never go anywhere as a result."

But that was the only concession she was prepared to give. "I'm sure that when I check up on your story, Mr Andrews, I'll find that you weren't in the country when your sister disappeared. But what about Mrs Farsley? How do I know that she isn't involved?"

Pete coughed indignantly, regaining some of his courtroom poise. "I've heard, Lieutenant, that you have CCTV footage of the abduction. Was my wife shown in any of that?"

"You know very well she wasn't, but she could have hired people; they were professional."

"To do what?" said John. "Kidnap the sister we haven't seen for ten years? That's patently ridiculous and you know it."

Roper ignored him. "You said your sister's name was Paola. What's her surname?"

"Well, originally it was Andrews, obviously. But the last time we met, it was Fisher," said John, picking out the first name that came into his head. "However, the Fisher she was married to was a creep so I doubt they are still together. The marriage was pretty rocky even then."

"Where was she born?"

"As it happens, she was born in Italy — our parents travelled a lot with their work. Sara was born here in the States. She met Pete when she was a student in Boston."

"Is that right, Mr Farsley?" said the lieutenant to Pete.

"Yes, it is," he said, unhappy about the lie.

"When was that, exactly? I'll need to check it all out, just for the paperwork, you understand."

Her tone told them she didn't believe a word of their story.

"Er, in the early nineties," said Pete. "Sara is the older sister."

The lieutenant grunted. "So why do you think your sister has been abducted, Mr Andrews? What do you know about this mystery man who has apparently taken her? Charles Creed. A man who doesn't seem to exist and who has also disappeared. Twin brother of a man who happened to be in the area at the time. I don't suppose you know him too, do you? Does the name Adam Fowler mean anything to either of you?"

John and Pete shook their heads unconvincingly.

"I really have no idea, Lieutenant," said John, once he found his voice again. "I have no idea what my sister has been up to for the last ten years, where she's been or why she ended up here."

Sharon Roper stared menacingly at him for a few moments, trying to force him to look away, but he held her eyes.

"Or why she's been taken out of the country?" she said eventually.

"Out of the country?"

"Yes, our latest enquiries have come up with a flight out of a private airfield a couple of hours from here where passengers fitting the description of Creed and your sister left soon after the time of the incident. The operations manager there is in deep shit, I can assure you, since he wilfully impeded this enquiry by lying to us first off, telling us there'd been nothing going out that evening. It took hours of valuable detective time to go indirectly through hundreds of manifests and route records to identify the private jet that seems to have spirited your sister away. I hope neither of *you* is holding anything back."

She paused to let the implied threat sink in.

"Where was it going, this jet?" said John.

"You don't know?"

"I know nothing about any jet, Lieutenant."

"Mmm. Well, the interesting thing is that a strong attempt was made to disguise the route. On paper, it was bound for a small island in the Caribbean, but in reality, it was headed further east."

"Europe, then," said Pete. "Whereabouts, exactly?"

"No, not Europe, Mr Farsley, at least I don't think it counts as Europe. My geography's not too hot."

"I don't understand," said John.

"Algeria, Mr Andrews. It flew to Algeria."

The sound of John's mobile ringing cut through the tension in the gallery. He pulled the phone from his pocket and glanced at the screen. Jacques' name was displayed in large letters. Aware that the detective standing behind him was trying to see the phone's screen, John was silently thankful he hadn't put the name Adam Fowler against the number.

He raised his eyebrows, trying to look surprised. "I think I need to take this, Lieutenant," he said, and pressed the respond button without waiting for her to answer.

"Jacques! What a surprise. It's been ages. Where are you?"

Jacques' reply was immediately guarded, his voice low. "Philippe, I take it there's a problem," he said, using the seventeenth century French that they still used occasionally. "Can anyone hear what I'm saying?"

"No, no," said John in English. "I'm in Cape Cod."

"OK," continued Jacques, "I take it you think it unwise not to speak in English. Presumably we shouldn't come near the gallery."

"No, not at all," said John. "I'm in an art gallery, you're not interrupting anything." He glanced at Roper. "I'm sorry, Lieutenant," he whispered, but loud enough for Jacques to hear, "it's an old friend calling out of the blue."

Roper glowered at him, not believing him for a moment.

"I hear you," said Jacques. "My friend the lieutenant's there asking awkward questions. Say nothing if I'm right."

John remained silent.

"OK," continued Jacques. "Can you get out of there? Does she have any reason to hold you?"

"No, no," said John, "I can return to Boston straight away. We can meet in a couple of hours. Yes, that would be brilliant. I can't believe we're both in the same place at the same time. I'll call when I'm—"

"Don't overdo it, Philippe," said Jacques, interrupting. "The car is still where we dropped you. Get here as quickly as you can."

John cut the call. "Sorry, Lieutenant. It was an old friend I haven't heard from for ages."

"Name?" said Roper.

"Lieutenant, I don't thi—" started John, but then change his mind when he saw the threat in the lieutenant's eyes. "Jacques Bognard," he said.

"He's French?"

"Canadian. Look, Lieutenant, that call was unexpected. We'd hoped to spend longer here today, perhaps even see my sister's house, if that's possible. But I really must get back to Boston. Could we see you tomorrow?"

"Come to the police department," said Roper grudgingly. "In the meantime, let me have your cell number, in case I need to talk. Here's my card. And yes, we can go to the house. The techs have finished there now. Are you sure you don't have time today?"

John glanced apologetically at his phone, indicating the call he'd just received. "Sorry," he said. He looked at the card and called Roper's number. When her mobile rang, he cancelled the call. "There, Lieutenant, you have my number."

He turned to Mary Murphy. "It's very good of you to keep the gallery running, considering what's happened."

"I wasn't really sure what to do," she replied. "And now, well …"

"John," said Pete. "We should go. The traffic can get busy." Like Jacques, he was concerned John was saying too much.

"I'll see you tomorrow, Lieutenant," said John as he turned to leave.

"Make sure you do, Mr Andrews. We still have a lot to talk about."

She watched as John and Pete left the gallery. "Follow them, Kevin. I want to know if they're meeting anyone here. I think we've just been told a crock of shit. And get on to checking Andrews' story. And the Farsley woman's."

As the door closed after the detective, she turned to Mary Murphy. "What do you think, Ms Murphy? You knew Naomi Tripley, or whatever her real name was. Pretty well, I should think, having worked with her for a couple of months. Is anything Andrews said likely to be the truth?"

Mary was shocked. She had taken the whole story at face value.

"Well, Lieutenant, I … yes, I think there's no doubt that Mr Andrews and Naomi are related. There's a lot of similarity in their looks and even their mannerisms. And then there are the eyes, of course. I think he is very likely to be her brother."

"Mmm," muttered Roper, distracted. "I'd love to know who called him. I have Andrews' number now, I'll contact the phone company, check his call records."

She started to punch some numbers but was interrupted by an incoming call.

"Lieutenant." Detective Mullins voice sounded in her ear, his tone full of urgency. "Andrews and Farsley just got into a large black limo that I swear is the one Fowler was using when he was released. I couldn't see into it because the windows were tinted. But I've got the plates and I'm running a check now."

"Why am I not surprised?" said Roper. "If the number comes back as Fowler's car or a car he's using, put it out on the wire and get them stopped. If they all know each other, there must be a lot they aren't telling us." She paused. "You know, Kevin, I think we made some progress this afternoon, thanks to Ms Murphy alerting us."

As the car door closed, John sat back in his seat and breathed a sigh of relief. Then he turned to Jacques. "We need to go immediately," he said. "Claudia was right: I should never have gone there. Paola's assistant was straight on the phone as soon as she saw my face. I thought the lieutenant was going to hold us on some trumped-up charge."

"You're forgetting I'm a lawyer, John," said Pete. "She would have been hard pressed."

"How far is Logan airport?" asked John.

Jacques shook his head. "We're not going to Boston, mon ami. I thought this morning that your visit to the gallery might produce problems, so I organised a jet from an airfield very near here. We'll be on the way within the hour."

"Can't be soon enough," said John. "Next time, Claudia, I'll listen more closely to your advice."

"You know," said Pete, "as long as we can get on that plane and go, the hassle will have been worth it. The lieutenant gave us some very valuable information."

"She did?" Jacques was surprised that she'd told them anything.

"Yes, she let slip that they now know that Dayton and Paola left the country on the night of the abduction. And not only that, they were headed for Algeria."

"Algeria?" echoed Claudia.

"Yes," replied Pete. "After leaving a false trail to some Caribbean island. I wonder why they are going to Algeria."

"Oh, I doubt very much it's their final destination," said Jacques. "It's almost definitely just a conveniently quiet place where Dayton happens to have some connections that will smooth the way for him. Remember that both he and I are originally Greek. We have darker complexions than you, John. He probably does business there and finds it easy to slip in and out. As it happens, I've also used it, from time to time."

"Really?" said Claudia.

Jacques' reply was an enigmatic smile. "Yes, really. From there a boat across the Mediterranean to Spain or Sardinia isn't a problem. You're right, Pete, the risk was worth it. We now know that Dayton's destination was very likely Europe. Pete, you look worried."

"I am," said Pete, puckering his lips. "It's not going to take long for the lieutenant to discover that John's very convincingly delivered story was a pack of lies. And in addition to that, she'll quickly discover I was lying to her about Sara. Whatever happens now, both Sara and I could find ourselves in trouble. I've no desire to be disbarred."

"I doubt it will come to that," said Jacques.

"How can you be so sure?"

Jacques smiled. "I'll have a little word with Digby Smith. I'm sure that he will be able to have the lieutenant's wings clipped. I'll call him once we're in the air. Rest assured, Pete, that our dragon of a lieutenant will be breathing fire of frustration before very long."

John sat back in his seat and looked relaxed for the first time since he'd climbed into the car.

"I think maybe I should call my Digby as well. He's bound to lecture me about my foolhardy behaviour, but even he will agree that we've made progress." His gaze drifted down from Jacques' face and he raised a quizzical eyebrow, a smile spreading slowly across his face.

"What is it, mon ami?" said Jacques.

"You look ... different. You've changed your clothes." He nodded his approval. "They suit you. Less—"

"Like a favourite uncle?" suggested Jacques, affecting disinterest with a slight toss of his head.

"Yes," said John. He turned to Claudia. "What happened?"

Claudia took Jacques' hands and looked into his eyes. "I took Jacques shopping while you were in the gallery. I'm afraid I left the favourite uncle in the fitting room and came away with this younger model. Don't you think it's an improvement?"

"Without a doubt," chimed in Pete. "The only problem is that you three youngsters are making me feel old."

"I'll talk to Sara if you like," said Claudia, reaching out to make an adjustment to the collar of Jacques' polo shirt.

Jacques raised his hands to take hers. "You know, Dr Reid," he said. "If I didn't know better, I'd say that you were flirting with me."

"Then I'd say that you don't know better, Mr Bognard," replied Claudia as she leaned forward to kiss him lightly on the lips.

Chapter Thirty

With a take-off time of four in the afternoon and an eight-hour flight to the small commercial airfield at Carlisle in the north of England, the arrival time for the Legacy 650 Executive jet Jacques had chartered would be around five in the morning local time.

"By the time Crawshaw, my driver, has whisked us down to Thirlmere, we'll be ready for an early breakfast," Jacques told the others as the jet reached its cruising altitude. "Perhaps you should call Lola, John, before it gets too late in the UK. After that, the seats in this little bird are extremely comfortable, so I think we shall all be able to enjoy a few hours sleep."

"After the nervous tension of our meeting with lieutenant Roper and more than a little concern as to whether we'd get out of the country before she put us on a stop list, I think some R&R will be very welcome," said John as he reclined his seat. "I'll call Lola now, if you will show me how."

Four hours into the flight, Claudia awoke with a start, wondering where she was. Then, as she turned her head in the softness of the small pillow Jacques had rested on his shoulder, she remembered. She smiled, stretched her legs briefly, and then snuggled back into the embrace of Jacques' arm wrapped around her.

Jacques felt her move and kissed the top of her head. "Are you awake, chérie?" he whispered.

"Mmm," she sighed very quietly as she reached to take his other hand. "No, I'm not."

Jacques leaned his head back into his own pillow and listened to her soft rhythmic breathing, a contented smile on his face.

Later, she stirred again, this time lifting her head to look into Jacques' face. His eyes were open, watching her.

"Have you slept?" she said softly, the sleep still in her voice.

"I've been luxuriating in the pleasure of listening to you sleep, chérie," he said. "It's very relaxing."

She smiled and kissed him.

"You know, I've been thinking," she said, resting her head on his shoulder again.

"Oh dear."

"No, not about, you know, anything to do with Paola. About us."

"That's nice."

"Do you know what I want to do when we reach England?"

When there was no reply, she lifted her head and saw a look of amusement in his eyes.

She traced a distracted finger on his cheek. "I didn't actually mean … but well, yes, that would be nice … in fact, more than nice. What I meant was I really want you to meet Sally and Ced. They're my closest friends in all the world and I can't wait to tell them about us, for them to meet you. They know about you, of course, from your friendship with John, but you've never met them, have you?"

"No, chérie, as with you, our paths haven't crossed in the three years since I rediscovered Philippe. But, of course, I know all about Ced's brilliant computing skills. I'd love to meet them both. Why don't we drive down to see them once we've freshened up at the Andrews' cottage?"

"Yes, that would be brilliant," mumbled Claudia as she nestled back against his shoulder and sleep overtook her again.

"That's settled then," said Jacques. "But in the meantime, I think I'll doze for a while and think about your other suggestion."

"Sal, it's Claw."

"Claw! Where are you? I've been trying to call you but I keep getting your answer message. What's going on?"

"I've been in the States."

"Really? Why?"

"It's a long story Sal, and it's far from over. I can tell you all about it when I see you. Which is why I'm calling. Can we drop in later, around lunchtime?"

"We?"

"Yes. We."

"Claw?"

"It's another long story, Sal. Well, not so long, actually, in fact, it's all happened rather fast. I want you to meet Jacques."

There was a moment's silence at the other end while Sally processed the name.

"Isn't Jacques the name of that friend of John Andrews? The one from … Claw! You're not telling me that … Christ, Claw! I mean, he's … Wow! That's amazing! Claw, say something."

"I don't need to. You're having a perfectly good conversation with yourself."

"Claw!"

"Yes, it is John's friend. Sal, I'm so happy."

"I'll bet you are. He's loaded, isn't he?"

"Sally Moreton!"

"It's Sally Fisher now, Claw, or have you forgotten?"

"It's Sally Moreton when you make comments like that! Now, can we come and see you?"

"Claw. I can't wait. Actually Claw, what have you been up to? Ced's been tearing his hair out for the last couple of days. It couldn't be connected, could it?"

"What do you mean?"

"Someone's trying to hack into his program."

Despite their best intentions, Jacques and Claudia didn't manage to escape the Andrews' cottage until shortly before ten thirty. Crawshaw had delivered the party to Thirlmere at six thirty, by which time the entire house was up and waiting for them, including a very sleepy Matt. By the time Jacques had been introduced to the other members of the Farsley family and then kidnapped by Sophie and Phoebe, who insisted on showing their favourite uncle their latest dolls, and Claudia had been taken aside by Lola, Lily and Sara for an excited interrogation, and finally all eleven of them had indulged in the usual Andrews breakfast, the hours had slipped away. It was only with firm promises that they would return the next day that they were allowed to leave.

As Crawshaw pulled up outside the Fisher's town house in Knutsford in Cheshire, Sally came running out to meet them followed by Ced, who was carrying their one-year-old daughter, Claudia-Jane, in his arms.

"Claw!" cried Sally, throwing her arms around her diminutive friend. "This is just … amazing."

As Ced caught up, Claudia turned to Jacques to introduce him and suddenly burst out laughing. "Oh my God," she hooted, "I feel so tiny!" At slightly short of five foot one, Claudia was a foot shorter than Sally while Ced and Jacques were six-four and six-five respectively. "Let me hold Claudia-Jane while I'm still taller than she is."

Before they headed inside, Jacques went back to the car to retrieve a huge bunch of flowers for Sally and a large fluffy pink rabbit for Claudia-Jane.

Claudia was incredulous. "When did you get those?"

Jacques tapped the side of his nose. "My car has magic powers, chérie. Now, I realise that we have serious business to discuss, but I hope we might also be able to relax later. Might I put a couple of bottles in your fridge, Sally?"

Sally took his arm in both of hers and marched him towards the house. "You can fill my fridge as full as you like." She turned her head back towards Claudia. "Sorry, Claw, I'm stealing him."

Ced looked at his daughter and sighed. "Oh, my little one, what can I do to protect you from your shallow mother?"

Claudia-Jane ignored him as she continued stroking her rabbit.

After the introductions and more hugs for Claudia from Sally, they settled in the living room where both Claudia and Jacques related the story of Paola's abduction and all the events that had happened since. As they were talking, Claudia realised that in the euphoria of their arrival, she hadn't really looked closely at Ced. He looked drawn, preoccupied, and lacked some of his usual sparkle. But he was now listening very carefully to what they were telling him, showing a particular interest in Marcus Dayton's greasy-haired geek.

"So let me just recap," he said as Jacques finished telling them about Dayton taking Paola out of the US to Europe. "Dayton learned about Paola through the notes from the psychiatrist—"

"From her book first and then later from the notes," said Claudia.

"Right. But the way the Farsleys found out was from old online newspapers with reports of the fire and then they found the psychiatrist and then the book, which is the other way round. So in order for Dayton to have learned of the book, he must have been searching the Internet for … what? Reports of people who claim to be old, presumably through medical or psychiatric papers? If that's the case, then he must have had a computer whizz to make the searches. Now, from the psychiatrist's book, they would have learned about Paola and the fact that she was claiming to be other artists in the past. The psychiatrist obviously didn't believe her, but Dayton did. She was exactly what he was looking for. However, when he couldn't locate Paola, he turned his attention to Sara. But then Paola turned up and now he's taken her."

"Yes," said Claudia. "Actually, the psychiatrist thought Paola was dead, but it's possible that Dayton didn't believe it. I think he located Paola in South America, in Brazil, in fact, but she managed to get away with a false identity, so she must have had some good connections there—"

"Which Dayton didn't know about so he lost her," interrupted Ced.

"Right," continued Claudia, "but then he found her again quite quickly. I wonder how he managed that."

"And how did he locate her in Brazil?" added Jacques.

Ced stood and paced the room while he turned over ideas in his mind.

"D'you—" started Claudia, but stopped when Sally held up a hand. She shook her head and indicated they should let Ced think.

Suddenly Ced spun around and clapped his hands. "Images!" he announced. "It must all be through images of her. Claw, you said something before about photographs in the psychiatrist's file. Have you seen them?"

"Yes, Pete showed me the copies of the files and the book the day before yesterday when we got back to Boston. We both saw them." She reached out and touched Jacques' arm affectionately.

"And?"

"And, well, there were loads of black and white photos of Paola when she was Annie Carr taken with the psychiatrist in the seventies when she was young. Paola of course looked no different from now, judging from a photo that Pete showed me of her taken recently with Sara."

"And Dayton has seen these shots from the seventies?"

"Yes, he broke into the psychiatrist's offices and copied everything."

"Exactly!" exclaimed Ced.

They all looked at him, waiting for a further explanation.

"Don't you see? Once he'd got the images of Paola, he could use them as a basis to search the Internet. He'd have the names of Paola's past identities from the files, so for the more recent ones, he could find photos of them and confirm his suspicions, confirm that Paola was them."

"Mali Whittaker and Dolores di Napoli," said Claudia.

"Who?"

"They were two of the names in the notes in the file."

"Wasn't Dolores di Napoli a silent movie star?" asked Sally.

"She was," said Jacques. "I remember her well. In fact, I met her at a reception in Hollywood in, let me think, it must have been around 1915."

"You met her!" Sally's jaw dropped.

"It was the briefest of encounters, she was whisked away by some producer. Of course, with the fashions of the day, we both looked very different."

Ced shook his head in astonishment, but he wasn't really interested in the reminiscences.

"When she disappeared," he continued, "Dayton would have got his computer bloke to continue searching modern day sources as well. Every source he could find. He must have come up with an image of her in Brazil, but before he could get to her, she must have found out and escaped."

Jacques nodded as it all fell into place. "And then he found her again through an article in the Cape Cod newspaper that included a photo of her, the one that John said the lieutenant showed him yesterday."

Ced sat down and put his chin on his hands. "So he's using some form of image comparison program. If that's the case, why is he so interested in mine?"

"Oh, I'd forgotten!" exclaimed Claudia. "Sal said you'd been hacked."

"An attempt has been made but so far they've failed to get the program," replied Ced through clenched teeth. "I've put in some very sophisticated security, much of which the hacker did get through, but when that happens, firstly all sorts of alarm bells go off that he can't avoid — some he won't even know about — and secondly he'll be led down all sorts of blind alleys, some of which are supposed to lead me back to him, although that part's failed so far."

"The image comparison software he's using must have been very good to have found Paola in the first place," said Jacques.

"Oh, yes," agreed Ced. "In fact, more than very good; I'd say it's state of the art. It must have been written by Dayton's man, who's obviously pretty special."

"As you said," added Sal, "it makes you wonder why he's interested in yours."

Ced tapped his fingers together in thought. "Well, his routines are probably geared towards photo comparison, whereas mine centre on brush strokes and the like."

"But he's got Paola," objected Sally. "What else does he want?"

"Oh my God!" Claudia's eyes were wide in horror as she cupped her hands to her open mouth.

"What, chérie?" said Jacques.

"He's looking for John," said Claudia.

"I thought he didn't know about John, or the others," said Jacques.

"He doesn't, or at least he didn't. And I don't think that Paola would tell him since it would also lead to Sara, as well as Lily and Phoebe." Claudia ran a hand through her hair, her eyes flickering as she searched her memory. "There was something in the notes. What was it?" She took hold of Jacques' hands and put them together in hers as she stared into his eyes for inspiration. Then her eyes sparkled.

"Stefano Crispi!" she said. "That's it! John was Stefano Crispi when he was married to Paola's mother, um … Francesca, that was her name … and in Dr Wright's notes on Annie Carr, Annie told her that her father's name was Stefano Crispi. Dayton will have seen that."

"I don't see——" started Sally.

But Claudia was now in full flood. "Dayton doesn't know if Paola's father is still alive or even if he was the same as she is, but perhaps she's said something to indicate he might be. Or maybe Dayton's just decided to cover all the angles. So he starts with Stefano Crispi, who was an artist, and he assumes that since Paola has remained an artist her father might be as well, he then searches for other artists who painted in the same style as Stefano Crispi. That could lead him to whoever he is now, if he's still alive. To John, in fact."

"And to do that," continued Ced, "he'd need my program."

"Exactly!" Claudia's eyes were wide, the flow of ideas racing through her mind. "Rather than write a program that is far more sophisticated than his photo comparison one, Melliff has looked around to see what's out there. And of course he's found out about you. Now he can't just approach you, so he'll try to access your program. Not so much to hack it or steal it, but perhaps to see what you've been running."

"Shit!" Ced stood suddenly. "He'd find loads of comparisons with all the artists that John has been, but, hey, he wouldn't find John."

"Why?" said Jacques, frowning.

"Because I've deliberately written routines to isolate John from any of his former personas. If a comparison's made between John's work and, say, Crispi's, or Perini's or Moretti's, the results will be negative. It was done to protect John, although not from someone deliberately trying to find him, rather from his being accidentally discovered."

"So all John's previous personas would match, but not John's," said Jacques. "Does that include the one immediately before John?"

"Yes. His name was Matthew Allen, but he was pretty obscure."

Jacques didn't like it. "I think that Dayton would smell a rat if it all grinds to a halt with this Matthew Allen. When—"

"In the 1990s," said Ced, anticipating the question.

"In the 1990s?" repeated Jacques. "He'd either think that Allen had died, or rather been killed, or that the next persona, John, was deliberately being hidden. I'd think that. Tell me, Ced, how have you communicated with John about this?"

"How do you mean?"

"Phone calls? Emails?"

"Both yes. But I think I've got that covered."

"You mean the hacker can't read your emails?"

"No, he can't. I go to great lengths to prevent that. Nothing to do with John in fact, but because of my clients and the fact that most of my work is crime related. All my incoming emails are automatically moved to another computer through a one-way link. That computer isn't connected to the Internet and nothing on it can be read online. At the same time, the incoming email is deleted from the live computer, so my inbox is effectively always empty. The only way anyone could read my emails is to break in here and read them. And they'd never find their way into the computer; I've got some of the best security there is on it."

"What happens when you want to reply?" asked Jacques.

"Replies go out of another account that is proxied and encrypted."

"What if the hacker went to John's computer? Would he be able to read the mail you send to him?"

"In theory, yes, but all the emails are encrypted to a very high level. And the algorithm constantly changes, so he'd only get fragments at best."

"Sounds sophisticated," said Jacques, impressed.

"It's actually ridiculously anal," said Ced. "But it's the only way."

Claudia was thinking through other possibilities. "Do you think he might have stolen a copy of your program to make his own comparisons?" she asked Ced.

"No, I'm sure he hasn't from the record of the intrusion. And now he can't. I've isolated everything so the program is never actually online. It's a nuisance since it adds extra manual transfers, like with the email, that take time, but it means it's secure."

"So where does that leave us?" mused Sally.

"It leaves me somewhat more reassured," replied Ced, taking her hand. "Having talked all this through, I now know what was going on and I'm confident that what they are hoping to find hasn't been found and won't be found, not from my system."

"It's important that we are very careful," said Jacques. "Dayton knows about Sara and her family, but not where they are at the moment. He may or may not know about John and his family, although he must suspect that John exists. But he almost definitely won't know about the four of us. We want to keep it that way."

Claudia agreed. "Yes, absolutely. Now, as we said before, neither John nor the others are likely to be under any immediate threat, not until things don't go according to whatever plan he has for Paola. So I don't think we need to call John; we can bring him up to speed tomorrow. And we have, apparently, got Digby's contingent lurking in the woods as protection."

"So we can relax." Jacques smiled and squeezed her hand.

"Now Ced, before we sample the champagne, I should very much like to look at your program. Would you mind giving me a demonstration? I have one or two paintings that I'd love to test for authenticity, if you wouldn't mind."

Ced showed Jacques upstairs to his study while Sally took the opportunity to grill Claudia. Having tried many times over the years to find someone with whom Claudia clicked, and failed every time, she was delighted with her best friend's romance.

"So where do you keep these paintings, Jacques?" asked Ced as they sat in his study in front of a bank of hi-res computer monitors. "I'm afraid I don't really know anything about you. Do you normally live in this country?"

"These days I do, for the most part," replied Jacques. "I have done for a good number of years now. I have an apartment in London where the security is good enough for me not to have to worry about them. I keep quite a few there rather than at the house; I think that security in houses is always so much more problematic. Obviously there are some at the house, since I want to see them, but not the really valuable ones."

"Where's the house?" asked Ced, suddenly wondering what 'one or two paintings' actually meant.

"The one I use most is near Richmond Park. There's also one in Scotland that I love for relaxing. Unfortunately I don't get there as much as I'd like since I spend much of my free time on the water. The sea is a second home to me. I've always sailed."

"And what are the paintings?"

"Oh, the usual names. There are some Rembrandts, Vermeers, a variety of Renaissance painters, including a couple of da Vinci cartoons that are unknown to the world. There's some relatively modern stuff as well: Renoir, Monet, Manet, that I mostly bought around the time they were painted, although not always from the artists."

"So ... it's more than one or two."

"Er, yes, I suppose it is," laughed Jacques.

"Have you always been interested in art?" asked Ced.

"To my regret, I haven't, no. It was Philippe who sparked my passion, when I saw him painting portraits of Mathilde, my wife."

"Philippe?"

"Er, John. Philippe was his name when I first knew him in the seventeenth century."

Ced shook his head; he still found what he knew about John and the others very hard to understand.

"So how many paintings are we talking about?"

"There must be close to a hundred scattered around. When I know I'm not going to see them for a substantial period, which can happen in my life, given that in the past I have had to leave one country for another for many years, in those circumstances I'll secure them in vaults. I hate doing that; paintings are to be viewed in my opinion, but to protect them it's necessary. With my love of the sea, I have sometimes spent many months on board a boat of some description, which is hardly a good environment for a work of art that you want to see preserved for as long as possible. Anyway, despite knowing the provenance of many of them, there are still a good few that I should love to have authenticated. Could I send them here?"

"Er, I don't think I'd like to take responsibility for a collection of old masters," spluttered Ced. "Suppose we were burgled?"

"That's a good point, although I do have many of them tagged with a microchip that will announce their location to within five metres anywhere in the world. The battery lasts for more than twenty years, so there would be a good chance of recovery."

Ced was amazed. "I've heard of tagging, of course, but that sounds very sophisticated; very cutting edge."

Jacques smiled. "I have a company that develops these things. At present I'm the only one using this particular prototype, but I'm sure that once we've ironed out the few remaining wrinkles, such as making them undetectable and irremovable, they will sell well."

"Even so," replied Ced, "I think I'd rather examine them somewhere very secure. I have a good friend who works at the National Gallery. Placing the paintings there would be about as secure as you can get."

"As long as they give them back," said Jacques. "I know what the British are like. They seem to think that all priceless art should be in state buildings in London."

After Ced had shown a fascinated Jacques around his program, they returned to the living room where Jacques opened the champagne with due Gallic ceremony.

"I thought you were Greek," teased Claudia.

"Chérie, I have been so many nationalities that I find it hard to keep count. But I do like the style of the French and in the last thousand years or so, I have lived in their country quite a lot."

He looked slightly bemused for a moment as both girls giggled and blew raspberries at him, and then he caught Ced's eye and grinned.

"Right," said Sally. "You'll both stay for dinner. In fact, stay the night if you want."

"Dinner would be wonderful, Sal, but we'll decline the offer to stay," said Claudia, looking up at Jacques with a coy smile. "I want to show Jacques my little house at Combrook."

"Ah," said Sally.

Chapter Thirty-One

Marcus Dayton's conversation regarding his suspicions over the existence of John Andrews worried Paola. She refused his offer of dinner and another cosy evening by the fire in his dining room and went to her room to think things through. She was unsettled and she wanted to identify what was playing on her mind. After half an hour of pacing and going over all the conversations she'd had since arriving at the house, her thoughts started to crystallise, She began to realise that it wasn't that she perceived Dayton as a threat to her father — she could see no reason why Dayton should want to harm him — and it wasn't her two half sisters, Lily and Phoebe — she had never met the child and had no feelings for her, and as for Lily, in the brief time she had known her, she had found her rather fawning in her affections for their father. No, she realised, it was Sara who concerned her.

In as much as Paola could feel guilty about anything she had done in her life, she felt guilty over the way Sara's childhood had turned out, guilty about not returning to the US to find her until it was too late. She did not want Dayton spreading his attempts to produce a child with their traits beyond herself; she found it distasteful enough that Dayton should contemplate what he was intending for her regardless of her objections. Sara had only recently discovered her strange traits and was still coming to terms with them. She had a loving husband and family; she must not be taken by Dayton.

Paola had to warn Sara, but how? Escape was the most obvious option, but Dayton was dangling this carrot before her in a way that told her it was far more difficult than it appeared. She had looked for telephones in the house but had found none, and none of the staff appeared to carry cell phones, just radios. Perhaps the guards had cells.

When she thought of the guards, she realised that they were the other thing that had bothered her. In fact, more than bothered her. If she was honest with herself, she was spitting. If Dayton was telling the truth, then she had been outwitted by at least one guard, probably two. Her pride in her skills was more than bruised. She would put things to the test the following day, even though she knew Dayton would expect her to try something.

The following morning was cold, only a few degrees above a frost. Paola rummaged in the wardrobe and dressed warmly. She wanted to be able to move fast, but if she did manage to escape, she had no idea how long she might be in the forest: she had no desire to freeze. Rather than waste time over breakfast, she went to the kitchen where she surprised the cook by demanding some bread and fruit, some of which she ate, and the rest she stuffed into the pockets of her jacket. Then she was off. She wanted to get into the woods to a particularly dense stand of trees she'd found where she could wait and listen.

She reached the spot within ten minutes and settled into a position where she could not be seen, and she waited. She had seen no activity near the house as she left, but she was sure that the cook would have alerted the guards, if they hadn't already been watching her. After twenty minutes she became aware of movement nearby that she was certain wasn't anything on four legs going quietly about its business. She listened carefully, but the movement stopped. Someone was waiting her out. The day was getting no warmer. She looked up and saw squadrons of menacing clouds vying for position as they skittered and bumped through the sky. The trees started to murmur as the wind got up, the rustling masking any other sounds. Time to move. She left her hiding place and darted through the undergrowth, moving silently and disturbing nothing until she reached a second dense clump of trees, this one centred around a fallen trunk overgrown with bramble and creepers she had found the previous day. She was quickly hidden. After a few minutes, she became aware again of the same quiet movement as before, and just as before, it stopped. She frowned. She had seen no one, even though she had looked back several times, waited, checked. She couldn't have been in view and she was sure she had left no trail.

The second vantage point was in the direction of the south gate, the one Dayton would have expected her to approach. Perhaps whoever was following her was anticipating this. So for her third move, once the breeze got up again, she headed in a different direction, into a part of the forest unknown to her. She found a suitable spot, secreted herself in it, and waited. Within a few moments, she again heard a slight movement about twenty metres away, after which there was silence.

She exhaled soundlessly, her frustration increasing. Either her tracker was very good or … She looked down at her clothes and the lightweight boots she had chosen. Then she realised what was happening. None of this gear was hers; Dayton had provided everything. She slipped off her left boot and examined it thoroughly. Nothing. Then she repeated the search on the right boot, and found it. There was a miniature tracking device embedded under the insole. She smiled grimly; her tracker was no better than the others; it was simply that he had electronic help. She removed the bug and placed it under a rotting log. Then she looked down at her clothes. What would she do in Dayton's position? Reluctantly, given the temperature, she peeled off all her clothes one piece at a time, checking every pocket, seam and zip. She found two more bugs, one in an inner seam in her jacket and one in a seam in her bra. She put them with the first one and dressed as quickly as she could, checking everything carefully once more as she did.

Once she was warm, it was time to put her findings to the test. She waited again, impatient for the trees to mask any sounds. As soon as they stirred, she was on the move, skipping five hundred metres through the forest until she found another suitable hiding spot. She settled and waited. This time there was nothing. She smiled in satisfaction. She had him. But he would soon become suspicious if the bugs registered no more movement. She had to confront him.

Choosing a wide arc, Paola circled back to a spot beyond the previous hiding place until she located her tracker. He was half-hidden between the boles of two wild oaks and a large heather. From his slightly agitated movements, he appeared to be starting to wonder if she was where the bugs said she was. Paola silently crept up behind him. At three metres away, too far for him to swing and kick, she said in a soft voice, "Lost someone?"

The guard spun around, his dark eyes a mixture of shock and anger. He stood, pocketing the tracking monitor as he did to free up both hands. He was around twenty years old and tall: about six foot five like Dayton. He faced Paola, holding his well-toned arms out slightly from his sides, flexing his fingers, his mouth a sneer.

"Not any more, bitch," he said in English, his accent New Jersey.

"That's not very friendly," said Paola cautiously. She was surprised at his accent, and there was something familiar about his face.

"I'm not paid to be friendly," he said, shifting his weight from one foot to the other.

"Didn't your boss say you had to be nice to me?" Paola was noting every twitch of every muscle.

"He didn't say nothin' about being nice; he just said not to kill you. Didn't say nothin' about not hurting you though, if you try to get away."

"Then I'd better be a good girl," replied Paola, her tone steely. "You're a long way from home, sonny boy, won't your mommy be missing you?"

From the black cloud that descended on the young man's face, she knew she'd hit a nerve.

His face hardened. "She ain't sayin' nothin', not since you killed her, bitch."

"Killed her?"

"Yeah, you deaf? You killed her at your house. Don't you remember? Or do you cut so many people's throats that you forget them?"

"That woman with Dayton in Cape Cod was—"

"My mother. Yeah. And you cut her down."

"It was self-defence."

"She was only going to sedate you."

"How was I to know that?"

"There's self-defence and there's cold-blooded murder, bitch. My mother was a good woman. It weren't easy for her."

"She didn't strike me as a good woman. And I couldn't care less if it wasn't easy for her, I'd do the same again." Paola had fixed her eyes on the man's, the expression on her face menacing, intimidating. He was young; perhaps he would be susceptible to her stare. She wanted to rile him, make him angry. *Angry people are careless.*

He closed his right fist and balled it into his left palm, closing his fingers over it as he took a slight step forward, then another.

All the while she'd been standing there, Paola had been partly concealing her left hand. Just before approaching the man, she had stooped to pick up a handful of almost dry, powdery earth.

She saw a tightening of his shoulder muscles as he prepared to swing a punch. It was time. She hurled the handful of earth at his eyes and in the same moment she launched her right foot in a powerful kick to his groin. Her aim was good and the man doubled over, one hand rubbing furiously at his eyes while the other clutched at his manhood. Knowing he wasn't seeing her clearly, Paola sidestepped, spun around and swung another hard kick at the side of his head, connecting with his temple. He grunted and fell sideways, a hand reaching for the point of impact. Paola wasn't angry; she was calm and anything but careless, but her survival instincts were deadly as the demon in her took over. She picked up a thick length of broken branch from the ground, swung it high over her head and smashed it down on the man's skull. The wood had a pointed protrusion on one side, the hardened remains of a smaller branch. It made the weapon as deadly as any axe. The protrusion penetrated three inches into the man's brain, rendering him totally helpless. But that didn't stop Paola from delivering three more skull-crushing blows, just to be sure.

It was all over in seconds. Paola stood over the body, a snarl coming from her throat, her lips pulled back over her teeth. She remained motionless, clutching the branch in both hands until her breathing subsided and the sounds of the woods returned, the wind rustling the branches of the trees.

Paola threw the branch to one side and bent over the body, going through the jacket pockets. She was hoping to find a cell phone but there was just his damn radio attached to a loop on his belt. She knelt and put her arms around his waist to feel what else was attached to his belt. Nestled in the small of his back was a leather sheath holding a knife. She unclipped its fastening and removed it. The weapon was a good one with a six-inch, double-edged steel blade; expertly honed.

As she sat back on her heels balancing the knife in her hand, she heard a crack from behind her as something stood on a twig. She started to stand, turning as she did, and she was knocked backwards by a whirl of arms and legs crashing into her. She hit the ground hard, landing awkwardly and winded, momentarily trapped beneath her attacker. She flexed her body, ready to launch a counter attack when she noticed that her attacker wasn't moving. It was then that she realised that she was still gripping the knife handle, its blade buried in her attacker's chest. She rolled the body off her and sprang to her feet, her eyes searching the space around her for signs of anyone else. But there was no one. She looked down at the body and started in surprise. Lying on her back at Paola's feet was a woman in her early twenties, dressed for tracking like the guard. She thought she had seen most of the guards and so far they had all been men. This young woman, her face frozen in shock at the moment of her death, was not unlike Paola herself. Her black hair was longer and her skin darker, but the oval of her face was similar, as were the high cheekbones and small, attractive nose.

Paola stared at the body, trying to control her breathing. The girl's death had been a total accident. However, when she considered it, while the attack had been wild and ill-considered, the girl clearly had every intention of killing her. If Paola hadn't been holding the knife, there would have been a vicious struggle, but the outcome would have been the same: the girl would have died.

She glanced at the guard's body and remembered what she'd been doing when the girl appeared out of nowhere. Perhaps she had what Paola was looking for. She felt through the girl's jacket and smiled. A cell phone. It was turned off, presumably as a precaution against a ring tone shattering the silence of the woods. She pressed the button and it powered up. The battery seemed good and within ten seconds, two bars of a signal appeared. She stared at the screen. Who was she going to call? She didn't know any numbers. She felt a slight panic rising as her eyes flashed around the trees. Was that someone else? No, it was just some animal. Who the hell could she call? Although John had normally called her, she'd also called him several times from Cape Cod, so why didn't she know his number? Of course! Lily had programmed the number into her contacts list. Damn! There must be someone. She had to know someone's number. The gallery. What was the number for the gallery? Again, it was programmed into the list. She stared at the phone's screen, almost crying in frustration. Then she remembered. Rodrigo. Why did she remember his number? She didn't know why but she did. It had been one she'd always punched in rather than speed dialled. She just had, dozens of times. But Rodrigo Barros, Paola's devoted friend and confidant in Brazil for more than twenty years after she fled the US, now a comandante of police in Rio de Janeiro, was thousands of miles away, possibly still in bed asleep. Would this phone even make international calls? What the hell was the code for Brazil? +55, that was it. She punched the number. A series of disconnected squeaks and disembodied screeches sounded in her ear and then to her relief she heard the dialling tone. It rang and it rang, and it continued ringing. Come on! Eventually, after thirty frustrating seconds, there was a click.

"*Alô.*"

Paola immediately broke into Portuguese. "Rodrigo, it's Cassie."

"Cassie? What—"

"Listen, Rodrigo, I'm sorry but I'm in a jam. I need you to call someone in England but I don't have his number. His name is John Andrews. Have you got that?"

"Of course Cassie, but—"

"Just listen, Rodrigo. Can you tell him I'm in Italy being held by Dayton? I don't know where exactly but it's very wooded and rugged. It could be somewhere in Tuscany. It reminds me of when I was in a convent."

"A what!"

"Long story."

"OK, listen, Cassie, that name, do you have any other information?"

"Yes, he knows me as Paola and he lives—"

The phone beeped and went dead. Paola stared at the screen in horror. The battery still registered as half full; it must have run out of credit.

She wanted to smash the phone but then thought better of it. She pressed a few buttons and erased the call memory, switched it off and placed it back in the dead girl's inside pocket. She then remembered the tracking device monitor the guard had been carrying, found it and turned it off as well in case it emitted a signal that located it. She looked down at the bodies. The guard was already half-hidden in a pile of fallen leaves and Paola quickly excavated a shallow pit next to him by scooping away more leaves and earth. She rolled his body into the depression and then turned her attention to her other victim. She bent over and removed the knife from the girl's chest. Should she keep it? She decided against it, tossed the knife onto the guard's body and then dragged the girl's body to lie next to it. She completed the job by piling earth and leaves on top of both bodies. At least they would not now be seen by accident.

There was a flash of lightning followed in five seconds by an enormous crack of thunder. The clouds had come down, plunging the forest into a sinister gloom. She was about to run back in the direction of the route to the fence when she remembered the bugs.

They would be found near the body. She hurried over to where she had been hiding earlier and retrieved them from under the rotting log. She'd put them back in her clothing later. There was another flash and this time the thunder followed in just two seconds. As the electric crackles and crashes reverberated around the forest, the rain started, turning from a few hesitant drops to torrential in a matter of moments.

She ran through the woods until she came across the track that she knew led to the south gate. She peered through the rain; it was like being underwater and if anything, it was getting heavier. Her head turned from one direction to the other. Should she continue in the direction of the gate and try to escape, or give up and return to the warmth of the house?

The voice came out of nowhere.

"Signora!"

Paola jumped in shock. She hadn't seen him coming and the noise of the storm drowned all other sounds.

She turned. It was another young guard, but with his mop of tight black curls this one looked distinctly more Italian. She tensed, for a moment regretting leaving the dead guard's knife with his body, but the man's body language indicated no threat.

"You should return to the house, signora," he shouted, leaning towards her. "This storm is bad, it could be dangerous in the woods; sometimes trees are struck by lightning."

"Were you following me?" yelled Paola.

"No, signora, I was looking for you. And for my colleague, Jason. Have you seen him? He's my age. Americano."

Paola shook her head.

The guard shrugged. "Oh well, he'll find his way back. He's brilliant in the woods; he can track anything. You wouldn't have known he was there if he was standing right behind you."

Chapter Thirty-Two

By the following morning, the violent storm had subsided to a squally downpour that continued with dogged persistence. Paola sat alone at the small breakfast table that had been set for her in the smaller sitting room, looking out of the windows for a break in the clouds. She suddenly saw a mud-sodden guard come running out of the woods waving his radio in what looked like frustration, as if to indicate it had succumbed to the onslaught of the weather. He was gesticulating wildly back into the trees and shouting. Five other guards ran from the left side of the house to join him and the party set off into the woods.

The maid who had just come in with Paola's breakfast was even more sullen than usual and seemed far more interested in the activity outside than in attending properly to the table. As she poured Paola a cup of coffee, her hand slipped and the hot liquid slurped into the saucer, splashing onto the starched linen tablecloth.

"Careful, you idiot," admonished Paola. "If you want to join those mud-soaked novices, feel free, otherwise, watch what you're doing."

The maid gave a swift, mocking curtsey. "Pray forgive me, Your Grace," she said, making no attempt to hide her insolent tone as she mimicked Paola's flowery sixteenth century Italian. "I trust thou hast not suffered any inconvenience as a result of my unfortunate incompetence."

"Get out before I throw the coffee pot at you," stormed Paola.

The maid scurried away, a grim but victorious smile on her face.

Paola glanced at the breakfast selection but she was distracted. She knew that a human form of the storm was about to enter the room and she anticipated it would be every bit as wild. She wasn't wrong. Two minutes later, the door from the corridor crashed against the wall and Marcus Dayton burst in.

"What the hell have you done, you stupid woman!" he railed.

Paola raised her eyebrows innocently as she concentrated on choosing a piece of fruit. "I don't know what you mean."

"You've killed two guards, that's what I mean! In cold blood! They've been searching for them for half the night, despite the foul weather, and they've just found them. One beaten to death and the other stabbed in the heart! Christ, Paola, what were you thinking of? They want to call the police; have you arrested!"

"Now that *would* be interesting." Paola looked up and caught his eyes. "Tell me, how would you explain my presence here?"

"Oh, don't worry; it's not going to happen," growled Dayton. "They know that, but given the background of most of those guards, they are going to want to mete out some form of retribution. Their way."

"Then you'll just have to protect me, Marcus dear. I'm a valuable commodity. Maybe you can sit outside my room with a shotgun."

"Why did you have to kill them, Paola? They were so young. Still under training."

Paola snorted her derision. "I think the millennia are catching up with you, Marcus. You're getting soft. You're a risk-taker, or have you forgotten? When you take risks, play with fire, sometimes you get burned. Or your minions do. Come on, Marcus, they were cannon fodder you sent out to test me and they failed."

"You heartless bitch!"

"Now, now, Marcus. That's what he called me. And look what happened."

"What do you mean, that's what he called you?"

"Marcus, I didn't approach the guard with the intention of killing him, or even hurting him. He turned on me, threatened me, and was about to attack me. I'm pretty good at reading the signs, you know. He's not the first man who's thought his superior height and strength would be enough to get the better of me. As far as I was concerned, I had to protect myself. It was self-defence."

She paused, pursing her lips.

"OK, perhaps I went a bit far; you know what I'm like. But it was clear to me that he hated me and regardless of your instructions, I think he might have either killed me or severely injured me, despite the consequences. Actually, Marcus, I'm staggered. You ask me what *I* was doing. What the hell were *you* doing employing him here as one of the squad watching me? The woman who killed his mother? You must be mad!"

Dayton surveyed her from under his eyebrows, his mouth pinched and his nostrils flared like a bull considering mayhem. Paola calmly buttered some toast while she waited for his anger to subside.

Finally he sighed heavily, pulled out a chair and sat at the table opposite her. "I see now that it was a huge mistake. But he showed promise, Paola, and Edith was quite persuasive. I thought that his resentment towards you would give him an edge, ensure that he was thorough."

"Thorough enough to kill me?"

"I don't think it would have come to that. And he was excellent in the forest; he could track someone all day and they'd never know. He's been tested on a number of occasions by his colleagues."

"Come on, Marcus, he wasn't that good. You know he cheated, don't you?"

"Cheated?"

"There had to be something giving him that edge. I learned my craft in the forests of Germany in the early 1700s, and I'm good. I'm like a wraith when I want to be. I can move in total silence and remain invisible. There had to be another reason for him finding me and I found it, or rather, them."

Dayton looked puzzled.

"Bugs, Marcus. There were bugs planted in my clothing. He was simply following their signals. Any idiot could do that. He was like so many people in this weird century of dumbed-down humans, slaves to their electronics: he relied totally on the stupid screen in his hands and forgot to use his eyes and ears. I've done you a favour."

"I'd still have preferred to fire him rather than bury him," muttered Dayton darkly. "Bury them, I mean," he added as he remembered the girl. "What about the girl, Paola, why did you kill her?"

"That was a total accident. I was holding the knife when she threw herself at me. She was actually quite good; I didn't hear her coming until she was flying through the air. The next thing I knew she was lying dead on top of me. Who was she?"

"She wasn't supposed to have been out there. Apparently she and Jason were an item, which was completely against the rules. If I'd known, I'd have fired them both."

He paused while he poured himself some coffee. "Paola. I didn't know about the bugs. Jason clearly had his own agenda. I apologise."

"No harm done. At least, not to me," shrugged Paola.

"Nevertheless, I think it would be better for you to remain in the house for a few days until the other guards have calmed down. I suspect they didn't know about Jason using bugs; they certainly haven't mentioned finding a receiver."

"I left it on his body so they would definitely have found it. I think your squad needs a bit of retraining, Marcus."

"I'll read them the Riot Act, for certain. In fact I think I'll replace them all; they're damaged and in danger of losing their focus on what's important. But I still want you to remain indoors."

"Mmm. I can only read so many books curled up by the fire. Maybe I'll start painting while I plot your downfall. Actually, I'd love to spend some more time looking at your art collection. May I do that? I promise not to damage anything." She raised her eyes to him, her lips pressed together in a coy smile. "I think you know that

I regard works of art like those as almost sacred; even if many of them are of you. I could never do anything to them."

Dayton thought about it for a moment. "Yes, of course you may. But I'd like something in return. Will you let Dr Ronaldi make some measurements, readings, whatever it is he needs to do? Nothing invasive. Can you agree to letting him do that without terrorising him?"

Having obtained Paola's agreement, Dayton left her to her breakfast and made his way to his private office on the first floor of another wing of the house, a room about which Paola knew nothing. As he locked the door behind him, he glanced across at the monitors of two super-fast computers that were each separately and securely connected to the Internet through scrambled data lines. But instead of sitting down, he walked over to the window and stared at the Tuscan landscape stretching away into the distance, the rain having finally eased into a light drizzle.

Although Paola was coming round to accepting she had little choice in complying with his plans, the incident the previous day had worried him. He would be reorganising the men who worked in and around the house, redeploying most to other locations, replacing them with a more experienced group from a house in the south he sometimes used. He would have to hope that despite the strong feelings all his guards had for Edith Cooper as a mentor, the replacement group would more readily regard her death as one of the risks of their trade. However, the killing of Edith's son and the girl, both of whom had shown such promise in training, would hit his colleagues hard. They would know that if they let their guard down for a moment with the unpredictable Paola, they could be risking their necks. Dayton was no longer confident that he could trust his men not to kill Paola and make it look like an accident. And until Ronaldi had secured a supply of Paola's eggs, her well-being was essential. Even then, there were no guarantees that his surrogacy plans would work; he needed Paola around and healthy for some considerable time. If he should lose her, his plans would come to nothing and he would have to start again. So why not improve his chances of success? Why not have Sara at the house as originally planned? From what he had seen, she was far less volatile. She might act as a calming influence on Paola and at the same time make Paola think that she was only part of the scheme, not its centre of focus.

He put his hands on a windowsill and took the weight of his body, stretching his arms and then his back and neck. He would be risking Paola's ire if he abducted Sara: she would be wild with rage to start with. But in the longer term she might be more disposed to being compliant, knowing that if she weren't, Dayton would turn exclusively to Sara. Sara would also be company for Paola, he thought; they were after all mother and daughter, and yet they hardly knew each other. They would obviously plot together; Paola would redouble her efforts to escape. But Dayton knew that escape was impossible, despite the problems the previous day. There were still many systems in place about which Paola knew nothing.

He walked over to the main desk and sat down, staring at the blank screens that were waiting patiently to burst into life as soon as he touched a trackpad. He picked up a telephone handset and stared at the buttons, still undecided. What was stopping him? Dammit! It was Paola and the thought of her anger. Abducting Sara would carve an even bigger distance between them than now. In his heart, he knew it was Paola he wanted as the mother of whatever offspring Ronaldi could conjure with his techniques, even though she wouldn't actually bear them and, according to his original plans, would have nothing more to do with them once a successful conception or conceptions had been achieved. Despite her wilfulness, her intransigence, her unpredictable behaviour and her tendency to kill when threatened rather than simply disarm or disable, he was becoming fond of her. He doubted that he could ever feel like that about Sara. He didn't even want to. So perhaps Sara was a better choice overall: he could remain entirely detached. But then what would he do about Paola? He could hardly release her.

He exhaled loudly, popping his lips. What to do? He thought of the incident the day before, of Paola's attitude and general disdain for her situation. She really did need to be taught a lesson, to be shown that she couldn't ride roughshod over the staff or him. He punched a number and then the connect button.

Palo Melliff was ensconced in his new computer heaven, surrounded by banks of the best of everything that would aid him in whatever task his boss set him, each task more demanding than the last. And the latest one was a tall order, even for Melliff. He knew his limitations, or at least he knew when an ask was too much. This one was crazy. Write a program to compare the artists of every portrait he could find painted in the last five hundred years? It was laughable. Just the notion of comparing them was totally ridiculous. He knew nothing about art but he had quickly realised that it was nothing like comparing photographs. For the first time, he felt that he was going to fail. But Marcus Dayton didn't accept failure; the word didn't seem to be in his vocabulary.

He could always disappear. He had made a pile out of Dayton and another pile by watching the way the man invested and then following his example. Carefully, of course, so that Dayton wouldn't notice. But he didn't want to disappear. Apart from anything else, Dayton had long arms; he was bound to catch up with him sooner or later, and that might be messy. So instead of disappearing, he had turned up the volume of the Bach fugues blasting through his soundproofed eyrie in a separate suite of offices in the Trevelyan building and processed alternative ways around the problem. That was how he had found Ced Fisher and his brilliant program. He couldn't believe his luck when he read about what it had achieved. It was perfect even if what Dayton wanted to do with it was nuts. It would surely be child's play. The geek who wrote this program was probably so in love with the lines of software that security would come a poor second to the execution of all the program could do.

How wrong had that been?

Since finding Ced Fisher, Melliff had spent days in increasing frustration trying to break into Ced's computer and examine the program, only to watch door after door and firewall after firewall slam in his face. His attempts were made doubly difficult since it was clear that Fisher's computer didn't just rebuff attempts at breaking in, it launched all-out counter attacks. Melliff found himself constantly fending off streams of data thumping into his system trying to locate, identify and destroy it. Even his unprecedented multitasking skills, which saw him controlling three massive screeds of computer code scrolling at blazing speed down his screens as he quietly issued commands through the microphone attached to his headset, were stretched to the limit.

He was, therefore, more than a little irritated when his phone rang, its screen telling him that it was his boss, Marcus Dayton. He had no choice but answer and watch in frustration as the lines of code he had been orchestrating tumbled out of control before his eyes.

"Melliff."

"Boss, Mr Dayton, sir, it's really not the best time. I—"

"This is important, Melliff. I need to know if the Farsleys have returned to their house in Boston."

"No, Mr Dayton, sir, they haven't. There's a sitrep from the watchers; you have only to click—"

"The sitrep's hours old and I need up-to-the-minute data. I need to locate Sara Farsley. Immediately, Melliff; it's of vital importance."

"But Mr Dayt—"

"You are to drop everything else you are doing and devote all your energies to finding her."

"But Mr Da—"

"All your energies, Melliff. It's more important even than the portrait comparisons I want done. By the way, how's that going? I'd like a result as soon as possible. But this is even more importa—"

"But Mr D—"

"There are no buts, Melliff, I need it done. What's so difficult? We know they went to England, don't we? Focus your search there."

"But Mr Dayton, I know ex—"

"Know what, Melliff. Exactly what do you know?"

"I know that I don't need to set up a search for Sara Farsley. I know exactly where she is."

"What! Why the hell didn't you tell me before?"

"Well, it's not easy when you've worked up a head of steam, boss, Mr Dayton, sir. And I only found out a little while ago."

He paused and was surprised when there was nothing but silence on the line.

"Boss? Mr Dayton, sir?"

"I'm waiting for you to tell me, Melliff."

"Oh yeah. Right. Well, I remembered that the Farsley girl Julie is always on her smartphone. When one of our watchers followed her into Boston, she—"

"Yes, Melliff, I know all that; it's ancient history."

"Right. So I reckoned that she would be texting her friends, wherever she is. And I was right; she texts all the time. And just to make things even easier, she posts on Facebook."

"Do you have an address?"

"No not yet."

"I thought you said you knew exactly where she was."

"Well, almost exactly. I'll have an address very soon."

"Good. In the meantime, I'll mobilise a team."

"What for, boss, Mr Dayton, sir?"

"Never mind what for, Melliff, just do your job. Now, although you don't have an address, do you know roughly where she is?"

"Of course. She's in or near a village called Grasmere in Britain's Lake District. She's mentioned several times that it's really cool."

"What's she doing there?"

"I don't really know. Sounds like a sort of family reunion."

"Interesting. And you're sure that her mother is there?"

"Pretty sure, yes, from a couple of things that were said in the texts."

"It must be her husband's family. Unless ... Check him out, Melliff; see if he has any British roots. In the meantime, I have some arrangements to make."

Chapter Thirty-Three

When she heard the tyres of an approaching car on the gravelled road leading to the cottage, Lola looked up from the recipe on her iPad and through the window. She smiled at the double toot that sounded and turned to John.

"That's very jaunty for our Crawshaw. He must think he's one of the family."

John walked over to the window to watch Claudia and Jacques as they got out of the car. "I wonder how they got on at Ced and Sally's. I'm surprised they didn't phone."

"I'm not," said Lola, a cat-like, all-knowing smile appearing on her face.

John turned to her, picking up on her tone. "Really?"

"Look at Claudia, John. She's not walking; she's floating. And Jacques can't keep his eyes off her."

She slipped her hand around John's waist and leaned her head on his shoulder. "I love you, John Andrews," she said dreamily.

"I love you too, sweetheart. What's brought this on?"

She punched his arm lightly and then squeezed it.

"It's so ... I don't know ..." Her voice cracked and she sniffed.

"Tears, Lola? It's not like you to be so emotional."

"You don't get it, do you?" she said, her head still pushed against his shoulder.

"Of course I get it. They're in love."

"I know they are, John. But think about it. When we first got together, one of the things that I couldn't get out of my mind on the days when I believed your story was how many other women there had been. How many other wives, lovers etc. Was I just one more? You made me feel very special but I couldn't work out how you could, I don't know, love me as much as you'd loved all the others. But seeing Jacques with Claudia, it suddenly all makes sense. After all, he's five times older than you and probably had far more wives, families and lovers. And yet, look at him. He looks like it's all so new, like it's never happened before."

"You can tell all that from watching them for five seconds?"

"Oh, John, stop being such a man! Of course I can! And it's wonderful."

John turned her to him and wrapped his arms around her, a large grin on his face. "I know exactly how he feels. I wake up every morning feeling like that."

She punched him again. "Soppy idiot!"

Claudia was still floating when she came into the kitchen holding Jacques' hand.

"Hi," she said, trying to sound nonchalant but still blushing slightly. "Sorry we're a bit late. Jet lag and a spot of shopping."

"I can see that," said Lola giving her a hug, "I noticed yesterday that there had been some adjustment to Jacques' wardrobe. And now you're wearing jeans, Monsieur Bognard. That's a first. You'll be turning up next time with a tattoo and piercings."

"He certainly won't," said Claudia rather more forcefully than she intended. "Well, maybe an earring." She looked up sheepishly at Jacques who was shaking his head very slowly.

"There's a great fire roaring in the sitting room," said Lola. "Why don't you three sit yourselves down in there while I make some tea?"

"Brilliant," said Claudia. "Can I help?"

"No need, thanks, Claudia. Go on through; I'll be there in a moment."

"Is everyone out?" asked Jacques.

John nodded. "Yes, the Farsleys have taken the girls and Lily to Keswick for lunch. Afterwards, they were going to treat the girls to an adventure place a few miles along the road from there. It has a large indoor space so it's open throughout the autumn and winter."

"Mmm," replied Jacques, pursing his lips.

"Is that a problem?" said John, picking up his friend's worry. "It'll be dark fairly soon, so I'm sure it won't be long before they're back."

"No. No, I'm sure it's not," said Jacques, but he didn't sound totally convinced. "OK, let's go through to the fire and we'll tell you about our conversation with Ced and Sally yesterday."

"So we were right to worry about Dayton looking further than Paola," said John after Jacques related the story of the attempts to hack into Ced's program. "He knows about Sara, of course, but it won't be long before he finds out about me, and that will lead him to Lily and Phoebe. I'm glad I called Digby about the potential threat."

"Has he acted on your request yet?" asked Jacques.

"Yes," said John, "he took it very seriously."

"There're a couple of spooks holed up in the woods with their binos trained on us right now," added Lola, waving her arm generally in the direction of Thirlmere. "I'm having to keep the bedroom curtains closed."

"Are they following you when you go out?" said Claudia.

Lola shook her head. "I doubt they would follow me since I'm of no interest to Dayton. Lily has looked for cars following her, but she's seen nothing. And I've no idea if Digby has anyone watching Phoebe at school. He's not likely to tell us."

"If they're good," said Jacques, "you'd never see them. Surely you haven't actually seen anyone in the woods?"

"No, of course not. It's just that Digby told John they were 'in place'." She wiggled her index fingers to mime speech marks.

"You can rest assured he will have someone watching Phoebe," said John, touching Lola's arm.

"I know, darling," she said. "What concerns me is how long is all this going to go on. Digby can't deploy people to watch you all for ever."

"No," agreed John. "Dayton needs to be found, and Paola needs to be freed. Maybe this Melliff person could be a way to him." He turned to Claudia and Jacques. "Did Ced have any idea where he was operating from?"

"No," said Claudia. "He's tried to locate him, of course, but he said that Melliff has covered his tracks too well. Ced reckons he must be something of a genius to have achieved what he did with finding Paola in the first place, and from the sophistication of the attack on the program. Fortunately Ced's a genius too, and he'd already anticipated much of what Melliff attempted in attacking his computer."

"Two geniuses squaring up against each other," said Lola. "It's like some gladiatorial contest."

"And just as serious," added John darkly.

"He's probably still in New York," said Jacques. "He could even be in the Trevelyan building. It's a hi-tech hub and would have the facilities Melliff would need. If Dayton rented other space there, it would be through completely different channels that have no connection to his MDCorp company. I'll ask Max to check out all the other tenants, but if there's one thing I've learnt about my twin brother, it's that he's devious. So I'm sure wherever he is, Melliff will be invisible to any checks."

"Maybe I can ask Digby if he can make any enquiries through his US counterparts," said John.

The sound of a car on the road outside interrupted their conversation. Lola got up to look through the window. "That's everyone now," she said, the relief sounding in her voice. "Thank heavens, I suddenly don't want to have any of them out of my sight."

A little over three thousand miles away in New York, Palo Melliff issued an instruction to one of his computers through the microphone attached to his headset, his eyes still roaming his monitors. "Text the boss. Tell him I have some news."

Within minutes, Dayton was on the line from Italy.

"What is it, Melliff?"

"I got the address where Sara Farsley's staying, boss, Mr Dayton, sir. It's some house near a lake called Thirlmere. It's in the Lake District, like the daughter's texts said."

"Whose house is it?"

"It belongs to a John Andrews. He lives there with his wife and kids. He's an artist."

"An artist. That's interesting."

"Yeah, and it gets better." Melliff was relishing being in a position to deliver his information slowly, knowing Dayton would be impatient for everything as quickly as possible.

Dayton knew the tone in Melliff's voice. He'd heard it before and he was quietly excited. "I'll just let you talk, Melliff, it might be quicker."

"OK, boss, Mr Dayton, sir. Him being an artist like Annie Carr, I thought he would be worth looking at. I checked for a website but interestingly, for an artist, there's not much, just the address of a gallery in the Grasmere place that Julie Farsley mentioned. No photo of him, just his name and the details of the gallery. So I went back to the data I got from Fisher. There wasn't much since he'd blocked all access to his emails. But the name John Andrews was there, in what I call shadows of information that remain when stuff is moved or deleted. No details, but the name came up quite a lot. They must either know each other pretty well or Fisher has done some work for Andrews. So I tried to look at Andrews' phone records, which is a bit tricky from here but I usually find ways in. However, not this time: they are completely blocked. I reckon this Andrews has connections in high places for that to happen."

Dayton was getting frustrated. He knew from Melliff's tone that there was good news coming and he didn't want to listen to all the minutiae of the chase.

"Where is this leading, Melliff?" he growled.

Melliff grinned at the monitor, pleased that he wasn't on a video link.

"Getting there, boss, Mr Dayton, sir."

"Today, Melliff, today, if you'd be so kind."

"Well, the next thing I did was to look back at Sara Farsley's calls and Andrews' number comes up a lot in the last coupla months. Nothing before. So then I wondered if Andrews travelled. Now this bit was a bit tricky, since again the information has been filtered. There was nothing in any airline data, but there was something from US Immigration."

"You got into US Immigration records?" Dayton was incredulous.

"It's something I've been working on for a while. I thought it might be useful. Anyway, Andrews has visited the US several times in the last three years and Boston very recently."

"Do you know where he's been staying?"

"Of course, it's on the forms. In New York he always stays with a woman called Lily Saunders. And guess what, she's also an artist. Not only that, but her website has no photo of her."

"So she's some lover? Who is she?"

"Not a lover, at least I don't think so. I needed to stretch my legs so I went to her gallery. Her assistant said she was away for a few weeks visiting friends in England—"

"Everyone's visiting friends in England."

"Precisely, boss, Mr Dayton, sir. Anyway, I found the address where she lives and last night I called into her apartment. I have a friend who's handy with locks, like you are."

"Skip the flattery and cut to the chase, Melliff."

"Struck gold. In a drawer by her bed I found some photos of a lady I assume to be her with Sara Farsley and Annie Carr."

"Annie Carr. You mean Paola was with them!"

"Yeah, and someone else who must be Andrews since there are several other photos of him with Saunders. What was really interesting, boss, Mr Dayton, sir, was their eyes."

"Their eyes?" Dayton was on the edge of his seat.

"All four of them have the same eyes. That weird pale grey that we noticed about Carr."

"Have you run the photos through your program, Melliff? Compared the faces?"

"Mr Dayton!" Melliff paused again, allowing the gentle admonition hang in the air. When the only reply was an icy silence, he continued. "Of course. They're all related. Even the Saunders woman, whose Asian features cloud the issue a little."

"She's Asian?"

"Eurasian, I'd say, given that she's probably Andrews' daughter. Half Chinese, at a guess."

"So we have another one. I want to see these photographs, Melliff."

"They should be in your inbox, boss, Mr Dayton, sir."

Melliff could hear Dayton tapping on a keyboard and imagined him sitting back in satisfaction.

"Got them," said Dayton. "Fascinating, Melliff. I'll print them out."

Chapter Thirty-Four

Although Dayton's UK team arrived in the Lakes within hours of being briefed, their leader insisted that they take their time before making any move. He didn't know the reasons behind the instruction to abduct Sara Farsley, but from Dayton's tone and the few background details he had imparted, Paul Westerly's professional nose told him to take extra care.

Posing as hikers, two of the team scouted the area around the Andrews' cottage while Westerly stood by on the Keswick–Grasmere road where he could see any cars that left the cottage and any vehicles that seemed to be following them.

The hikers were under strict mobile phone and radio silence, breaking it only with coded beeps on the radio to advise Westerly that a vehicle was leaving the cottage. But that didn't stop them listening. Included in their kit were digital and analogue radio receivers to monitor anything transmitted locally. However, Digby Smith's team were also careful, their encrypted and compressed routine messages to HQ being transmitted only once a day at five in the morning, the equally brief encrypted responses coming back on a different frequency after exactly ten minutes. All other messages were, as for Westerly's team, coded beeps lasting only fractions of a second. Hence the hikers had to wait through a long cold night before being rewarded with their first interception.

"Five o'clock on the button and precisely six hundred seconds between the end of the first message and the start of the reply," mused Doug, the elder of the two hikers. "This whole thing smells of the security services. Given this terrain, Lennie, whoever's sending these must be close by. Get over to that ridge, we'll get a fix from the next message and triangulate it. If he's as close as I think he is, we'll pinpoint his position to a couple of feet."

Unlike Doug, who seemed to revel in spending hour upon uncomfortable hour motionless in a bush or behind a pile of rocks in freezing, wet conditions, Lennie preferred action. He cast a rueful eye on the ridge, knowing what the next few hours would bring. He was right, but his frustrating and cramped wait in the mist and cold was worth it; the triangulation from the exchange the following morning told them that their man was six hundred metres away, more or less where they had predicted, in line of sight with the cottage.

Three and a half hours later, Doug picked up a beep from the man's radio that coincided with a car leaving the cottage. Lola was taking the girls to school. Back on the main road, Westerly noted the car heading towards Keswick and sent an instruction to the fourth member of his team, who was waiting in the town, to pick up the car and watch for any third party interest. Sure enough, Debbie, the fourth member, noted an apparently innocuous saloon car fall in behind Lola and station itself outside the girls' school, remaining there when Lola returned home.

This intelligence was duly reported to Westerly and followed up in another two hours when Debbie called him on his encrypted line to say that both girls' classes appeared to have left the school in separate groups. "Probably field trips into the town," she told him. "Interesting thing is that our friends only trailed after the younger girl's class. I got a good look at the kid as she passed me; pretty little thing, startling pale grey eyes."

The observations continued for the next four days, much to Dayton's frustration as he waited in Italy. He had agreed that following the problems that had accompanied his involvement in the aborted abduction of Sara in Boston and the successful but messy taking of Paola in Cape Cod, he would leave this job to the pros. But that didn't stop him pacing the room and barking orders down the phone to Westerly when he could. Paola noticed a change in him and wondered what was going on.

During the four days, Claudia and Jacques left for London, since there was nothing they could achieve by remaining in the Lakes. Claudia needed to report to the prof, who had returned from Australia and was puzzled by her prolonged absence, while Jacques reluctantly tore himself away from Claudia for as few hours as necessary to keep his multifarious business activities running smoothly.

Meanwhile, John was continuing to find it very hard to concentrate on his normal routine. What had promised to be a golden time of getting to know the daughter he had been convinced was alive had turned into a nightmare. He felt increasingly under siege, knowing that Dayton would be closing in on him but not knowing what he would then do. In the past, John would have disappeared, removed himself to another location and another identity. On this occasion it was too complicated. Now he knew what it was that Dayton wanted, John was also worried about Lily and Phoebe, particularly Lily since she would make a perfectly good alternative for Paola or Sara in Dayton's eyes, once he knew of her.

None of this was lost on Pete who was equally concerned for Sara, and he and John would spend hours in John's study discussing options while they waited for a breakthrough from Ced, who was trying and so far failing to locate Melliff, in the hope that he would lead them to Dayton.

John wanted to close the gallery. It was late autumn, there wasn't much trade and he thought it would be safer for Lola and the others to remain at home. But Lola was having none of it.

"We can't just sit around all day, John, we'll go crazy. We should have faith in Digby's security detail. Lily is sure that she's spotted the ones who follow her and I think I know the car that follows the girls and me to school. It sits there keeping a watch on Phoebe. As for Sara, there's obviously a team for her as well. So really, I'm sure it's perfectly safe for me, at least, to go to the gallery, since no one's interested in me. And Lily, Sara and Julie want to help. Digby's people are professionals, John, they know what they're doing."

And all the while, Paul Westerly continued to wait and watch as he learned the routines, absorbed the ways of the village, the comings and goings of the women to and from the gallery, and most importantly, he watched Digby's watchers until he felt he could predict their movements.

On the fifth day after his arrival in the Lakes, Westerly informed his team that he was changing the status of the operation from passive observation to potential completion of the brief: from now on, as and when an appropriate opportunity arose, they would act.

For Lola and the others, the morning was no different from any other recent morning. Lola had taken the girls to school and, having satisfied herself that Phoebe's minder, as she had taken to calling him, was parked outside the school, she returned home to pick up Lily, Sara and Julie to head for the gallery. John was intending to drive in after taking a call from Ced about progress, while Pete and Matt were taking advantage of a break in the weather to go hiking around Helvelyn.

Lunch in the gallery invariably comprised homemade rolls filled with local cheeses, fresh salad and a selection of prosciutto and other salumi from Gordon's Village Store about three hundred metres along the road, next to the Green Man pub. Julie would go with either Lily or Sara to fetch them, but today, she and Lola were ensconced in the studio working on a project to computerise stock and sales. It was one o'clock and Sara was hungry. She looked over to Lily, who was busy trying to persuade their first customer that day that she should buy a dramatic winter panorama of Derwent Water, and indicated that she was off to Gordon's store.

Lily looked concerned, not wanting her to go alone, but Sara pulled a face and put her hands on her stomach. "I'll just be a few minutes," she whispered from behind the customer. "Gordon knows our order and has probably made up the rolls already." She paused and then added, "And I'm starving," mouthing the words dramatically rather than speaking them. The shop doorbell tinkled as she left and Lily turned her attention back to her customer.

That morning's shift of Digby's watchers comprised two twenty-five-year-old women who had been in the service for three years. They were diligent, resourceful, skilled in unarmed combat and already veterans of 'watching grass grow' assignments, or 'wag-grows', as these tedious surveillance tasks were informally known. Both were sitting in a car fifty metres from the gallery. Michelle, assigned to Lily, was in the driver's seat quietly watching the gallery door, while Natalie, Sara's watcher, was checking data on her iPad.

"There's your girl, Nat," said Michelle, her hand moving to the ignition as she saw Sara emerge from the gallery. Then she paused. "Christ, she's on her own."

"Shit," said Natalie, putting down the iPad. "You stay here; I'll follow her on foot. She'll only be going to the village store."

She got out of the car, slung the long strap of her handbag over her head so that she had both hands free, and fell in about seventy metres behind Sara.

Across the road from the gallery was the Grasmere village green. In the summer, lunchtime would normally see it packed with tourists picnicking, poring over maps or simply relaxing after a hard morning of walking in the hills. Late autumn was entirely different, and although it was dry and the scudding white clouds held no threat of any rain, there was just one hardy soul sitting on a bench seat reading a book, her bicycle leaning against its stand in front of her. While to any casual observer, Debbie's eyes may have appeared to be focussed on the open book in her lap, they were concentrating mainly on the door of the gallery, with the occa-sional flicker towards the grey saloon parked down the street. She had identified the watchers three days before. They were rank amateurs in her opinion and she felt completely in control.

When she saw Sara leave the gallery on her own and head towards Gordon's store, she moved her eyes to the car. Sure enough, just one of the two occupants was out and on foot, striding after her charge while trying at the same time to look casual. Sensing this could be the opportunity, Debbie pressed the button of a tiny radio transmitter in a ring on her left hand. In the rear of a white van parked outside the Green Man pub, three men tensed as the signal sounded on the speaker of a receiver mounted in the roof. Paul Westerly smiled. "Ready lads?"

Debbie watched as Sara followed her normal routine of walking along the left side of the road to within about fifty metres of the bend that blocked the view of the village store from the gallery, checking the road for traffic and then crossing it. Debbie jumped on her bicycle and pedalled up the road, keeping Natalie, the watcher, just ahead of her.

Natalie walked on, beyond where Sara had crossed and then glanced back down the road. She noted only a woman on a bicycle about twenty metres away, but she was moving slowly, giving her plenty of time to cross. She turned her attention back to Sara who was now disappearing around the bend, walking past a motorcyclist who had stopped to study a map. Natalie stepped off the curb.

There was no shout, no alert, just the bicycle slamming into her, taking her totally by surprise and knocking her down. Her instincts cut in and before her head could hit the ground, her arms were out, but then the full weight of the bicycle and its rider caught up with her, propelling her left hand and wrist into the tarmac surface, shattering her wrist bones. She yelled in pain as the bicycle flattened her and Debbie's well-aimed forearm crunched her head into the ground, stunning her, skinning her nose and forehead, and splitting her lip. Debbie was on her feet in an instant, stamping on the bicycle frame as she rose, which jammed one of the pedals hard into Natalie's kidneys.

Debbie quickly pressed the button on her ring twice to indicate a 'go' and then turned her attention to her quarry.

"Christ, what were you thinking of?" she yelled as she yanked the bicycle from Natalie's sprawled body. She stepped forward, holding out a hand as if to help her victim, but as she did, she stepped down hard on Natalie's foot, turning it horribly sideways against her ankle. She heard a snap and another yelp of pain.

By then, two bystanders had rushed up to the two women. Debbie clutched her side as if winded. "She just stepped out in front of me," she wheezed. "I didn't stand a chance. I think she might be hurt. Could someone call an ambulance?"

She'd been keeping half an eye on the grey saloon, knowing it would be only seconds before it roared past to take over following Sara.

"Maybe this person can help," said Debbie, stepping farther into the road and directly in the car's path.

"Look out!" someone yelled.

The car screeched to a halt, stopping inches in front of her. The angry driver threw open her door and stormed out. "You idiot! I nearly knocked you down!"

Debbie ignored her and pointed at the battered mess that was Natalie lying in the road in front of them.

"I think she's hurt," she repeated, still clutching her side.

Michelle brushed passed her and bent down. "Nat, are you OK? How can—"

She paused in shock as Natalie turned her head to reveal her bloodstained face. Through the blood pouring from her lip, she slurred, "Mish, shtop her."

"What?"

"Shtop her!" croaked Natalie as forcefully as she could, lifting her one good arm towards where Debbie had been standing.

As the light dawned for Michelle, she was vaguely aware of the sound of a motorcycle. She sprung to her feet, spinning to face Debbie. "Where—"

Her question died as she saw the motorcycle accelerating away down the road with Debbie on the pillion seat.

"Well, I'll be," said one of the many passers-by who had now gathered. "Did you see that? That bloke just roared up, she jumped on and off they went."

"Jesus!" yelled Michelle as she took off, sprinting in the direction of the village store.

. . .

Moments earlier, unaware of the mayhem breaking out around the bend behind her, Sara had been passing the Green Man as she headed towards Gordon's store. She could see Gordon's large white Labrador sitting outside. It lifted its head in her direction, expecting to be stroked once she reached the store.

A large white van was parked in the pub's car park, close to the road. As she walked past it, its engine suddenly fired and she looked up with a start.

"Mrs Farsley?" The voice came from behind her.

She jumped in surprise; she hadn't seen the man walking round the side of the white van.

"Er, yes," she said, her eyes wary as she turned to face the man.

The man reached inside his jacket and produced a leather pass holder. He flipped it open to show her.

"Detective Sergeant Watkins, madam. I'm with the Cumbrian police. I'm afraid there's been an incident back at the house. Would you mind coming with me?"

"An incident? What's happened?"

"If you'd just get into the van, madam."

"I don't know. Shouldn't we go back to the gallery?"

Confused, she took a step back and turned in the direction of Gordon's, but there was now another man blocking her way. "I think the van would be easier, Mrs Farsley," he said.

She turned again, only to find the first man was now inches from her. She was penned in and she started to panic. Then she felt a jab in her arm and the man immediately started to blur. She was aware of two strong arms lifting her towards the side door of the van … and then of the van interior spinning fast … and then nothing.

The white van's side door slammed shut. The vehicle pulled into the road, turned right and accelerated away. By the time Michelle came pounding around the bend, it had disappeared from view, the only thing now moving being Gordon's Labrador as it settled back down on its belly, disappointed at having missed out on a stroke.

Chapter Thirty-Five

Lily's customer had decided to 'think about it' and was just leaving the gallery when the ambulance sped past, its wee-warring siren shattering the peace of the village. Lily looked up the road in the direction the ambulance was heading and saw the crowd gathered near the bend.

"Lola!" she yelled. "Something's happened. I'm going to check Sara's OK."

"No, Lily!" cried Lola, running from the studio. "I think I'd better go. It could be, I don't know, a trick. I think you and Julie should go into the studio; I'll put up the 'closed' sign and lock the gallery door. I'll be back straight away." Her eyes roamed the counter by the cash register. "Where did I put my phone? And my keys?"

"Here," said Julie, locating them immediately and handing them to her. "Look, why don't I go?"

"It's fine, Julie, really," said Lola. "Just go with Lily into the studio and make sure the rear door's locked. This one too."

She turned, rushed out of the door, locked it and pounded up the road.

Pushing through the crowd, she was just in time to see a stretcher being lifted into the rear of the ambulance. She couldn't make out who the injured person was but she was sure that it wasn't Sara. At that moment, Michelle barged through the crowd waving her ID at the ambulance staff. Lola immediately recognised her as one of the minders she'd seen on security detail over the past few weeks. The woman was talking agitatedly but quietly on her phone and did not appear to have noticed Lola.

"What happened?" Lola asked one of the passers-by as she suddenly realised who the injured woman was. A shiver shuddered through her body.

"Poor thing," said the elderly woman she'd spoken to. "A bicycle knocked her down. It must have hit her pretty hard; she's in a right mess. And then the woman on the bike, who seemed to be hurt as well, just jumped on a passing motorcycle and raced off. Very strange, dear."

Lola hardly heard the last few words as she turned to run. Sara must still be at Gordon's; she had to be at Gordon's. She had to find her.

She sprinted the hundred metres to the store and burst through the door.

"Hello, Lola, I was ju—"

"Gordon. Is Sara here? My American friend? You remember her?"

"Yes, of course I do, Lola. I've got some rolls all ready. Would you like to take them? There's—"

"Yes. No. I don't know." Her eyes made a frantic search of the shop. "Gordon, have you seen her today? She was coming here to collect the rolls."

"No, Lola, she's not been in. Mind you, I was out the back fetching some more … Lola?"

Lola had no time for Gordon's ramblings. As she ran from the store, she punched Sara's mobile number on her phone, but all she got was an unobtainable message. She ran back to the ambulance where there was now a police car and two other grey saloons stopped close to where the bicycle was still on lying on the ground. PC Jeff Roberts was peering at the bloodstains on the road as if they were going to impart some sort of wisdom to him, while a man in a grey suit was talking fast to Michelle.

Lola walked up to them, breathing heavily from her two sprints. "Sorry!" she said, interrupting them. She paused to gulp some air.

Then she remembered who they were and dropped her voice to a forceful whisper. "I know who you are and if you don't know already, Sara's disappeared." She eyeballed Michelle. "I've locked the gallery. Lily and Julie are in the studio." She waved her arm in the direction of the village store. "She didn't make it as far as Gordon's."

Michelle fixed her eyes on Lola, her nostrils flared. Lola could see she was fighting to control her emotions.

"Thank you, Mrs Andrews," said the man calmly. "Well done. Perhaps you'd like to go back to the gallery now. We'll be along in a moment to escort you all home."

Lola wanted to scream at him about the urgency to start looking for Sara, but his tone and body language told her to hold her tongue. She sighed in frustration and ran back to the gallery, pulling out her phone again as she ran and pressing the buttons for John's number.

When they arrived back at the cottage, John ran to meet them. "No sign?" he said as Lola got out of the car.

"Nothing," she replied. "We ran round the entire village, at least until Digby's man caught up with us. He seemed cross that we hadn't waited at the gallery. But when Lily wasn't absolutely certain that Sara had headed off in the direction of Gordon's, we had to check, just in case she'd had a notion to, I don't know, go shopping or something."

"I'm not surprised he was cross. He's made one huge cockup; he didn't want another."

"Yes," said Lola. "I was on at him immediately about the girls and he said he'd been in contact with his people outside the school and everything was fine. He suggested that rather than worry the girls, it would be better to leave them be. He didn't seem very impressed when I said I hoped that his people there were more competent than the two in Grasmere."

John took her hand. "I think that Sara was the only target. It's probable that Dayton either doesn't know about Lily or Phoebe, or if he does, he isn't sure whether they have our DNA or not. In any event, Digby has assured me that security will be stepped up."

"Hmm," snorted Lola. "Stable bloody doors."

"It must have been a well-planned operation," said Lily as she helped Julie out of the car. Julie's face was red and blotchy from crying. "I mean, it all happened so fast."

"Yes," agreed Lola, turning to take Julie's other arm. "And they meant business. You should have seen that girl who was tailing Sara. She looked more like she'd been run over by a bus than a bike."

"They must have been watching us and Digby's people for some time," said Lily, looking nervously across the fields to the woods beyond Thirlmere.

"Have you spoken to Pop and Matt?" said Julie, swallowing her tears.

"No," said John, "I've tried his phone several times but he must be in a dead spot. The signal can be pretty terrible in the valleys." He put his arm around her and walked her towards the cottage door. "Come on," he said, "let's get into the warm."

"What else did Digby say, John?" said Lola as she followed them into the kitchen.

"Well, he was clearly very shocked. He already knew about it when I called; his people must have contacted him immediately. He said they'll be checking all the ports and airports, particularly the airfields for private jets. He thinks that given the operation with Paola, it's likely that they will try to take Sara to wherever she is."

There was a cry from Julie as emotion took over again. "I should never have let her go out on her own. It's all my fault. You don't think they'll hurt her, do you?"

"Julie," said Lola, sitting down next to her and taking her in her arms. "It was far more my fault. I was distracted with that stupid computer thing. But listen, from what we know about why they took Paola, they certainly won't want to hurt your mom; it's the last thing they'll want."

As Lola was comforting Julie, John tried Pete's number again.

"Ah," he said, looking over to Lola, "it's ringing at last." He paused. "Pete. It's John. Listen, something's happened."

. . .

By six that evening, Pete, Matt and Julie were gathered around a blazing fire in the living room with John and Lola. Lily had volunteered to field the girls in their bedroom.

Pete had hardly sat for a moment since he and Matt returned earlier in the afternoon. He was now pacing the floor, impatient, restless.

He suddenly stopped by John's chair. "John, I'm really concerned that we should inform the US authorities as soon as possible. After all, Sara is a US citizen who's been abducted in one overseas country and probably taken to another. If anything happens …" He faltered.

John sighed. He understood Pete's point of view but he knew that Digby would never agree.

"Pete," he said, "we've been over this and there's really nothing to be gained. Perhaps if we knew where Sara and Paola are being held, it would be different. But for now, what reason could we possibly give for what's happened? Digby has us all tied up in the Official Secrets Act and wouldn't ever agree to my even being interviewed by the US authorities, let alone telling them anything."

Pete wasn't convinced. "I'm a lawyer, John, and under US law—"

"Which doesn't apply in this country, Pop," interrupted Matt. "John's right, you know, there's nothing the Feds or anyone could do here except throw their weight around, which would probably just make things worse."

Pete sighed and reached out to touch Matt's arm. "Yeah, I guess you're right, Matt. Wise words from a young head. It's just I feel so helpless."

"We'll know more once Digby gets back to us," said John. "Meanwhile, I know he has already sent a team to scour the woods out there to find where Dayton's people were hiding. He thinks they will have left something behind, something perhaps with DNA on it that his forensic people can examine. Maybe it will lead back to a person or people, if they have criminal records. If they can be picked up and leaned on, it could lead to Dayton."

Pete looked sceptical. "If they're as good as they indicated this morning, I doubt they'll have left so much as a hair out there," he said.

Their conversation was interrupted by John's phone ringing. He checked the screen and pressed the answer button. As he put the phone to his ear, he looked up at the others. "Digby," he mouthed.

He spent most of the next five minutes nodding and grunting. Finally he thanked Digby and rang off.

He sat down next to Lola, his eyes on the carpet, his expression heavy.

"It's probably, no, it's almost certainly as we thought," he said. "The police were quick to get to all the small airfields, concentrating on those that service private jets. They've checked through all the manifests from airports in the immediate area. Digby reckons that if they intended to head out of the country, they would have arranged a flight from somewhere no more than two hours' drive from here, probably far less. There were four flights that took off between the time Sara was taken and when the police started physically searching waiting aircraft. All were from Carlisle airport which, as you probably know, is about an hour away. Of the four, three had landed before the police could alert anyone. But one of those was to City airport in London and it was perfectly bona fide, as was another to the Isle of Man. And the one that hadn't landed was checked by the French authorities. It was bound for Lyons and again it was legitimate. That just leaves the fourth, which was a medevac to a small airport in Holland. The passengers were a doctor, two uniformed female nurses and an elderly woman on a stretcher. The paperwork had her as a Dutch national, but when the Dutch police followed up with the hospital that had supposedly arranged the medevac, there was no record, and later they found that the woman whose name was on the documents had died some years ago."

"So she's gone to Holland?" asked Matt.

"I doubt that's the final destination," said John. "All they needed to do was get her to the continent and for that, they would want to be in the air for as short a time as possible. Once they're on the road, there are no border checks anymore in Europe, apart from going in and out of Switzerland, so they can drive anywhere they like in the EU with impunity."

"So what do we do now?" asked Matt.

John shook his head, an expression of helplessness on his face. "I really don't know. Apart from making sure that Lily and Phoebe are well protected, all we can do is wait."

Chapter Thirty-Six

Two days later, Paola was pleased to find Marcus Dayton sitting at the small breakfast table that had been set up at her request in the sitting room. He hadn't joined her for breakfast for the past several days, making the excuse that he had urgent business that needed his personal attention. Paola wondered if this was true or whether he was still angry with her for killing the guards. Whatever the reason, she was finding her confinement to the house particularly tedious and she was concerned that if Dayton brooded, he might want to constrain her movements even further. She needed to turn on the charm and try to be less argumentative, less hostile. When she entered the room and saw him sitting there quietly buttering some toast, she realised she had actually missed his company, so being pleasant to him would require little effort.

"Marcus." She smiled and touched his arm. "This is a welcome surprise. Where have you been for the last few days? I've hardly seen you."

"I've, er, I've been rather busy," he said, a note of suspicion in his voice. He glanced up at her, and then turned from his toast to busy himself with pouring some more coffee. He lifted the pot. "May I pour you a cup?"

"Thank you, Marcus. One of the aspects of this prison that I really enjoy is the coffee. And of course the first one of the day is always special."

"This is hardly a prison, Paola. I doubt that even the most liberal of those institutions offers the luxury of this house."

"Just calling a spade a spade, Marcus." She smiled sweetly. "And like most prisoners, I am getting rather stir crazy. Could you possibly consider relaxing your rules and letting me into the grounds again? I promise not to hurt the guards."

He gave a short, dry laugh. "That's very reassuring, but I'm more worried about them hurting you. As I've already explained, I have no wish to lose you."

"How very sweet of you, Marcus. But if you're worried, why don't you come with me? The fresh air would do you good and you can be my protector. None of the guards would dare to make a move with you around."

"I'll think about it," he said, studying the pattern on his bone china cup. "However, I can't this morning; I have things to do."

He looked across the table at her relaxed and smiling face, and he felt his pulse increasing. He put down his coffee cup, worried that his grip might snap the handle. Then he leaned forward and propped his chin on his hands, his elbows resting on the table.

"Dammit, Paola," he said with a deep sigh. "You're such an enigma. I mean, look at you. You're an exceptionally attractive woman, who, to all intents and purposes, is around thirty years old. You're in your prime. You're witty, charming — sometimes, you're intelligent, and I think when you want to be, very caring. And yet when you're threatened, you're utterly ruthless and totally without compassion. I can't believe that having waited so long to find someone else who was like me, when I do, she turns out to be homicidal."

She laughed. "I'm not homicidal, Marcus. I just have a strongly developed sense of self-preservation."

Dayton grunted.

"Marcus, is something wrong? I mean, I know you're angry with me about the guards, but I think there's something else. You seem distracted, brooding almost, despite your attempts to flatter me."

She tilted her head at him, fluttering her eyelashes. "Do you really think I'm exceptionally attractive?"

"Stop flirting, Paola. You worry me when you're being so nice. I suddenly want to know where all the sharp knives are."

He straightened in his chair. In spite of what his heart might be telling him, his head demanded common sense. He was going to have to tell her, and he knew it would probably fracture the fragile relationship they had developed.

"I understand from Dr Ronaldi that you're still not being very cooperative, despite our agreement."

"You mean the one about me being allowed to roam the grounds?" she bristled, tossing her head dismissively. "Anyway," she continued, remembering that she was trying to be nice to him, "I don't know what you mean. I let him take his measurements every day."

"He tells me he needs more than just your blood pressure and heart rate. He needs to examine you more thoroughly, Paola. Internally. And that you won't let him."

"I'm sorry, Marcus, he just gives me the creeps. I'm not used to dealing with doctors since, like you, I have no use for them. No doctor in nearly five hundred years has ever come close to doing what he wants to do."

"But you've had children. Several children. Surely—"

She shook her head. "All delivered by midwives. It's different when it's a woman dealing with you, completely different. When it's some fawning little man with probing fingers ..." Her voice trailed off as memories of various priests pretending to perform exorcism while assaulting her appeared in her mind.

Dayton looked away as he gathered his thoughts; he was finding the conversation uncomfortable. Paola studied his face and misinterpreted his silence.

"Don't look like that, Marcus! I'm not a prude and I'm not frigid. My years in nunneries took away none of the healthy sexual appetite you'd expect from an exceptionally attractive woman in her prime." She flutter her eyelids at him before continuing. "It's completely different when it's your lover or husband. But that ... Ronaldi ..." she shuddered. "Couldn't you have got a female doctor?"

Dayton shrugged. "I'm afraid that I didn't give it much

thought. Obviously nowhere near enough. After all, a doctor is a doctor. And as I've told you, Ronaldi is the top man in his field, and it's a field that seems to be dominated by men. I think a female specialist would have been far harder to—"

"To what? Bribe? Coerce? Intimidate? Corrupt?"

A chill descended on Dayton's features, his eyes hardening. "I can't get anyone else, Paola, so I'm afraid that I'm going to have to insist that you cooperate."

"Well, I won't. And if those buffalos of nurses try to hold me down, they will come out of it badly."

"No, Paola, they won't. No one else is going to get hurt and I'm not going to take the easy way by sedating you. You *will* cooperate."

"God, Marcus! Are you deaf or just stupid?"

"Neither, as you well know. The thing is, Paola, I have a trump card in my deck. One that will overcome your objections."

Paola felt a sudden rising alarm. "What have you done?" she yelled.

As Dayton put his hands up, palms facing her, the door to the sitting room flew open and Dayton's head guard stepped quickly into the room, his eyes scouting the space, his body tense, expecting trouble.

"It's OK, Maurizio," said Dayton, "Ms Santini and I are just having a healthy discussion." He glanced down at the table. "Are you having any breakfast, Paola?"

She remained silent, staring at him darkly.

He stood. "You can always come back for it. In the meantime, perhaps you'd be good enough to come with me."

He bowed very slightly and indicated the door with his left hand.

The anaesthetic had worn off hours ago and, while she was still sleeping, the constraints had been removed from Sara's wrists. She was now awake, wondering where she was. She remembered nothing of the journey and apart from two huge nurses who had brought her a tray with soup, some bread and a jug of coffee, she had seen no one. She thought the nurses' behaviour had been rather odd. She had been sitting on the bed when they came in and the leading one had immediately held up a hand to tell her to remain where she was. The one with the tray had followed warily, placing the tray on a table at the far end of the room. When Sara made to get off the bed and ask them where she was, they scurried away quickly, locking the door after them. That had been a couple of hours ago. Since then, she had been doing some serious thinking as she stared through the barred window at the formal gardens and the autumn landscape of forested hills. The room was well heated, but it was obviously cold outside. The view offered her nothing, although from what she could see of the building from peering through the window, the place she had been brought to was large and old. To be still in England or even in the British Isles made no sense: Jacques had been certain that Paola had been taken to somewhere in Europe. Sara was sure that she must have been brought to the same place.

She was somewhat reassured by the fact that she wasn't bound in any way, although she was nevertheless confined in a locked room. She applied her lawyer's mind to her situation, considering what might happen next and what she should do: how she should behave and what she should say. She thought through everything that John and the others had learned so far, and more specifically, what they knew about Dayton and what Dayton might or might not know. How comprehensive was his information? Did he know that he had a twin brother who was still alive, a twin brother he had never met? Jacques hadn't known, it had been a total surprise to him, so the chances were that Dayton also didn't know. Which meant, of course, that Paola didn't know. In the brief time Paola and John were together or in one of their phone conversations, John might have told her about his enduring sea captain friend who was, like him, immune to ageing, but at that time none of them knew about Dayton. And Paola had been abducted before the connection between Jacques and Dayton was discovered.

Sara was sure that very soon Jacques' double was either going to walk through the door or she would be taken to him. She felt it was important that she didn't appear to recognise him. Knowledge was power, and the small amount of knowledge she had about Dayton and Jacques might be useful, might give her an edge. She would keep it in reserve.

What about Paola? Should she tell her? Of course she should. Paola was her mother and must be desperate to escape from this nightmare situation. But would she even be allowed to see Paola?

The thought of it as a nightmare triggered the memory of why she was there. She felt a cold tremor shudder through her body. He wants me as breeding stock, she thought. The bastard, what was he intending? Or rather, how was he intending it? Surely he wasn't expecting her to offer no resistance? Was he going to have her held down, strapped to the bed while he …? That was ridiculous. There was no guarantee that it would work. Was she going to be kept there for months, years perhaps, until she got pregnant? Pete had said something about it not being possible; something that Claudia had told him. Recessive genes, he'd said. Her knowledge of genetics was sketchy at best; she wished she'd asked Pete more about it.

Another thought struck and she looked down at her clothes in horror. Maybe he has already … while she was unconscious. But the clothes were what she had been wearing when she was taken. She was sure that they hadn't been removed or disturbed. She had a vague memory of being helped to the bathroom, but she was sure the person was a woman, and she had been returned to her bed.

Her thoughts, so controlled at first as she had analytically examined her situation, were now cascading out of control. Her heart had started to race and suddenly the room, which was quite large, felt horribly claustrophobic. She needed air …

She jumped as the sudden sound of a key turning in the door lock shattered the silence. She had been pacing the floor, but as the door opened, she backed against the wall furthest from it, her eyes wide with panic, like cornered prey before the inevitability of slaughter.

One of the two huge nurses came in and then stood aside, her back to the open door. She was followed by the even taller figure of … Jacques! Sara gasped involuntarily. But then she saw the livid scar on his cheek, the wound still not healed. And she saw a coldness in his eyes that she had not seen with Jacques. So this was Marcus Dayton. How could two men with essentially identical features have such a different mien? She swallowed. He mustn't know, not yet, that her reaction was because of his features.

"Mrs Farsley. Sara," he started, offering her a formal nod of his head. His voice was quiet, controlled, with the vaguest hint of a non-English accent. "I—"

But he got no further with whatever he was going to say as the sombre, quietly threatening mood of the room was shattered. Paola had followed Dayton into the room, and the sight of Sara leaning hesitantly against the far wall triggered an explosion.

"You bastard! I'll kill you!" she screamed as she spun towards Dayton, her right hand whipping across his face with a vicious slap.

Dayton had been expecting her reaction and he tried to ride the slap. He failed, but he still managed to follow it immediately by grabbing both Paola's wrists, spinning her and immobilising her from behind, her arms now crossed in front of her. He was strangely reassured that her attack had been with her open hand rather than with tearing nails. Paola lifted her legs and tried to kick backwards at him, but as she did, he forced her downwards so that her legs were pinned to the floor while he knelt behind her. Still she wriggled and squirmed, but his hold was strong and he knew she wasn't going to break free.

"Paola! For Christ's sake! Stop it! Don't destroy everything we've achieved. Think of your daughter. Think of Sara."

"How could you? *How could you?*" Paola's anger was rising again.

Dayton pulled hard on her arms. "Paola!" he said firmly. "You gave me no choice. I can't play this game of cat and mouse with you and Ronaldi forever. I want results. And simply threatening to bring Sara clearly wasn't enough. She had to be here."

"And how long are you going to keep us?" Paola yelled, still wrenching impotently against his grip. "You know very well that what you're trying to achieve could take months, years perhaps. Even then there is no guarantee of success. It's one thing to hold me against my will, but Sara has a husband, kids. They'll be beside themselves with worry. This is too cruel, Marcus!"

She slumped, but Dayton wasn't about to relax his grip. He was aware that Paola knew all the tricks.

"The ball's in your court, Paola," he said calmly. "Cooperate, and show that you intend to continue cooperating, and Sara can go."

He felt a change in the tension of her body. It was as if the fight really had gone out of her. "Dammit, Marcus, let go of me. I'll stop fighting. Let me talk to my daughter."

He cautiously slackened his grip, ready for any tightening of her muscles. He glanced over to where the nurse was standing and noted she was poised, prepared for action at the first sign of a move from Paola. He suddenly let Paola go, stood up and took a step back, watching, waiting, but there was nothing. Finally Paola dragged herself to her feet, walked two paces and sagged onto the bed, her arms folded defensively across her chest. She lifted her eyes to his. "Just get out, Marcus!"

Dayton stood his ground for a moment and then decided it best to leave the two women alone. He tossed a glance of instruction to the nurse and she followed him out. As the door closed behind them, Paola turned to her daughter who was still standing at the far end of the room, her back against the wall.

"Sara, I'm so sorry. It should never have come to this."

Sara walked over to her and sat down, taking her hand.

"Paola …" She paused, hesitating, undecided. Then she said softly, "Sorry, I can't call you Mom, it seems just too strange. Oh, gosh, I'm not thinking. Perhaps you'd prefer—"

"No, Sara, you're right. You can't call me Mom any more than I can call you Serena. Those days are gone."

"But I can still hug you," said Sara as she put her arms around her.

Paola put her head on Sara's shoulder and they sat motionless for a few moments.

"Are you all right, Sara? They haven't hurt you?"

"I'm fine, and I'm very relieved to see you. I was a little groggy when I woke up, but my head's clear now. I realised that I must have been brought to the same place as you. You see, we've worked out what's going on, or rather, Claudia did."

Paola sat up straight and turned to her. "Who's Claudia?"

"She's the geneticist who profiled John's DNA, pursued him, worked out why he and therefore we are like we are."

"Yes, I remember now. John mentioned her name."

"We know that Dayton is the same as we are and that he wants children with our traits, especially since the death of his daughter."

"You know about that too, do you? You've obviously been working hard behind the scenes."

"You'd be amazed. But what concerns me is what Dayton has done already. I mean …"

Paola gave her a slight smile as she slowly shook her head. "Don't worry, he hasn't raped me, if that's what you mean. In fact, he's trying his hardest to be honourable, if abducting and imprisoning someone can be honourable."

"Who's this Ronaldi he mentioned?"

"He's some kind of expert in IVF. Marcus wants him to harvest my eggs and fertilise them in his laboratory using Marcus's sperm. He then plans to implant them in someone else he's got ready and waiting. A surrogate mother."

"I see. So he wants a child or children from you, and he assumes that they will be like us, but he doesn't want you to carry the baby or to be involved with them?"

"Yes, that's about right. He says that once he's achieved his goal, he'll let me go."

"But that could take years. In fact, Claudia thinks that it won't work at all. Something to do with recessive genes."

Paola shrugged. "She could be right. After all, if our genes were more dominant, the world would be populated by people like us, and it's not. But there must be a chance it would work, surely. After all, we exist."

"Maybe," said Sara. "I'm afraid that science and I have always been strangers." She looked around the room. "I assume he's brought me here to increase his chances of success? Two sources instead of one."

"Actually, I don't think so, not for the moment, at least. You heard him: if I cooperate, he'll let you go. Your presence is a way of forcing me to comply."

"Do you think he would? Let me go, I mean."

Paola shook her head. "I really don't know; he's a hard man to predict. I've got to know him quite well in the short time I've been here, I've made a point of it, tried to get under his skin. It's strange. Behind that ruthless, calculating exterior, there's a sad, vulnerable and rather lonely man. I can understand that, being so old myself, although he's far, far older. It kind of goes with the territory. But I think that finally having a daughter who was like him, and then losing her, has affected him profoundly."

"You sound like you almost agree with what he's done," said Sara, unable to keep the surprise out of her voice.

"Hardly. And I can assure you that I've given him a hard time."

"So I take it you haven't been cooperating."

Paola smiled grimly. "Ronaldi is a creepy little man who just makes me shudder. The thought of him touching me is utterly repugnant. I've had endless rows with Marcus about it, and during those he's threatened to abduct you to try to force my hand. But I didn't think he would; I really didn't think he would. That's why I'm so sorry, Sara. I underestimated him. If I'd cooperated, then you wouldn't have been taken."

"I don't blame you. Why should you cooperate? But now he has brought me here, what do you intend to do?"

"I'm thinking of saying I'll go ahead and then killing Ronaldi. That should delay things."

"Killing him!" Sara was shocked. "I don't think that's a good idea. That would be murder; you'd be answerable."

Paola shrugged. "I doubt it. Anyway, I've already killed two of his guards. Marcus was cross, but he seems to have gotten over it."

Sara was shocked. "You killed someone here. Paola, I—"

"Look, Sara, I've been in situations like this before. Abducted, I mean. Had men try to force themselves on me. Some succeeded, but they all regretted it."

Sara was shocked by the coldness in Paola's eyes as past scenes were clearly playing in her mind. When she spoke again, her voice was distant, tinged with a mixture of regret and threat. "I'm afraid I'm not quite the daughter that John thinks I am. As well as his traits, I have inherited my mother's ruthless single-mindedness."

"That's one way to put it," said Sara. "Look, I really don't think you can kill your way out of this. Firstly, Dayton could just turn his attention to me if he thought I would be less hostile, or he might write both of us off and turn to Lily or even Phoebe." She dropped her voice, suddenly worried that they might be overheard. "Does he know about them yet?"

"I don't think so. But you're right: he's bound to find out about them before long. But Phoebe's just a child, Sara—"

"He's waited two and a half thousand years, I don't think waiting a few more for her to grow up would worry him if he thought it was a better alternative."

Paola got up and walked to the window, looking for inspiration in the wintery landscape.

"I'm going to have to string him along to buy some time. I think I can stretch the Ronaldi thing for a little longer," — she shuddered again — "maybe, maybe not. I can't kill Marcus since I know that if he dies, his guards here would kill me for certain, and possibly both of us. So we'll have to escape. It's the only option."

"Surely this place is very well guarded."

"It is, but the estate is huge and there are only so many guards. I'm good in the forest, as I suspect you are. I think we could shake them off and get to the fence easily enough."

"So long as by shaking them off you don't mean killing them all."

"Needs must, Sara. I wouldn't expect you to be party to dealing with any … confrontation."

Sara watched as Paola concentrated her mind on a strategy. She was shocked at the calm way this woman, her mother, talked about cold-blooded murder. She knew from Dr Wright's notes that when Paola was Annie Carr she had killed to survive. But this cold-heartedness, a glibness almost, in the way she considered killing someone who was in her way, Sara found abhorrent. Did Paola actually enjoy killing?

"What happened with the guards you … killed?"

"There were two, a young guard and his girlfriend. She was also a guard, but under training. I was exploring the forest, with Marcus' consent. The young man tracked me down but I outwitted him. He went for me. I can assure you he had every intention of inflicting serious harm; I had little choice." She thought back over each of the skull-crushing blows she had delivered. "In fact, no choice at all."

She continued to replay the scene in her mind. "Then the girl came at me out of nowhere. I was holding the guard's knife and she literally impaled herself on it."

Sara was about to ask for more details when there was a knock on the door and the two huge nurses came in, their eyes wary.

"Ah," said Paola, "Tweedledum and Tweedledee. What do you want, you oafs?" she spat at them, repeating it in Italian.

The one closer to Paola replied at length. Sara didn't understand what she said but she thought the tone sounded sarcastic. She watched for Paola's reaction.

"One day …" snarled Paola, glaring at the nurse. She turned to Sara. "Marcus wonders if we would like to join him for tea in the sitting room," she said, her voice also inflected with sarcasm. "You'd think we were guests in some country hotel, not victims of his scheming. Let's go, we mustn't keep our host waiting."

Chapter Thirty-Seven

Paola walked into the sitting room as if she were mistress of the house, while Sara hovered by the door.

Marcus Dayton stood to face them.

"Paola. Sara," he said, the wariness clear in his voice.

Paola ignored him and sat down on one of the large sofas next to a coffee table set with cups, saucers, and a bone china teapot. She sat back, crossed her legs and sprawled an arm along the back of the sofa.

"How disappointing, Marcus, I thought we'd be in the large sitting room."

"We can easily go in there if you want, Paola," said Marcus, somewhat bemused by her mood.

"It doesn't matter," replied Paola, keeping to her dismissive tone. "Sara, come, sit here, you can see the view. Even in this cold season it's really stunning."

Sara glanced hesitantly at Dayton. He held out an arm towards the sofas, bowing his head very slightly. Sara sat down, surprised by Paola's display of bonhomie.

"Shall I pour?" said Paola, leaning forward. Then she paused. "No, Marcus, you're our host, you do it."

Dayton made to bend over the tray when Sara interrupted. "I'll do it," she said, wanting to occupy herself as she gathered her thoughts.

"Thank you, Sara," said Dayton. "I feel I owe you an explanation as to why you're here."

"I know very well why I'm here," said Sara icily as she weighed the teapot in her hand, surprising herself with thoughts of dashing it against Dayton's head. "I assume the penalties for abduction and forcible detention are as strict in this country as in the States. Not to mention anything else you have in mind. You'll be going to prison for a long time once the authorities catch up with you. And they will, have no doubt about it."

Dayton's smile was patronising.

"No, Sara, they won't. Catch up with me, I mean. There will be no cavalry of any nationality riding over the hill. I have far too many safeguards in place. But I do apologise to you. I certainly didn't want to inconvenience you by bringing you here. I had hoped to come to an arrangement with Paola, but ..." He shrugged.

Sara banged the teapot down on the tray. "Do you honestly think that my husband is sitting at home doing nothing? You may think you have 'safeguards' in place, but I can assure you he'll be moving heaven and earth—"

"Sara," Dayton interrupted, his tone still patronising. "If heaven and earth comprises the people who were assigned to protect you, I'm sorry to tell you that they are not up to much. My team had no problem outwitting them."

He paused, his eyes boring into Sara's. "Mind you, they were clearly well connected. It makes me wonder just who this John Andrews you've all been clustering around really is."

Sara felt as if a bucket of icy water had been flung in her face. She clenched her jaw, trying her best to retain her courtroom mask, but she knew the alarm must be showing in her eyes. Paola felt the same. This conversation had gone far enough. She decided to stop it there.

"That's enough, Marcus, you're a bastard and I'm not through with you, but for now you have the upper hand. I've come to a decision. I will cooperate with you, or rather with that revolting creep of a doctor. But there are conditions."

Dayton raised his eyebrows slightly and waited.

"In return for my cooperation," continued Paola, "I must have a full return of my freedom to explore the estate. If I spend another day cooped up in here I'll be climbing the walls. Sara must have the same freedom. We want to go for walks whenever we choose and remain unmolested by your hounds. Tell them to keep their distance."

Dayton nodded. "That seems reasonable; I appreciate your change of heart."

"You haven't given me much choice," growled Paola. "Now, there's another condition. I want a sensible timeframe for Sara's release. You are not to keep her here for any longer than necessary. And I want you to somehow communicate with her family that she is alive, safe and coming home soon."

"I can't give you a timeframe, Paola, you know that," replied Dayton, shaking his head.

He turned Sara. "I apologise, but you must understand that I have reservations about sending you on your way just yet. I have to see something positive coming out of all this. If I release you now, I'm concerned that Paola will revert to her previous position."

"I've told you I'll cooperate," snapped Paola. "Surely once your little man has got what he wants, Sara can go."

"It's not as simple as that, Paola. Dr Ronaldi will of course obtain sufficient eggs for multiple attempts, but if they all fail, he would need to come back to you. I don't want him finding you resistant if he approaches you a second, or third or fourth time."

"So what are you saying?"

"I'm saying that once we have a successfully fertilised egg implanted in the surrogate mother, then I can consider releasing Sara."

"But that could take months."

"Possibly, but I am quietly confident. Dr Ronaldi is very competent, as I've told you."

He held out his palms. "It's the best I can offer you. But in answer to your, what shall we call them, conditions? Please feel free to explore the grounds and the woods to your hearts' content, both of you."

Sara's eyes flickered between Dayton and the woman she was

finding it increasingly difficult to believe was her mother. She was trying to understand the dynamics of their relationship, the mood of which seemed to change by the minute. Dayton's overall game was clear: he was used to getting exactly what he wanted and he was not prepared to stop in this venture until he had succeeded. But Paola's position was confusing. Some moments she appeared almost intimate with her captor, others aggressively antagonistic. Which of them was real? Was either of them?

Paola suddenly jumped to her feet. "We shall," she said. "Come on, Sara, let's find some warm clothes and give the guards some exercise."

The following morning after breakfast, the two nurses escorted Paola to a part of the house she had not been allowed to see before. It was a small wing on the first floor comprising four rooms fitted out as a state-of-the-art clinic. She was shown into a spotless examination room from which she could see through a half-glass wall into a laboratory next door. The laboratory contained several deep freezes, centrifuges, microscopes, an array of glassware and the inevitable computer monitors. One of the nurses pressed a switch by the door and a set of blinds swished across the glass, closing off the view of the laboratory from the examination room. The nurse indicated a folding screen and tossed Paola a gown.

"Take off your clothes and put that on," she grunted. "The dottore will be along in a moment."

Paola looked warily at the stirrups that would support her legs for the examination. She shuddered and walked behind the screen.

When she emerged wearing the gown, the larger of the two nurses told her to lie on the examination table and wait. As she did, Paola studied the movements and body language of both nurses. They appeared to be relatively relaxed, giving her no more than the occasional glance.

"Ah, Ms Santini, we meet again. How good of you to grace my humble clinic." Dottore Ronaldi had slithered quietly into the room, taking Paola by surprise. She turned her head to see he was dressed in a white, waist-length jacket that buttoned on his right side up to the neck, and white trousers. A white paper cap covered his hair while a mask covered the rest of his face below his blood-shot, bright blue eyes. He snapped on a pair of disposable rubber gloves with an almost gleeful panache.

"Shall we begin? I just want to make a preliminary examination today, firstly with a speculum and then with a camera attached to an endoscope. Entirely painless, I can assure you."

"Spare me the gory details, Ronaldi," snarled Paola.

She slowly lifted her hands from where she had held them together over her stomach and put them loosely behind her head. She grasped the pillow and pulled it under her neck. "Much more comfortable," she said.

"Excellent!" Ronaldi bobbed his head enthusiastically as he unsealed a packet and removed what seemed to Paola to be an enormous disposable speculum.

He glanced at the nurses and shifted into Italian. "Now, if I can ask you two ladies to lift one of Ms Santini's legs each onto the rests, we'll begin."

The nurses did as they were bidden, half turning their backs to Paola.

Ronaldi started to walk around to the foot of the examination table to commence his work.

"Oh, dottore," called Paola very quietly, "there's just one thing …"

"Yes, Ms Santini?" said Ronaldi. He paused and then walked back to the head end of the table. He bent towards Paola, his eyes crinkled in a benign smile. "What is i—"

He never saw Paola's fist as it launched from behind her head and crashed into his beak of a nose. As he catapulted backwards across the examination room, a red stain spread rapidly across his face mask. He made no sound; he was unconscious from the blow before he collided with the trolley carrying the monitor for the endoscope, both trolley and doctor tumbling and skidding across the floor.

Paola didn't pause to watch. She snatched her feet from the

hands of the two nurses, using the momentum and her arms to push herself up to a sitting position. She had calculated exactly where she was going to grab their gowns and her hands shot out. Taking a handful of gown in each hand, she pulled sharply downwards, thumping the two nurses' heads together with a sickening thud. She knew it wouldn't be enough to knock them out, but they would be dazed. She was off the table in a flash and round to the end. One of the nurses was recovering quite quickly, but Paola just had time to grab her hair and smash her head down onto the head of the other nurse. Two more powerful crunches of skull against skull and both nurses slithered unconscious to the floor. Paola walked calmly over to Ronaldi and ripped off his face mask. She didn't want him to choke on his own blood. She massaged her fist with her left hand as she looked at the mess his nose had become. It'll recover, with surgical help, she thought as she flexed her fingers.

She ripped off the examination gown, recovered her clothes from where she had left them in a neat pile behind the screen, and dressed. As she walked past the spread-eagled limbs of the unconscious nurses, she spied a tray of surgical instruments on a small trolley in the corner of the room. She picked up a scalpel and weighed it in her hand as she turned to look again at the nurses. Smiling to herself, she tossed the scalpel back into the tray and quietly left the room.

Marcus Dayton was on his own in the sitting room, Sara having decided to take her breakfast in her room: she had no desire to spend time in her captor's company. His face immediately registered his surprise as Paola walked through the door.

"That was quick, I thought—"

"Change of heart, Marcus, I couldn't go through with it, not with Ronaldi."

His faced darkened as he saw the redness on the knuckles of Paola's right hand. "What have you done?" he said angrily.

"Calm down, Marcus, nobody's badly hurt. I'm sorry, but I'm just not convinced by IVF; it's all rather too clinical for my taste."

She walked over to where he was now standing and stopped in front of him. "Anyway," she said as she looked up into his eyes, "I've had a much better idea."

Chapter Thirty-Eight

It had been a week since Sara's abduction and there had been nothing. No news, no communication. Nothing. John had called Digby every day, his own desperation compounded by Pete pacing the floor and muttering darkly about contacting the Feds if the Brits were getting nowhere.

Claudia and Jacques had returned from London to offer their support, and Jacques in turn had been badgering his own Digby to the extent that the normally unflappable Whitehall ghost had insisted that everything possible was being done and that the constant calls were only interrupting his concentration.

The reality, which neither of the Digbys wanted to admit, was that they were drawing blanks with every avenue they tried. Their dealings with other police forces and their shadowy opposite numbers around Europe were always delicate, given their trade in highly classified information. In this case, the need for total secrecy regarding the reasons for the abductions and the genetic traits of the two women was only making their lives even more difficult.

At the Andrews' cottage in the Lakes, the mood varied from sombre to fractious. Julie had reacted badly to her mother's abduction, blaming everyone in turn, but mainly herself. As her younger brother, Matt became her whipping boy even though he had been roaming the hills when the incident occurred. He had now taken to avoiding her wherever possible, disappearing for long walks around Thirlmere to brood.

Lily had taken on the role of surrogate mother/big sister to Julie and was trying whenever she could to pacify her and reason with her. Long walks taken in a different direction from Matt's were her prescription, if only to help keep a distance between Julie and the others. After the fiasco with Digby's team, a new team was in place and the walks were not allowed without a female officer accompanying them directly and two innocuous-looking but highly capable young men following at a distance. Julie had worried about the woman Natalie, but was told that her injuries were not as serious as first thought, although the truth was her wrist and ankle would never be quite the same and the embittered security officer was destined for a desk-bound future.

Lola worried about her girls but accepted that rather than confuse them further by keeping them from school, it was better for them to continue with their normal routine and head off to Keswick every day with their minders in tow. Their headmistress had been told that for unspecified reasons, threats had been made to the family and that there would be a need for covert security around the school. She had no choice but to cooperate, but given the intensity of the security, she wondered just who the Andrews were, postulating theories to her husband of their being in a witness protection programme. Despite the squad assigned to the girls, Lola still worried every moment they were out of her sight.

John had decided to re-examine everything that had happened to date in their search for Paola, starting from the time when Sara had first approached Ced Fisher regarding paintings. He had drawn up a huge flow chart on several sheets of newsprint that were now draped around the living room, having been forced inside the house from his preferred venue of the garage by the cold autumn weather. He had read and reread Nancy Wright's notes on Annie Carr, trying to put himself in Marcus Dayton's head; he had pored over everything with Pete until they were climbing the walls with frustration; and he had made long calls to Ced to try to get some insight from the cyber attacks on Ced's computer and program that might lead them to the culprit. Likewise, Jacques had kept Max on the case in New York, but he too was getting nowhere. Every apparently new trail led them all down endless blind alleys. It was futile and they knew it, but they kept at it, just in case there was something, anything.

It was the middle of the afternoon and John was in the living room with Pete, Jacques and Claudia when he heard the phone ring in the kitchen. Lola appeared at the door, having grabbed the handset as she headed out of the kitchen on her way to Keswick to fetch the girls from school.

"John, there's someone on the phone asking for you. He sounds, I don't know, Spanish. His English certainly isn't up to much."

John took the phone.

"Hello?"

The reply was in slow, broken English.

"*Alô*. Hi ham looking for a Senhor John Handrews. Er, ha you—"

"I'm John Andrews, how can I help you?"

"Er, do you 'ave ha daughter call Paola, Senhor Handrews?"

"Paola! Yes I do!"

Everyone in the room turned to John, an electric silence of anticipation freezing them. They hardly dared to breathe.

"Senhor, hi hapologise; my English ees no good. Hi call from Brazil—"

"Brazil!" exclaimed John. "I—"

"Philippe," interrupted Jacques, stepping forward quietly. "I speak Portuguese. Perhaps I could—"

"Yes, yes, of course," said John. "Here, if I press this button, I think it goes to speaker."

"Senhor," said Jacques in Portuguese, "I am a friend of John Andrews and I speak your language. What is it that you want?"

"Ah," replied the caller as he relaxed into his native tongue, his voice suddenly filling the room. "Thank you, that helps. I am sorry, Senhor, but I'm afraid my English is non-existent. You see, Cassie and I always spoke Portuguese. Unlike me, she was very good with languages."

"Cassie?"

"Yes, but I think you know her as Paola. Is that correct?"

"John Andrews' daughter is Paola, yes. Do you have any information about her?"

"Yes, Senhor. I am a policeman in Rio de Janeiro; my name is Rodrigo Barros. I was a friend of Cassie's for many years when she lived here in Brazil. She left here in a hurry some months ago, senhor, but she called me unexpectedly about ten days ago with a message for John Handrews, her father. But the phone died before she could tell me very much."

"A moment, Senhor Barros," said Jacques, seeing the eagerness to know what was being said in all the eyes focussed on him. "John and others are listening. I want to translate what you've said."

"Ten days ago!" cried John, once Jacques had rapidly repeated the conversation so far. "What's taken so long?"

Jacques went back to Portuguese. "Did you say ten days ago, Senhor Barros?"

"Yes, I'm afraid I did. I apologise but you see there are a great many men with the name John Handrews in your country and I didn't even know where in the country the right one might be. I have spent a large number of hours on the phone and I regret to say that many of the other John Handrews are not so polite. Even for me, finding you has been difficult, and I am a policeman."

Jacques explained again in English to the others.

"What was the message?" said Claudia through her teeth, her fists balled in excitement.

Barros heard her and picked up her meaning from her tone.

"She says she is in Italy. She doesn't know where but she thinks it might be Tuscany. It is very wooded and rugged. She said it reminded her of when she was in a convent. And she said she was being held by a man called Dayton. Does that name mean anything, senhor?"

"Yes," said Jacques, "it certainly does. We knew already that Dayton had taken her, but it confirms that it's our Paola who called you and where she is. How did she sound?"

"She sounded like Cassie, senhor. She is a very strong woman, very resourceful." He paused. "Senhor …?"

"Bognard," said Jacques, "Jacques Bognard. I apologise, I didn't introduce myself."

"Senhor Bognard. I know about Cassie, about her life, I mean. Her long, long life. I have heard her speak a number of languages, some of which she learnt a very long time ago." He paused before adding, "Your Portuguese, Senhor Bognard, is exceptionally elegant, especially for a foreigner, but it's also from another time. I suspect you too must have learnt it a long time ago." Jacques took Claudia's hand and squeezed it, his eyes moistening. Rodrigo Barros' voice then filled the room again. "It has been a pleasure to talk to you, Senhor, and to Senhor Handrews. Please keep me informed about any progress in your search for Cassie; she is someone who is very special to me." He recited a number.

"Thank you, Senhor Barros," said Jacques quietly. "Thank you very much."

Jacques turned to the others and repeated the entire conversation again as Claudia hung onto his arm.

"John!" cried Lola, running to him.

"I know," he said, holding her tight. "This is it, a turning point."

He held out an arm towards Pete. "We're going to find them, Pete, both of them. We'll get Sara back, and Paola. We'll do it."

"I must call the kids," said Pete. "I wonder if their phones will be working in these damn hills."

"I'll ask one of the detail outside to contact their people with their radios," said Lola. "God, look at the time. I must fetch the girls." She kissed John, her eyes radiating her excitement, then she rushed from the room.

"He knew," breathed Claudia quietly. "That policeman from Rio, he knew. About you, I mean, Jacques, and of course about John."

Jacques put an arm around her. "He was a clever man, Claudia, and a good friend to Paola."

"We've got to go to Italy," said John. "We can't stay here."

"But where?" said Pete, "Italy's quite a big country."

"I think Florence would be a good place to start," said John, "somewhere we can base ourselves. Paola has suggested somewhere very wooded and rugged, which means it must be high. It could be Tuscany, or somewhere in the Apennines. If we use that information as a starting point, it should help. From the sound of it, Dayton must be holding her somewhere deep in the country, perhaps in a large house with its own grounds big enough for none of the neighbours to be suspicious. We'll get some maps. I'll call Digby, see what he says. Perhaps the Italian authorities can help."

"John," said Jacques, "I shall of course come too. I have some contacts in Italy."

"I think you mean *we* shall of course come too," added Claudia. "You're not leaving me behind, Jacques Bognard!"

Digby Smith was rather circumspect. "The Italian authorities are not easy to deal with John," he said down the phone once John had repeated the conversation with Rodrigo Barros. "The problem is that they have so many police forces all of whom spend a great deal of time competing with each other. As for their more … clandestine people, shall we call them, I've always found them very difficult. Nevertheless, I'll try to find some information about the larger estates. I think your idea that Paola and Sara are being held somewhere like that is a good one. However, some of these places go back centuries, and the families can be very closed, very secretive, especially when it comes to dealing with the authorities."

"And I imagine there are quite a few," added John, suddenly having visions of needles and haystacks.

"Surely," agreed Digby, "but sit tight, John, I'll get some people onto it."

"We're certainly not sitting tight, Digby; we're heading off to Florence as soon as we can organise it. Tomorrow morning at the latest, maybe even tonight."

"John, I really don't think that rushing off to Italy is going to help."

"Well, I can't just sit here, Digby, and nothing will stop Pete. It's his wife we're talking about."

"Who is going, exactly?" sighed Digby, the resignation sounding in his voice.

"Apart from me, there's Pete, Matt, Jacques and Claudia. I'm not sure about Julie yet."

"OK, but definitely not Lily, John. It's too risky. I'm afraid I must insist that she remain behind."

"My thoughts entirely, Digby," agreed John. "Lily has agreed to stay with Lola, who of course won't be going because of the girls."

"Naturally," said Digby. "Now, John, there is one thing I want to double check before you rush off, so I should suggest you don't leave until I have an answer."

John was puzzled. "What do you need to check?"

"The Rodrigo Barros person."

"What about him?"

"I need to confirm his bona fides, John, and confirm that the person you spoke to was actually Barros. I have to consider the possibility of a smokescreen; that this story isn't something that Dayton has dreamed up to send you off on the wrong tack."

"That would be staggeringly devious, Digby," said John, taken aback at the thought.

"It would be, John, but in my world, I cannot afford to take anything at face value. I'm just crossing Ts and dotting Is; I should not be doing my job if I didn't."

Chapter Thirty-Nine

"Sal, it's Claw."

"Claw! Hi, any news?"

"Sort of, yes. John had a call out of the blue from a policeman that Paola knew when she was in Brazil."

"Brazil?"

"Long story; she used to live there. Somehow, she managed to call this bloke a few days ago. Maybe she didn't know John's number. Anyway, she must have got hold of a phone, but it died on her before she could say very much. But she did get as far as telling him she was in Italy."

"Italy? You're joking."

"Why should I be joking? We thought it very likely she was in Europe."

"I know, but that's where Ced is."

"In Italy? You're joking. I'm there too. In Florence."

"Florence? You're jo— Claw, this conversation is getting ridiculous. Ced's in Florence to meet his Italian art expert friend, Corrado Verdi, the one who looks like an ageing gigolo."

"You could say that about many of the men here, Sal, but I remember you talking about him, of course. You spent your honeymoon at his villa, didn't you?"

"Yes, but he wasn't there."

"I should hope not."

"No. Anyway, he called Ced a few days ago to invite him to see some paintings that have been restored in a church in Florence. Apparently it's a once in a lifetime opportunity to get up close to see them. Ced jumped at the chance, especially since Corrado of course has a personal guided tour to see them."

"Too good to miss, I'm sure. Listen, Sal, I wanted to ask Ced if his investigations into the attacks on his program have shown any Italian connections. Jacques suggested I call."

"He hasn't said anything, but I suppose it's possible. But there's no point in calling his mobile since he's switched off roaming. He's paranoid about the ridiculous charges that mount up when you're overseas. However, he's done something to it that lets me call him, just in case there's an emergency, you know, with Claudia-Jane. Ced hates her being out of his sight. I can contact him and tell him to call you. Who's with you, Claw?"

"I'm with Jacques, of course. And the other men: John, Pete and Matt. They didn't want Lily to come, for obvious reasons, and Julie's in a bit of a mess over her mother. She can't stop beating herself up about it and she reckoned she'd only be in the way. I think Pete was secretly pleased since when she's in the Lakes, he doesn't have to worry about her."

"So why Florence?"

"John's pretty convinced that they are being held in Tuscany and in makes a good base. He got hold of some detailed maps and we've been looking for all the remote places that are very wooded. John and Jacques have gone over to Siena today to see a couple of large estates that looked possible candidates, while Pete and Matt are up in the Chianti hills being guided around by a satnav. Over the last couple of days, we've covered much of the southern part of Tuscany. I think we're heading into the Casentino tomorrow, wher-ever that is."

"What about you?"

"I was supposed to be going with Jacques and John, but I was feeling rough this morning so I decided to stay back at the hotel."

"Rough ...?"

"I think it was some prawns I ate last night, Sal, nothing else!"

"Right."

"Sal!"

"What? Look, I'll contact Ced and tell him to call you. He'll be amazed to find you're there. How are you feeling now?"

"Much better thanks. In fact, I'm heading down for an early lunch."

"Great. How's Jacques?"

"Wonderful. I'm so happy, Sal. And of course I'll be even happier once Paola and Sara have been found and we can all get on with our lives. You should see this hotel, Sal. Jacques really doesn't do things by halves."

"That's brilliant, Claw, it's about time you found Mr Right."

"I can't believe it, Sal. I keep pinching myself just to make sure I'm not dreaming. I don't know why Jacques should be interested in me."

"I can't work it out either. I mean, plain little you, all goofy and boss-eyed. Retiring wallflower. Very strange."

"I mean it, Sal. You know, he's, well, seen so much. When he talks about the past, you'd be staggered who he's met and been friends with. It's like a Who's Who of history. And then there's me ..."

"Well, he might have been around the block, but I saw the mistiness in his eyes. When he looks at you, it's the real thing, believe me. You jammy bugger. I want the cast-offs each time he buys you a new piece of jewellery. Nothing fancy, just a few carats."

"I'll see what I can do, Sal. But in the meantime, can you call Ced? Oh, and big hugs for my little namesake."

"Sure. Love ya, darlin'."

Claudia put down the phone and walked over to the window. The view from the top-floor suite in the Grand Hotel looked out across the glistening waters of the Arno to the timeless jumble of terracotta rooftops spreading into the distance, their pastel tones accentuated by the soft autumn sunlight. It was only the constant rumble of traffic that told her she was in the twenty-first century rather than the fifteenth. A few hundred metres to her left was the Ponte Vecchio, buzzing as ever with tourists. After their arrival the previous evening, she and Jacques had walked there to see it and make an initial sortie to the gold shops. Pleased with what they saw, they continued on to the Duomo and climbed the Giotto-designed campanile to admire the cathedral's magnificent brick dome. Designed and built by Brunelleschi, it was completed in 1436, just nine years after John Andrews had been born in San Sepolcro.

She was startled out of her reverie by her mobile ringing. She thought at first it was Jacques enquiring for the fourth, or perhaps fifth, time that morning how she was feeling, but the caller display showed a different number.

"Claw! Hi, it's Ced, how are you?"

"Ced! That was quick. I'm fine, thanks, much better."

"Have you been ill?"

"No, just a tummy bug."

"What do you mean 'that was quick'?"

"Well, I only spoke to Sal a few minutes ago; I didn't expect a call quite so quickly."

"I haven't spoken to Sal, Claw. I was just calling you about something."

"I thought you'd turned off your phone. Sal said I couldn't call you."

"Doesn't stop me calling you when I want to, Claw, Now listen, I'm sure I've just seen this Marcus Dayton person."

Two days earlier, Ced had been scanning rapidly through hundreds of lines of code on his monitor: searching, checking, refining, modifying, and then sending the latest foot soldier of code on its way. His search for Palo Melliff had been relentless but he was getting nowhere. He thought he'd switched his mobile to silent, but the insistent beat of the intro to his favourite Eliza Gilkyson track that served as his ringtone jangled through the room, shattering his concentration. He picked up the phone in some annoyance, but then smiled when he saw the caller's name.

"Corrado! What a pleasant surprise. It's been ages. How are you?"

The liquid, Latin tones of Corrado Verdi's musical voice sounded in his ear.

"Cedric!" he announced, as ever pronouncing the name according to the Italian rules, and since no self-respecting word should end with anything but a vowel, adding the hint of one to finish it. "Chay-dric-a!"

Corrado's English was, in fact, perfect and his pronunciation excellent, but he liked to play.

"My dear boy, it has been too long. I think that fatherhood has distracted you. How is my beautiful cherub? And of course, her divine goddess of a mother?"

"They're both very well, Corrado," laughed Ced. "We were talking about you only a couple of days ago, wondering when we might see you. Any chance of a trip to this neck of the woods?"

"To England?" Verdi made the suggestion sound as absurd as if Ced had asked him to meet on Mars. "But Cedric, the weather."

"It rains in Italy too, Corrado."

"There is no rain like British rain, Cedric," said Verdi, the finality of his tone dismissing any further discussion on the topic. "No, I have a far better proposal. You have heard about the Gaddi restoration?"

"At Santa Croce in Florence? Of course I have, yes. I've been meaning to make time to see it. The opportunity to get so close to those amazing fourteenth century frescos won't occur again for possibly hundreds of years. Once they've taken down the scaffolding, that'll be it."

He smiled to himself. Unless you happen to be John Andrews, he thought. If John misses it this time, he can catch it the next time it's restored. But for us ordinary mortals ... However, while Verdi knew of John, he didn't know about the consequences of John's DNA and therefore Ced couldn't voice the thought.

"It's just that I'm always so busy, Corrado," he continued.

"I am not surprised with the genius of your little program, Cedric. But I should like you to think about taking a couple of days off, soon if possible. You can fly into Florence, or Pisa if you prefer, where I shall of course meet you and we shall have our own private Gaddi tour. You will bring Sally and Claudia-Jane, I hope."

"Corrado, that would be brilliant, but we haven't actually got around to getting a passport for Claudia-Jane yet, and anyway, she's a bit young for Gaddi."

While they were talking, Ced was tapping on his keyboard.

"OK, Corrado, what about the day after tomorrow? The flights on the budget airlines into Pisa are much cheaper than the major airlines' routes into Florence itself. There's a really early flight from Liverpool which is perfect; the airport's only half an hour away. I can get that and then the bus from Pisa to Florence."

"Perfetto, Cedric. Even sooner than I'd hoped. But the bus is out of the question; I wouldn't hear of it. I'll pick you up at Pisa."

"Do you still have your little blue car?"

"Of course, Cedric, of course."

"Can't wait," replied Ced.

He rang off and in his next breath he was calling out to his wife.

"Sal! Guess what?"

"Your short-term memory's got even shorter?" suggested Sally as she appeared at his study door. "I told you I was trying to get Claudia-Jane down for her afternoon sleep. If your yelling has woken her, she's all yours, buster."

"Sorry, Sal. Listen, that was Corrado on the phone. He's asked me to go to Florence to see the Gaddi frescoes, the ones in the Basilica of Santa Croce. I've booked a flight for Wednesday."

"What's so special about them that you have to go now? They're not going anywhere, are they?"

"What's so special? Well, firstly they're brilliant. They show the Legend of the True Cross and they were painted by Agnolo Gaddi in the mid-1380s in the high chapel of the church. That's the central and biggest chapel. Many of the other frescoes in the place were painted years earlier by Giotto, so the whole place is oozing early Renaissance. Giotto was Gaddi's father's godfather."

"All very fascinating, marathon man, but like I said, why now?"

"They're over thirty metres high, Sal, so the detail is hard to see from the ground. But for the last seven years, they've been under restoration, so the whole chapel has been covered in scaffolding. The restoration's now finished, but the authorities have decided to keep the scaffolding in place for a year and allow guided groups to view the frescoes at close quarters. I mean, less than a metre away, Sal. It's a unique opportunity."

"I thought John's friend Piero painted the Legend of the True Cross."

"He did, the one in Arezzo, about seventy or eighty years after Gaddi's. There are quite a lot of Legend cycles around, in fact. Piero would have seen Gaddi's several years before he painted his version, when he went to Florence as a young man. I've got a feeling John was with him on one occasion. Imagine that, Sal."

"Yes, that bit still blows my mind."

"Mine too. Anyway, Sal, Corrado's got his own private guided tour and he's asked me to go with him. I'll only be gone for one night."

"Well make sure you bring back a nice big cuddly toy for Claudia-Jane. But not the statue of David. Far too graphic for a girl of her tender years."

The flight from Liverpool arrived ten minutes early at nine-thirty and following an all-too-brief but exhilarating dash along the autostrada in Verdi's Maserati, Ced and Verdi were being greeted by their guide, Antonio, for their eleven o'clock appointment. Ced had hardly got his breath back from the car ride when he found himself climbing the scaffolding, his eyes hungrily taking in the brilliance of the colours and detail revealed by the restoration.

"This is truly amazing, Corrado," he gasped. "This must be how they were when they tripped off Gaddi's brush. To be so close, it's like standing alongside the man."

Verdi smiled, enjoying his friend's enthusiasm. "It is a wonderful opportunity, Cedric. Just think; these frescoes have been discoloured for centuries with the grime of a candlelit atmosphere. This is the first time almost since they were painted that their true magnificence has been observable."

"I hope they are now banning the use of candles," replied Cedric.

"Mmm. Hard in a Catholic church, my friend, it's something of a tradition. But you never know."

Their designated hour went by in a flash, leaving Ced yearning for more.

"I'll have to come back, Corrado, an hour just isn't enough. Maybe I'll join one of the public tours."

He turned to the guide. "I'm surprised that there aren't queues out of the door for your tours, Antonio. When is this open to the public?"

"Almost every day, signore. It's just that sometimes a morning is reserved for private viewings for VIPs such as the dottore and yourself." He bowed his head slightly towards Verdi and then continued. "There are a number of benefactors to the world of art who contribute generously to projects such as this. It is our pleasure to return their kindness by arranging individual tours, should they wish them. In fact, a guest earlier this morning is one such benefactor who has underwritten a number of significant projects in this and other churches."

He glanced past Ced's shoulder. "Ah, there he is now. After seeing the Gaddi frescoes, he told me he wanted to immerse himself in the Giottos in the other chapels here in the basilica."

Ced turned to follow his gaze and immediately raised his eyebrows in surprise.

"Oh, I know him. How strange, I didn't know he was in Florence. He's the fiancé of a very good friend of mine. At least, if he isn't yet, I think he soon will be."

He walked over to a tall man about ten metres away.

"Jacques! What a surprise. I didn't know you were here. Is Claudia with you?"

Marcus Dayton turned to face him, his forehead furrowed in a suspicious frown.

"I think you have mistaken me for someone else," he said.

Ced then saw the livid scar on Dayton's face and the darkness in his eyes. They were the same jet as Jacques' eyes but unlike Jacques', this man's eyes radiated no warmth.

Ced gulped. The conversation he'd had with Jacques back in the house in Knutsford played in his mind; did Jacques say that

Dayton didn't know he had a twin? Shit, he thought, I've well and truly blown it.

"Oh, sorry, yes … of course. How stupid of me," stuttered Ced. "Now I see you full face, you're nothing like my friend. It was just in this dim light, in profile …"

The guide unwittingly came to his rescue. He smiled as he addressed Dayton in Italian. "Were the Giotto frescoes as you remembered them, Signor Constantine?"

Dayton seemed to ignore the man for a moment, then he shifted his eyes to him and replied, also in Italian.

"They were, Antonio, thank you, although I think that your experts should consider some of them for cleaning as well. I should like to see them attain the magnificence of the Gaddis. Now, if you'll excuse me, I have a lunch appointment."

He gave a slight nod of his head to the guide, threw another puzzled glance at Ced, then turned and strode for the door.

Ced watched him go, a feeling of panic rising in his gut. He needed to do something.

"You look troubled, Cedric," said Verdi, strolling up to him. "Who was that person? He didn't seem very pleased to see you."

Ced turned to Verdi, his eyes betraying his bewilderment. His mouth worked at a few words, but nothing emerged. Finally he took a deep breath. "Corrado, I can't really explain, but I need to make a call very urgently. Could you do me a huge favour?"

"Of course, Cedric, what—"

"Could you follow that man? Discreetly, of course."

Verdi narrowed his eyes. "That sounds very cloak and dagger, Cedric. Certainly I'll follow him, but you'll have to tell me later what's going on."

"Yes. Right. Of course," replied Ced, turning towards the exit.

He hurried off, wondering absently what sort of tale he could spin for Verdi.

"Marcus Dayton! Where? How do you know?" Claudia was stunned.

"I know because he looks just like Jacques, except he's got a scar on his right cheek."

"Scar?" Claudia's head was spinning. "Ced, where are you?"

"I'm in Florence."

"Yes, I know that, so am I. I mean where exactly are you?"

"You're in Florence?"

"Yes, didn't Sal tell you?"

"I haven't spoken to Sal, not since I arrived here this morning."

"Oh, right, you said."

"Why are you in Florence, Claw?"

"Paola and Sara are here. Well, not here in Florence. I mean they're in Italy. We've had confirmation."

"Wow! Are you on your own? Where's Jacques?"

"He's with John searching the countryside near Siena. I stayed at the hotel, so yes, I'm on my own at the moment."

"Which hotel?"

"The Grand, it's by the Arno, not far from the Ponte Vecchio."

"Very smart. Look, that's not far away. I'm outside Santa Croce. Corrado is following Dayton. I think he told the guide he was meeting someone for lunch. Why don't you jump in a cab and meet me here?"

"I'm on the way."

Claudia ended the call, grabbed her bag and ran out of the door.

Ced had crossed the large piazza outside Santa Croce to the road that ran across the end, figuring that would be where Claudia's taxi would appear. He was pacing the street, staring at each vehicle that passed, when there was a toot from behind him. Claudia brought the classic red Vespa motor scooter to a halt a few inches from his feet and grinned at him.

"Claw! What the hell are you doing on that?"

"There were no taxis. I was desperate. This belongs to an American tourist who rented it. He'd just got back to the hotel. I pleaded with him and he let me borrow it along with the helmet."

"Do you know how to drive it?"

"Of course I do! My brother was crazy about motorbikes; still is. I used to ride with him when I was a teenager. I got my licence before he did. Where's this man who you think is Dayton?"

"Verdi has followed him to a restaurant. He just texted me the name. Here, I found it on my phone. There's a map." He held up his phone.

"Where are we?" said Claudia. "Oh, yes, down there. Looks easy enough."

"Yes, I reckon it's about ten minutes' walk."

"It'll only be two on this. Jump on."

Ced looked hesitant. "I can't, Claw. No helmet. We don't want to be held up by some traffic cop. Anyway," he grinned, "if I run, I'll probably beat you."

"You're not that fast, Ced Fisher."

"OK, but I won't be far behind. I'll just text Corrado and tell him to meet you by the door. Do you know what he looks like?"

"Fifties, swept back grey hair, immaculately dressed. I've seen a photo."

She revved the engine, twisted the left grip to put the scooter into gear and shot off.

After some very Italian overtaking and a close encounter with a group of Chinese tourists oblivious to any traffic as they snapped each other on their phones and cameras in front of anything and everything, Claudia saw Verdi standing in the shadows of a doorway just before the restaurant. He stepped forward as she stopped next to him.

"Signorina Reid," he said, bowing his head and sweeping a hand through his leonine grey hair. "I have long wanted to meet you but I never thought it would be in so a clandestine manner. How exciting that you have arrived in such an Italian way; I feel as if I am in a film by Fellini." He leaned forward to whisper in Claudia's ear, every bit the secret agent. "The man Cedric asked me to follow is in that restaurant there, lunching with an art dealer I recognise. A complete shark, he always charges absurd prices. I remember—"

"Do you think he saw you following him?" said Claudia, cutting through Verdi's ramblings.

"Signor Constantine? No, I was very careful; I'm sure he was completely unaware of me." He rocked his head in a slight swagger, proud of his skills and wanting to leave Claudia in no doubt as to his competence.

"Constantine?" said Claudia, confused.

"That is the name by which the guide addressed him. Is that not his name?"

"It's not the name that—" Claudia started to reply but she was interrupted by a toot from behind her as a large limousine nudged past and pulled up outside the restaurant. A driver jumped out, opened the rear passenger door and waited. A moment later, Marcus Dayton emerged from the restaurant and without a glance in their direction climbed straight into the car. The driver closed the door, got back into his seat and the car sped away.

"Oh my God!" cried Claudia. "I'll have to follow it." She looked back over her shoulder but there was no sign of Ced. She revved the scooter. "Tell Ced I'll call him," she shouted to Verdi as she accelerated away.

"But signorina ... be careful," called Verdi as he stood helplessly watching the scooter disappear.

Chapter Forty

The previous day, Paola had gone to Sara's room at noon and knocked on the door.

"Sara, it's me," she called.

"It's not locked," called Sara as she opened the door to let Paola in. "They don't seem too bothered about keeping me from wandering around."

"No, although there is more security than you'd think at first sight," said Paola, moving over to the window. "Why are you hiding in here anyway? It's much more comfortable downstairs in the sitting rooms."

"Once you'd gone off with those two hulks of nurses, I didn't want to be alone with Dayton. I know that he intends to keep both of us here for a long time, but that's no reason for me to be nice to him. It would be like condoning what he's done, and I refuse to do that. How did you get on? I was surprised that you agreed to the examination."

Paola shrugged. "I realised that there was little choice. Dayton intends to have his way and if that's the case, I'd rather minimise the discomfort. I certainly don't want to be restrained or locked up anywhere. The examination wasn't as bad as I thought."

"I guess I've been lucky. My gyny's always been a woman. I can sympathise with how you feel."

"I just never think about doctors. Why should I? The only

reason I would need one is if I broke something. And, surprisingly enough, that's never happened. Not once in nearly five hundred years."

"Quite a record."

"Look, I've been thinking. After I'd seen Ronaldi, I spoke to Marcus, gave him another lecture about you and how unreasonable he's being keeping you here. It didn't seem to have much effect but what he did tell me is that he's going away for a couple of days. There're some paintings that have been restored in Florence that he wants to see. He's very knowledgeable about art, although unlike the Andrews clan, he doesn't appear to have any talent himself."

"Neither do I, I'm afraid," laughed Sara. "Unfortunately, that's something I didn't inherit from you, although having seen a lot of John's work recently, I'm developing a better eye. And having watched him in action, I'm in awe of his talent. He painted a portrait of Julie that is breathtaking."

"Yes," said Paola softly, almost wistfully, "he's incredibly gifted." She paused, refocussing her thoughts. "Anyway, I think that we should take advantage of Marcus' absence to try to get out of here. The guards are not, in my opinion, as good as they think they are and I think that together we should be able to outwit them."

"I hope that by outwitting them, you don't mean killing them," said Sara.

"Not unless it's absolutely necessary," said Paola, her tone businesslike, as if killing guards was a completely acceptable possibility. "But I'll probably have to bang some of them over the head."

Sara pursed her lips; she was clearly not happy with the prospect of the violence that didn't seem to bother Paola at all.

"The point is," continued Paola, "if Marcus is away, we can roam the land without his interference. I've been thinking back over what I've seen of the perimeter fence and there might be a chance. There were only two guards at the post I saw and with two of us, we should be able to create some sort of diversion."

"You make it sound very easy, Paola. From what Dayton said, the security is very sophisticated."

"It's only as sophisticated as the people who operate it, and from what I've seen of them, they are local yokels. Look, we've got nothing to lose; they're not going to kill us. The worst thing that can happen is that they stop us and bring us back here. They have strict instructions on how far they can go with us, whereas we can do what we want with them. It must give us the upper hand."

"When do you want to try it?"

"No time like the present. I suggest we have some lunch since we might not eat properly for a day or so. I'll pick up some chocolate bars and some cheese to nibble on later, but we can hardly wander out with a hamper of food. We'll need to wrap up well. I don't know how extensive these forests are beyond the fence, but there's a good chance that we might have to hide out for a while before we reach civilisation, and it's cold at night. We'll have to be careful who we approach once we're beyond the fence; they might be in Dayton's pay."

They spent the half hour following their lunch raiding their respective wardrobes for a selection of warm clothing, after which they left the house through the doors from the smaller sitting room.

"Marcus asked me to inform the guardhouse if we were going outside," said Paola as they made their way along the paths bordering the more formal parts of the garden, "and I did just that. Once we get into the woods, we'll see how they react."

As soon as they were out of sight of the house, Paola led the way to the spot where she had previously hidden and watched. It was well chosen: they could see all the paths running from the gardens into the trees while remaining invisible themselves. Sure enough, after a few minutes, two guards could be seen walking briskly from the house in the direction of the main path into the woods.

"We'll let them get ahead of us," whispered Paola, "and at the same time check that there are no others following."

She turned to Sara and grinned. "How are your forest skills? Have you used them much since Colorado?"

Sara smiled. "We'd take camping trips when the kids were young and I'd run rings round them with my tracking. They could never find me, but I always found them. They were pretty nonplussed that a mere mother could get the better of them. I think Pete's backwoodsman instincts were offended as well."

"You certainly move very quietly, which is probably the greatest skill," said Paola as they made their way from their hiding place, now satisfied that only two guards had been dispatched.

"That and observation," replied Sara. "If you don't know what's out there and where, you're at a total disadvantage."

Keeping away from the main path, they took a parallel track to follow the guards. Within a few minutes, Sara, who'd taken the lead, put her hand up to warn Paola, and then she pointed. The two men were standing at a fork in the path, clearly discussing which way to go. They looked slightly agitated, having found no sign of the women. The men were suddenly wary, one indicating to the other not to speak. He made a few signs to his colleague and then touched his wristwatch, holding up his hand and opening and closing it twice to indicate ten minutes. They were clearly splitting up to scout the paths.

As they moved off from the fork in opposite directions, Paola touched Sara's shoulder to indicate she should squat down and wait while she followed the guard who had taken the left path. Sara's eyes indicated concern. She dragged her hand across her throat and then wagged her finger at Paola. Paola smiled and put her hands together by the side of her face, reassuring Sara that she would only render the guard unconscious, not kill him.

After five minutes she was back. Sara had heard nothing but from the confident set of Paola's jaw, she knew she had successfully subdued the first guard. Paola tapped her jacket pocket and partly lifted out the guard's radio set to show Sara. She then nodded in the direction of the other path and they set off.

They quickly caught up with the second guard. He had moved about five metres from the path and was peering into a dense patch of undergrowth. Paola put out a hand to stop Sara and then indicated a stand of trees where she should wait. The guard was only twenty metres away from Sara when Paola landed the blow from behind. Sara didn't see it but she heard it and winced. When it was followed by three more blows, she stepped out of the trees. "Paola!" she whispered as loudly as she dared. "Stop!"

She saw Paola turn towards her, her nostrils flared, her eyes fixed in a distant stare. She dropped a log she was holding and walked back to Sara.

"You said—" started Sara.

"He'll survive," muttered Paola.

"It didn't sound like it, and that was some piece of wood," said Sara. "I think we need to check he's all right."

She took a step towards the spot where the guard was lying in the undergrowth, but Paola took hold of her arm to stop her.

"I said he'll survive. I just needed to teach him a lesson."

"Why? He's a guard, not an enemy soldier."

Paola's mouth was downturned with bitterness. "He cornered me in one of the corridors at the back of the house. Last week. Thrust me up against a wall with one hand around my throat and the other between my legs. Told me he'd kill me for what I did to the other guard, whatever the consequences."

"You didn't report him to Dayton?"

"I thought I'd deal with it in my own way."

Sara didn't want to let it go. "He didn't look very murderous just now when he was crossing the garden."

"Looks can be deceptive," muttered Paola. "Come on, the daylight won't last for ever."

She strode along the path, keeping to the left of Sara to block her view of the guard.

They walked along in silence for about five minutes until Sara suddenly stopped.

"Paola, I really don't think we should continue. How many more people are going to die?"

Paola spun around to Sara and put her hands on her shoulders and fixed her with a harsh stare, their eyes only inches apart. "Keep your voice down!" she hissed. "How many times do I have to say it? I didn't kill them; they will survive."

"I wish I could believe you, but I saw those blows. They were sickening."

Paola tightened her grip, turned Sara around and gave her a

shove along the path. "Go check then, if you're so concerned. But believe me, we're running out of time and we won't get another chance. Do you really want to stay here for months, years perhaps? Because that's what our host has in mind. I've spoken to him at length, remember, you haven't. I've seen inside his head. He's ruthless and he'll do anything to achieve his goal."

Stumbling slightly from the shove, Sara stared along the path, but the spot where the guard had been hit was too far away. She thought of Pete and how much he must be worrying. Then she thought of Julie and Matt. She couldn't subject them to months of anguish. She'd rather be dead and have them know that. At least they could grieve and move on. But hostage for who knew how long? No, it was unacceptable.

She turned to Paola, her eyes on the ground. "Sorry," she said. "You're right. Staying here is not an option. We have to escape." She paused and sighed heavily. "But please, Paola … Mom … please, these men have lives too. Show them some compassion."

Paola took a step towards her daughter and held out her arms. "I'll try," she said, "but the number one priority is escape. Now give me a hug."

They clung to each other while Paola stroked her daughter's head and hair. "It'll be OK," she whispered. "We'll get there."

When they reached the part of the fence with the gate and guard-house that Paola had seen previously, they stopped and watched from the cover of the trees. Paola produced the binoculars from her pocket and scanned the scene. Then she passed them to Sara.

"Two guards, as before," she said. "They don't seem to be doing much. It must be nice and warm in there or one of them would be on patrol."

Just then, they heard the rumbling of a diesel engine in the distance that was quickly getting louder. There was a toot and a 4x4 flatbed truck appeared along the track on the outside of the fence. As it stopped in front of the gate, the door of the guard-house opened and the two guards emerged. The flatbed driver wound down his window and called through the fence.

"Delivery of repair materials for the interior trips, the ones that were damaged by the pig last week. About a kilometre along the path."

"You mean the pig we had for three dinners, two breakfasts, and several lunches," laughed one of the guards.

"What's he saying?" whispered Sara, very close to Paola's ear.

"Repairs," replied Paola. "I think they're coming inside."

They watched the guards disconnect the power supply to the electric fence and then open the gate for the truck to pass through. To Sara's surprise, they didn't immediately close it.

One of the guards jumped up onto the flatbed and turned to his colleague while nodding his head at the gate.

"OK with that, Franco? I'll hitch a ride with these two to the repair spot. I'm bored rigid sitting in there. My turn, huh, like it was yours last time."

"No problem," replied the guard casually. "Got word that the two bitches are loose in the woods somewhere, but Ugo and Aldo are trailing them. There's been no follow-up so they must have them covered."

With that, the truck drove off along the inner track.

The remaining guard suddenly shivered. He'd forgotten to put on his fleece-lined jacket and was feeling the difference in temperature between the snugly heated guardhouse and the forest as the afternoon rapidly cooled. He cast a glance along the track and then walked back inside, closing the door behind him.

Paola turned to Sara with a grin. "I won't translate all of that, but as one bitch to another, I guess we're in luck," she said, nodding towards the still-open gate.

"Let's go," she whispered. She crouched and indicated to Sara to do the same. With her hands and arms she indicated the route past the guardhouse and through the gate, telling Sara to stay as close to the building as she could to limit the guard's chance of seeing them.

"You first; I'll follow," she mouthed.

They moved sideways through the trees until they were as close to the guardhouse as possible while still in cover. With a swift glance up the track, Sara darted forward, staying very low; Paola followed closely behind her. As they drew level with the guard-house, they ducked down under the level of the windows, and then sprinted as best they could in a crouch position through the gate and over the outside track. Ahead of them now was a cleared area about thirty metres across, after which was the dense forest of freedom.

"Go!" hissed Paola. Sara stood up and started to sprint. It was only then that she saw the trip wires stretching out before her for twenty metres, a random pattern designed to upend the unwary as well as trigger the alarms. She caught one with her foot but kept her balance. There was no alarm! When the guards turned off the electric fence, they must have turned off the trips as well. She lifted her knees and started to trot through the maze of wires like a pony performing dressage.

Paola wasn't so lucky. She also saw the wires just as she started to sprint. She sprung off her right foot but her left then landed inches in front of the next wire. The spot where she landed was damp and her foot slid under the wire. The momentum of her body carried her forward but her foot was well trapped and she crashed to the ground with a yelp of pain.

Sara heard her just as she cleared the final wires and slid to a halt. She watched in horror as Paola tried to stand, only to fall again as her ankle collapsed under her. Without a thought, Sara ran back across the wires, catching a couple but acutely aware of keeping her footing as light as possible. She was back with Paola in seconds and helping her to her feet. "I've got you," she whispered, taking hold of Paola's left arm by the wrist and placing it around her shoulders.

"Come on!" she insisted.

"I can't," cried Paola, "I think it's broken."

Thoughts of doctors and tempting fate flashed across Sara's mind.

"We can do it," she said, but just as she did, her own left foot caught a wire and they both crashed down, Paola again yelping loudly with pain as her injured foot took the impact of the fall.

Sara was quickly on her knees and reaching out to Paola when a shout from the direction of the fence froze her to the spot.

"Hold it there, bitches!"

The remaining guard, now warmly wrapped in a fur-hooded, fleece-lined jacket, was standing by the gate and pointing a rifle at them. A wide grin spread across his face.

Sara was more surprised that he spoke in English than by the fact that he'd appeared from nowhere. She reacted angrily, yelling at him. "Don't just stand there, you ape, come and help! This woman is injured!"

There was a chuckle from the guard and he ambled forward to the edge of the trip wires. He was now about three metres from them.

"Keep his attention!" hissed Paola.

Sara glanced down and saw Paola's hand had closed around a rock and even now she was adjusting her position so that she could hurl it. Sara edged slightly away from her and the guard's eyes followed her. Paola was now on the edge of his vision.

"What are you waiting for, you moron!" screeched Sara. "Those wires won't bite! Watch them carefully and you won't trip."

The guard looked down to check his footing and at the same moment, Paola launched the rock. He was too focussed on his feet to even register it and her aim was perfect. The rock hit him squarely in the right temple and he fell as if he'd been shot.

It was Sara's turn to over-react. She jumped to her feet and rushed to the unconscious guard. She bent to pick up the rock and raised it above her head, ready to smash it down.

"Sara! No!"

For a moment, Paola could see herself reflected in Sara's face, the eyes that now bored into hers wild, feral.

"He's out cold, Sara," said Paola, keeping her voice as calm as she could. "There's no need for more." She lifted her arm. "I need your help."

Sara was still panting with raw emotion, but gradually her breathing returned to normal. She looked down at the unconscious man at her feet and then at the rock still in her hand. She threw it to one side, gulping in horror at the thought of what she had nearly done.

She ran over to Paola, watchful for the wires.

"I don't know how far I can get," said Paola.

"Well I'm not going without you, Paola," said Sara as she hooked her arms under Paola's armpits and tried to help her up.

"You need a crutch," she said, looking around. "What about that rifle? It'll do until I can find something longer."

She stood and was about to retrieve the rifle when there was a toot and the sound of the flatbed's engine reached them as it returned along the track.

"Shit!" cried Sara. "Come on, Paola, we can still make it."

She turned to see Paola shaking her head. "I can't, Sara. Give me the rifle. I'll keep them here while you escape. It's the only option. Quickly! Pass it to me!"

Without thinking, Sara did as she was told.

"Now go. Go!" barked Paola.

"Paola, I—"

"Go!"

"I'll get help. I'll be back. Don't let them hurt you."

"For Christ's sake, Sara, they'll be round that corner any second!"

Sara still remained glued to the spot, her legs unwilling to move. Her breathing had increased again and her eyes were darting in panic. She knew she had no option. She turned, picked up her feet, danced across the trip wires and fled at full tilt into the forest.

Chapter Forty-One

Marcus Dayton's black BMW 7 Series saloon negotiated a number of side streets before joining the Florence inner ring road at the Viale Amendola and heading towards the Arno, meeting it at the Torre della Zecca Vecchia, part of the old city walls. There it turned left onto the Lungarno Del Tempio, heading east.

One hundred metres behind, hair flying out from beneath her crash helmet, Claudia was hunched over her scooter's handlebars, willing every set of traffic lights the car crossed to stay green until she reached them. The crisp autumnal air felt like sharp needles piercing her eyes. She wished she'd thought of putting on the sunglasses that were sitting back in her room. As she roared past the Torre della Zecca Vecchia, she ignored the traffic lights that had just turned red and found herself heading straight for the side of a taxi that had shot from the Lungarno to her right. She hit the brakes and swerved, but her teenage years of racing her brother paid off and she quickly straightened up. She gulped nervously as the taxi driver treated her to a blast of his horn. He accelerated away from her, gesticulating angrily from his window. In braking, she had lost some distance and Dayton's car seemed to be disappearing. She changed down and twisted the throttle, the tiny engine screaming its anguish as she dragged every ounce of power from its tortured piston. After another near miss at a small roundabout that was home to the Folon statue La Pluie, she raced flat out towards the junction with the Via Marco Polo. The traffic lights here were just turning from green to amber, not something that would normally deter Florentine drivers, but the elderly driver of the battered Cinquecento with ancient Florence plates that was now directly ahead of Claudia knew the limitations of his vehicle. He applied the brakes and the car shuddered to a halt. Claudia had to make the lights but the Cinquecento was hogging the outside edge of the lane, making overtaking impossible in the narrow gap between the car and the large blue bus that was also slowing next to it. She checked the other side: there was no room to pass on the road, but there was a footpath and no pedestrians. She leaned sharply to the right, lifted her front wheel up the kerb and bumped up onto the narrow footpath. She wobbled precipitously past the Cinquecento and bounced off again into the junction.

Another large blue bus that had just crossed the Arno on the Via Marco Polo bridge was waiting at the lights, intending to turn left and head into Florence. Seeing the bus slowing to his left, the driver anticipated the change of lights and started to edge out. "Madonna!" he yelled as the tiny Vespa appeared out of nowhere and almost disappeared under his front wheels. He slammed his foot on the brake, causing several standing passengers to lurch forward into each other. The driver was by now half standing to scream abuse at the scooter as it shot away, the angry yells of the passengers ringing in his ears.

"Sorry!" cried Claudia, with a wave of her hand, her voice lost in the noise of the traffic and the continuing plight of her engine, but her concentration was still on Dayton's car as she prayed that there were no police cars to witness her driving.

The traffic thinned slightly as the road followed the Arno out of the city and once again she settled to a distance of about a hundred metres behind Dayton's car. She glanced up at a direction sign that gave the normal endless list of destinations, the topmost of which was Pontessieve, fifteen kilometres away.

In a moment of panic, Claudia wondered how much fuel the scooter had. She hadn't anticipated a lengthy ride when she'd virtually hijacked the machine from the American tourist. She glanced down at the speedometer to find the gauge. It registered full, but then she noticed that as she slowed on a bend, the gauge's needle moved toward half full, and then towards empty as she slowed further. Accelerating away from the bend, the needle moved confidently to the right, hitting full as Claudia's speed topped out. She pulled a wry face: the gauge seemed to be at one with the speedometer and was therefore useless. How long she could continue her chase after Dayton's car was in the lap of the gods.

By Pontessieve, where the river Sieve flowing from the hills of the Casentino meets the Arno, the road had a distinctly Alpine feel, a river valley carved into steeply undulating terrain, much of it covered with fir. The main road bypassed the town, negotiating several roundabouts and a 700-metre tunnel before heading north-eastwards and upwards into the Casentino. The gradient added further to the scooter engine's stress as well as to Claudia's: the increasingly windy road meant that Dayton's car, now over two hundred metres ahead, often disappeared for several seconds at a time. She thought of stopping to call Ced — her other thought of calling Jacques would involve too much explanation — but she would be bound to lose Dayton. Twelve kilometres farther on at Contea, Claudia saw Dayton's car turn right off the main road in the direction of Londa. There was little traffic now and with the increase in elevation, the air was cold. Claudia shivered under her thin jacket. A kilometre after Londa, the car turned left onto a narrow lane. The Vespa followed.

The poorly surfaced lane, slippery with damp leaves and a light mist, climbed through a series of tight bends. Claudia was concentrating hard on maximising her speed without losing control when, as she came rather too fast round a right-hand bend, she looked up to see the car stopped immediately ahead of her. Standing next to it was Marcus Dayton.

Claudia braked hard and skidded the scooter to a halt, stopping just short of the car's rear bumper. As she put her foot on the ground, she was aware of another man moving from the side of the road to stand immediately behind her, blocking her in.

"Can I help you, young lady?" said Dayton.

Claudia opened her mouth to vent her anger but the shock of Dayton's appearance left her gulping air. Everything about him was Jacques: the face, the build, the way he was standing, even the tone of his voice. But then she saw the scar on his cheek and the coldness in his eyes, and she realised just how different he was. She found her voice.

"You could move your car for a start," she said indignantly. "That's a very dangerous place to stop. If a truck comes roaring round that bend, he'll take me out and your car as well."

"Unlikely on this track," said Dayton, amused by her intensity. "Now, I'll ask you again, can I help you?"

"What do you mean?" said Claudia. "How did you know I was English?"

Dayton smiled at her. "You've been following me all the way from the restaurant in Florence and I overheard that grey-haired gigolo talking to you as I left. He had followed me in a very bumbling and obvious way from Santa Croce, and he in turn was with the Englishman who spoke to me there. So, you see, it wasn't too difficult to work out you were connected. When my driver saw you struggling to keep up, I was intrigued, so I instructed him to take this route and not to lose you. Usually by now we would be gliding at high speed down the autostrada, but I realised that you can't use the autostrada on that thing. So, what is it that you want?"

"I don't know what you mean. I'm on my way to, er ..." She faltered and Dayton waited.

When she said nothing more, he offered her a cold smile. "Yes, where are you going?"

"It's none of your business," she stuttered. "Now please, I have to go."

"I don't think so, young lady. This day is just too full of coincidences. I'm followed by an Englishwoman shortly after being mistaken for someone else by an Englishman. He seemed very convinced that I was this other person, which of course set me wondering. Just who are you, signorina?"

"No one," said Claudia defensively, "I mean, I'm nothing to do with you. I have no idea who you are and I'm certainly not following you."

Dayton's expression was pure condescension. "I'm afraid you are a poor liar, young lady. Now, this is a very quiet road. If I were to take your keys and drive away, it would be a while before some passing tractor came by to offer you a lift, and of course you wouldn't know where I'd gone. But suppose we were to bump into each other again. Would you start charging after me?" He nodded. "I suspect you would, so I think it would be better if we stop playing games and you come with me now."

Claudia tried to wheel the scooter backwards, but the man standing behind her stopped her with one hand in her back while he leaned over and removed the keys from the ignition.

"My driver will push your scooter into that clump of trees over there. It will be perfectly safe," continued Dayton.

He turned towards the car, his arm out to indicate the rear door.

"I'm not getting in there with you!" cried Claudia, a shudder of panic lurching through her.

The driver took hold of the scooter's handlebars and jerked the machine up onto its stand with Claudia still sitting astride it. Then he gripped her upper right arm firmly.

"Ouch!" she yelped, trying to tug herself free.

"Please don't resist," said Dayton, "my driver is very strong." The driver pulled her from the scooter and pushed her towards the car. Dayton opened the door and suddenly she was inside it, the door slamming after her.

Dayton made his way round to the other side and climbed in next to her while the driver pushed the scooter away from the road. Dayton held out his hand. "Your bag, please."

Claudia took hold of her bag with both hands and clung to it defensively, but the steely glare in her captor's eyes told her she had no choice. She bit on her top lip, realising she was close to tears as her breath came in short, rapid bursts. She reluctantly pulled the strap over her head and handed the bag to him.

"Thank you," he said. "That's much better."

He glanced through the bag's contents and removed her mobile phone. He powered it down and slipped it into his pocket.

He smiled as he peered back into the bag. "Since I doubt your phone has been specially modified, I don't need to go through the charade of removing the SIM card and battery like they always do in the movies. It's quite untraceable now."

He retrieved her passport and opened it. "Now, let's see. Claudia Natasha Reid. Mmm. Pretty names. May I call you Claudia, Miss Reid, or do you prefer Natasha? No, I think you'd use Claudia."

He then noticed a plastic ID card that had tucked itself into the front page of the passport. "Oh, I see, it's Dr Reid. My apologies. You are a geneticist, judging from the name of this laboratory. How very interesting."

The driver's door closed with a sharp click as the driver settled back in the car. He slipped the car into gear, turned it around, and they headed back along the lane.

"Where are we going?" said Claudia. "You can't just take me."

"I can, Dr Reid, and I am. We have quite a way to go to my house in the country. It's very secluded. But don't worry, I mean you no harm. I just want to have a little chat."

As he was talking, he dipped deeper into the bag and pulled out a photograph. His eyes widened in surprise as he saw his own face smiling back at him. The photo showed Jacques Bognard with his arm around a carefree-looking Claudia as they sat in a restaurant. He turned his eyes to Claudia.

"This really is very interesting, Dr Reid. Do you still claim you weren't following me? Who is this? His name please. He is your husband? No, I don't think so, you are not wearing a ring and you English are so particular about that. And anyway, you are blushing." He turned his attention back to the photo, fascinated by the resemblance. "So, a boyfriend? A lover? How romantic. And you just happened to be in Florence."

Claudia took a breath and set her jaw. She had taken the plunge when she charged off after the car in Florence with no thought of the consequences. She'd half thought that Ced might have appeared chasing after her, but he hadn't. It didn't matter;

there was no further point in trying to hide things from this man, or in lying to him. She would continue with the plunge.

"No, Mr Dayton, I don't just happen to be in Florence," she said through clenched teeth.

"Ah, you know my name," interrupted Dayton.

"Of course I do. We were in Florence looking for you."

Dayton looked puzzled. "Really? Why Florence? I seldom go there."

"We knew you were in a region of Italy with terrain like that around Florence, the hills of Tuscany. It seemed a good place to start."

Dayton smiled. "Well, you did strike lucky, didn't you, you could have been floundering for weeks. I wonder what the chances are of your friend bumping into me on the one day I'd decided to take up the Santa Croce restoration committee's offer to view the frescoes. But tell me, why are you looking for me?"

Claudia found herself losing patience. "Look, I'm being open with you. Don't insult me by acting innocent. You know very well why we're looking for you. You have taken both Naomi Tripley and Sara Farsley against their will. I want to know why."

Dayton studied Claudia's eyes, which were flickering from his to her hands and back again.

"You are a brave young woman, Dr Reid, to be making such accusations on your own. No one knows you are with me. If you were to disappear into the Tuscan countryside, never to be seen again, there is nothing to connect you to me."

"There certainly is. Ced will know by now that I have followed you, and he will have told the others."

"The others. So there are more people involved than just this person who seems to be my twin. What did your friend say his name was? Jacques, was it? I shouldn't be too confident about them finding me, Dr Reid. I am a past master at disappearing."

"Don't threaten me, Mr Dayton, I know what you're capable of and since you seem reluctant to admit it, I'll tell you why I think you have taken Naomi and Sara, and I'll tell you why you are wasting your time."

Dayton looked askance. "Wasting my time?"

"Yes, wasting your time!" She paused, checking her tone. She didn't want to get angry but the fear of the precarious position she had landed herself in was in danger of overwhelming her. She ran a hand through her hair.

"Look, Mr Dayton, I can understand that you are not used to explaining about yourself to anyone, I mean really explaining about yourself, particularly to a complete stranger. But you must realise that since I know your brother, your twin brother, that I also know all about you, about your rare DNA and the fact that it has enabled you to live so long. I know how old you are and that you were born on an island in the Aegean Sea, and I know that you were separated from your parents at birth and never saw them or your twin brother again."

Dayton was astounded but he didn't want to show it.

"That's absolutely fascinating, Dr Reid, but we are straying from the point. What did you mean when you said I was wasting my time?"

Claudia turned her head to look out of the window. The Tuscan countryside was now flashing past. She had no idea where she was and the names she saw on occasional signposts meant nothing to her; they all seemed to be very similar to each other. She turned back to face Dayton and spoke to him in as even a tone as she could muster.

"I know what you are hoping to achieve by taking Naomi and Sara. You want children who are like you. You want to replace the daughter you had who was killed."

She saw the surprise register in his eyes.

"I've been to your offices in New York and I saw her photo," she continued. "I can understand your grief, but wanting to have children with both Naomi and Sara, it's, well, apart from the moral abhorrence of that idea, that you should want to force yourself upon them, I'm sorry to tell you that what you are trying to achieve is impossible. You see, there can be no offspring from a man and a woman with your type of DNA; your genes are mutually destructive. It's like matter and antimatter, the egg simply can't be fertilised by the man's sperm."

Dayton sat back. The coldness had gone out of his eyes, which

Claudia found disconcerting: with just a slightly puzzled expression on his face, he was even more like Jacques. He looked down at his hands and then at hers, which were firmly clasping each other in her lap. For a moment it seemed as if he was about to take hers in his.

"You are wrong, Dr Reid," he said softly. "Quite wrong. About forcing myself on either Naomi, as you call her — she is Paola to me — or Sara. It was never my intention and it still isn't. You seem to think I am some kind of ogre, but I can assure you that I'm not. It is true that I intend to get my way, to produce a child or children who are like me, in the same way that Paola's father has, but not that way. I intend to take advantage of modern medical science and Paola is now willing to cooperate."

"Really! I'm surprised," said Claudia. "At least I think I am. But as I've said, you are wasting your time and causing a lot of grief, not only to Paola and Sara, but also to their families."

Dayton still refused to believe her. His tone changed, hardening again. "How can you be so sure, Dr Reid?"

"I'm sure because I'm a geneticist working in a cutting-edge laboratory with one of the world's most eminent professors of genetics. We made a study of ... your brother, and more recently of Naomi — Paola." She suddenly realised she was on thin ground. The studies had been on John and Lily; neither Jacques nor Paola had been involved.

"Now I know you are lying to me," retaliated Dayton. "You might have had time to study my brother, although why I can't imagine, but you certainly haven't had time to study either Paola or Sara. I have had them both under my close scrutiny for some time now, since before you even knew of them, and neither has been in touch with you or your professor. So in view of that, I have no reason to believe you. No, Dr Reid, it was a nice try, thinking that with your apparent naïvety and feminine charm you could trick me into believing your fairy story. However, I am sorry to disappoint you but you have stumbled across the wicked witch."

He paused, running through in his mind exactly what Claudia had said, processing the alternatives. He nodded slightly as the logic seemed to fall into place.

"Unless, of course, you have made a study of some sort. That would mean that since you haven't had time to study Paola and Sara, there must be others. I know about Paola's father, of course, John Andrews, but as a man he is of no interest to me. No, there must be other females. His children, perhaps, or my brother's, or both. There are others, aren't there Dr Reid, and you have made a rather pathetic attempt to keep it from me by lying about your genetics. I'm right, am I not?"

Against all her personal expectations and with her heart pounding at the thought that she might have compromised Lily and Phoebe, Claudia kept her cool. She eyeballed Dayton and shook her head very slightly.

"No, Mr Dayton, you are not. You were right the first time. I made up the science to try to persuade you to release them. But think about it, if there were others, how many would there be? This incredibly rare condition you have would cease to be rare. We'd be seeing people with your traits popping up all the time. A new species even. You know that's not true. You have only had one child like you in all your long life, and despite what you think, your brother has had none."

Dayton's smile was cold. "Good attempt at diversionary tactics, Dr Reid, but you see, I do believe you about making some studies, which means that you must have made them on Andrews and at least one other female. So whether or not you were lying to me about the results, you have confirmed that there are others."

Claudia desperately wanted to change the subject. The conversation was going round in circles and she was getting confused. The scientist in her was beginning to question her own results. They had certainly been convincing enough for John's and Lily's DNA, but what about Jacques'? She tried to remember the sequencing. Jacques' rare alleles were more or less the same as John's so the conclusions had to be valid for Jacques as well. The more she recalled the results, the more she was convinced that what she had told Dayton was true: he was wasting his time trying to produce offspring with either Paola or Sara, whichever way he planned to do it.

She glanced up at Dayton to find his eyes fixed on her. It was as if he was trying to read her mind. "Where are they, Mr Dayton?" she said. "Paola and Sara. Where are they? Are you taking me to the same place?"

To her surprise, Dayton's face relaxed and he smiled at her. "Yes, Dr Reid, I am. We are going to my house, which is, as I told you, very secluded. The chances of it being found by John Andrews or my brother are minuscule."

"And how long do you intend to keep me there?" Claudia had sudden visions of years passing with her in captivity while Dayton insisted on continuing with his pointless attempts at producing offspring.

"That depends on the success of what I have in mind, which in turn depends on you, Dr Reid."

"On me? Why?"

"You are a geneticist, Dr Reid, an expert working in what you yourself have told me is probably the most advanced research team in the world. You can give me the benefit of that expertise and join forces with my own expert in IVF, Dr Ronaldi. You may even have heard of him."

Claudia hadn't, but she said nothing, wondering what Dayton was going to say next.

"You see, I don't believe your results, Dr Reid, I think that what I am trying to achieve is possible. What it needs is a more genetic approach. I have no doubt that once you and Dr Ronaldi have compared notes, you will be able to come up with something that will improve the chances of success. You have given me hope, Dr Reid. It is very fortunate that you decided to follow me today."

Chapter Forty-Two

Sara pounded into the depths of the forest as fast as the dense undergrowth would allow, weaving past bramble, ducking branches, leaping over rocks. She knew that running at this pace she would not be able to hear anyone following since the only sounds she was really aware of were her own gasps for breath and the blood pumping in her ears. She also knew that if she continued at this pace she would soon be exhausted. However, the good thing was that the truck wouldn't be able to drive through this terrain: the men would have to follow on foot.

After several hundred metres, she stopped and tried to slow her breathing, gulping air as quietly as she could. She listened, but she could hear nothing except a light breeze in the trees. Her time in the forests in Colorado as a child came flooding back to her. She had survived there, avoided detection through cunning. She had left no trails except false ones, and she had learned to move silently. She could do it again. It meant moving with a careful footfall, not running flat out, and taking note of everything around her: a badly placed foot on a dead branch could send out a crack loud enough to betray her.

She moved on, farther and farther away from the fence, stopping every few seconds to listen and to check that she had disturbed nothing, given no indication of where she had been. She was torn between making a wide circle back to the fence, with thoughts of trying to rescue Paola, or forging on to get help as Paola would have wanted. But who could she ask? She was concerned that a man like Dayton would have the local authorities in his pocket, that if she walked into some police station, she would be kept waiting while Dayton was informed and he would send someone to take her back. That couldn't happen: there wouldn't be another chance since Dayton would be bound to keep both her and Paola under much tighter security.

She stopped for the twentieth time to listen, glad that Paola had insisted on her putting on a thick padded jacket. The light was starting to go and it was getting colder; a sky of marbled slate and gunmetal was closing in, threatening rain. She had just one chocolate bar that Paola had thrust into her hand before they left, but nothing else. She tried to remember how big Italy was, whether it was likely that these woods went on for hundreds of miles or whether she would soon find an end. Whichever it was, she couldn't continue once it was dark; she needed somewhere to settle down for the night, a dense clump of trees, preferably with some cover.

She broke from the trees onto a narrow track that seemed to come from the general direction of Dayton's estate. She must have been inadvertently following parallel to it as she made her way through the denser woods. This would make the going slightly easier, but she would also have to be extra careful since anyone following could move faster and more quietly along the track. She continued warily for about a kilometre when out of the corner of her eye she saw a hut hidden in the trees about a hundred metres from the track. In the rapidly fading light, she had almost missed it, but having seen it, she felt it beckoning her.

Checking constantly that she was leaving no trail, she quickly covered the distance to the hut and tried the door. It was unlocked. The inside took her by surprise: it was clearly used as an occasional refuge. There was a low canvas camp bed slung across some folding supports and a pile of blankets on a wooden chair next to the bed. In a small cupboard against one wall were several cans of sausages and beans, a can opener, and even three unopened plastic bottles of mineral water. She shook her head. This was like a five-star hotel compared with how she'd thought she'd have to spend the night. There was an oil lamp hanging from the roof, but she didn't dare light it in case the guards were following her. She opened a couple of cans and wolfed down the contents. Slightly more relaxed, she unfolded some of the blankets to make the camp bed more comfortable and then lay down, tuning her ears to the forest outside, trying to pick up any sound that might be her pursuers. But she could hear nothing except the natural sounds of the woods. She was quickly asleep.

Sara was awoken the following morning by a shaft of sunlight streaming straight into her eyes through the hut's only window. She sat up with a start and almost overturned the camp bed. She had no idea what time it was but to her horror she realised that the sun must have been up for at least a couple of hours. She should have been long gone, but at least the lack of company might mean that no one was out looking for her. That thought surprised her since Dayton would definitely want her to be found. Perhaps Paola had somehow managed to overcome all three of the guards. It seemed unlikely, but Paola had shown extreme cunning in dealing with the guards the previous day and she was utterly ruthless. If that were really true, perhaps Paola had managed to hobble into the forest herself. Should she go back to find her? Sara tossed the idea around and decided that if Paola had managed to make her way into the undergrowth, she wouldn't have got far since her ankle was in bad shape. So even if she had overcome the other guards, a search would already be underway for her by now, and given that the sun had been up for some time, the chances were that she'd been caught.

However, if the guards hadn't been searching for Sara the previous night, they surely must be by now. She had to leave and distance herself from the estate. She opened another can of sausages, less appetising now she wasn't so hungry, tucked a bottle of water into her jacket and left the hut.

She made her way back to the track she'd found the previous evening and began jogging steadily along it. The track wound along the contours of the land and slowly descended to a stream that ran along the valley floor. Alongside the stream, the track widened, now substantial enough for an off-road vehicle to drive along it. She would have to be careful, but at least this must mean that she was closer to some sort of civilisation. Suddenly, not too far away, but off the track, she heard a female voice talking firmly to someone. She stopped and listened. There was just one voice and the language was English, and whoever it came from was staying in the same spot. She walked slowly and silently towards the voice, hoping that the person it belonged to wasn't talking on a phone or a radio to someone she might alert.

She rounded a bend in the track and immediately ahead she saw a woman of about sixty positioning an easel on which stood a large blank canvas stretched on a frame. Sitting on a chair watching her was a Yorkshire terrier with a pink ribbon tied in a bow on top of its head. The woman was in earnest conversation with the dog, seemingly seeking its help in deciding the optimum position for her canvas to capture the scene stretched out before her. Sara realised that the forest had suddenly thinned. Along the valley were several fields, one of which had a small pond, the fortunes of which must have depended on the level of water flowing in the stream next to it. With a backdrop of fir trees and wild oak, the latter still bearing a golden cloak of dying leaves, it was an attractive scene of bucolic harmony dappled by the clear autumn sunlight, the previous day's clouds having departed to threaten elsewhere.

The dog barked just as Sara coughed quietly.

The woman spun around. "Oh, my dear, you took me quite by surprise," she said as she patted the terrier's head. "I don't usually meet anyone around here except the odd hunter, and they're so noisy that I hear them coming for miles. It's a wonder that they ever catch anything."

She looked Sara up and down. "Heavens, dear, you are rather bedraggled. Are you all right?"

Sara nodded, the tension of the potential threat the woman might have posed now evaporated.

"Yes, thank you, I'm fine. But I do need to get in touch with someone. You don't happen to have a cell, do you?"

"A what, dear? Oh, you're American. I've heard that word on the television. I—"

"I mean a phone," said Sara.

"Yes, of course you do. Well, you're in luck, I do have one, but I'm afraid the chances of it working here are pretty slim. No one seems to have told the Italian telephone companies that this country has hills and valleys where mobile signals bounce around until they disappear to wherever these things disappear. There just aren't enough masts around."

As she was speaking she was rummaging through a large leather bag. "Here it is," she said, producing an ancient-looking phone. "Just as I thought," she added, peering at the screen, "not a bar in sight. Would you like a cup of tea, dear? You look as if you could do with one." She produced a Thermos flask from the bag and unscrewed the cup. "I've only got ginger, don't like the builder's stuff myself. There are some tea bags in the box by the paints." She pointed with the Thermos flask to a folding table she'd set up for the tools of her morning's work.

"Thank you, thank you very much," said Sara. "That would be wonderful."

"Excellent," beamed the woman. "Now, tell me, what's a pretty young American woman like you doing deep in these woods? Did you get lost?"

Sara seized the opportunity to fabricate a story. "I did," she said ruefully. "I took a long hike yesterday afternoon, dropped my map somewhere, not that I really knew where I was on it anyway, and ended up stuck in this forest. Luckily, I found a hut back there where I spent the night."

"Lucky indeed," agreed the woman. "It was a cold night. Nearly abandoned the idea of coming this morning. Then when I woke up and saw that it was going to be such a lovely day, I changed my mind and here I am." She held out her arms and smiled. "So, I'd imagine you have people who might be worried about you."

"I do," said Sara. "My husband. He'll be worried sick. How far is it to the nearest village? I should be able to call him from a bar. All these villages have bars, don't they?"

"They do, but it's about five miles. Bit of a hike. Listen, my wagon is just along the way. I'll take you if you like. I can leave my stuff here; it'll be quite safe unless it gets knocked over by a wild boar." She chortled quietly at the thought.

"Would you? Would you really?" gushed Sara. "Gosh, I'd appreciate it so much. You really are very kind."

During the drive to the nearest village, Sara learned that the woman was called Dorothy. "Dot, for short, although there are some heathens around who call me 'Dotty' on account of some of the out-of-the-way places I end up painting." She was an English-woman who had lived in the area for twenty years making a living from her paintings, many of which were shipped to a gallery in London for sale. "Quite a following back there," she said. "Just as well. The Italians don't seem to appreciate them."

On reaching the tiny village of Molino di Sant'Agata, Dorothy parked her wagon — an ancient Land Rover Defender — opposite Bar Rita, one of three commercial premises in the village, the other two being a butcher's shop and a shop specialising in local honey. Sara eased her way from the discomfort of the passenger seat. She was convinced the battered vehicle must have been built before the concept of suspension was ever conceived. Dorothy retrieved her phone from her voluminous bag, checked the signal and tossed it to Sara.

"There we are. Five bars. You should be able to reassure your hubby now. Sit yourself down here; I'll get some coffee. Espresso all right for you?"

"Actually, I'd prefer Americano, if that's OK," said Sara, catching the phone and sitting at one of the two tables outside the bar.

She looked at the keys and realised she didn't know a single number in Italy. Why should she? She'd been abducted in the Lake District and brought straight to Dayton's house. What was Pete's US cell phone number? Try as she may, she could only think of some of the digits. Then she remembered. The Lakes. She knew John's landline number. She jumped up and ran after Dorothy.

"Dot," she called through the bar's doorway, "Is it OK if I make an international call? I'll pay for it."

"Go ahead," said Dot, breaking off from a conversation with the bar owner. "Call my agent in London all the time. They pick up the tab, so don't give it another thought."

Sara rushed back outside, punching the numbers. After three rings, Sophie answered. "Auntie Sara!" she cried as soon as she heard Sara's voice. "I— Oh, Mummy!"

Lola had grabbed the phone from her.

"Sara! Where are you? Are you OK? Christ, we've been so worried."

"I'm fine, Lola. I'm in Italy. I managed to escape from where I was being held. Is Pete there?"

"He's in Italy with the others looking for you and Paola. Paola phoned someone in Brazil of all places and told him she was in Italy, so they've gone to try to find you. Are you with Paola?"

"No, but I was. She fell when we were escaping. I think she broke her ankle. She insisted that I carry on and now I'm glad I did because I think I can find my way back to Dayton's house."

"Excellent. Look, you probably don't have John's number, or any of the others, do you?"

"No, that's why I called you. Can you give them to me?"

"Give me a second; I need to look at the contacts list on the mobile. Have you got a pen?"

"I'll get one," grabbing a napkin to write on.

"Are they all here in Italy, Lola? Lily as well? I don't think—"

"No, Lily stayed here. Digby wouldn't allow her to go, for obvious reasons. Julie stayed too. She was in a bit of a state after you were taken. She's better now, but she'll be jumping for joy when she knows you're OK."

"Can I speak with her?"

"She's at the gallery with Lily and now, of course, one of the minders. Still got your pen? I'll give you the number."

"OK, but can you call her and tell her? I need to get in touch with Pete and the others before I do anything else. Tell her I'll call as soon as I can."

"Right. So where exactly are you, Sara?"

"Oh, gosh. I don't know." She looked up to see Dorothy carrying two coffees to the table. "Dot, where is this place?"

"Molino? It's about twenty minutes from Anghiari. Do you know where that is?"

Sara shook her head.

"San Sepolcro?" suggested Dot.

"San Sepolcro?" echoed Sara.

"Did you say San Sepolcro?" said Lola.

"Yes," said both Dorothy and Sara at the same time.

"That's where John was born," said Lola.

Chapter Forty-Three

Claudia drifted from a troubled sleep full of half-formed images: racing through the countryside at high speed on a massive Harley-Davidson motorcycle with extended sportster handlebars that she was fighting to control; Jacques speaking in a strange accent as they raced along in a car; Jacques turning to her, his face hideously disfigured by a jagged scar running from above his eye down to his jaw; Jacques laughing tauntingly, jeering at her desperate attempts to persuade him she was not lying to him.

She opened her eyes but she could see nothing. The images receded but were still an echo in her semiconscious mind. Her mouth was dry, very dry. She was lying on a bed. There was no noise, nothing. She must be in a room. Where?

She sat up and her head started to spin. Why was she so woozy? She tried to stand, but her legs wouldn't hold her, so she sat again. She rubbed her eyes and the back of her neck. She walked her hand along the top of the bed towards the head end. She found the wall and then a light switch. She pressed it. The room was suddenly bathed in a soft, yellow light. She blinked, waiting until her eyes adjusted, and then looked around. The room wasn't large, perhaps four metres long by three wide. There were doors at either end and a window in the wall opposite the bed, the outside world screened off by large internal shutters. Apart from the bed, which was single size, the only furniture was a tall wooden wardrobe and a nightstand.

Her next attempt at standing was more successful. She made her way over to the window, twisted the wooden stop holding the internal shutter closed and opened it. She was greeted by a panoramic view of a forest extending to the horizon, a sea of golden brown in the sunlight. Below her were some formal gardens, low box hedges and clusters of lavender, flowerless now, trimmed back for winter.

Where was she? She ran her hand through her tangled hair and she felt an urgent need for a brush and a mirror. Looking over at the smaller of the two doors, she hoped it was a bathroom; she had suddenly realised that she needed that too. She opened the door and found she was right. Not only that, the bathroom was fully equipped with toiletries, brushes and combs.

She emerged feeling fresher, her hair and teeth brushed and her face washed. As she walked back to stare out of the window, she tried to remember the events of what had presumably been the previous day.

Fragments of her dreams of racing through the countryside flashed in her mind, but now the Harley had been replaced by a small red motor scooter, a Vespa. Why was she finding it so hard to remember? She realised her mind was still far from clear so she sat down on the bed and put her head in her hands, rubbing her eyes with her fingers.

Dayton. She had chased Marcus Dayton after Ced had called her at the hotel. She had taken the red Vespa from a bewildered young American, pleaded with him, promised him heaven knew what, and then roared off through the city. She'd found Ced, who had refused to join her on the scooter, which was just as well since it was hardly more powerful than her father's lawnmower, and then she'd met Ced's friend. What was his name? Verdi. Yes, something or other Verdi.

While they were talking, Dayton had walked out of a restaurant. Even though she'd known he was Jacques' identical twin, seeing him in the flesh had still been a shock. But it wasn't until she caught up with him, or rather he stopped to let her catch him, that she saw how someone identical to another could also be so different. Dayton had forced her into his car and then calmly informed her that he expected her to help some IVF expert in his work. She'd told him that his quest was futile and why. But she had fluffed her story, left it with gaping holes, and worse, she had more or less let him know about the existence of John's other daughters, Lily and young Phoebe. Dayton had scoffed at her, told her she was lying, and now she was here.

But how did she get here? She had no memory of arriving, no memory of anything beyond their conversation in the car. She stood and walked over to the window, running her hand through her hair as she tried to coax the memory from where it was lingering somewhere in the recesses of her mind.

Dayton had asked her if she was cold after her long ride in the chill of the lower reaches of the Casentino. He had produced a cashmere shawl from somewhere and she had wrapped it around her shoulders. Then he had opened a compartment in the rear of the seat in front of him and taken out a flask. Coffee. He had poured her coffee. He'd poured himself one too, but he'd set the cup to one side. Claudia had welcomed the thought of a hot drink; the chill had got to her. After a few sips of coffee she remembered nothing else, except a gentle hand relieving her of the cup.

So that was it. He had drugged her, which was why she was so groggy. God, she was gullible! She shook her head in disgust at herself. What was going to happen now? She was locked in a room. Or was she? She rushed over to the door and turned the handle, but the door didn't move. She kicked it in frustration. "Anybody there?" she yelled. "You can't just leave me here. I want to know what's going on? Hey! Anyone!" She kicked the door again and yelped.

She sighed heavily and marched back to the window. It was not only locked, it was barred. And even if she could have climbed out, it looked like she was on at least the third floor of whatever this place was.

She thought back to when she had first seen Dayton outside the restaurant. Verdi had seen him too and he had called out to her as she charged off. Surely he must have called Ced immediately. But what use was that? Neither Verdi nor Ced would have any idea of the direction she'd taken. But at least he knew, which meant that Jacques and the others would know. They were actively scouring the countryside for large, well-guarded estates. Surely it would only be a matter of time until they found this place. Wouldn't it?

However, Dayton wasn't stupid. He'd know what was going on. What would she, Claudia, do in that situation, given he had what appeared to be huge resources at his disposal? She'd up sticks and go somewhere else, that's what she'd do. He was bound to have other houses in other countries, probably in this one too. He'd go to one of those and take her with him. And, of course, Paola and Sara, both of whom were presumably here in the house. Claudia wondered if that were true. Were they here, perhaps being held in rooms like this? Maybe they were close by.

She went back to the door and banged hard on it with her fists. "Paola! Sara! It's Claudia! I'm here too! Dayton caught me!"

She stopped, listened, but there was only silence. Damn, she thought, frustrated. Well, she decided, gritting her teeth, if Dayton did decide to move somewhere else and take them with him, she'd resist. She wouldn't let it happen without a fight. She'd read Paola's account given to Nancy Wright of the way she'd resisted attacks over the centuries. She'd do the same.

She was musing over this, boosting her own confidence, when she heard some movement outside the door followed by the sound of a key turning in the lock. She spun round to face whoever it was coming in.

The door opened and a huge woman dressed as a nurse came in. Her enormous size made Claudia look like a child by comparison. She had a large bruise on her face, just above her right eye. She glowered suspiciously at Claudia and then took a step back against the open door to make way for yet another equally huge nurse, this one also sporting an angry bruise on her face. The second nurse was carrying a tray with some covered dishes and a china jug with a lid. She placed it on the bedside table.

Completely stunned by their size, Claudia found herself unable to speak. She had plenty she wanted to ask them, but no words would come as she opened and closed her mouth. The nurses backed out of the room, not taking their eyes off Claudia until they were closing the door.

Claudia lifted the covers from the dishes to find soup, some cheese, tomatoes and fruit. She replaced them. She didn't feel hungry. She recalled the end of the conversation with Dayton in the car, him telling her that she would be required to join the IVF expert. Then she thought about the two huge nurses with the bruises on their faces and wondered if the marks were Paola's handiwork. She shook her head in frustration: there was no way that she, Claudia, could ever get the better physically of those two. Resist? She wouldn't stand a chance. Her fists would be no more effective than feather dusters.

She sat down hard on the bed, the hopelessness of her situation suddenly overwhelming her. She put her head in her hands and cried.

Chapter Forty-Four

The group of ageing locals, village men who spent their days solving Italy's problems while drinking their coffees, aperitivi and digestivi at Bar Rita in Molino di Sant'Agata, watched in bemusement as in fairly rapid succession three cars screeched into the village and braked to a halt outside the bar. First to arrive by ten minutes were Corrado Verdi and Ced in Verdi's powder blue Maserati. This in itself was enough to keep the locals arguing over its merits for the rest of the day. Ignoring them, Ced and Corrado rushed into the bar to find Sara sitting nervously in the corner — she had retreated there after Dorothy suddenly remembered that she was expecting an urgent call from her agent on her house phone and had to leave.

Sara had never met either Ced or Corrado, so she was initially concerned when they appeared through the door. However, Ced's artistic eye recognised her features immediately and he walked over to her with a broad, reassuring smile on his face.

"You must be Sara," he said. "I'm Ced, Claudia's friend, and this is Corrado Verdi."

"Yes," said Sara, the relief sounding in her voice. "Lola called a little while ago to say you were coming. I'm so pleased to see you." She reached out to touch Ced's arm, as if to make sure he was real.

"It's OK," said Ced softly as he took her hand. "No one can hurt you now."

.   .   .

The previous day when Ced had run flat out through the back streets of Florence after Claudia's scooter and turned into the narrow viale where Verdi had followed Dayton, he had seen a very bewildered-looking Verdi standing outside the restaurant.

"Where's Claudia?" he shouted, pounding up to Verdi. He feared the worst since there was no sign of the motor scooter.

Verdi shook his head. "I have no idea. The man I was following came out of the restaurant a few moments after the young lady arrived, jumped into his car, and she roared off after him. In these back streets, they could have ended up going in any direction."

"How long ago?" demanded Ced.

"No more than a couple of minutes," said Verdi.

"Then let's get back to your car and hunt around the town. There must be a chance we'll spot them," said Ced, very much doubting there would be. The thought of Claudia following Dayton alone made him feel sick with worry.

Verdi's car was illegally parked outside Santa Croce, but owing to his status with the church and his renown in the art world, his car was immune from any form of ticket. They hurried back to it, Ced urging the unfit Verdi along. Verdi collapsed into the driver's seat, raising his arms in a gesture of hopelessness. "Where shall we start?" he said breathlessly.

"I don't know," replied Ced. "Is there a wider road where we could at least get a better view than in these back streets?"

"Yes," said Verdi. "It's only a couple of minutes away."

As Verdi drove onto the Viale Amendola, Ced pulled out his phone and hit the buttons for Claudia's number. He let it ring and ring, but there was no answer. Her phone was in fact ringing away in her bag as she drove towards Pontessieve, but with the noise of the scooter and the traffic, she had no chance of hearing it.

After redialling several times as they scoured the Florentine streets, Ced decided to call Jacques. The phone was answered after just one ring, the surprise at seeing Ced's number on the caller display sounding in Jacques' voice.

"Ced! How—"

"Jacques. There's no time for niceties. Where are you?"

"In Italy, in the countryside north of Siena. What's happened?"

Ced explained the events of the past two hours as briefly as he could, finishing by saying, "I can't forgive myself. If only I'd jumped on the back of the scooter. At least we'd be following Dayton together."

There was a brief silence at the other end of the phone while Jacques thought through the options. Then he asked, "Where are you now exactly, Ced?"

Ced looked out of the car window. "Exactly, I'm not sure, but we're basically in the middle of Florence. Looks like the inner ring road. Yes, there's a sign for Santa Maria Novella station."

"OK, you keep searching the streets while John and I head back to Florence. I'll call Pete and Matt and get them back too. We're staying at the Grand. I'll call you when we arrive and we can all meet up to decide what we do next."

After continuing their search for nearly an hour, Ced and Verdi decided it was futile and they made their way to the Grand Hotel. They pulled up outside the main entrance where the doorman immediately took a solicitous interest in the Maserati. They left him drooling while they headed up to Jacques' room, arriving only minutes before Pete and Matt.

"Any news?" asked Pete breathlessly as Jacques opened the door for them.

Jacques shook his head, the worry over Claudia's disappearance etched into his face. He introduced Ced and Verdi to Pete and Matt and the six sat down to compare notes.

As they were talking, John noticed Verdi taking more than a passing interest in his face. Verdi was unaware of John's history; he knew only that John was a brilliant artist. However, with Verdi's encyclopaedic knowledge of Italian art, and in particular his intimate familiarity with the Piero della Francesca painting 'The Awakening' in which John's face featured as one of the shepherds, he was starting to join up a few dots. John thought it best to pre-empt his questions so that they could remain focussed.

"Corrado," he said. "You are probably wondering exactly what's going on, over and above the abduction of Pete's wife and my ... of Paola. I know that despite having helped Ced enormously with the identification of a number of paintings three years ago, you haven't been told very much."

Verdi brushed a hand through his leonine hair, lifted his shoulders and pushed his head forwards. "I only know that whatever story is behind it, it is rather sensitive," he said. "I have no wish to pry; you clearly have your reasons."

John smiled. Verdi's body language was screaming that he would love to be told. "That's very diplomatic of you, Corrado. However, when this is all over, I'll sit down with you and explain a few things. Given your involvement, I think you have a right to know. But for now, may I ask you to accept anything odd about Jacques and me that you hear, and even about Sara and Paola?"

Verdi lifted his shoulders in acquiescence.

John had several large-scale maps of Tuscany spread out on the floor in front of them. A number of areas had been inked in with felt-tip pens of various colours, indicating places they had already searched, towns and extra-urban locations that were population centres and therefore of no interest, and tracts of land that still needed to be explored. He pointed to the maps as he explained their progress to Ced and Verdi.

"Our results so far have eliminated much of the western side of Tuscany and now have us homing in on the Casentino and areas east of that in the Apennines, heading into Le Marche. That was based on what Paola told Barros, although she could have been mistaken since there is other similar terrain in the north of Italy and farther south. However, now that Dayton has been spotted in Florence, it would appear that she was right, so I think we should continue our search as planned."

Pete glanced at Jacques. "How certain are we that Dayton has Claudia?" he asked hesitantly.

"I think we must assume it," said Jacques. "She followed Dayton's car and since then she hasn't been answering her phone. Is there any way we can track it?" he added, turning to Ced.

Ced shook his head. "Not if it's turned off, no. I can call a colleague in the UK to check it out with some tracking software on the computer in my office, but frankly, if she's not answering, my guess is that it's been switched off."

"Where did she get the scooter from?" asked Matt.

"Good point, Matt," cried Ced, springing to his feet. "She sort of borrowed it from an American tourist here, outside this hotel. It was a fairly classic scooter, not a modern one. Perhaps someone at reception might know who rented it and where he got it from."

He rushed out of the door. John watched him go and then decided to follow. He wanted to call Digby to ask for whatever help he could offer, which might include tapping into the Italian police system to check for any scooters that had been found, or worse, involved in accidents. He didn't want Jacques to be party to that conversation for the time being.

He caught up with Ced in the hotel lobby. "Anything?" he asked.

Ced nodded. "The scooter rental was arranged here at the desk. They weren't over-impressed that Claudia commandeered the thing, but they did give me the number."

"Let me have it," said John. "I'll see what Digby can come up with."

"Do they have traffic cameras here, like they do in England?" asked Ced. "Digby might be able to persuade them to look for the scooter."

John shook his head. "No, not as far as I'm aware. Italy isn't nearly so big brotherish. I know what you mean: in England there are so many traffic cameras that it's hard to drive anywhere without there being some sort of digital record of your vehicle. Here the system isn't as extensive. It you don't go into historic centres that are restricted and you don't break the speed limit, you can pretty much drive around in total anonymity."

They walked from the lobby into the street and watched the evening traffic along the now dark Lungarno. Each time a scooter or small motorcycle passed, they looked up expectantly.

"This is stupid," growled Ced. "Let's go upstairs and make a plan for tomorrow."

· · ·

There was nothing back from Digby Smith by the time Ced and Verdi left to head for their hotel. They had agreed to meet the others the following morning at eight and to divide up the Casentino into three areas to improve the speed of the search. They had been on the road for two hours when John received the call from Lola to say that Sara had escaped and that she was near Anghiari. Ced and Verdi's search area was the closest to the village where Sara was waiting and hence they arrived first.

"Do you know where Pete and Matt are?" Sara looked expectantly at the two men as Verdi brought three coffees to the table.

"They'll be here very soon," replied Ced. "John called them before he called us. It's just that they've been looking in an area a bit farther away from here."

He paused. "Sara, you know that Claudia's missing as well as Paola, don't you?"

"Yes," said Sara, "Julie told me. John called Lola last night. Whatever was Claudia thinking of, following Dayton like that?"

"That's Claudia," said Ced. "She would never have passed up that opportunity. I just wish I'd jumped on the back of the scooter, although I'd probably have slowed it down."

Corrado shook his head. "No Cedric, I should have gone with her. I could have made some calls while we followed."

"Hindsight's a wonderful thing," said Sara ruefully. "I take it there's no news."

Ced shook his head. "No, but assuming that Dayton has her, it would seem reasonable to assume that he's taken her to the same place where you were held. Actually, Sara, it's brilliant that you've escaped. It's really going to narrow the search. As far as I can tell, for John and the others it's been like looking for a needle in the proverbial haystack. What time did you leave the house with Paola yesterday?"

"In the early afternoon."

"So if Dayton brought Claudia to the house, you wouldn't have seen her since you'd already gone."

"I guess, yes."

"How far away do you reckon Dayton's house is?"

"From here? I don't know. Maybe ten, fifteen miles. Not far. If I could study a detailed enough map, we should be able to locate it."

"I'll fetch mine from the car."

As he stood, he heard a car roar into the village and screech to a halt outside the bar. Doors slammed and suddenly there was Matt bursting through the door.

"Mom!" Matt rushed across the bar, scooped Sara from her chair and buried his face in her neck. Then Pete arrived and threw his arms around both of them. "Sweetheart—"

Sara burst into tears. "Oh, Pete, Matt, I can't believe you're here."

"Are you OK, Mom?" said Matt. "He hasn't hurt you?"

"I'm fine, really. Apart from injecting me with something to knock me out for the journey, I've been treated well enough."

As they were hugging and Sara was alternately stroking their cheeks and wiping her eyes, John and Jacques arrived. The small bar now seemed very congested. Two of the local clientele stuck their heads through the open door to see what all the fuss was about, but since they only spoke the local dialect, neither of them ever having ventured beyond San Sepolcro in their entire seventy-plus years, they had little idea what was going on.

"Sara," said John, "it's wonderful to see you. You're not hurt in any way?"

Sara smiled and shook her head.

"Lola said Paola was injured," continued John.

"Yes, there were trip wires outside the fence. She snagged one and fell quite badly. I think she might have broken her ankle; if not, it's severely sprained. She couldn't walk on it." She looked shame-faced. "I'm sorry, John, she insisted that I go on. I wanted to stay, to try to help her. She tried to walk with me but it was no use."

"She was right," said John. "If you had stayed, both of you would have been caught and we'd be no further forward."

Jacques touched John on the shoulder. "The maps, mon ami," he said quietly. "I think we have no time to waste. I don't want

Dayton to anticipate our arrival and disappear with Claudia and Paola."

"I agree," replied John. "We need to make a plan immediately. I'll get them."

While John went to the car, Jacques put his arms around all three of the Farsleys. "Sara," he said, "I can't say how pleased I am to see you here safe and sound. You had a remarkable escape. How did you manage it?"

"It was all down to Paola; she's really quite amazing. And then finding Dot this morning was another stroke of luck."

"Dot?"

"An artist I bumped into. She brought me here."

"Where is she now?"

"She had to leave, but she said she'd be back later."

"Interesting," said Jacques. "I'd like to talk to her."

John spread the large-scale map of the immediate area he'd fetched from the car across one of the bar's round tables. He found Molino di Sant'Agata and drew a ring around it with a red pen. "Are you up to looking at this map and helping us to locate Dayton's house?" he said to Sara.

"Of course," said Sara. "I'm as keen as anyone to find it and get Paola and Claudia out of there."

As she sat down at the table, she looked at her husband. "Can you call Julie, sweetheart, tell her you're here with me? She's desperate to hear."

Jacques turned to John. "The Three Musketeers have expanded to seven, mon ami, all searching for Paola and our super-sleuth. But I think it would be unwise for the entire band to continue the search."

"Well, don't think you're relegating me to the sidelines," said Pete. "We've come a long way together."

"I know, Pete," said Jacques, putting a hand on his shoulder. "But with the three of you here safe and sound, and with your lovely daughter safe back in England with Lola and Digby's minders, your family is now whole again. I think it would be unreasonable to separate you again and subject you to any further risk.

And anyway, we shall need someone here to assist Corrado with any advice or dealings with the authorities."

He glanced over at Verdi. "Do you agree, Corrado, that it would be better for you to remain here as a point of contact?" Verdi nodded, the relief clear on his face.

Jacques smiled and turned again to Pete. "I think it is now down to John and me. We'll locate the house and find a way of rescuing them."

"That's nonsense, Jacques," said Ced. "You can't have just two musketeers. And you won't, not while I'm around. I'll replace Pete in the ranks. I feel totally responsible for Claudia being taken by Dayton and I can't sit back and watch from the sidelines while you two go after her and Paola."

"I don't know, Ced," said John. "I know we worked as a team before when you and the prof rescued me from Peterson, but this is all very different."

Ced shook his head. "Peterson was crazy, John, ruthless, and would think nothing of killing anyone who got in his way. I don't think that Dayton is quite as crazy as that. He may want what he wants very much, but I doubt he would kill us to get it."

He turned to Sara. "What do you think, Sara? You've met him."

Sara sighed. "I don't know. He's certainly single-minded and relentless in pursuing what he wants. But I think he would stop short of murder." She paused, her eyes flicking hesitantly to John and then looking away. "However, there has been some loss of life."

"You mean the woman in Cape Cod?" said John. "Surely that was self-defence on Paola's part."

"Yes," said Sara, although her face betrayed her lack of conviction. "It probably was." She paused, looking down at her hands. "There have also been a couple of incidents here," she added quietly.

"What sort of incidents?" said John.

"Let's just say that there are fewer guards now than when Paola arrived, and a couple of other staff who never want to see her again. My mother is an interesting person."

"OK," said Jacques. "Let's look at the map and decide on what we're going to do. Then we'll know what resources we'll need."

He pointed to the circled village. "This is where we are, Sara. You say the artist brought you here. How long did that take?"

"It was about twenty minutes," said Sara as she studied the terrain around the village. "Let me see, we came in from this direction. There was a river, well, a stream really, where I met Dot. Oh, heavens, there are rather a lot."

She went silent as she pored over the map, running her finger in several directions. Finally she said, "I think it could be around here. This looks like a very extensive area of woodland, the largest on the map. I know from what Paola said that the estate is huge. Is this a house, to the northern end of the woodland?"

The others looked closer. John sighed in frustration. "These maps are good, but they are based on old military surveys. We could do with something more up-to-date."

Ced straightened up. "No problem," he said, pulling out his phone. Then he changed his mind and turned to the door. "I've got my iPad in the car. Its screen is much bigger than a phone. Let's have a look at Mr Google's satellite version."

He was back in an instant, his attention entirely focussed on the tablet's screen.

"Here we go," he muttered, glancing over at the map on the table. "Let's see, here's the village … if we scale back, then … over here a bit … yes, there's that area of woodland. And yes, that is a house, a pretty big one I should say. Here, Sara, what do you think?"

He moved next to Sara as the others clustered round. "Does that look familiar?" he said.

Sara studied the satellite photo and zoomed it in with her fingers. "That's it!" she cried, looking up, her eyes excited. "No question. The gardens immediately outside the house are quite formal: low box hedges and things. I've only seen part of it, but this side," — she pointed to the south side of the house — "is where we walked into the woods."

She zoomed the image back and moved it around. "I wonder if we can see the fence. Gosh, the woods really are dense. Paola said they were. But there's a track around the fence that should show up. Look! It's here, I think. Yes."

They traced what was visible of the fence and then followed Sara's best guess of her route through the woods beyond the fence to where she met Dorothy.

"You did well, Sara," said Jacques. "It would have been all too easy to go round in circles."

Sara grinned. "I had some good training in Colorado back in the seventies."

"The seventies?" said Verdi in astonishment as he computed the numbers. He had assessed her age as early thirties at the most, and given Matt's age, assumed she must have been a very young mother.

"I told you it was complicated, Corrado," said John, raising his eyebrows in amusement.

Verdi shook his head. "Maria Madre di Dio e tutti i Santi," he muttered.

Jacques stood back and put his hand on John's shoulder. "I think we have two choices, mon ami," he said. "We either go back through the woods and try to penetrate the fence, although I suspect that would now be very difficult, especially since Sara and Paola managed to breach it once, apparently through incompetence on the part of the guards." He paused, pursing his lips as he considered the options.

"Or?" said John.

"Or we drive up to the main gate, which appears to be a couple of kilometres to the north of the house, according to this satellite photo," he said.

"The woods would seem to be the better option," said Ced. "We might be able to find some weakness in the system."

"Paola told me that there are cameras along the fence, and a load of hi-tech security stuff," said Sara.

John shook his head. "I don't think we have the time to scout through the woods and hope for something to turn up with the fence. We would run the risk of being stuck there while Dayton goes out of the main gate with Paola and Claudia. By the time we got in, we could find just an empty house."

Ced wasn't convinced. "We can't just drive up to the main gate and tell them we have an appointment to see Dayton," he said.

Jacques smiled. "Ah, but I think we can, Ced. You see, we have a secret weapon, at least as far as the guards are concerned."

"What sort of secret weapon?"

Jacques held his arms out wide. "Me," he said.

Chapter Forty-Five

"I don't understand. How can you be a secret weapon?"

"Ced," laughed Jacques, "for someone so intelligent, you are being rather slow to catch on."

Ced's face was a picture of incomprehension as he glanced around at the others. John's face was as inscrutable as ever, Sara and Pete had a knowing look and even Matt seemed to get it. Only Corrado Verdi looked as if he no longer understood English at all.

"Think about it, Ced," continued Jacques. "Think back to Santa Croce. What happened there?"

Slowly the light dawned. Ced nodded. "Yes, of course. I thought Dayton was you." He banged the heel of his right hand onto his forehead. "He's your twin brother, your identical twin brother. You're right, but I'm not just being slow, I'm being totally thick." Then he realised the implications of what Jacques was saying. "Jacques! You're not considering posing as Dayton, are you, showing up at the gate and expecting the guards to let you in? Surely there'll be some sort of record saying whether he's there or not?"

Jacques shrugged. "Who knows? It depends on whether he's come and gone today. And whether the same guards are on duty. We already know that they are not as good as expected. Look what happened at the gate in the fence when Sara escaped. It will all be in the perception. If they think the person they see is Marcus

Dayton, then whatever their contrary information is, they'll think there has been a mistake. They'll perhaps think that Dayton has left by another gate and that his departure has not got onto whatever system they have."

Ced still wasn't convinced. "Isn't it going to appear strange for you to be on foot?"

"I agree, that would be strange. But why should I be on foot? Perhaps Sara can help us here."

He turned to Sara who was sitting between Pete and Matt, holding hands with both of them. "Did you see any vehicles parked, Sara? Corrado's sharp eyes have told us that yesterday Dayton was using an expensive BMW, a black one. Could you perhaps have seen others?"

Sara thought about it. "I saw some cars parked at the side of the house when I looked back from the woods. It was some distance. There were three, I think. They looked like fancy 4 by 4s, but I've no idea what sort."

"What about the vehicle that showed up at the gate in the woods?" said John. "Lola told me you'd mentioned one."

"It was a pick-up, navy blue with a red stripe. A Mitsubishi. I remember the badge now. We had a Mitsubishi a couple of cars ago."

"Then we need a Mitsubishi pick-up," said John. "That would be perfect. The guards would just think that Dayton had been looking around the fence, perhaps left the estate through one of the gates in the fence rather than the main gate."

"What about clothing?" asked Matt. "Don't you think it would be better to be wearing something similar to what Dayton wears? And what about John and Ced? Are they going to be hiding, or should they be dressed as guards and one of them driving the flatbed?"

"That's good, Matt," said Jacques. "You're really getting the hang of this. Any tips, Sara?"

Sara inhaled deeply as she thought about it. "I've only seen Dayton a couple of times and that was indoors. He was wearing grey, medium-weight slacks, rather like those you're wearing, Jacques. Those would certainly do. Let me see, what else? Yes, he was wearing a ribbed beige sweater, quite heavy duty, military style. But there's one thing you must remember."

Jacques raised his eyebrows in question.

"Dayton has a large scar down his right cheek from a recent wound. I think it was Paola's handiwork."

"Ah," said Jacques, "that would explain the blood at Paola's house in Cape Cod. She cut him."

"Yes," said Sara. "So you'll need to remember to keep a hand over that part of your face when you see the guards."

"Talking of the guards, what were they wearing?" asked John.

"Navy combat trousers, boots and dark blue padded jackets," said Sara, picturing the guards at the fence. "Oh, and plain, dark blue baseball caps."

"No writing or logos?"

"No, nothing. Harder to see them, especially in poor light."

Jacques turned to Verdi. "Corrado, would you mind asking the bar owner where the nearest place is to buy this sort of stuff? And to rent a pick-up?"

Pleased to be of use, Verdi walked over to the bar and talked to the barman. After a brief but animated discussion, he returned to the table.

"San Sepolcro," he said as he sat down. "There's a small industrial estate on this side of the town as you approach from Anghiari. He said there's a superstore there that has that kind of clothing, and there's a heavy-duty vehicle rental place next door."

"How far?" said Jacques.

"About half an hour."

"Perfect. John, Ced, let's go." Jacques turned to the others. "It might be wiser if you went back to Florence, got out of this area," he said.

Pete shook his head. "No way, José. We're staying put. You might just need back up."

An hour and twenty minutes later, a dark blue pick-up driven by Ced braked to a stop outside the bar. John's rental car with Jacques in the passenger seat was just behind him.

"Wow!" said Sara as the three of them walked into the bar, all wearing the new clothes they'd just bought. "That was fast. And boy! Do you three cut the mustard. Two regular guards and a dead ringer for Marcus Dayton. This could work."

Jacques smiled. "Let's hope so. We've been discussing what we'll do once we're in and it occurred to me that I might have to continue my impersonation in front of one or two people. How similar is my voice to Dayton's?"

"The overall tone is very similar," said Sara. "But whereas from time to time when you're not being very proper English you have a hint of a French accent, Dayton's accent is slightly Germanic. Just a hint. Not like some German in a 'Hollyvood vore film'," she mimicked. "Far more subtle."

Jacques laughed, amused by her assessment of his normal accent. "You mean perhaps a little like this," he said, trying the flat accent of a non-native-English speaker from central Europe.

Sara nodded. "Perfect."

"Good," said Jacques. "Then let's not waste any more time. We need to go."

Sara looked at them uneasily. "Are you sure this is the best approach? Doesn't this country have some sort of law enforcement we could tap into? I've seen Dayton's guards. They're big and rather mean looking. You could be walking into a huge amount of danger."

John nodded. "You're right, Sara, we could. But we have to act now. I can't imagine even trying to explain what's happened to one of the local police forces; it would be way outside of their comfort zone. And anyway, Dayton has probably ingratiated himself with anyone important around here. They wouldn't take kindly to one of their sacred cows being criticised. No, if we went down that route, Dayton would just evaporate with Paola and Claudia while we were wrapped up in bureaucratic wrangling."

Sara sighed deeply. "I guess you're right." She stood and hugged the three of them in turn. "Do be careful," she said, swallowing hard.

"We shall," said John. "And rest assured, when we return, it will be with Paola and Claudia. That's a given."

Sara bit her lip and held up both hands with fingers crossed.

"Make sure you do," said Pete, slapping John on the back. "Heck, I really think I should be going with you."

"We've been through that, Pete," said John. "It'll all be fine, don't worry."

It took thirty minutes to drive the narrow winding roads that led up to the main entrance of Dayton's estate. Ced was at the wheel with John sitting in the middle of the cab and Jacques on the right by the passenger door. Both Ced and John were wearing dark glasses and the baseball caps they'd bought, while Jacques was wearing neither. He wanted the guards to see his face and for them to be convinced that whatever their information said to the contrary, the man before them was their boss.

They knew from the satellite photo that the house was about two kilometres inside the estate. Their plan was that once they'd crossed the first hurdle of the guards, Ced and John would get out of the pick-up about five hundred metres from the house and Jacques would drive on alone. Anyone he encountered would just think Dayton was going about his normal business.

"I'm feeling confident about the first part," said Jacques when they were about a kilometre from the gates to the estate, "but short of beating a hasty retreat, what will we do if the guards don't fall for me being Dayton? Or, for that matter, if they are suspicious of you two?"

Ced cast him a casually confident smile. "We'll bluff our way as far as the guardhouse where we'll sort them out, assuming there aren't too many. John and I have a history with guards, Jacques. We make a good team, don't we John?"

"No problem," said John, punching his right fist into his left palm.

In the event, it went remarkably smoothly. As they approached the gate in the high wall of the estate, Ced hit the horn to announce their arrival and swung the pick-up in towards the entrance.

A single guard carrying an iPad emerged from the gatehouse. As he peered in through the driver's window, Jacques leaned across John to talk to him, his right hand casually covering his right cheek. Startled, the guard's attention was now fully on him.

"Signor Dayton," he said, speaking Italian. "I was not expecting you. They didn't tell me at the house."

Without missing a beat, Jacques answered in fluent Italian, reading the guard's name badge as he did.

"No problem, Mario. I decided to make an inspection of the perimeter. After yesterday, we can't be too careful. I left through the south gate."

The guard nodded furiously. "Yes, signore. Of course, signore." But instead of moving, he remained rooted to the spot.

"Mario," said Jacques.

"Yessir!"

"The gate?"

"Oh, pardon, signore," he said, flustered. He ran to the gatehouse and pressed a button. The gate swung open and Ced hit the throttle. In the mirror, he could see the guard taking out a walkie-talkie as the gate shut behind them.

"He's on the radio," he said. "Presumably to the house."

"Then I'll drop you two fairly soon and drive up to the house alone," said Jacques.

"Just as well you speak the lingo," said Ced.

Jacques smiled. "Fortunately, I have a few up my sleeve," he said.

The gravelled drive curved through a number of bends as it climbed steeply towards the house. After the fourth tight bend, Ced looked up from the satellite image on his phone and announced that he and John should get out.

"This is the last of the serious bends before the house. After this, the road straightens as it gets onto the ridge. There's still good tree cover here; John and I can work our way quickly to the rear of the house. If Claw and Paola aren't locked up — and Sara told me that Dayton has been allowing Paola access to the downstairs sitting rooms — there's a chance we might see them."

He stopped the pick-up and got out, followed by John. Jacques moved across to the driver's seat.

"Phones on vibrate only?" he said.

"Yes," they both replied.

"OK, I'll leave the key in the footwell under the mat. If you need to leave in a hurry, especially with the women, do it. Don't wait for me. I'll find my own way out."

With that, he drove off towards the house while Ced and John hurried into the cover of the trees.

Seeing no point in announcing his arrival too loudly on the noisy gravel, Jacques stopped the pick-up about fifty metres from the house. He climbed out quietly, leaving the keys as arranged. He looked around. Three vehicles were parked close to the house: the large black BMW saloon and two high-end Toyota Land Cruisers, also black. Apart from the cars, there was no sign of anyone. He looked up at the house. It was a large, three-storey rambling affair, built mainly of local stone with terracotta tiles on the various roofs. It had a quiet authority that made Jacques think that it was no ordinary grand Italian country house, that the external impression was a façade hiding more than beamed living spaces and bedrooms. He estimated that there could be upwards of fifty rooms. More of a palazzo than a house, he thought.

Cursing the gravel, he trod as lightly as he could towards the huge dark walnut double main door that was accessed by a flight of wide, semicircular stone steps. The door was unlocked, opening silently when he turned the handle and pushed. Inside was a large rectangular entrance hall with an ornate wooden staircase on the right climbing through one half-landing to the first-floor rooms. The stairs leading up to the top floor were not immediately obvious.

Ahead, and more or less opposite the entrance, was a partially open door that appeared to access a corridor. To the right of it was an old stone fireplace with an armchair on either side.

He paused, listening, but he could hear no one. He continued on, but when he was about half across the hall, urgent footsteps sounded on the gravel outside, heading towards the house. He darted towards the corridor, but before he could reach it, the main door flew open.

"Signor Dayton!" cried a voice in Italian.

Jacques spun around. Two guards were standing by the door looking hesitant.

"What is it?" he said.

"Is everything all right, signore? It's just that the main gate called. We didn't know you'd left the estate."

"I haven't." The voice boomed across the hallway from where its owner was standing on the half-landing of the stairs.

The guards looked up in confusion at the owner of the voice and then back to Jacques.

"Don't stand there you idiots!" bellowed Marcus Dayton as he marched down the remaining stairs. "Seize him!"

The guards didn't move. Processing the conflicting information their eyes were feeding their limited brains was proving too much.

"He's an impostor, you fools!" shouted Dayton. "Use your eyes!" He turned his head slightly to show them his right cheek and pointed to the long scar running down it. It was enough for the guards. They darted forward and seized Jacques firmly by the arms. Both guards were well built and nearly as tall as Jacques; he made no attempt to resist.

Dayton crossed the hallway and stopped a couple of metres in front of Jacques. He slowly surveyed the brother he'd only recently learned existed and of whom he had seen just one photograph, the one he'd found in Claudia's handbag.

The corners of his mouth lifted in a slight sneer. "Jacques Bognard. My long-lost brother," he said in English. "We meet at last after two and a half thousand years. There can't have been many brothers in history who could have said that."

Ever cautious, Jacques' eyes flicked to the guards. Dayton laughed mockingly. "Oh, you needn't worry, these apes don't speak a word of English. I make sure of that when I employ them."

Jacques said nothing. He was still shocked at the sight of this man standing in front of him, a man who seemed identical to him in every way, apart from the scar.

Dayton looked around, as if considering the armchairs. Then he made a decision. "Bring him through here, into the rear sitting room," he ordered, and marched off ahead of Jacques and the guards.

The guards pushed Jacques forward and the three of them followed Dayton along the corridor and into the smaller of the two sitting rooms.

"Sit him down by the desk," said Dayton, nodding towards a chair at the library end of the room.

Jacques was pushed down hard onto the chair and the guards took up position, one on each side of him, their hands initially on his shoulders until he shrugged them off.

"You were quicker than I expected, brother," said Dayton as he sat down in a leather office chair on the other side of the desk.

"You knew I was coming?" said Jacques, still fascinated by Dayton's face.

Dayton laughed scornfully. "You think I'm stupid? Your lanky friend mistakes me for you at Santa Croce after which your girl-friend follows me through the Tuscan countryside. And then once we'd made each other's acquaintance, she tells me all about your little group. Of course I was expecting you. But I must congratu-late you on your planning; you moved quickly and you even dressed the part. Tell me, where are the two clowns who came with you?"

Before Jacques could answer, Dayton waved a hand dismis-sively. "No matter, the guards will find them soon enough and enjoy roughing them up a little. They have a few scores to settle after the activities of the last few days."

It was Jacques' turn to scorn. "I hope they are good enough. From what I've heard, Paola has outwitted them every time."

Dayton's features darkened. "That woman's a murdering bitch," he snarled.

"Maybe," retorted Jacques, "but she seems to have picked up a few survival skills." He turned his head to look up at the guard on his left and then to the other before he added, "It goes with the territory."

Dayton shook his head. "Don't get any ideas, these two are better than you might imagine. Anyway, survival is one thing. I've no doubt we have both had to make difficult choices at times through the centuries. The difference with Paola is that she seems to enjoy it."

"You don't seem very enamoured of the woman you've apparently chosen to be the mother of your children."

"I don't have to like her. I simply need her to perform a function. After that, I'll send her on her way."

"In case you don't know, you could be disappointed."

"Yes, your little girlfriend tried to spin that lie as well. I'm afraid she wasn't very convincing."

"You probably intimidated her, but she was telling the truth, I can assure you."

"That I doubt," sneered Dayton, "but I don't blame her for trying. She was merely trying to secure Paola and Sara's release."

"Well, thanks to the incompetence of your guards, Sara managed to secure her own release."

Dayton grunted. "That was more Paola than Sara, but fortunately, Paola had a little accident. However, it has been a lesson learned. I can assure you that the opportunities for escape will be far more limited where we are going next."

"And where is that?" Jacques felt a chill of concern run through his body. He knew that Dayton's resources were probably even greater than his own.

"Not a piece of information I'm willing to share, even with my brother," said Dayton. "However, I hope your girlfriend's skills are as good as you think they are since how long she remains my guest will depend completely on her scientific competence."

"What do you mean?" yelled Jacques. "How long are you intending to keep her?"

Dayton's smile was cold. "As long as it takes, my dear brother. You might think that I have rather base intentions for Paola, but don't worry; I do not intend to lay a hand on her. She will be attended by a world authority on IVF who will in turn be assisted by your geneticist. Dr Claudia Reid is going to have to find some way to circumvent the problems she claims prevent my sperm fertilising Paola's eggs. I have time and so does Paola. Let's hope it doesn't take the rest of Dr Reid's life."

"You're insane!" Jacques started forward in the chair, but immediately two strong hands clamped onto his shoulders to secure him.

"On the contrary, I'm simply someone who yearns to have a family. For my whole life, I have been under the impression that I was alone, a one-off. Of course, like you, I have had many ordinary children, but they didn't really interest me. Then Emma proved to me that I was wrong, that I wasn't some freak of nature, and having tasted that sweet dish of parenthood, I shall not be content until I have repeated it, preferably a number of times. Paola will provide the means for that and Claudia will provide the method.

"Surely, my brother, you have yearned to have children like yourself, have you not? Your friend John Andrews has had several, I believe. How many, I wonder? Maybe I need to gather them all together to maximise my chances."

"Over my dead body," snarled Jacques.

"If necessary," returned Dayton. "Now, pleasant though it is to talk, especially after such a long time, I'm afraid that I have to go. You see, Sara's escape yesterday and your irritating escapade to find Paola have left me vulnerable. I suspect that you have already informed the authorities of my location and that sooner rather than later we'll have them banging on the gate. I can't be here for that and neither can Paola or Claudia. It's such a bonus to have her along, you know. No, we are leaving within the hour and this time I can assure you that you'll have no chance of finding us. The next time you see your girlfriend, brother, will depend on her skills."

"It doesn't have to be like this, Marcus," pleaded Jacques. "I'm sure that some more sensible arrangement could be made. Why can't we all sit down like civilised people and discuss it? It's people's lives you are talking about, Claudia's, Paola's, the people who love them."

Dayton shook his head. "You haven't gained much wisdom in your two and a half thousand years, brother. I can't believe how dissimilar we are. Surely you've learned that in this world you can trust no one except yourself. We are not like other human beings, you and I, we are special and we have both accumulated the wealth to get what we want, whatever that may be. If they knew about us, the rest of the human race would simply want to kill us. We're a threat, don't you see, a threat because we're different. You can't trust them, brother. All you can do is pay what's necessary, buy what you want and leave them behind."

Jacques looked down. He was disgusted. "You're pathetic," he said. "But you are right about one thing, Marcus. I have accumulated much wealth; I am indeed extremely rich. I can assure you that I shall find you; there are only so many places to hide on this planet. You'll leave a trail and I'll find it."

"I look forward to the challenge," sneered Dayton. "Of course I could just kill you now, which would ensure that you don't become an irritation. But unlike Paola, I am not a murderer. I stop short of that unless I really have no choice. Make sure you leave me a choice, brother."

He turned his attention to the guards and spat an order. "Keep him here. Use whatever force is necessary."

The older of the two guards' smile was a vicious sneer. "Will do, boss." He grasped Jacques' shoulder, pushing him hard into the chair.

As Dayton made to leave, there was a commotion from the terrace outside. Four guards were marching along with John and Ced stumbling in front of them. Both were handcuffed, their hands behind their backs. The guard who seemed to be in charge opened one of the terrace doors and pushed the two captives in.

"What have we here?" said Dayton. He walked up to Ced and pulled off his dark glasses. "Ah, the young man who mistook me for Jacques. Well, take a good look, because this is the last time you'll ever see me."

He turned to John, who was no longer wearing his dark glasses. They had been knocked off when the guards had caught him as he and Ced were making their way around the edge of the trees to view the rear of the house. Dayton stood close to John, studying his face, a half smile on his lips.

"Yes, of course, now I see it, it's perfectly clear. You are Paola's father, John Andrews. At least that's who you are now. What was the name Paola gave for her father? Stefano Crispi? Yes, that was it. So Mr Andrews, what a pleasure to meet you. I wish we had more time to chat. I'm intrigued; just how many daughters do you have who share our unusual traits? Apart from Paola, of course. I suspect the Eurasian woman must be one. What about those girls in the Lake District? Maybe I should get to know them."

John struggled against the grip the guard had on his arm, but with his wrists handcuffed, the effort was futile. He glowered into Dayton's eyes. "Touch any of my children, Dayton, and I'll kill you."

Dayton shook his head. "Empty threats, I'm afraid, John. You don't mind if I call you John, do you?"

"I mind very much," snarled John.

Dayton shrugged his indifference and checked his watch. "I'm running out of time," he said. He turned his attention to the lead guard. "Sit them down there on the sofas. It shouldn't take four of you to control them. Leonardo, go and fetch the two women. Bring them here." He nodded his head towards the guard's holster. "Keep them covered with your gun. The taller one can be fiery, as you know."

The guard left and Dayton walked over to the desk to press a button on an intercom.

"Is the car ready?" he barked.

"Yes, signore," came the reply.

He walked over to the windows and stared at the view. Then he returned to stand in front of Jacques. "It's very inconvenient to be leaving this house, brother. I hope you're satisfied by all the trouble you've caused me, you and your friends."

Jacques lifted his chin to him. "I told you, Marcus, it doesn't have to be like this. Not everyone is your enemy."

Dayton looked at him piteously. "Poor fool," he said, and strode across to where John was now sitting uncomfortably on the sofa, his wrists still handcuffed behind him.

"I have a couple of your paintings, you know, John. One, from when you were Tommaso Perini, is here. It's brilliant. The other is, well, it's elsewhere. It's a Moretti. Wonderful brushwork."

John's cold stare failed to register on Dayton, who gave him a benign smile. "You know——" he continued, but he was interrupted by the door from the corridor crashing open. He turned to see the guard Leonardo pushing Paola and Claudia into the room.

Paola's wrists were also handcuffed behind her back and there was a large red mark on her right cheek. Claudia wasn't constrained, but she looked terrified.

"Claudia!" cried Jacques.

Claudia gasped and made to run forward, but the guard grabbed her arm.

"Let her go, Leonardo," said Dayton.

Claudia rushed to Jacques who pulled her onto his lap and threw his arms around her.

"It's all right, chérie," he said. "No one's hurt."

"Paola!" admonished Dayton. "What now? Have you been fighting again?"

"It was the nurses, boss," said Leonardo, who was gesticulating with his gun. "She thumped one real hard, hurt her. The other managed to land a punch and get the cuffs on her. It was just as well I got there 'cos I think they was going to knock her about a lot more." He gave Paola a shove and she stumbled forward. "On the other hand, p'raps it was a shame I got there. The bitch might have got what she deserves."

"That's enough, Leonardo," said Dayton. "Paola, sit over here. How is your ankle?"

"What the hell's going on, Marcus?" growled Paola, her attention on Jacques. "Who——" Then she saw John trying to stand, but the guard closest to him pushed him back down.

"Paola," said John, "are you badly hurt?"

Paola lifted her eyes to his. Her breathing was shallow and her stare seemed to last an eternity, but finally she just shook her head. "I'm fine," she whispered.

Dayton moved round behind Paola and took the handcuff link in his hand. "Time to go," he said. "Leonardo, bring her," he said, nodding towards Claudia.

"No!" cried Claudia. "Jacques!"

Jacques enveloped her with his arms, but one of the guards behind him pulled out his gun and pointed it at his head.

"Release her," he said.

Jacques shook his head. "You'll have to shoot me," he said.

On the other side of the room, Ced had been quietly adjusting his position on the sofa. As everyone's attention turned to Jacques, he lashed out with his right foot, connecting hard and accurately with the groin of the guard standing in front of him. The guard yelled and doubled up in agony. As he did, Ced threw his legs up and backwards in a kind of backflip and kicked the guard behind him squarely in the jaw. The guard fell over backwards, his head colliding with a credenza as he fell. John picked up on the action and started to stand. But the guard, Leonardo, lifted his gun to fire.

"No!" yelled Dayton. Leonardo's attention was distracted, but the gun still fired, the bullet thudding harmlessly into the wall at the far end of the room. Incensed, the guard with the gun trained on Jacques raised it to aim at John. Sensing this, Jacques reached up and grabbed the man's arm. The gun fired but again the bullet went well wide of the mark. The guard wrestled his arm free and swung his fist, still clenching the gun, at Jacques' head. As the blow connected, his gun fired a second time. There was a scream as Jacques fell to the floor, taking Claudia with him.

"Enough!"

The cry froze them all in their tracks as Dayton caught their attention. He had grasped Paola firmly around the waist with his left arm while in his right hand he now held a gun that was pointing straight at her head. She was struggling wildly but he was too strong. "Stop!" he yelled. "You!" he gesticulated to the guard behind John. "Cover them!" The guard ran round in front of the sofa and pointed his weapon at John and Ced.

"Leonardo!" commanded Dayton. "Bring the girl."

Leonardo took a step and then stopped. "Boss," he said. "She's been hit."

Dayton tightened his grip on Paola as he looked down at Claudia. Blood was oozing across the floor from under her.

The guard pulled Jacques' unconscious body away from Claudia.

"How bad is it?" said Dayton.

The guard bent down and carefully turned Claudia. "It's her shoulder, boss, but she's bleeding a lot."

"Shit!" yelled Dayton. Then he turned to Leonardo. "You! Go and get those damn nurses."

"Let me help!" cried Ced, springing to his feet. "I can staunch the bleeding."

The guard standing next to him went to hit him with his gun but Dayton stopped him. "Let him help!" he cried. "Uncuff him!" The guard followed his orders as Ced looked urgently around him. His hands now free, he snatched a cloth from a side table, scattering its contents on the floor, and rushed over to Claudia. He quickly assessed the damage, balled the cloth and pressed it against the wound.

"Claw," he said, brushing the hair from her face.

Claudia's eyes winced in pain and then opened. "Jacques?" she whispered.

"It's OK, Claw, you'll be fine," said Ced.

"Where's Jacques? I heard a shot," insisted Claudia.

"He's OK, Claw," said Ced, glancing at Jacques who was stirring on the floor next to him. "He's here."

He looked up. "Dayton—" he started, but there was no sign of either Dayton or Paola.

Chapter Forty-Six

John stood and turned to the guard behind him.

"That woman needs help," he yelled. "Uncuff me! *Now!*"

The guard's face registered his incomprehension.

"Now!" repeated John, switching to Italian and indicating the handcuffs. "Remove them!"

Still the guard hesitated. He turned to his colleague, looking for support. The guard Ced had kicked in the jaw was sitting on the floor behind the sofa, massaging his bruised face. He waved his hand towards John, nodding.

Once free, John rushed over to where Ced was kneeling next to Claudia.

"Dayton said something about nurses," said Ced. "Perhaps we should take Claudia to them rather than wait. This wound needs attention now."

"You're right," replied John as he helped Jacques to a sitting position.

"I'm fine, Philippe," said Jacques, massaging his temple. "Help Ced, I'll follow."

John stood and turned to the guard, ignoring the gun still aimed at him.

"Take us to the nurses!" he ordered brusquely in Italian.

The guard backed up a step, but John followed, pointing at the gun. "And put that away before anyone else gets hurt!"

"Do what he says," said the guard by the sofa.

"Come," said the guard by John, and headed for the door.

"Ced," said John. "If you carry her, I'll keep the cloth pressed against the wound."

Ced lifted Claudia into his arms and followed the guard through the door, with John leaning over him protecting Claudia's shoulder. He glanced back and saw an unsteady Jacques getting to his feet to follow.

They rushed along the corridor and into the entrance hall. The guard was at the foot of the stairs.

"Turn right at the top, signore, follow the corridor to the end, go through the door, turn left and the clinic is the last door on the right. The nurses should be there."

Not questioning why the guard wasn't going with them, Ced bounded up the stairs with John still leaning partly over him, struggling to keep up. As they reached the first door, Ced spun around and pushed it open with his back, before turning again to run on, following the guard's directions.

They burst into the clinic expecting to find the guard Leonardo and the nurses, but the room was empty.

"What the hell's going on?" said John.

"Doesn't matter," replied Ced as he placed Claudia on an examination table. "I want to get this wound sorted."

"Ced?" Claudia lifted her head.

"It's OK, Claw, I know what I'm doing. When Sal was pregnant with Claudia-Jane, she insisted that I went on a whole load of first-aid courses just in case we were stuck in the middle of nowhere when Claudia-Jane decided to arrive. I'm practically a trained nurse. Let's cut this blouse away from your shoulder."

He took a pair of scissors from a trolley by the table and carefully exposed the wound.

"Can you grab some gauze, John?" he said. "I'll mop it up and then clean it. Sorry, Claw, this will probably sting like hell, but you'll be pleased to know that it's only a flesh wound. It's not too deep, just a lot of blood, that's all." He grinned at her. "God, you're a loony. I can't leave you alone for a minute."

"I was protecting my man," said Claudia, her eyes looking past

Ced's shoulder. Ced turned to find Jacques standing behind him, his hand resting on Claudia's knee.

"Chérie?" he said.

"How's your head?" she asked.

"Better than your shoulder." He smiled softly at her and then turned to Ced. "Let's get that covered and bandaged, shall we?"

Once Claudia's shoulder was bound, Ced fashioned a sling. "Lie still for a while, Claw," he said as he turned to inspect Jacques' head.

"Don't be stupid," said Claudia, sitting up, "I'm as right as rain."

John reached out to help her as he saw her wincing.

"Do you think you can walk, Claudia?" he said.

"Of course," she said, trying to stand. "Perhaps an arm to lean on would help. I really think we should see what's going on. Where did Dayton go with Paola?"

John shook his head. "The last I saw in the confusion downstairs was that he virtually dragged her through the door. She was trying her best to fight him off but he had a strong grip on her."

"What happened to the guards?"

"I've no idea. We'll head back the way we came, but we must stick together."

"Don't worry, mon ami," said Jacques, holding an ice pack Ced had found to his head. "I'm not letting Claudia out of my sight."

They walked back along the corridor to the stairs leading up from the main entrance, checking in a number of rooms as they went. Those that were unlocked were empty. At the top of the stairs, John peered over the railings to the hall below.

"Wait!" said Claudia.

"What is it, chérie?" asked Jacques.

"We need to go up there," said Claudia, indicating the upper floors. "That's where I was held. Sara must be there somewhere too. I haven't seen her but I've just realised that she wasn't with Paola when they brought us down."

Jacques stroked her hair. "Sara is safe, chérie. She escaped. That's why we're here. She helped us locate the house."

"Escaped? How?"

"We'll explain later." John smiled and put a hand on Claudia's arm. "Come on, we really need to find out what's going on."

Once downstairs, Ced nodded towards the corridor leading to the rear of the house. "I'll go and check the room we were in," he said.

"No, Ced." John was shaking his head. "We stick together. We'll all go."

The door to the sitting room was wide open. Ced peered round the frame from the corridor and then walked in. "There's no one here," he said, running a puzzled hand through his hair. "Looks like they've all gone."

"That's ridiculous," said Jacques. He stared down at the bloodstain on the wooden floor, unconsciously pulling Claudia closer to him as he did.

"Careful," she whispered.

"Sorry, chérie." He removed his arm and kissed the top of her head. "There were three vehicles outside when I arrived. Let's see if they are still there."

As they left the house through the main door, Jacques could see the pick-up fifty metres away where he'd left it. But both Land Cruisers and the BMW had gone.

John ran across the gravel to the side of the house. "The guards must have somewhere they use as an office," he called. "This could be a trick to make us think they've gone. Dayton could be hiding with Paola."

"Philippe!" cried Jacques, but John ran on. "I'll go after him," said Ced, running off in the same direction as John.

Jacques shook his head. "They won't be there, chérie," he said to Claudia. "I'm sure of it. Dayton has outwitted us and he still has Paola."

. . .

Later in the bar at Molino di Sant'Agata, Sara was fussing around Claudia who was adamant that she was fine.

"There's no need for a doctor right now, Sara," she insisted. "Ced's done a good job; Sally has him well trained."

Pete was pacing the floor. "Don't you think we should go back to the house?" he said to John. "There must be some indication of where Dayton's gone."

"I searched pretty thoroughly, Pete," said John. "We all did. Once we were sure that they'd all left, we went back in looking for an office, a study, somewhere that might have papers or a computer with information on Dayton."

"And what we found was weird," continued Ced. "The computers we found in what must have been Dayton's office were completely empty. It was like they were brand new, fresh from the factory. The drives were all professionally wiped. The only way I could tell that they weren't straight out of the box was that the keyboard showed signs of use, and the mouse. There was a very sophisticated modem too, packed with security. So he must have been up to something there, connecting with someone, but whoever and whatever, there's no trace."

"And there were no papers?" Pete was incredulous.

"Nothing," said John.

"What about the rest of the house?" Pete wasn't giving up.

John shook his head. "Shut down, all systems switched off. It's …" his voice trailed off.

Pete stopped pacing to look at him. "John," he said, pulling up a chair next to him. "We won't give up, but perhaps it would better to—"

"Call Digby?" interrupted John. "I have. He had already dispatched a couple of people, it's just that this all happened too fast. They're going to meet us back at the hotel in Florence as soon as they arrive."

They were back in Florence by nine o'clock. Jacques organised a light supper for them in his suite while he took Claudia to a private clinic three streets away. The very discreet doctor who owned the practice was an old friend. After a thorough examination and fresh dressings, Claudia's wound was declared superficial and she was reassured that there would be only the slightest of scars.

"I think I should prescribe something for the shock, signorina," said the doctor. "From the brief details Jacques has given me, you have had a traumatic experience. I can quite understand why you don't want the police involved, but—"

"I'm fine, thank you, dottore," interrupted Claudia. "I just need a glass of wine and a good night's sleep. I'm not a great one for pills."

Jacques gripped her hand, wanting to hold her tight but frightened in case he hurt her.

The doctor smiled. "You are a brave young woman," he said. Then turning to Jacques, he added in Italian, "Look after this treasure, my friend, she is a rare find."

"What did he say?" asked Claudia as they left.

"He suggested I get you drunk."

Claudia nodded her approval. "He's my kind of doctor," she said, squeezing his arm.

The following morning at seven thirty, Ced was dressing in the room at the Grand Hotel that Jacques had insisted he move into the previous evening. Corrado Verdi was in the room next door. Ced's head was still buzzing with the events of the previous day, events that had continued to be discussed late into the night.

As he poured himself some coffee from the pot that had been delivered a few minutes earlier, the phone rang. He thought it might be Sally checking up on him again.

They had talked until late the previous evening over several calls. Ced had been elusive to start with, playing down the dangers, but Sally had phoned Lola to compare notes with her following her own long calls to John, and she had immediately called Ced back to badger him for more details. When he had reluctantly told her about Claudia, she had burst into tears.

"Guns! Ced, I can't believe it! I thought the Peterson thing had been bad. Ced, hon, you must promise me you'll never, ever, take these risks again. I can't begin to think … I mean … Ced!"

"It's all right, Sal, no harm done. Claw's fine and Jacques will never let her out of his sight again."

"It's you I'm worried about, Ced."

He had let her give vent, sipping quietly at his wine and feeling justifiably chastised, but knowing full well he wouldn't have taken any other course of action.

But it wasn't Sally on the phone, it was Jacques.

"Good morning, Ced."

"Hi, Jacques. How's Claw?"

"Well rested, thank you. Listen, I think something's come up. Digby has arrived from London and he's with John. He wants us all to meet in John's room."

"Digby?"

"Yes."

"Christ."

"Yes."

"I'll be straight there."

He put down the phone and stared at the receiver. For the first time since he'd watched Claudia drive away from him on the motor scooter outside Santa Croce, he felt truly scared.

The door to John's suite was ajar and Ced walked straight in. He was immediately surprised to see an attractive young woman sitting next to Sara, holding her hand, her face a mask of concern. Sara looked up and smiled softly. "Ced. This is Julie, my daughter."

Ced frowned, not understanding. "Hi," he said, "I—"

"Good morning, Ced," said Digby, turning from where he had just poured some coffee.

"Digby, I—"

"Julie!" Claudia's voice stopped Ced short. She had just walked in with Jacques. "What are …? Jacques, you didn't tell—"

"I didn't know," said Jacques.

"I'll explain in a moment," said Digby. "We're just waiting for Signor Verdi."

"Corrado?" Ced was surprised.

"John insisted," said Digby, shaking his head slightly. It seemed to him that his flock just kept increasing. "He's just been signing some papers."

"Oh," said Ced.

There was a light tap on the door and Verdi walked in, nodding his head to everyone. Ced had never seen him look so out of his depth. Matt vacated the spot where he'd been sitting next to Pete on one of the sofas and settled himself on the arm of the other sofa where Sara was sitting with Julie.

"Good," said Digby, "we're all here."

"What about John?" said Jacques.

"He'll be joining us shortly. I've already briefed him. He's with Lola in the next room."

"Lola?" they all said together.

"Yes," said Digby. "She flew over with me early this morning. Along with Miss Farsley." He nodded towards Julie.

Digby put down his coffee cup and turned towards them, steepling his hands to his mouth as he prepared to speak.

He sighed and looked slowly at each of them.

"I know what you've all been through in the past forty-eight hours and I understand just how difficult it has been; how worrying, for some of you," — he caught Julie's eye as she gripped Sara's arm — "and how dangerous for others." Claudia's eyes roamed the floor and then she turned her face into Jacques' shoulder.

"I regret to say," continued Digby, "that following yesterday's events at Marcus Dayton's house, there has been an outcome that was entirely ... unexpected." He paused, searching for the right words.

"I'm afraid there is no easy way to say it. About half an hour after Marcus Dayton left you, having forced Miss Santini into his vehicle with him, his vehicle went out of control on a precipitous and badly maintained road in the hills above his estate. The road was unmetalled, its surface merely loose gravel, and the edges on most of the corners were entirely unprotected. At the point where the vehicle left the road, there was a sheer drop of some two hundred feet into a gorge. For reasons that are not yet understood, the vehicle burst into flames on impact and the ensuing fire was so extreme that both Dayton and Miss Santini were burnt beyond recognition. It would appear that there were some jerry cans of petrol stored in the vehicle that exploded in the fire, adding to the severity of the damage."

There was total silence in the room, the shock tangible, like jagged shards of ice slicing into each of them.

Jacques was the first to speak. "You are sure about the vehicle? It couldn't have been—"

"We are certain. One of the few pieces of the vehicle that remained undamaged was the rear number plate. It must have flown clear on impact. Among the very few documents that have been recovered from the house was a log at the main gate giving the numbers of the vehicles registered there. The vehicle was one of the Land Cruisers."

Claudia rubbed her forehead with her right hand; her left was still strapped in the sling. Her forensic training was streaming questions through her brain as she analysed the information Digby Smith had related to them.

"Digby," she said, her voice whisper, "you said that the bodies were ... burnt beyond recognition. How ... How sure—"

"That they are Dayton and Miss Santini?"

"Yes."

Digby paused again as the gruesome details he'd been given flashed across his mind. The bodies had been crushed on impact and then bathed in a sea of flammable liquid. It had been an inferno and little remained apart from the partly melted remains of the handcuffs Paola had been constrained with, and one of Dayton's boots that had at some stage in the fire been partially protected by other debris falling on it. Otherwise, there was no clothing, there were no bones, no teeth to compare — not that either one of them would have had dental records anywhere — and nothing from which any DNA might be recovered and profiled.

Digby knew that because of her professional background he

could explain these details to Claudia. But to the others? Such horrors were, in his opinion, best left unsaid; there would be enough nightmares.

"We are sure," was all he said.

The silence was shattered by a rasping cry of anguish, a deep intake of breath followed by an unearthly wail. Ced was kneading his fingers tightly into his hands, his arms and body shaking.

"The bastard!" he cried. "The bastard! The bastard!" His words blurred into his tears. "We tried … we tried so hard … we …" He slipped to his knees from his chair and buried his head in his arms, his body continuing to shake. Jacques knelt on the floor next to him and enveloped him in his huge embrace as Claudia also knelt and took his head into her lap as she bent over him, cradling it as she shared his grief. The Farsleys followed, gathering around them, holding them. Somehow, Sara gently moved arms aside and positioned herself by Ced, so that when he finally sat up, she was there, in front of him. He looked at her and fell into her outstretched arms. "I'm so sorry, Sara, I'm so sorry."

Sara shook her head, no words coming as she hugged him tightly. Her eyes were open, staring, unseeing. But spinning and swirling in her mind among the sweet, childhood memories of Annie, her mother, were the more recent memories of the unpredictable, dangerous woman who had returned to her, the real Annie, the real Paola, the real Cassie and all the others, the woman she was sure she had witnessed mercilessly killing two guards and whom she knew had killed others. And whispering insistently from the tangle of images was a voice unbidden that she wanted to reject but couldn't. Perhaps it was for the best, said the voice, perhaps it was for the best.

As Ced slowly stopped shaking, Sara lifted her eyes and saw that John had come into the room. He was holding Lola's hand but his focus was locked on her, his granddaughter. Their eyes met and in that moment, Sara knew that John understood, that he had heard the same voice.

Chapter Forty-Seven

2014

Claudia was watching with a mixture of amusement and the awe of a new mother as her daughter Mathilde's eyes slowly failed in their attempt to resist closing in sleep. The three-month-old Mathilde's twin brother, Philippe, had long given up the struggle and was purring softly, the gentle breeze wafting through the large aft stateroom fluttering the cotton gauze of his cot in time with the soothing rocking of the yacht at anchor. Claudia reached out to touch Philippe's tiny feet, knowing it wouldn't disturb him. If she tried the same thing with Mathilde, the lullabies and coaxing of the last twenty minutes would have all gone to waste: the little girl would immediately be wide awake.

Claudia knew that the ninety-five-foot *Pelagios'* 300 horse power engines were turning over deep in the hull, ensuring the vessel's intricate network of mechanics and electronics were maintained at optimum performance at all times, but she could hear nothing. The state-of-the-art acoustic engineering that Jacques had incorporated into his very particular design meant that there was no dull throb and no vibration. Her eyes flitted around the luxury of the stateroom; it was a far cry from the smelly, cramped craft her parents had rented for holidays on the Norfolk Broads when Claudia and Simon, her brother, were children.

Pelagios was Jacques' pride and joy. He was in his element at sea, having spent much of his long life sailing the world, and he was totally at one with the ocean, knowing instinctively how to react to it in any situation. This huge yacht had been designed by him to be sailed single-handed in almost any weather, not that he would be testing his skills with his precious family on board. Their sailing was for now, at least, confined to the Mediterranean, and only then when that capricious sea was in a benign mood.

Claudia's eyes fell on three framed photographs mounted on the stateroom wall to one side of the king-size bed. They had been taken at the Andrews' cottage in the Lake District during the celebration of the twins' birth. None of the assembled company had any religious beliefs, but the equivalent of the christening, where the twins were formally named, and their guardians, their secular godparents, were recognised, was as serious and meaningful as any religious ceremony. There seemed to be an abundance of guardians: John, Lily and Sara were the obvious choices along with Sally, Ced and Pete. Lola had tried to decline on the grounds that the twins carried the same rare traits as Jacques and would therefore outlive her by millennia, but she was overruled. Not wanting to be left out, Sophie, Phoebe, Claudia-Jane and Julie were declared guardian sisters, while Matt was a guardian brother.

Claudia had worried that the ceremony might be tinged with sadness: the twins' birth had been less than eighteen months after the traumatic events in Italy that had resulted in the tragic and horrendous accident that killed both Paola and Marcus Dayton, and her pregnancy was a reminder of the reasons behind Dayton's abductions. However, Jacques was quick to reassure her that John had come to terms with Paola's death far faster than anyone expected. In the days and weeks following the crash, first in Italy and then back in Thirlmere, John had talked openly about it to both Jacques and Lola.

"It's hard to accept that after five hundred years of feeling in the depths of my soul that Paola was alive, and then, having found I was right, she was snatched from me," said John.

They were spread around the soft comfort of the sofas in the Andrews' large sitting room, a roaring fire helping to insulate the cottage's interior from the effects of the bitter January winds battering the hills and ripping freezing spray from the numerous bodies of water that gave the area its name.

"You know, the more I think about Paola," he continued, "the more I realise that she was an enigma, possibly damaged by events, but more likely a result of her genetics."

"Of course she was a result of her genetics, John," said Lola. "They were pretty weird, like yours are. Do you think that she found the whole age thing too hard to cope with, that perhaps she had one too many run-ins with scheming men she had to contend with?"

John nodded. "As I say, she was possibly damaged by events, but I didn't actually mean my genetics, crazy though they are, I meant her mother's."

"Francesca?" said Jacques.

"Yes," said John. "Francesca was a difficult woman, to put it mildly, the complete opposite of her sister Anna, who was delightful in every way, and, sadly, very unappreciated by her husband, Gianni, my grandson. She deserved better, to be honest. She was very loyal to me, unlike Francesca. But that isn't the extent of it. You see, what I didn't know at the time I fell rather stupidly into my marriage with Francesca was that her scheming, her paranoia, wasn't exclusive to her. She came from a line of what you might call disturbed women. If anything, it was Anna who was the odd one out. Their mother was pretty scheming too, although that wasn't unusual in those days when it was a mother's duty to find a suitable husband for each of her daughters, but Francesca's grandmother, her mother's mother, was, by all accounts, completely evil, as was her mother before her. The grandmother was long dead by the time I met Francesca, and the family never talked about her."

"Tell us more, John," said Lola, leaning forward. "You've never mentioned this before."

"No, I haven't. I suppose not knowing anything about Paola, I formed a picture in my mind of the daughter I wanted her to be, rather like another Lily, I suppose, and of course the two rascals upstairs. It wasn't until I read the notes of the interviews with

Nancy Wright that a few dim and distant bells started to ring, and even then I rejected them."

"So what was it about Francesca's grandmother?" asked Jacques.

"Apparently she was crazy. Dangerously so. Her first child died in odd circumstances — she was suspected of smothering it — and there were numerous other unexplained deaths in the household, mainly relating to servants and their children. Nothing was ever proven, but when Francesca's mother was born, she was immediately removed from her mother and given to a wet nurse. Her mother was sent away by her father and never seen again. Obviously that resulted in many other stories, but most smacked of speculation and gossip rather than having any substance. However the fact remains that Paola's grandmother was seriously unhinged, and perhaps some of that rubbed off on Paola. We'll never know."

"That's terrible, John," said Lola. "I mean, these days, whatever demons bugged her mind might have been treatable with, I don't know, modern psychiatric medicines?"

"It's possible, I suppose," agreed John. "'Chissà?' as they say in Tuscany. Who knows? What I do keep thinking of is how Paola behaved with us in the brief time we knew her, me especially since I spent more time with her or talking to her on the phone than anyone else in the family."

He looked up from the flames to find both Lola and Jacques staring in rapt attention. He smiled. "Psychology one-o-one, courtesy of John Andrews," he said as he bent forward to place another log.

"Initially, I think she was, like me, very overcome with the emotion of our meeting. In that first phone call that Lily put through, she called me Tata, using the Neapolitan dialect for Daddy. It was wonderful, the most amazing echo from the past, although of course she had never actually called me that since we'd never met. And then a day later when we did meet, when I flew to Boston, it was a very emotional time. But now that I think back on it, I was seeing that time, and Paola, in the way I wanted it to be, not necessarily how it was. You see, I think there was always a reserve there, a distance. Whether it was because she couldn't come to terms with the fact that she suddenly had a family: a father, a daughter, grandchildren, plus all the other complicated relationships, or whether there was something darker than that, I don't know. Paola knew what she was like, she knew there was an unpredictable and potentially dangerous part of her nature that could surface at any moment. Look at Sara's account of how Paola dealt with those two guards. Sara is convinced that she beat them to death, despite Paola's protestations that she didn't. And she'd already killed others there as well as beating up the nurses and a doctor."

"The accounts in the psychiatrist's notes are quite a chronology of violence too," added Jacques. "And having read through them a couple of times, I can't help but feel that they were incomplete."

"I have no doubt you are right, Jacques," agreed John, nodding in resignation.

"Paola did effectively save the other guard though," said Lola, thinking back to Sara's account of her escape.

"Yes," said John, "she did. However, I suspect she did that more for Sara than out of compassion for the guard. She knew that Sara wasn't like her, that Sara is a loving and caring wife and mother. She knew that in the cold light of day, Sara wouldn't have been able to live with herself if she'd killed that guard in a moment's madness. Paola was protecting her own."

He paused. Then he leaned forward in his chair and took Lola's hand. "Don't get me wrong, I'm not saying in any way that she deserved to die, nor am I saying that her death means nothing to me. On the contrary, it's a tragedy and I would do anything to replay those final moments at the house and change the outcome, to overpower Dayton and free Paola. What I am saying is that I don't know how close we would have been, once the initial euphoria of meeting each other had worn off, whether we would have even liked each other. Does that sound unfair, heartless?"

"No, mon ami," said Jacques, "it doesn't. We have both met many people during our long lives, you and I, and I think we have learned not to take people at face value: the demons lurking beneath the surface of some people might later emerge and cause us all sorts of grief. What happened is that you met someone who'd been around for five hundred years that you'd never met before who happened to be your daughter. That meeting came with no guarantees: Paola had long been her own woman."

Mathilde had finally given up the fight and was sleeping quietly. Claudia stood and walked softly over to the photographs. She looked at the faces of the people she had come to love more than any others and she thanked her lucky stars for the remarkable sequence of events that had brought them together. She reached out and touched the image of John's smiling face, his arms in the photograph around his wife and three daughters, Lily, Sophie and Phoebe. She thought, as she often did, of that day in the Lake District when they had first met, of his resistance to her questions that served only to increase her resolve to learn more about him. She thought about the young Phoebe, five at the time, and the painting she'd bought of her and the events that had unfolded following that, of her own persistence, and of Ced's and the prof's brilliance, and how it had all combined with almost disastrous consequences. Her fingers lingered on John's face; they had become the closest of friends and she loved him dearly. Then her eyes shifted to Jacques' smiling face, his pride only too evident as he stood with both the twins cradled in one large arm while the other was wrapped around Claudia. She sighed in happiness and decided it was time to go on deck and hug the man she loved so much.

As she turned to the steps that led up from the stateroom to the aft cockpit, where she knew Jacques would be methodically checking the seemingly endless ropes and pulleys that he controlled so effortlessly when they were sailing, her eyes fell on the screen of her laptop. A panel flagging a message had just popped up: there was an email from the prof.

She leaned over the laptop and tapped a couple of keys to call up the email and then she entered a series of passwords to unscramble the encrypted message. Like all missives from Professor Frank Young, it was short and to the point. She read it through and her eyes widened. Then she read it again. Typically, the prof was giving her a set of facts but at the same time leaving something out, something to challenge her mind. She read it a third time and then sat down on the bed as she thought through the information. Her eyes flickered around the room and then she smiled and raised her eyebrows. Very interesting, she thought, on both counts.

"Are the twins asleep, chérie?" said Jacques as Claudia emerged into the cockpit.

"Yes," she said. "Finally. You know what Mathilde is like. She doesn't want to miss a thing. She's only three months old but she already has a very knowing look in those dark, dark eyes that are so much like her father's."

"She may have her father's eyes," he laughed, "but the rest is entirely down to her mother."

He stood up from the winch he'd been tinkering with and gathered Claudia into his arms. He had never loved anyone more in his long, long life, not even his beloved Mathilde from Marseille in the 1600s. When Claudia had suggested, no, insisted, that their daughter be called Mathilde, he felt his heart was going to burst. As for Mathilde's twin brother, well, he just had to be Philippe.

Claudia squeezed him and then stood back to admire the view. They were moored in a small bay of an unpopulated island in the Dodecanese, only fifty nautical miles from the island where Jacques had been born two and a half thousand years before. That island now boasted a population of over a thousand who relied almost entirely on the tourists who flocked there in the summer months. Jacques and Claudia had explored it, looking for the spot where the sacred ground might have been, but afterwards, they didn't want to stay. They preferred to remain private, separate from the crowds, and they sailed away, literally into the sunset, to their present location. There was little on this island to attract anyone and there were no other boats moored there. It was the way they liked it.

"This is paradise," said Claudia, sighing and hugging her husband again. Then she sat to watch as he resumed his tinkering.

"I've just had a very interesting email from the prof," she said.

"Really, chérie? What does the dear man have to say?"

"He's revised his opinion on the likelihood of someone like Marcus Dayton, or you for that matter, having a child with Paola or any of the other women in her line. He says he was wrong before."

"Wrong?" Jacques stopped what he was doing and looked up in surprise.

"Yes. You see, once we had the data from John and Lily indicating that their genes would be mutually destructive, we assumed that it would apply to Dayton as well, and of course to you. For the prof, that was quite a sloppy conclusion since he never actually did the work to confirm it; there were too many other more important avenues to follow. Well, recently, I think simply because he realised there were Ts uncrossed and Is undotted, he went back and did the tests he should have done in the first place. It's complicated and time-consuming work, which is probably why he'd put it on a back burner. Obviously he doesn't have Dayton's DNA, at least not enough for the work, but he does have plenty of sample from you which he checked out against Lily's DNA. It turns out that the alleles in your family tree are subtly different at significant places from the Andrews strain. So although he was right that there could be no offspring from a union, however it was achieved, of a man and a woman both from the Andrews line, for a man from your line and a woman from the Andrews line, he's shown that an offspring is perfectly possible, and that offspring could well have a gene set that carries the rare traits of both parents."

"So if Dayton had continued with his surrogacy plans, he might have succeeded," said Jacques.

"I think it's more than might have; according to the prof, there's no reason why he wouldn't have succeeded."

"How very sad for him."

"Perhaps."

"Why only perhaps?"

"Well, there's a second part to the prof's email that is very intriguing. Typically he has set me a problem rather than giving me the answer since he knows I've always like crossword puzzles."

Jacques tilted his head in question. "You've lost me, chérie."

Claudia smiled mischievously.

"I sometimes think about that huge house in Tuscany where Dayton took me and where he kept Paola and Sara," she said.

"I'm sure you do, chérie," said Jacques. "It still gives me nightmares when I remember that day."

"I don't mean that," said Claudia.

Jacques narrowed his eyes as he looked into his wife's earnest face. She was biting her bottom lip, a sure sign that her scientific mind was working overtime, either nagging away at a problem or checking her solution was correct.

"You remember what Digby told us about the house after that terrible day when Dayton and Paola were killed," said Claudia.

"You mean about when his people went back the following day to examine it thoroughly?"

"Yes. It was a team from London, all very clandestine. He said it was tricky since they had no authority there — they weren't there in any official capacity — and they thought it was only a matter of time before the Italian police would arrive, once they had connected the burnt-out Land Cruiser with the house."

"Didn't Digby's people find they couldn't get into part of the house?"

"Yes. They found a door in the larger of the two sitting rooms on the ground floor that led into a tiny vestibule that had a massively thick steel door preventing them from going any farther. There was no handle and there were no hinges. They waved some sort of gizmo at the door and found that it was controlled electronically, but they had no time to investigate it."

"Why was that?"

"Because they were interrupted. Not by the police as they expected, but by a small team of business types, a woman and two men who told them in no uncertain terms that they were trespassing, that the house, grounds and woods had been taken over by a business research academy that was very private, very discreet. Digby's people were then immediately ushered from the grounds, much to Digby's irritation."

"Yes, I remember now. It was all rather strange."

"It was more than strange for two reasons that the prof has

now given me. Well, he's given me one and left me to work out the other. He and Digby have become rather friendly, which is pretty weird when you think about it. It would be a bit like having a shadow as a friend. Anyway, Digby has told him that he has never been able to find out anything about the organisation that now occupies the house, even with all the resources and contacts he has at his disposal. It's like they don't exist. Apparently he was quite forthcoming about it to the prof and he didn't object to the prof telling me. He said that although his Italian counterparts have told him very clearly to back off, he's convinced that the place has nothing to do with their normal covert operations. He told the prof that he's aware of those, even the ones he's not supposed to know about."

Jacques laughed. "So what is the problem he set you, my super-sleuth?"

Claudia gave him her Mata Hari look and then poked her tongue out.

"Like I said. Crossword puzzles."

"He sent you a crossword puzzle?"

"No, of course not. But the solution to what he told me is like doing a crossword puzzle. It's all down to the name of the place under the new occupancy. It's now called Rompton Academy."

"Sounds innocent enough."

"Yes, but you remember Dayton's company in New York that we went to."

"MDCorp?"

"Yes. We always assumed that it stood for Marcus Dayton Corp."

"Doesn't it?"

"Not necessarily. This is what the prof said and then left me to work it out. Supposing the M in the name stood for Emma. The Italians do this with company names; they spell a letter like M in the way it's pronounced: M is Emme, pronounced Emm-ay."

"And F is Effe pronounced Eff-ay," added Jacques. "Mario Fellini the plumber would be EmmeEffe Ltd."

"Exactly. So if the M was for Emma, in a sort of twist of the

Italian idea, then MDCorp could stand for Emma Dayton Corp rather than Marcus Dayton Corp."

She paused and looked him in the eye, her own eyes sparkling. "Well," she said, "have you worked it out?"

Jacques shook his head.

"It could of course all be a coincidence," said Claudia, "but Rompton Academy is an anagram of Emma Dayton Corp."

Epilogue

Twelve hours later, several thousand miles away in the Caribbean, another yacht was moored in another small, sheltered bay off another small island, hardly moving on an almost glass-like sea that sparkled with the reflection of myriad stars on a moonless, cloud-free night. But unlike the *Pelagios*, this yacht had no sail. Designed and constructed by an exclusive Italian company on the coast of Italy north of Pisa, the 140-foot luxury motor cruiser *Emmagine* was built for comfort and performance, its three two-and-a-half-thou-sand-horse-power jet engines capable of maintaining a cruising speed of 45 knots that in calm waters would barely ripple a cock-tail. At anchor, it was a villa on the sea.

The lower deck had a huge stateroom, sizeable guest rooms and a gym aft, with forward galleys and crew quarters, while the main deck housed spacious living, dining and recreational spaces, all areas air-conditioned and fitted out in the highest quality hard-woods and softest hand-stitched leather. An eight-man crew catered to the owner's every need, including security, going quietly and effi-ciently about their business, shadows who were hardly in evidence yet always on hand.

On this sultry evening, both the owner and his partner had rejected the climate-controlled ambience of the main living room in favour of leather loungers on the forward upper deck. Marcus Dayton was sitting back enjoying the huge panorama of stars as he listened to Mozart piano sonatas playing quietly from speakers mounted invisibly in part of the nearby superstructure. Across the deck, Paola Santini was sipping a chilled sparkling water as she idly watched him. It was something she enjoyed doing whenever she could: Marcus was a busy man with extensive and complicated business commitments that saw him frequently travelling the world in his private jet, and these opportunities were few.

Until recently, Paola had often accompanied him, but in the past three months, she had cut back her travel, spending time on the boat or at the villa on their nearby private island. To the outside world, they were no longer Marcus Dayton or Paola Santini, their new names well established with suitable histories to match. But in the privacy of the boat or one of their homes, they preferred the names they had used when they'd first come to know each other.

It was during these restful evenings, as Marcus soaked up his beloved Mozart, that Paola would reflect on the turn her life had taken, a direction she liked to think she had chosen.

She had been incensed when Marcus had abducted her. She could think only of how she might escape and at the same time do him considerable harm, kill him if possible. Yet as she got to know him, despite her anger at what he was expecting from her, she found she was increasingly attracted to him. There was no denying he was a very good-looking man, which of course helped, and he was breathtakingly rich.

On the one hand, her baser, more calculating instincts told her that here was an opportunity not to be missed — win him over, take his money and run — while on the other, her more sensible side told her that there was no way she would get her hands on his money if he wasn't around: she couldn't have one without the other.

But then cold calculation gave way to desire overlaid with confusion. She thought of how she had felt prior to the abduction; her newly discovered family, the father she had never known, the father whose artistic talent outstripped hers and who would have willingly and lovingly guided her and coached her to reach new heights in her art. She thought of the daughter she'd accepted was dead who was in fact very much alive with her own loving family, a regular professional Bostonian with her regular professional Bostonian husband. She thought of her half-sister Lily and of her other half-sisters, her father's children by Lola. It had all happened so fast, all as a result of Nancy Wright finding her on Marconi Beach.

Actually, that wasn't quite correct. If she hadn't hung that portrait in the gallery window in Falmouth, the psychiatrist would never have found her. Why had she done that? She'd known she was tempting fate. But once it had happened, once the pieces all started to fall into place, it seemed like a helter-skelter she was careering down out of control.

She'd felt suddenly stifled, constrained, no longer in charge of her own destiny. She'd taken a step back, deliberately dragged her feet over completing the two paintings she'd promised. She could easily have asked her father to help and they would have been ready in a couple of days. But she hadn't asked him, very deliberately she hadn't asked him. Instead, she'd kept him and the others at arm's length, engaging in long phone calls every night to England that he seemed to enjoy but which she found increasingly overpowering. As the paintings neared completion, she had found herself dreading going to England to be with her family.

The music stopped. Marcus opened his eyes and looked at her. "Still plotting how you're going to bump me off, darling?"

She gave him a nonchalant shrug. "Oh, I've got that all sorted, sweetheart. I just need to perfect your signature so I can persuade the banks to part with your money."

"Which particular signature?" he said as he swiped a finger over his iPod to find another Mozart selection. He touched the 'play' arrow and settled back in the lounger. "You must make sure you use the right one or you'll be clapped in irons and never seen again." He closed his eyes and let the music envelop him.

She smiled at the banter, the same routine they often tossed around, knowing that in one universe they might actually mean it, but not this one.

Her mind returned to her train of thought. As her anxiety over how she would cope in England once she was surrounded by her new extended family had increased, suddenly everything changed. Marcus had abducted her. The incident had triggered her natural reaction: kill or be killed.

She'd shown no mercy towards Edith Cooper, nor had she ever felt a twinge of guilt since. She'd attacked and scarred Marcus, something she did slightly regret, although now, over eighteen months on, the scar was barely visible, a cosmetic surgeon's scalpel having helped it along. There had been another outburst of rage once Marcus had told her why he'd taken her, and she'd hardly been able to resist smashing a fist into the bony Ronaldi every time she saw him.

However, once she'd learned about Emma, learned the rationale behind Marcus' actions, she began to understand him, even to sympathise with him. Their conversations had been increasingly congenial, although she still nursed a yearning to escape, even if she then disappeared rather than going back to her new family.

She'd somewhat surprised herself at the extreme violence she'd dispensed to the guard who tracked her. It wasn't remorse — he'd clearly intended causing her harm — but her burst of brutality worried her slightly. Then there was the girl, which was a complete accident.

While she had used the girl's phone to contact Rodrigo Barros, at the same time she'd found herself wanting to appease Marcus when he was so incensed over the deaths. She didn't regret the deaths, but she did regret losing his trust.

The crunch had come when Marcus took Sara. Paola's initial anger had quickly given way to a realisation of just how serious Marcus was in his quest, and with this realisation came the surprising notion that she wanted to do her very best to help him. Sara had mentioned something about genetic tests and the whole exercise being futile, but Paola didn't believe her. What she did reject was the notion of IVF and a surrogate mother. If there was going to be a child with her traits, a child like Sara but also with Marcus' traits, Paola wanted to be part of the process.

Paola smiled to herself as she watched Marcus moving very slightly in time with the music. He loved Mozart, a love reinforced by a certain pride in the fact that he'd actually met the composer in London in 1765 when Mozart was a boy of nine.

Marcus' reaction to Paola declaring she had a much better idea after she'd floored Ronaldi and rendered the two nurses unconscious had initially been one of incredulity. She had taken his hand and led him off to an unused bedroom she'd found at the rear of the house where they spent the next two hours making passionate and very physical love.

After, Paola had lain in his arms as he gently stroked her hair. She'd turned her head to kiss his chest. "That wasn't too bad for someone of your advanced years, Mr Dayton."

He smiled. "My expectations wouldn't normally be too high when making love to a five-hundred-year-old woman, even one as well preserved as you, so I'm pleasantly surprised myself."

"Is that so?" she said, punching him firmly on the upper arm as she climbed astride him.

He had actually been very surprised at the ferocity and intensity of Paola's lovemaking. She had no sooner pulled him into the room and slammed and locked the door, than she was tearing at his clothes, her mouth greedily exploring his face, his lips, his neck. He had picked her up and almost thrown her on the bed, but she had wriggled from under him as she tore at her own clothes, her jaw set as her eyes fixed on his.

Free of their clothes, they had squared off against each other like two combatants, devouring each other with long, deep kisses and then rolling, turning, teasing, exploring each other's bodies until they were both slick with sweat, yet still hungry for more.

Dayton had learned much from many women during his two and a half thousand years, yet it had been almost two years since he had last shared a bed with anyone. On that occasion, desperate, angry and bitter after his daughter's death, he had unwittingly peppered the woman with bruises, deep thumb marks on her neck witness to just how close she had come to being throttled.

For Paola too, it had been some months. She had had a series of lovers in both Rio and São Luís, most of them dark, brooding artists with whom she had been mostly disappointed, although one, Fernando, had matched her in intensity and competence.

Now, as Paola rolled off Dayton, they both lay back, finally exhausted.

"An interesting change of heart, Paola," Dayton murmured softly in her ear.

"I figured that if you are intending to imprison me until you have an offspring, or at least until you are convinced that it's not going to work, I might as well enjoy it. After all, I could be your guest for a long time. And given the choice between your hands exploring me and Ronaldi's, well ..."

"And if you get pregnant, what then?"

"I don't know, I haven't thought that far ahead. But if I don't and you still want to explore modern alternatives, I insist that you find someone different from Ronaldi. A woman."

"I think I'll have to anyway, given how you've treated him."

As they lay there, they hatched their plan. Paola insisted that the price of her cooperation was that Sara must be released. He'd laughed out loud, "I'm impressed by your interpretation of the word cooperation."

"I've thought it through," she said. "I don't want to go back, I don't fit in with my family and I doubt I ever will. They are decent people with a great love for each other. They want, at least John wants, that I slot in with that, but I don't think I can. If I ever again find myself with my back to the wall — and I do seem to attract trouble — I know I'd fight and kill if I had to. I don't mean my family, but it might involve them. They don't deserve that kind of problem, to have to defend me, justify me, put up with me."

She paused and sighed. "And I don't think I want to live their sort of life; it's not for me."

He continued to stroke her hair. "I think you're being very hard on yourself, Paola. Are you sure this is what you want?"

"Yes. We're survivors, you and I, prepared to fight hard and dirty, so we understand each other. I know John's a survivor too, as is Lily, but not in the same way. I don't think our universes really overlap."

They talked through a plan where Paola and Sara would attempt an escape. The guards would be briefed and pretend to follow them. Paola would give the impression of taking out one guard and then another — a pretence that Sara was to find all too convincing — and then at the fence, the guards would act carelessly and the women would seize the opportunity to escape. Paola would feign an injury and appear to reluctantly send Sara on her way.

The plan had nearly backfired at this point when Sara was very tempted to kill one of the guards, but Paola had managed to intervene. John had later been close in his interpretation of this, although he'd misunderstood Paola's motives.

They knew that Sara would be more or less obliged to follow the path she'd taken through the woods, but as a precaution, they'd stationed guards to steer her if necessary. It hadn't been, and she'd found the hut that had been conveniently stocked with food and blankets.

The artist, Dot, had been called in. An occasional character actress who Marcus had used once in a while for various subterfuges, she had played her part well, guiding Sara to the bar in Molino di Sant'Agata, and then quietly disappearing.

The arrival of Claudia on the scene had been an unexpected complication. Marcus had gone to Florence, both to keep out of the way and because of a genuine desire to see the Gaddi frescoes close up. Bumping into Ced had confirmed what he had begun to suspect about a brother, while Claudia had been a diversion that required a certain amount of quick thinking.

Having caught Claudia, confirmed the existence of Jacques and then fed her some spiked coffee, Marcus had called Paola to brief her that things would likely all come to a head at the house very soon. They monitored events at the bar through a tiny microphone and transmitter that Dot had discreetly hidden and let John, Jacques and Ced think they had cleverly talked their way into the estate.

Marcus and Paola had carefully planned and arranged their exit strategy. In order to prevent John continuing his search for her, Paola suggested it would be better for everyone if she and Marcus appeared to be killed. Since the bodies of the two guards that Paola had killed were still in a deep freeze in a cellar at the house awaiting disposal, Marcus hatched the idea of the car crash using them. The girl was similar in size to Paola and the man, Jason, a similar height and build to Marcus, not that their sizes really mattered following their almost complete destruction in the ferociously intense fire.

The plan had nearly come to grief when the guards had become too enthusiastic with their guns. They were not supposed to be loaded, but somehow the instruction had been overlooked. Shooting Claudia was definitely not in the plan and it was down to good fortune that she wasn't more seriously hurt. As it turned out, her shooting provided a huge distraction, enabling Marcus and Paola to slip away more easily and enact the plan to fake the crash and explosion of the Land Cruiser.

As they drove away from the estate to the waiting plane at the small airfield outside San Sepolcro, Dayton had received a phone call. He listened intently throughout the call and finally just said, "Good. You may proceed."

Visibly relieved, he had turned to Paola. "Andrews and the others would never have noticed, but the sitting room activities were being followed by concealed, very tiny CCTV cameras. The guard watching the monitors has confirmed that our guests have taken charge of dealing with that pushy young woman, but also that her wound is only superficial. I have given the guards the instruction to vacate the place. Once they've gathered their breath, our guests will realise that they are alone."

"I'm pleased to hear it," said Paola. "That was too close for comfort. The last thing we wanted was for any of them to be hurt."

She touched Dayton's arm. "Marcus. I assume the house will soon be swarming with police, but are you really vacating it? What about all your art? You've collected that over centuries."

He shook his head. "Firstly, the police won't go near the place; I've got that sorted. Secondly, there will be some people turning up tomorrow to seal the house. It will be given another name and another apparent function. However, in reality it will go into hibernation until such time that I feel I, we, can go back there to live. Of course I'll pop in quietly every now and then to check, but you can rest assured that the paintings and sculptures will be perfectly safe."

"How long do you think it will be before we can go back there?"

He stared through the car window at the passing countryside.

"I should think about fifty years," he said, "just to be sure."

"Paola?"

"Sorry, I was miles away, literally." She smiled at him as he stood and walked over to her.

"Ready for bed?" he said, holding out a hand.

"Yes," she said, letting him pull her to her feet. "I'm really rather tired. These sultry evenings are wonderful for sitting out, but I need the soothing cool of the air con to help me sleep."

When Marcus said nothing, she looked up into his eyes. He was quietly watching her, a slight smile on his face.

"What?" she said.

The smile broadened. "I had a note from Melliff in New York. As you know, he has been keeping a watchful eye on the Andrews clan and also on my brother and his wife."

"The intrepid Claudia," said Paola. "Yes, she turned out to be quite a girl."

"She did. She and Jacques are in the Greek islands with their young twins."

"The ones who have both inherited his traits even though they are a boy and girl," she added wistfully.

He pulled her closer to him. "Melliff monitors her email. She received one today from Professor Young."

"The brilliant geneticist."

"Yes. Melliff said it took him ten minutes to decode, which given his skills means that it was impressively encrypted. What it contained is very interesting. You remember how I have said on several occasions that I doubted Young's conclusions about us having a child who would inherit our traits, that scientists aren't infallible, that they make mistakes all the time and are often guilty of applying the conclusions from one situation to another they think is relevant, when the reality is that their assumptions aren't valid?"

Paola laughed and poked a finger into his chest. "Wishful thinking Marcus. I doubt your rather superior attitude would apply to someone as eminent as Professor Young."

He waited until she lifted her eyes again to his, his own crinkling in amusement as Paola's widened suspiciously.

"On the contrary," he said at last. "In the email to Claudia, he admitted that he did make a mistake, that he had taken the conclusions from work he did on John Andrews' DNA and Andrews' daughter Lily, and assumed they would apply to my brother and me. He has now repeated the work using my brother's DNA instead of Andrews', and guess what? It is apparently perfectly possible for a man from my genetic line to have a child with a woman from your genetic line that would inherit our rare traits."

Paola's smile was pure amazement. "And with IVF, things could be controlled so that the fertilisation favoured our special genes."

"Exactly," he said. "Of course, with a natural conception, because only half of my DNA has the rare traits, and only half of yours has as well, there would be a possibility of the child just being like any other ordinary human being."

"It's possible," she said, gently patting the large round bump in her belly. "I guess we'll find out in two months' time."

Afterword

When it was self-published in 2015, this novel was called Murderous Traits. It was the third part of the Rare Traits Trilogy, the first book of which, Rare Traits, was self-published in 2012, and the second, Delusional Traits, in 2013.

I had always had a lurking doubt about the titles and indeed the covers — cover fashions change, especially in the fast-moving world of self-publishing. Further dissatisfaction with the covers of my other four novels, and indeed the title of one of them as well has now, in 2021, resulted in a total rethink.

As a result, the Rare Traits Trilogy has become a series: The Dust of Centuries, and the three books that so far comprise it are now Quincentenarian, The Delusion Gambit and Fatal Consequences, each of them with completely redesigned covers. Does this mean that there might one day be a fourth book in the Dust of Centuries tales? I'd like to think there might, but for now, don't hold your breath.

I hope very much that you enjoyed reading Fatal Consequences as much as I enjoyed writing it. If you did, I should be extremely grateful if you could spend a few moments posting a rating and perhaps even a review on one or more sites of your choice. It needn't be long; one word will do — preferably a favourable one! Genuine reviews, however short, are worth a lot.

And equally as important, please recommend it to your relatives, friends and colleagues. While word of mouth is very helpful to the cause of any author, it is particularly so for self-published authors for whom marketing is that much harder. If you tell a few people about this book or any of my other books, and they in turn tell others, the word will spread.

You can find more information about all my books and other book-related stuff on my website at davidgeorgeclarke.com. If you are on FaceBook, Instagram, Twitter and/or Goodreads, I'm there too.

David Clarke

June 2021

facebook.com/davidgeorgeclarkeauthor

twitter.com/clarkefiction

instagram.com/clarkefiction

goodreads.com/davidgeorgeclarke

Acknowledgments

As with the first two novels in The Dust of Centuries series, Fatal Consequences, could not have been completed without the help and encouragement of many people.

First and foremost, I could not have continued down my novel-writing journey without the constant support and encouragement of my wife, Gail. She is always there as a sounding board for ideas, a critical and constructive reviewer of drafts, and an enthusiastic supporter of the project. More than anyone, this book is dedicated to her, with love.

Much of The Delusion Gambit was set in the United States and since this book continues where that book left off, some of its early chapters are also set there. Once again, without the critical eyes of a number of American friends, I should not have been able to extricate myself from the huge number of semantic, geographic, linguistic and cultural holes that I managed to dig for myself in the first draft. My grateful thanks are therefore due to Anne Mensini, Sanford Foster, and Wendy Bearns, all three of whom put me straight on innumerable matters, as well as raising many salient points about the plot.

Thanks for an early edit, and for very positive comments, are also due to my son-in-law, Simon O'Reilly — the fastest copy editor in the East!

A number of others have kindly read through the book in draft form and all were very positive and helpful in their comments. Thanks go to Cedric Harben; my sister, Jill Pemberton; my daughter, Lea Woodward; and my stepdaughter, Zoe O'Reilly.

Two other friends volunteered to use their professional experience to proofread and copy edit printed versions. Luci de Nordwall-Cornish provided me with a duly and brilliantly marked up script in record time; thank you, Luci. Then Janette Lesser applied skills honed many moons ago when working for a well-known publisher and proved that none of those skills has lost its edge over the decades. Thank you, Janette, for the huge amount of time and effort you put into the task. Thanks as well to Danny Lesser for duly scanning the marked-up pages in Tel Aviv and sending them to me. A truly international operation.

My thanks are also due to Paula Svensen for her professional copy-editing services. Paula was a great find and a pleasure to work with. Your many, many suggestions have made a huge difference to the final product.

Final thanks for proofreading services go to my dear friend Linda Davy in Hong Kong. Linda's remarkable eagle eye picked up many points very late on in the preparation process that would otherwise have slipped through the net. I am indebted to her.

I have continued to borrow the names of my grandchildren for significant characters in the plot. Lily, Phoebe, Frank and Digby arrived in Quincentenarian and Mali joined them in The Delusion Gambit. With the arrival of grandchild number six, Samson, a place had to be found for him in Fatal Consequences and what better place that for his name to be the real name of one of the Digby Smiths. To them all I say that I hope that if one day you read this book, you will be amused, even though your namesakes in the book are in no way meant to be like you.

Finally I should like to thank the characters in the book who all came to life for me as they appeared. Good or evil, I enjoyed my time with them all. For the time being, I shall miss them, but they'll be back!

In the meantime, look out for one or two of them in the Cotton & Silk Crime Thriller Series.

David George Clarke

AN IMPERFECT REVENGE

If you would like to listen to a free audiobook version of AN IMPERFECT REVENGE read by the author, scanning the QR code above with the camera on your phone will take you to a link to sign up to the clarkeFiction newsletter and download the file. You will also be guided to the BookFunnel app for listening to the book.

Synopsis of An Imperfect Revenge

On assignment to review Villa Brocanti, an up-market agriturismo resort in Tuscany, travel writer Evie Lorrigan explores the dense forest surrounding the Brocanti estate and finds the boarded-up ruin of a palatial villa.

Her journalistic antennae piqued, she breaks in and what she finds is chilling. Prevented from leaving by doors with no handles closing behind her, she has little choice but to make her way through one room after another, each one decorated with extraordinary trompe l'oeil paintings. Lured onwards and upwards, she finally becomes trapped in an attic room with the gruesome remains of a man from a bygone era.

And no one knows she is there…

Enjoy!

A Final Word

Do you have kids or grandchildren, a favourite godson or goddaughter, a class of kids you teach or support in some way? My wife Gail is an author and illustrator who has published ten beautifully illustrated children's books. They are written in rhyme that children from 4–9 years just love reading or having read to them.

Patrick's Birthday Message
Searching for Skye — An Arctic Tern Adventure
Cosmos the Curious Whale
The Chameleon Who Couldn't Change Colour
Sharks — Our Ocean Guardians
[The Shark Guardian Series Book I]
Jed's Big Adventure
[The Shark Guardian Series Book II
Ndotto — An Elephant Rescue Story
Mischief at the Waterhole
Dormouse Snoremouse
Meerkat's Exciting Adventure

You can find more details on Gail's website and YouTube channel:

www.gailclarkeauthor.com
www.youtube.com/c/gailclarkeauthor